**JAIMIE ADMANS** is a 32-year-old English-sounding Welsh girl with an awkward-to-spell name. She lives in South Wales and enjoys writing, gardening, watching horror movies and drinking tea, although she's seriously considering marrying her coffee machine. She loves autumn and winter, and singing songs from musicals despite the fact she's got the voice of a dying hyena. She hates spiders, hot weather and cheese & onion crisps. She spends far too much time on Twitter and owns too many pairs of boots. She will never have time to read all the books she wants to read.

Jaimie loves to hear from readers; you can visit her website at www.jaimieadmans.com or connect on Twitter @be_the_spark.

T0312528

# Also by Jaimie Admans

*The Château of Happily-Ever-Afters*
*The Little Wedding Island*
*It's a Wonderful Night*

# The Little Vintage Carousel by the Sea

## JAIMIE ADMANS

ONE PLACE. MANY STORIES

HQ
An imprint of HarperCollins*Publishers* Ltd
1 London Bridge Street
London SE1 9GF

This edition 2019

First published in Great Britain by
HQ, an imprint of HarperCollins*Publishers* Ltd 2019

Copyright © Jaimie Admans 2019

Jaimie Admans asserts the moral right to be
identified as the author of this work.
A catalogue record for this book is
available from the British Library.

ISBN: PB: 978-0-00-833086-6
EB: 978-0-00-829696-4

Typeset by Palimpsest Book Production Ltd, Falkirk, Stirlingshire

*For Mum and Bruiser.*

*You will forever be my little family who
I wouldn't change for the world, now and always.*

# Chapter 1

Why does every man in London think that eight o'clock on a warm June morning is the ideal time to remove their shirt and get on the tube? I consider this as I peel myself away from a sweaty back and turn around to find myself face to face with someone's wet armpit. There's often a good time for shirtlessness, but the middle of rush hour on a crowded train is not it.

I sigh and stare at my feet. Every morning I get on this train and get off feeling like a floppy sardine that's just been let out of a tin and probably smelling worse. All to go to the soulless office block of the women's magazine where I work as a fact-checker, and then do the exact same thing at half past five with all the other sweaty, irritable commuters who would really love nothing more than to poke their boss in the eye and run away to a beach somewhere.

Someone stands on my toe and a handbag hits me in the thigh as someone else swings it over their arm. Ow. Only four more days to go until the weekend, and then I can have two whole days of not having to leave the flat and face the crowds of London. Two whole days of uninterrupted Netflix, apart from when Mum calls to update me on my ex-boyfriend's latest news, which she knows because they're still online friends even though I deleted him over two years ago.

I jump back as a briefcase threatens to take out my kneecaps. There's got to be more to life than this.

I look up and my eyes lock on to a man near me. Train Man is going somewhere today. Usually he only has a backpack with him, but today there's a huge suitcase leaning against his leg, rucksack straps over both shoulders, and a holdall bag hooked over one arm. He's standing up and holding on to a rail like I am, his attention on the phone in his hand, the lines around his eyes crinkled up as he looks down at it, and the sight of him makes something flutter inside me.

I see him quite often, but he's always already on the train when I get on, and we're usually much further apart. Up close, he's even more gorgeous than I'd always thought he was. He's got short brown hair, dimples denting his cheeks, and the kind of smile that makes you look twice, which I know because he's one of the rare London commuters who smiles at others.

The noisy tube train full of other people's body parts in places you don't want other people's body parts, the noise of people sniffing and coughing, an endless medley of beeps as people play with their phones, snippets of conversation that aren't meant for me … they all fade into the background and the world turns into slow motion as he lifts his head, almost like he can feel my eyes on him, and looks directly at me. If it was anyone else, I'd look away instantly. Staring at strangers on the tube is a quick way to get yourself punched or worse, but it's like a magnet is holding me, drawing my gaze to his, and his mouth curves up a tiny bit at each side, making it as impossible to look away now as it is every other time he smiles at me.

I feel that familiar nervous fluttering in the deepest part of my belly. It's not butterflies. My stomach must have disagreed with the cereal I shoved down my throat before rushing out of the flat this morning. Even though it's the same fluttery feeling I get every time I see him and he sees me. Maybe it's because I'm never usually this close to him. Maybe those dimples have magical powers at this distance. Maybe I'm just getting dizzy from looking up at him because I'm so short and he's the tallest person on the train, towering above every other passenger around us.

His smile grows as he looks at me, and I feel myself smiling back, unable not to return his wide and warm smile, the kind of smile you don't usually see from fellow commuters on public transport. Open. Inviting. His gaze is still holding mine, his smile making his dimples deepen, and the fluttery feeling intensifies.

I feel like I could lean across the carriage and say hello to him, start a conversation, ask him where he's off to. Although that might imply that I've studied him hard enough on previous journeys to work out that he doesn't usually have that much luggage. And talking to him would be ridiculous. I can't remember the last time I said hello to a stranger. It's considered weird here, not like in the little country village where I grew up. People just don't *do* that here.

He's wearing jeans and a black T-shirt, and he tilts his head almost like he's *trying* to hold my gaze, and I wonder why. Does he know that I spend most journeys trying to work out what he does, because there's no regularity to his routine? I'm on this train at eight o'clock every morning Monday to Friday, I look like I'm going into an office, but he's always in jeans and a T-shirt, a jacket in the winter, and sometimes he's on this train a couple of times a week, sometimes once a week, and other times weeks can pass without me seeing him. I don't even know why I notice him so much. Is it because he smiles when our eyes meet? Maybe it's because he's so tall that you can't help but notice him, or because London is such a big and crowded place that you rarely see the same faces more than once.

His dark eyes still haven't left mine, and he pushes himself off the rail he's leaning against, and for a split second I think he's going to make the move and talk to me, and I feel like I've just stepped into a scene from one of my best friend Daphne's favourite romcom movies. The leading couple's eyes meet across a crowded train carriage and—

'The next station is King's Cross St. Pancras.' An automated voice comes over the tannoy, making me jump because everything but his eyes has faded into the background.

I see him swear under his breath and a look of panic crosses his face. He checks his phone again, turns around and gathers up his suitcase, hoists the holdall bag higher up his arm, and readjusts the rucksack on his shoulders.

I feel ridiculously bereft at the loss of eye contact as the train slows, but I get swept along by the crowd as other people gather up their bags and make a mass exodus towards the doors. He glances back like he's looking for me again, but I'm easy to miss amongst tall people and I've moved from where I was with the crowd. He looks around like he's trying to locate me, and I want to call out or wave or something, but what am I supposed to say? 'Hello, gorgeous Train Man, the strange short girl who's spent the entire journey staring at you is still here staring at you?'

I'm not far behind him now, even though this isn't my stop and it's clearly his. I can see him in the throng of people, his hand wrapped around the handle of the huge wheeled suitcase he's pulling behind him as the train comes to a stop.

As if the world turns to slow motion again, I see him glance at his phone once more and then go to pocket it, but instead of pushing it into the pocket of his jeans, it slides straight past and lands on the carriage floor at the exact moment the doors open and he, along with everyone else, rushes through them.

He hasn't noticed.

Without thinking, I dart forward and grab the phone from the floor before someone treads on it. I stare at it for a moment. This is his phone and I have it. He doesn't know he dropped it. There's still time to catch up with him and give it back.

Zinnia will probably kill me for being late for work, and I'm still a few stops away from where I usually get off, but I don't have time to wait. I follow the swarm as seemingly every other person in our carriage floods out, and I pause in the middle of them, aware of the annoyed grunts of people pushing past me as I try to see where he is. I follow the crowd off the platform and up the steps, straining to see over people's heads and between shoulders.

I'm sure I see his hair in the distance as the crowd starts to thin out, but he's moving faster than a jet-powered Usain Bolt after an energy drink.

'Hey!' I shout. 'Wait up!'

He doesn't react. He wouldn't know who I was calling to, if the guy I'm following is even him.

'Hey! You dropped your—'

Another passenger glares at me for shouting in his ear and I stop myself. I'm already out of breath and Train Man is nothing more than a blur in the distance. I rush in the same direction, but those steps have knackered me, and the faraway blob that might still be the back of his head turns a corner under the sign towards the overground trains, and I lose sight of him.

I race ... well, limp ... to the corner where I saw him turn, but the station fans out into an array of escalators and glowing signs and ticket booths, and it's thronging with people. I walk around for a few minutes, looking for any hint of him, but he's nowhere to be seen. In the many minutes it's taken me to half-jog half-stumble from one end of the station to the other, he could be on another train halfway across London by now.

I pull my own phone out and glance at the time. I'm twenty minutes late for work, and still three tube stops and a ten-minute walk away. Zinnia is going to *love* me this morning. I put my phone back in my pocket and slide his in alongside it.

I'll have to find another way to get it back to him.

I could just hand it in at the desk in the station, but he'll probably never see it again if I do that. If I dropped my phone, I'd like to think that a stranger would be kind enough to pick it up and attempt to reunite it with me, rather than just steal it.

Why shouldn't I do that for Train Man?

There's something about him, there has been since the first time I saw him standing squashed against the door of a crowded train, right back in my first week at *Maîtresse* magazine. I know Daphne's going to say that this is the universe's way of saying I'm supposed to meet him after all the smiles we've exchanged, although she regularly says that when she's trying to set me up on dates, if she's not too busy reminding me of how long it's been since my last date.

But it doesn't mean anything. He isn't even going to know that I'm the girl he smiles at sometimes. I'm sure I can just get an address and pop the phone in the post to him.

Simple as that. It won't be a problem.

# Chapter 2

'Let me get this straight,' Daphne says as I sit in her office at *Maîtresse*, mopping sweat off my face from the rush to get here just-regular-late instead of monumentally going-to-be-fired late. 'A stranger made eye contact with you, on public transport, in London?' She screws her face up. 'What kind of weirdo is this?'

By the time I've finished recounting my tube journey, she's leaning over her desk, one hand rubbing her pregnant belly and one fanning her face. 'Oh my God, Ness, I take it all back, he's not a weirdo at all, he's Train Man.' She elongates the middle of both words to make it sound like she's swooning.

It might not be the *first* time I've mentioned Train Man to Daphne.

'This is like the start of a chick flick. I'd force you to watch this with me if it came on TV.'

'And I'd humour you and spend the whole film picking apart the inaccuracies, because we all know that happily-ever-afters don't happen in real life, and those daft romantic films are pure escapism, a million miles away from anything that could ever happen in reality.'

Daphne is so pregnant that she can barely get comfortable and she shifts in her chair again, still fanning a hand in front of her

7

face, and I'm unsure if it's because she's getting hot flushes or because she thinks my morning is so swoonworthy. 'The universe wants you to meet this man.'

I knew she'd say that.

'No, it doesn't. He doesn't deserve to get his phone crushed by a stampede of people, but that's as far as it goes. This is not one of your romantic stories.'

'It could be like *Sliding Doors*.' She ignores me. 'Maybe you split in two as the train doors closed and there's a whole alternative universe where you did catch up with him and—'

'I could definitely do with splitting in two. Would the other one take half my body weight so I'd never need to go to the gym again?'

'You don't go to the gym, Ness, you just feel guilty for *not* going to the gym.' She points a swollen finger at me. 'And don't try to divert the conversation. This is something special. In the other universe, the one where Gwyneth Paltrow cuts all her hair off and tells her cheating boyfriend where to go, your fingers could've brushed as you handed his phone back and he could've halted his plans to immediately take you on a date, and …'

I glance at the time on my phone again. 'Well, my alternative-universe self works a lot faster than me. I went down the wrong escalator and got stuck for ten minutes trying to get back up. I bet she didn't get her toes run over by three separate suitcases either.'

'Your alternative-universe mum is probably already buying a hat. Can you imagine what your mum will say when you tell her about this? She'll start a national campaign to find this man.'

'That's why *no one* is telling my mum in a million years. If she finds out—'

'She'll love it, just like all our readers will,' Zinnia says, appearing in the doorway of Daphne's office. I hadn't even realised she was listening. 'I was about to tell you off for being late, Vanessa, and then you come in with an incredible story like this.'

'It's not a—'

'This *is* just like *Sliding Doors*, but it's real,' she says, her face lighting up as much as the Botox will allow it. 'It's just the sort of romantic story our readers would fall head over heels for.'

'The romantic tale of soulmates torn apart by closing tube doors.' Daph sits up. 'What if now you have to find him in this universe and catch up with the other universe or you'll be torn apart forever?'

'I think that's pushing it a bit, don't you? There were no magical sliding tube doors. I'm just not fit enough to chase someone through a train station.'

'Oh, don't talk about pushing.' Daph groans and rubs her belly again. 'And everyone wants love like in the movies, but you never try to find it. Movie characters don't just sit around expecting love to find them in the most romantic way—'

'Unrealistic way,' I cut in. 'Although I wouldn't mind my hair being as good as a Nineties Gwyneth Paltrow.'

'Yes!' Daph says. 'But that's how it is when you find "The One". The universe rearranges itself to throw you into each other's paths. Just like when I met Gavin. Ridiculous, inconvenient, all-consuming love, in the words of Carrie Bradshaw. This could be your chance.'

Zinnia points a bony finger at Train Man's phone, which is still sitting in the middle of Daphne's desk like it might burst if someone pokes it. 'Can you get into that?'

'No, it's locked.'

'Well, get it unlocked, woman. How else are you going to get it back to him and feel the sparks of your fingers brushing as you stare deeply into his eyes and fall in *lurve*?'

Zinnia is probably a typical magazine editor; picture Meryl Streep in *The Devil Wears Prada*, but with more hair product and brighter clothes. Thankfully she's a bit nicer than Miranda Priestly, and she runs a fortnightly women's magazine instead of a haute couture fashion mag, but she only employed me because Daphne persuaded her I had all the qualities needed in a fact-checker, like being fastidious and meticulous, when the only thing I'm fastidious about is making sure there's not a *scrape* of Nutella left at the bottom of the jar and I'm definitely not meticulous about setting my alarm in the mornings, and the more days that I underestimate the amount of time it takes to commute through London, the more likely Zinnia is to realise that Daphne was just trying to help her best friend get a job and I'm not actually that good at being a fact-checker. Or at getting here on time.

'You've got articles to check piling up on your desk, Vanessa. You could've finalised three stories in the time you've spent running around train stations this morning. Either get that unlocked and give me something that Daphne can write about, or forget it and get back to work.'

I should forget it. I should've handed it in at lost property in the station and been done with it. I lean over and pull the flat, black phone towards me. 'I suppose I could ask the IT guy to look at it.'

'Gosh, this is so romantic.' Zinnia clasps her hands together. 'Maybe you'll have some sort of spiritual connection and you'll just subconsciously know his password.'

'Oh come on, it's asking for a four-digit code. There are endless possibilities and the phone will probably lock us out after three attempts.' I pick it up and run my fingers across the blank screen. I would *love* nothing more than to have a look through it and prove to them both that he's undoubtedly married and his best quality is probably trying to pick up women on trains that his wife doesn't know about. I need to forget all about Train Man *and* his phone. Besides, he was around my age and *gorgeous*, there's no way he's going to be single too. I don't know what they're expecting to come out of this.

Daphne gets up and waddles around the room in another attempt to get comfortable. 'Try 1234,' she says with a laugh.

I type the numbers in. 'As if anyone would be that stup—'

The phone makes a jingling sound and pings into life.

Daph bursts out laughing. 'Seriously? The man *deserves* to have his phone stolen just for that. What's his credit card PIN – 5678?'

I suddenly feel really bad. Whoever Train Man is, this is his private phone. He wouldn't want a random stranger going through it, and I feel like some kind of criminal mastermind to have managed to unlock it. I'm going to be hacking the government next. Even though the government's security systems are probably slightly more complex than 1234.

'What did I tell you?' Zinnia sounds gleeful. 'Get into his pictures, quick. I want to see this dashing romantic hero.'

'What's that?' Daph peers over my shoulder.

'A train timetable,' I say, looking at the jumble of numbers and times still onscreen from the last time he looked at it. 'And not for the tube.'

'So he was catching another train. Maybe that's why he ran off so quickly.'

'He did look worried about something. And he did keep checking his phone. Maybe he was looking at the time. Probably to check that his wife wouldn't be home before his latest bit on the side left.'

'Nah,' Daph says. 'Things like this don't just *happen*. He's obviously single and looking, just like you.'

'I'm not looking.'

'I'm looking for you,' she says with a shrug. 'Same thing.'

'Anyone would think you didn't have enough on with swooning over your own husband and a baby on the way.'

'Girls, pictures,' Zinnia says before she can respond. It's not like it's the first time we've had this conversation anyway. It always goes the same way. Daph says I'm over the hill, I tell her there is no hill to be over because whether I'm thirty-four or fifty or seventy, I'm not interested in another relationship, and she says she thought the same thing until she met Gavin, and if I'd just put myself out there and give it a chance, I might surprise myself

11

and meet someone. I tell her how much I enjoy my own company and how nice it is to be single after spending so many years in a loveless relationship, and she tells me that was just one relationship and others will be different, ad infinitum. I can finish the conversation in my head without Daph saying another word, until she walks off muttering things like 'spinster' and 'cat lady'.

I'm obviously not moving fast enough because Daphne plucks the phone from my fingers and starts playing with it. 'I hope he takes a lot of selfies. I'm desperate to see this guy.'

'We shouldn't be going through his phone,' I try to protest.

'We're not. We're looking for a way to get it back to him. Via his photos. Ooh, and his notes. Oh, and we have to check his messages because there might be some vital bit of contact information in there.'

'And we're just nosy,' Zinnia adds.

Like I hadn't figured that one out for myself.

'Like you don't want to know too,' Daph says.

'Nope. I'm not looking. I'm not interested. I just want to get the phone back to him.'

Daphne makes various noises as she fiddles with the phone and I fight the urge to see what she's doing.

'Okay, well, he's not big on selfies, but we've got bigger problems than making eye contact on public transport. Are you sure he didn't strike you as a bit of a weirdo?'

'No, why?' I instantly imagine she's found a folder full of dick pics ready to send to unsuspecting women or something. No wonder he smiles at people on trains – he's probably assessing them for how happy they'd be to receive an unsolicited photo of his manhood.

'Nothing about him screamed weird fetishist or anything?'

'No. Why, Daph?' All pretence of not being interested falls away as I jump out of the chair and try to see over her shoulder.

'Well, he's got a real thing for wooden horses. Look at this. His phone is absolutely full of photos of bits of wooden horses.'

That's a bit weird, isn't it?'

'They're carousel horses.' I peer over one shoulder and Zinnia peers over the other as Daphne scrolls through his photos at the speed of light, each one showing similar pictures of wooden carousel animals in methodical stages, from perfectly painted to varying states of decay.

'And what's that? It looks like parts of a rollercoaster, and what the— Ooh, is that him?' She shoves the phone at me, showing a picture of Train Man in the distance, his arms outstretched on a sparkling carousel.

'He's definitely got some kind of weird fetish for those things,' Zinnia says.

'Or maybe he just likes that godawful old movie that you love.' Daphne elbows me in the ribs, knowing full well I can't retaliate while she's pregnant.

'Aww, stop mocking *Carousel*. It's a lovely film. One of the best.'

'Yeah, if you like things that are nonsensical, boring, and old. And then you have the nerve to complain that I like modern romcoms. Judging by these photos, I bet he *loves* that movie. Talk about your perfect match.' She takes the phone back and scrolls further through the photos, picture after picture of wooden things, half-finished paint jobs on carousel horses and other animals, and a few of various scenery, beaches and mountains and hills. Train Man must get around a bit.

'Well, he's definitely not vain – he's never taken a picture of himself in his life. Although he's got half his shoe in with one of these horse legs, which tells us *so* much.' Daph gives up and scrolls back to the photo of him on the carousel, zooming in on it and bringing the phone almost to her nose. 'He looks handsome, though. Good hair.'

'He had good hair on the train this morning.'

I don't realise I'm smiling involuntarily until I catch the knowing look on Zinnia's face. I blush and tuck my own shoulder-length lank hair behind my ear. 'Unlike my messy split-endy thing that needs a trim.' I always feel self-conscious of my hair around Zinnia, who never has a strand out of place. Mine still hasn't recovered from an ill-advised home highlighting kit where the streaks went orange so I dyed over them with a brown that was supposed to match my own colour but ended up going lighter because of the orangeness. Daph calls them lowlights; I call them 'can't afford to go to the hairdresser's'.

'You hate taking selfies too,' Daphne says. 'I can already tell this guy is perfect for you. Now, what next? Text messages?'

She's gone back to the home screen and is fiddling around in his message folder before I've even started to protest. 'We're just looking for vital contact information so we can get it back to him.'

'And evidence of a girlfriend because so far there's nothing,' Zinnia adds. 'He must be single or there'd be some photos of a girlfriend, boyfriend, or otherwise on there. My phone is packed with pictures of my husband.'

'And mine's packed with pictures of Gavin measuring things against my ever-expanding belly to show how big it's getting,' Daph says. 'Well, this morning someone called Jack texted telling Train Man "not to miss that bloody train". His parcel was "now with his local courier for delivery" last Thursday, he wished someone called Susan a happy birthday last week, and someone sent a message a fortnight ago asking if he wants to go on a fishing weekend in July, but he hasn't responded.' She glances at me over her shoulder. 'This is just as boring as your phone.'

'Still no girlfriend,' Zinnia says. 'Tell me this isn't looking more and more promising.'

'There's nothing here,' Daphne says. 'Funny pictures someone's forwarded him, the odd joke between mates, but absolutely no sappy love messages. Not even an "on the way home, see you soon" – and even I text Gavin one of them when I leave work every night.'

'It doesn't matter, I'm not interested.' I ignore the flutteriness again. There must've been something wrong with that cereal this morning. Nothing more.

'Right, notes. He could have written his address in there in case his phone ever got lost.'

'Daph! This is his private property!'

'Oh my God, Ness. He's a vegetarian too. He's literally the male version of you. Look, last week's shopping list.' She waves the phone in front of me. 'Halloumi cheese, Quorn sausages, veggie bacon, Coco Pops, Nutella, and Cadbury's Fingers.' She sighs happily. 'Any guy who buys Cadbury's Fingers is a keeper. They're your favourites.'

'He's probably buying them for his wife,' I say, even though warmth floods my insides. I'm not interested in men, but if I could invent a perfect one, that would be his shopping list. 'Besides, Cadbury's Fingers only mean he's a keeper if he bites both ends off and sucks tea up through it like a straw until it goes all melty and gooey on the inside.'

'No address then?' Zinnia asks. She's all about yoga and detoxing teas. She doesn't approve of chocolate. Daphne and I regularly joke that it's all a front and she often leaves abruptly so she can get back to the bar of Galaxy hidden in her desk.

'Nothing. What shall we do? Call the last number he dialled and see if they know how else to get in touch with him?'

'Oi!' I finally do protest. 'I'm the one who found the phone. I should be the one doing this. It's not right for us all to gather round it like some kind of soap opera.'

'Yeah, and I'm pregnant so you can't hit me to get it back.' Daph ducks behind Zinnia and pokes her tongue out at me. 'Right, call log.'

I sigh as I watch her go through the phone. 'Again, no repeat calls to any specific number. No late-night booty calls. Here, last number dialled was local. I'll ring it.'

She presses the dial button and puts the speaker on.

'Cheap N Easy Pizza is closed at this time. Try again after five-thirty,' a tinny voice comes through the phone.

Daph hangs up and bursts out laughing. 'The last thing he did was get a takeaway pizza. Ness, he's literally you. When did you last have a takeaway pizza?'

'The weekend,' I say, trying not to blush. 'There's nothing wrong with takeaway pizza. Not all of us have husbands who like to experiment with cooking gourmet meals for us, you know.'

'Not for my lack of trying to find you one,' she mutters. 'And I bet he even likes pineapple on it too.'

'There's nothing wrong with—' I start to protest but Daph drops her arm and I see an opportunity to snatch the phone out of her hand. 'Ah ha!'

'Okay, how are you going to find him then?' Zinnia asks. I'm surprised she's getting so involved in this. She loves anything to do with love, but she's not usually got much time for me. I'm supposed to be a fact-checker for *Maîtresse* but my heart's not in it. She knows it and I know it, and I'm not fast enough, thorough enough, or dedicated enough for her to like me.

'There's not even any social media,' Daphne says. 'I'm getting a bit worried here, Ness. Where's his Facebook app? No Twitter? No Instagram? You are sure he isn't a technophobe ninety-year-old, aren't you?'

'Well, maybe he just likes to keep things private. Not *everyone's* on social media. Some days, I think we'd all be a lot less stressed if we weren't. I don't have the Facebook app on my phone either.'

'See?' Daph holds her hand up. 'Perfect match.'

I sit there and scroll through the photos. He's certainly got a thing about carousels. Almost all his photos are of them. There are photos taken of aged photos depicting them in olden days, pictures of broken parts of various wooden animals, paint-chipped poles, carousels in fairgrounds, one on a pier, and there are other rides too. I spot what must be joints of a rollercoaster and possibly some tracks, what looks like antique furniture and old steam engines. I linger on the distant photo of him standing on a carousel for longer than could be considered normal. My heart is pounding harder just at the sight of him in a zoomed-in photograph.

I have to stop thinking about it. The sooner this phone is out of my hands, the better. 'Why don't I try texting someone on his contact list and ask them how to get in touch with him?'

'I volunteer my services while you go and get on with work,' Daphne says quickly. 'I'll find someone who can get in touch with him *and* verify his relationship status.'

'Chop chop.' Zinnia taps her wrist like I'm on a schedule.

I scroll through the messages again but Daph's right, there don't seem to be any ongoing conversations or anything other than perfunctory messages and courier confirmations, so I go to his contacts list instead, hoping it might be in some kind of most-contacted order but it's alphabetical.

'Just text the first one,' Zinnia says, and I get the feeling this has gone on too long for her. She's efficient and doesn't believe in wasting time, which is probably why she's the editor of a popular women's magazine and I'm the person who phones round publicists trying to find two sources to confirm that Brad Pitt's name is actually spelt Brad Pitt. Nothing is too pedantic in fact-checking.

I slide my finger back up to the top. 'Okay. Alan it is. Let's hope he's a good friend of Train Man.'

*Hello, I type out. I found this phone on the train this morning and I'm trying to get hold of the owner to give it back. Do you know how I can contact him?*

'Now we wait.'

Daph starts talking about the baby pressing on her bladder, but within minutes, the phone lets out a low jingling noise and lights up in my hand.

'Oooh!' we all say in unison.

I unlock the phone and blink in surprise at the reply. 'Oh. No "oooh" at all. Wow.' I ignore the growingly insistent chorus of 'whats'. 'That's not very nice.'

I read the text message from Alan aloud, cutting out some of the more, er, choice language. 'Eff off Nathaniel, don't involve me in whatever stupid game you're playing now.'

'Ooh, intriguing,' Daph says.

'Worrying,' I amend for her. 'What's he done to this bloke? What "stupid game" has he been playing before?'

'Why'd he bother to keep him as a contact if they hate each other so much?'

'A mystery,' Zinnia says. 'To solve.'

'Nathaniel is such a sexy name,' Daph says, fanning a hand in front of her face again.

'*That's* what you took from that message?'

'Well, at least we know what he's called now. Although I don't fancy texting dear old Alan back to ask for his home address or landline number, do you?'

I recoil at the thought. 'Don't you think we've invaded this poor man's privacy enough? We've been through his pictures, his notes, his messages; we've even managed to text his number one enemy. I should have dropped this phone straight in at lost property in the station. It has nothing to do with me if he gets it back or not.'

'There's an amazing story in this. It's so romantic. A man you've been silently flirting with on the train for months, eyes meeting across a crowded carriage, and now you being the one to spot his dropped phone and the quest to find this mystery man and return it ... Our readers will *love* it.' Zinnia looks between me and Daphne with an expression that means she's plotting something, and then her eyes settle on me. 'And you're going to be the one to write it.'

'Me?' I shake my head in an attempt to clear my ears because I'm definitely not hearing her right. 'Write what?'

'*This.*' She rolls her eyes, leaving me in no doubt about how dense she thinks I am for not getting it yet. 'The story of The Guy on the Train. It'll be like that novel but without all the alcoholism and murderyness.'

'Oh, it'll be so romantic.' Daph picks up a magazine to fan herself with. 'The playful flirtation, the eye contact, the smile, the dimples, the connection on a crowded train where the only thing anyone usually connects with is some drunken guy's leering or the smell of wee where someone's urinated on a seat. Again.'

'Yes,' Zinnia says. 'A story about being in the right place at the right time to pick up the mysterious gorgeous man's dropped phone and lose him by the whisper of a second in a crowded station. A romance for the modern woman who commutes to work every day on public transport. A magical connection with a stranger that could happen to any one of our readers at any moment.'

'But … I …' I have no idea what to say. I can't believe she's giving me a chance to write for *Maîtresse*. It's what I've been waiting for since I started here. Fact-checking was only ever supposed to be temporary, but in the two years since I started, it doesn't feel temporary anymore.

'I want this story, Vanessa, and realistically you're the only person who can write it. I know you joined *Maîtresse* with the intention of writing features for us, and I know you've been hoping for a promotion since your first day and you're probably wondering why I've always overlooked you, but the right way for you to prove yourself has never come up … until now.'

It's probably meant as a compliment but Zinnia only succeeds in making me feel about as important to this office as the persistent bluebottle buzzing around the water dispenser.

'I want this article on my desk today. We'll put it on our website straight away, and *if* it gets a good response, then you'll find your debut feature in print in the July issue of *Maîtresse*, and we'll talk about moving you out of fact-checking and into a feature-writing role. We can start with Daphne's maternity leave. You know she's disappearing on us next month, and you probably know that I haven't arranged cover yet. Impress me with this article, and Daphne's job is yours for the twelve months of her maternity leave. If you do well, we'll look into something more permanent.'

Daphne squeals in delight. 'I told you ages ago that Ness should do it!'

I'm, again, unsure of whether the idea that my best friend and boss have been talking about me is a good thing or not, but it makes me feel a bit irrelevant. Daph mentioned that I should talk to Zinnia about covering her maternity leave months ago and I never plucked up the courage – if she mentioned it to Zinnia around the same time then Zinnia clearly wasn't interested in the idea.

'It'll be a great start to a career as a writer here,' Zinnia continues. 'That's what you want, isn't it?'

'More than anything,' I say quickly before she has a chance to change her mind.

She nods once. 'Good. I'll forward this morning's articles to be fact-checked to one of the temps so you can give this your full attention. I think this is going to be really special. Two o'clock this afternoon and not a *second* later.' She goes to walk out but then spins on her heels and points a long red nail at me. 'And, Vanessa? Leave it open-ended. You're going to find this guy, and when you do, our readers will want to know about it.'

Daph barely gives her time to get out of earshot before she squeals. 'This is brilliant, Ness, well done!'

It *is* brilliant, I know that, but … a love story? Me? I'm the worst choice in the world to write a love story. I haven't even been on a date in over two years, as Daph reminds me repeatedly. She's the one who writes articles about love and romance and couples who meet in weird and wonderful ways. I just fact-check them, and I love reading them because my best friend wrote them, but Daphne can make a story out of anything. I don't know how to write this breathtakingly romantic article that Zinnia seems to want out of a guy I've looked at on the train a few times.

Daph's already scribbling notes for me in a notepad. 'Tell it exactly as you've always told me about Train Man. Focus on how his gaze makes you feel rather than how pretty his eyes are because you don't want his identity to be too obvious. And make sure to mention how single you are and how single he is, and how you'll meet when you give his phone back.'

'I've got to find him first. Alan certainly wasn't any help.'

'Someone else will be. You haven't got time to go through his contacts now, but after the article's done, then you can concentrate on finding him.'

'He's probably a psychopath,' I say. 'Eye contact on public transport is a big no-no.'

'*You* made eye contact on public transport with *him* too.' She sighs. 'You don't always have to think the worst of people, Ness.'

'I don't always think—'

'You thought that guy I tried to set you up with last month was a lunatic.'

'He wanted to go rock climbing for a date. Rock climbing, Daph! A coffee is a date, not clambering up a flippin' rock. Dating is bad enough without involving rocks and exercise.'

'You wouldn't have accepted even if he'd offered coffee and cake, just like you didn't accept the last guy I tried to set you up with, or the one before that, or the one before. It's been years since "poor Andrew"—'

'Just how romantic do you think Zinnia wants this to be?' I interrupt her. I know she thinks I was mad to break up with 'poor Andrew' and even madder not to want to find someone else, but I'm better off alone. 'Poor Andrew' proved that. Netflix is a much better companion.

'*So* romantic. She wants the love story of the year that's going to resonate with any woman who's ever been on a packed train.'

'That's exactly the point though, isn't it? It's just a story. A fantasy. It'd make a nice movie, but this sort of thing doesn't actually happen. It'd be great if he was the man of my dreams.' I pat the phone in my pocket. 'But he isn't. Stories like these are just stories. They're not real life.'

* * *

At five to two, I press send on my email to Zinnia.

**The Guy on the Train: A love story for our time, with a twist worthy of any Paula Hawkins novel**

*By Vanessa Berton*

*The unspoken rule of London transport: ignore everyone. No one else exists on the tube. The disinterested gaze at nothing in particular as long as it's not another human being is an art form that every person learns upon their arrival in the capital.*

*I have broken this rule. A man has broken this rule with me.*

*For a few months now, Train Man and I have looked at each other on the Victoria line. It's not every morning, far from it. Sometimes there can be days or weeks between our clandestine gazes.*

*I'm not a born Londoner. Would other Londoners turn on me if they knew that I regularly make eye contact with a stranger? Would they make me disembark at the next stop if they knew that we sometimes – and I can't believe I'm going to admit this – smile at each other?*

*There. I've said it. I've noticed that there are other people on the tube. One of them has noticed me. Sometimes we share a smile. And it's a very nice smile. It's a smile with dimples, and hair of the darkest brown, and dark eyes that smile too when they look at me. It's quite a feat to see me flustered and sweltering on a summer morning and not be scarred for life, but Train Man manages it. Each morning that I see him is just a little better than any other morning. I arrive at work with just a slightly springier step.*

*This morning was different. This morning, instead of being at* the opposite end of the carriage like I usually am, I was mere feet away from him, crammed against a sweaty shirtless body. Unfortunately not his sweaty shirtless body. That would've made the journey marginally more pleasant.

Our eyes met as usual. And his dimples at such close range were enough to make me take leave of my senses. I nearly spoke to him. Thankfully I stopped myself at the last second because I hadn't completely lost my marbles. But he nearly spoke to me too. In fact, we were barely saved from a lifetime of awkward conversation by arriving at a station – his stop today, but not his usual stop. Why is he getting off here when he doesn't usually? Judging by the suitcase and array of bags, he's obviously going somewhere, and judging by the panicked looks he keeps giving his phone, he doesn't have much time to get there.

I don't mean to watch him, but he's tall enough to unintentionally draw the eye, and I'm short enough to be hidden by other passengers, so he can't see me lurking behind him, watching the way long, sexy fingers wrap around the handle of his suitcase as he waits for the door to open. I see him give a final glance at his phone before he slips it back into his pocket. Except, he doesn't slip it back into his pocket. He thinks he has, but I'm the only one who's noticed that he missed, and in the clamour of the doors opening, he hasn't heard it clatter to the floor.

I grab it before it gets caught in the stampede, and make a split-second decision to run after him to return it, but I may have been slightly lax on my gym visits lately, and he runs out of there at a speed that would make Sonic the Hedgehog jealous.

I don't catch him. And I now I have his phone.

And I've managed to unlock it. I am inside the private life of Train Man. I've read his texts. I've seen his photos. I know what grocery shopping he bought last week and that he ordered a pizza last night. I know he likes the same things I like, that there are no texts to a significant other, and I've happened to notice on our shared journeys that he doesn't wear a wedding ring.

*Could a guy so friendly and gorgeous really be single? Could my silent flirtation with Train Man really mean something? Have we defied the laws of public transport because of a deeper meaning? Has the universe thrown us into each other's path for a reason that we can't yet see?*

*I have his phone. I have to get it back to him. But I have to find him first ...*

Daph warned me to only expect a response from Zinnia if she hates it, so I take the silence as a good sign and get on with fact-checking the stack of articles piled up in my inbox. Well, between obsessively refreshing the website to see when it goes live, obviously.

It's not perfect; I know that. I'm sure it'll fade into the depths of *Maîtresse*'s site and be read by approximately four people, three of whom will be me, Daph, and Zinnia double-checking ad placement, and any hopes of seeing my name in print and starting a real career will be gone forever. But it was fun to write, even if my promotion to features writer only lasts a morning.

# Chapter 3

I've just sat on the sofa and put Netflix on that evening, and I'm scrolling through the recently added things, having already watched pretty much the whole catalogue, when the phone rings. I've left Nathaniel's phone on the kitchen unit next to mine, and as I shove my microwave meal onto the coffee table and run to get it, I notice it's his phone that's vibrating across the counter towards the sink. I grab it and slide the screen up to answer without even glancing at it.

'Hi, this is Nathaniel's phone.'

'Hi, this is Nathaniel.' He pauses and my heart jumps into my throat. I pull the phone away from my ear and look at the number onscreen, a mobile number that's not saved in his contacts. It must be him on another phone. Maybe it's just as well I didn't know – he'd have rung off by the time I'd psyched myself up to speak to him.

'No, wait, it's Nathan. Only people who hate me call me Nathaniel. Where did you get that name from?'

'I texted the first name in your directory.'

'Who was … oh no, don't tell me. Alan? I take it he gave a suitably charming response?'

'He, er, didn't seem to like you very much …'

'The feeling's entirely mutual.' He sighs. 'What did he say?'

'Um …' I don't feel particularly comfortable repeating the nasty message. 'You'll see when you get your phone back.'

'Don't worry, "um" is more than descriptive enough.' He lets out a sad laugh. 'It's actually nice of you not to tell me. You are planning on giving it back then?'

'Of course I am! I have my own phone that I'd like to get away from half the time, I certainly don't want yours as well. I saw you on the train this morning. I was behind you when we pulled into your stop and you went to put your phone in your pocket but you missed. I picked it up before it got trampled or stolen. I've been trying to find a way to contact you all day.' *You know, between writing an article about how pretty your eyes are and examining every inch of your phone.*

'You're the girl I see sometimes, aren't you?' His breath catches in his throat and I get the sense that he's holding it, waiting for an answer.

At that caught breath, all of my doubts slip away. He does know me. I haven't imagined some connection between us. He smiles at me too. Whatever *Sliding Doors* magic Daphne keeps going on about, whatever else Zinnia wants me to write about him. It doesn't matter. Maybe they're right. Maybe this isn't just coincidence.

'We do see each other sometimes, yeah,' I say, hesitating a little because I'm not quite sure how to describe it.

He lets out a long breath and warmth floods my insides. He must've felt something over the months of our silent flirtation too. Not just that I was a weird public transport starer.

'What's your name?' he asks in a soft Yorkshire accent.

'Ness. Well, Vanessa, but everyone calls me Ness.'

'We have something in common then – full names we don't get called by.'

The way he says it makes me want to smile but I still feel like I need to explain myself. 'I tried to catch you, you know? But you ran out of there faster than the Road Runner.'

'Beep beep,' he says, doing a spot-on impression, and a giggle takes me by surprise because I used to love those cartoons.

'Yeah, sorry, I had a connection to catch and about three minutes to make it between platforms and that was without the tube being a couple of minutes late. Trains to this part of the country only run once a day. I couldn't miss it.'

'What part of the country's that then?' I grew up in a little village where my parents still live. I remember the days of one bus an hour and being completely cut off from civilisation. The constant trains and buses were one of my favourite things when I first moved to London, but even that's got old now. Sometimes I long for the days of one bus an hour and not being crammed into a tube train every morning like a limp flip-flop on a summer's day.

'A little village called Pearlholme. I bet you've never heard of it because it's so small that even people who live five miles away from it have never heard of it. It's on the Yorkshire coast, not far down from Scarborough.'

'I always hear people saying they love that part of the country.'

'It's perfect here. The beach is amazing and the village is so tiny. It's all cobbled streets and quaint cottages. There's one combined shop and post office, a pub, and a couple of beach huts on the promenade, and that's it. It's the perfect antidote to London. I've only been here a few hours and I feel better than I have in months.' He sounds like he's smiling as he speaks.

I wasn't expecting him to sound the way he does. His voice sounds warm and approachable, like a steady reassuring policeman, someone you'd be safe with. It matches the way his smile has always looked.

*'Are you on holiday?' With your wife? And children?*

'No, I'm working, although I've got a nerve to call it work, really. I'm restoring an old carousel by the sea. I'm literally on the sand. The beach is my office. It's amazing. It couldn't get any better.'

I find myself smiling at how happy he sounds. 'That explains all the pictures of wooden horses on your phone.'

'So you've been going through my pictures then, have you?' He still sounds jokey and not annoyed at all.

'I wasn't going through them, I was looking for a way of getting your phone back to you.' I don't mention *quite* how much time Daph, Zinnia, and I spent combing through his phone inch by inch this morning or that I'm already thinking about how smug I can sound tomorrow when I tell them the carousel horses aren't just a weird fetish.

'In my photos?'

'Well, you could've taken a picture of your house, couldn't you?'

'Hah. It's a crummy flat in an ugly block in London. The only people who'd take a photograph of it would be filmmakers for a documentary on Britain's worst housing.'

'Oh, I know that feeling.' I glance over at the bucket in the corner, catching a leak of unknown origin. The landlord, on the rare occasion I can get hold of him, promised to get it sorted last year. He hasn't answered his phone since. Perhaps I should stop the rent direct debit – that'd get him round here pretty fast.

'And I bet you pay enough rent to purchase a small car every month too, right?'

'Several small cars, actually.'

'You should see the cottage I'm staying in here. It's a holiday let that I've rented for six weeks, but I could live here for six months for the price of one month in London, and it's *gorgeous*.'

'Six weeks,' I say, trying not to think about a beautiful cottage by the sea or that gorgeous man in it. It sounds like the most perfect place and I suddenly have an overwhelming pang of sadness because I'm here and not there. 'You won't be back for ages.'

'No, the owner wants this thing restored by the summer holidays so I'm here until then. It's an incredible old carousel. I reckon it was carved entirely by one person, and it was found in an old ruin. The owner won it in an auction, and put it on the beach for the public, and their busiest season is once the kids break up from school so that's my deadline.'

So much for hoping to see him on the train again tomorrow morning to return the phone. 'Do you do this a lot then? I mean, all those pictures …'

'Yeah, mainly repairs rather than full restorations because there just aren't that many carousels to restore in the country – this is a rare treat for me.' He laughs. 'And yeah, I really am that boring. That's pretty much all I use my phone for, as I'm sure you discovered. Pictures of work.'

And keeping track of your shopping lists, of course. Which I know because you buy all of my favourite food.

'I must be creating such a good picture of myself here. All I do is moan about my flat and talk about work. Sorry, I'm sure I'm not usually this boring.'

'It's not boring at all. Pretty much all I do is work and moan about my flat too. At least your job is a lot more interesting than mine.'

'What do you do?'

'I'm a fact-checker for a women's magazine. I have to double-check everything that proper journalists write so we don't publish anything that's untrue. I want to be a journalist and I thought I'd get a chance to prove myself there, but it's been years now and all I am is basically a proofreader who does a *lot* of googling and phoning around to confirm quotes. I work a lot of overtime because I have nothing better to do and I keep hoping my boss will notice how dedicated I am.'

'I can't complain about my job. I work a lot of overtime because I *love* old carousels and mainly because if I'm working then I'm not sitting in my crappy flat thinking about how many places I'd rather be.'

'I know that feeling too,' I say, looking at the window, which gives me a marvellous view of the building next door. I can imagine what his view in that gorgeous cottage is like. 'Do you do anything other than carousels? There were some pictures that we— I— couldn't work out, they looked like bits of rollercoaster?'

'I'm glad you were so thorough in your search for my address.' He still doesn't sound annoyed by it. 'And yes, I'm not strictly carousels, although they're my speciality. I'm just a repairman in general, really. My firm restores all sorts of old things, from organs to engines to fairground rides, and yes, they were bits of roller-coaster but not rollercoasters as we know them now – the old wooden scenic railways that were popular in the early 1900s, the kind of thing anyone from a baby to a granny could enjoy a ride on, a real throwback to days gone by. I take a lot of pictures because you can rarely get parts in this day and age, and we usually have to find something similar and adjust it or make the parts ourselves.'

He suddenly stops himself. 'I'm sorry, I must be boring you senseless. I'm not usually this boring, honestly. And the fact I've said that twice tonight probably doesn't bode well. You're not busy, are you? I've been rabbiting on for ages and never asked you if I was interrupting something. You're probably sitting down for a nice dinner with your husband, and—'

I laugh at the mental image. 'No husband. I was sitting down with a microwave meal and Netflix. How's that for busy? Talking to you is much more interesting.'

He laughs too. 'You obviously don't know me well enough yet.'

I try to ignore another little flutter of butterflies at that 'yet'.

'And you've just described my average evening. Netflix and a sarnie. Sometimes I stretch to something really strenuous like cheese on toast.' He says it with a French accent, like a posh chef describing a gourmet meal, and it makes me laugh again, and I realise that I'm gripping the phone tighter because I don't want him to go yet. 'My brother bought me a chef's blowtorch once.

30

God knows what he thought I was going to cook with it. Beans on toast *on fire?*'

'You know what I don't get?' I say, trying to stop myself laughing again. 'Instant mashed potatoes. You sprinkle a little bit out of the packet into the bottom of a mug, and it makes six bowlfuls.'

'Oh, I *love* instant mashed potatoes,' he says. 'They're like the ultimate comfort food, and I can pretend they're healthy because they're vegetables. Powdered, reconstituted vegetables, but still. I'm spoiled tonight because the landlady at the cottage made me a macaroni cheese and left it in the fridge. At least I now know why she asked if I had any allergies. I wondered if she was planning on filling the roof with asbestos and painting the walls with lead or something. I'm just waiting for that to come out of the oven and I'm going to eat it in the garden with a cup of tea.' He pauses. 'You probably thought I was thirty-six this morning, but now I reveal I'm really an eighty-year-old woman in disguise. No wonder I like it in Pearlholme so much. Everyone seems to be elderly around here. You should've seen my landlady, bless her. She looked like she could barely carry the key when I collected it. God knows how she's still managing to cook huge casserole dishes of food.'

I laugh yet again. I'm not good at talking to strangers, which is probably quite weird for someone who spends a lot of time phoning strangers to confirm facts and double-check quotes in articles, but there's something about him that puts me completely at ease. I'm often on edge in my flat – you can usually hear the shouting of neighbours or fights in the hall, and it never feels safe here, but his warm accent on the other end of the phone settles something inside me.

'Thanks for picking up my phone this morning. I'm glad it was you. I mean … I saw you … We're usually much further apart … and I was in such a hurry … and I'm not even sure what I'm trying to say. Just thank you for grabbing it and trying to get it back to me. I assumed I'd been pickpocketed. I always think the worst of people and don't really trust anyone, so ...'

'My best friend has been saying exactly the same thing about me this afternoon.'

He does a soft snort. 'Ah, at least we can revel in our trust issues together. Which is, of course, a totally normal thing to talk to a complete stranger about. I don't talk to many people, as you can tell because I'm so bad at it.'

He's self-deprecating and rambly in the most adorable way. And I just ... don't want to stop talking to him. 'Well, that's three things we have in common – trust issues, full names we don't use, and being bad at talking to people. And for what it's worth, you're doing a great job so far. This is fun.'

I can hear the grin in his voice. 'Maybe it's because you're on my phone. I feel like I'm talking to myself.'

'Yeah, that must be it.' I'm sitting here smiling at my empty living room, which is not something that usually evokes a smile. 'How'd you manage without your phone today? Must've been tough – we're so used to always having them on us.'

'Oh, you have no idea. My train timetable was on it, directions, and the bus timetable to get into Pearlholme. I didn't even know the time because I rely on my phone instead of wearing a watch. I had to do the *unthinkable*. I had to stop strangers in the street and ask for directions.'

'Oh no, how did you cope?' I struggle to hold in a giggle.

'It was terrible! I had to make actual eye contact and every-thing.' He makes the noise of a shudder. 'Who does that in this day and age? It's what Google Maps was invented for – to prevent the rare occasion that you might have to speak to a random human being you don't actually know.'

'I remember that. It was always so annoying when you'd ask someone and they'd tell you the way, and you'd follow their directions and you were clearly in the wrong place, so you'd ask someone else and they'd tell you completely the opposite direc-tion from what the first lot had told you, and then you'd have to drive back past the first lot and wonder if you could casually push them over a bridge or something.'

He groans. 'I better not tell you that one of my favourite pastimes growing up was trolling people who asked for directions. They'd ask if I knew where a place was, and I act all authoritative and say, "Oh, yes, I live right near there; it's this way, take a left and turn down the lane." I'd direct them to, like, the middle of the nearest cow field. It was great!'

'Why?'

'I don't know. I grew up in a tiny village and life was boring.' He pauses. 'From the tone of your voice, I take it the correct answer is "because I was young, cruel, and incredibly immature, and got my jollies off by making other people's lives a misery"?'

'That's better,' I say, unable to contain my laughter. He's naturally funny but none of it seems forced. He seems like an old friend I've known for years.

A really hot old friend, obviously.

'I nearly had to go full-on retro and call the speaking clock to find out the time.'

'With what?'

'I hadn't even thought of that!' He laughs. 'See? That's how weird it is not to have a phone on you. I suppose I'd have had to find a relic of an old telephone box. Anything would be better than having to ask a stranger again. Starting conversations with strangers once in a day is more than enough.'

'So what phone are you on now? Did you have to borrow one?'

'No, I bought this ancient pay-as-you-go thing for fifteen quid. It's one of the old clamshell flip phones, if you can remember them. Colour screens had barely been invented and there's so much glare that you can't see it in daylight. Most people haven't seen one since 2003 but they like to keep up with the times around here.'

'And you managed to get that in Pearlholme? From what you've said, it doesn't sound modern enough for a phone like that.'

'Flipping 'eck, no. There's a slightly bigger village about five miles away. I got the bus there and found it in the chemist of all places. And when I got on the bus, the bus driver said, "You're the bloke doing up the carousel on the beach, aren't you?" and he refused a fare because the carousel will be good for the area. That's how archaic it is round here. I'd only been in town long enough to collect my key and dump my bags at the cottage.'

'I grew up in a village like that. I used to hate it, but sometimes the crowds of London make me miss it.'

'Me too. I'm from a village in South Yorkshire. I haven't lived there for a long time though.'

'Yeah, your accent kind of gives that away.' I try not to sound as spellbound by his accent as I am. I could quite happily sit here and listen to him read the phone book. 'I'm from Nottingham but it reminds me of home.'

'I hate London. You never really escape the feeling of loneliness there despite the fact you're constantly surrounded by people. I love going on jobs like this where I can get away for a while.'

'I'm so jealous. My office is a cubicle the size of a matchbox, and my choice of view is a white wall *or* a white wall with the scars of a thousand drawing pins being stuck in it over the years. Your job sounds like heaven.'

'I'm really lucky,' he says. 'If you ever want to get away, you should come up here. It's beautiful.'

'I'll add it to my list of destinations for holidays I'll never take,' I say, feeling more desolate than is normal when talking about holidays.

He sighs and the line goes quiet, but it doesn't feel awkward. I used to talk about nonsense to fill up uncomfortable silences with 'poor Andrew', but I feel content just listening to him breathe down the line.

It is a bit weird though.

'So how am I going to get this phone back to you then?' I say eventually. I don't want this conversation to end, but it seems stupid not to mention anything about it. 'I can keep—'

'Why don't you come and find me? It's kind of your fault that I lost it in the first place because I was distracted by you—'

'Oi! You can't blame me.'

He starts laughing, letting me know it was just a joke. 'Well, you want to give it back so badly, come up to Pearlholme and give it back. It's the most gorgeous village – you'd love it here.'

'I can't, Nathan, I'd never get the time off work and it's a long way and …' I trail off, feeling like I'm scrabbling for excuses. In reality, my heart has leapt into my throat and is hammering like a pneumatic drill. The idea of getting away, of going to a beach, a vintage carousel, and … him. The idea that he might actually want to see me …

'Yeah, of course. Sorry. It's been a long day of travelling. I've lost my grip on how funny my jokes are. I didn't mean owt by it.'

'I mean, I would, but …'

'No, no, I was just messing about. No one would be that much of an idiot. Don't worry about it. I'm sure you'll look after it for me.'

'Of course, but—'

'I'd better go before I make an even bigger fool of myself. It's getting late and I've got to start work at first light tomorrow. I need to strip the carousel to pieces and assess exactly what kind of condition it's in and what needs doing, and that macaroni cheese is bubbling away, ready to come out of the oven.'

'Thanks for ringing.' I try not to think about how jealous I am of his quiet cottage, homemade meal, garden, tea, and sea view. Nothing has ever sounded more appealing. I squeeze the phone tighter, hoping that I can somehow cling on to him a bit longer. 'I'm really glad you did.'

'Me too,' he says softly, and I can hear that smile in his voice again.

He doesn't say anything else and I get a sudden flutter that maybe he's doing the same thing as I am, hanging on that little bit longer.

This is all too weird. I can't remember the last time I talked to someone so easily. It's like something from a film, like those first exciting emails between Tom Hanks and Meg Ryan in *You've Got Mail*, and I'm sure I've got the same sappy smile on my face.

'I suppose I'd better say goodnight,' I say, feeling abrupt, but the longer I hang on to this call, the more real it seems, and this … whatever this is … how can it be real? Life doesn't happen like this. You don't smile at a stranger on a train and then they turn out to be the perfect match.

'Yeah, me too,' he says. Am I imagining how sad he sounds?

I could so easily ask him something else, anything else, just to stay chatting to him a bit longer, but I give myself a shake. 'Goodnight, Nathan. It was nice talking to you.'

*Nice*? It's the best evening I've spent in months. Years, maybe. Nice is how you describe the questionable jumper your nan knitted you for Christmas when she asks if you've worn it, not a warm, funny conversation with a gorgeous, sweet guy.

Even though I'm not interested in guys, no matter how gorgeous or sweet they are.

'Night, Ness,' he says. 'And thanks again. Don't let the bedbugs bite.'

'Don't let the sand fleas bite in that gorgeous cottage of yours.'

I can hear his laughter fading as he hangs up, and it makes me smile. Again. I've lost count of how many times he's made me smile tonight. He's better than anything I could've chosen on Netflix.

And no matter how *not*-interested I am in men and relationships, I grab my charger and breathe a sigh of relief when it fits his phone. I don't even know why I'm so relieved, but I know I want to keep it charged in case he phones again.

\* \* \*

About an hour later, after I've warmed up my microwave meal – living on the edge because the packet said 'do not reheat' – Nathan's phone jingles again. I trip over my own feet as I rush embarrassingly fast to get the message, still convinced it will be his girlfriend wondering where he is.

It's him again, a picture this time. I smile as I open it. He must be standing on the beach, and he's taken a photo of the sun setting over the ocean, almost pink sky and darkening clouds as the sun sinks into the sea, a jagged cliff to one side.

It's the most perfect view I've ever seen.

The phone jingles with another text message, and I smile again as I read it.

*This is my office. Not a drawing pin scar in sight.*

Two seconds later, it jingles yet again.

*And yes, that was taken with the bona fide VGA camera on this awful flip phone. That should go some way towards showing how beautiful it is here – it even looks good in 0.03 megapixels.*

What is it about this guy? Everything about him makes me smile.

And everything about him makes me want to throw caution to the wind and go to Pearlholme. But that would be stupid, right? I mean, it does look like a gorgeous place, maybe I really will add it to my list of potential holiday destinations, and Mum and Dad aren't too far from there; maybe I'll pop by next time I go up to visit them, see the carousel after it's restored and Nathan's long gone.

I couldn't go up there now, while he's still there. That's another thing that would only happen in one of Daph's beloved romantic comedies. Not in real life.

# Chapter 4

'Gimme that.' Daphne whips Nathan's phone from my hand before I've fully pulled it out of my trouser pocket.

'He texted you goodnight at half past ten last night *and* he put two kisses. If that's not a sign that he's into you then I don't know what is. Do you know how hard it is to get a goodnight text from a guy? Gavin doesn't even text me goodnight when he's away and we've been married for three years.'

'Everyone puts kisses these days. It's habit. It's a nightmare when you send a professional email and accidentally sign off with a couple of x's. I've done it loads of times.'

'I see you did it last night too.' She raises an eyebrow.

'Well, he texted me goodnight – it would've been rude to ignore him, wouldn't it?'

'And he put kisses so you just *had* to put them back, right?'

'You're reading way too much into—'

'And how long did you talk to him for last night?'

'About half an hour—'

She's into the call log before I can finish the sentence. 'An hour and thirty-one minutes! Ness, you've never talked to a guy for that long before! You dated "poor Andrew" for three years and you probably didn't talk to him for that long over the whole course of your relationship combined.'

'Which is a great clue to why it went wrong. And I didn't talk to Nathan for that long. It was nowhere near that.'

'It says it here in black and white.' She taps a nail on the screen. 'And it's Nathan now, is it? Not Nathaniel?'

'He doesn't go by Nathaniel. He prefers—'

'And this is where he wants you to go.' She zooms in on the beach photo and stares at it longingly, while I wonder why I'm bothering to tell her anything when she's going to draw her own conclusions from the phone anyway. 'It's beautiful. I'd be there in a heartbeat.'

'He doesn't want me to go there. It was a joke. I mean, he seems lovely and everything, but it's just so—'

'I know you, Ness. You only make those kinds of excuses when you really want to do something but you think you can't. Like that guy from Gavin's work I tried to set you up with last year. He friended you on Facebook and you liked the look of him but you found a snake-length list of excuses not to go on a date, even though there was a very good chance that you'd have had a good time.'

'This is not like that. There's no dating. The only thing he wants is his phone back. He's probably married anyway,' I say, even though I know Daph's right. It's just another excuse. No part of our conversation last night made me think he's married.

Daphne snorts. 'No way is the guy on the other end of that flirty, adorable conversation anything but single. He furtively wheedled husband info out of you, Ness. And he didn't even try to arrange any other way of getting his phone back. Assuming he assumes you *aren't* going to Pearlholme, he's got an excuse to call you again, hasn't he? You talked for hours with the intention of giving his phone back but you seem to have talked about everything *other* than giving his phone back; therefore you'll just have to talk again, won't you?'

My mind drifts at the thought of talking to him again and I

don't realise I'm smiling until Daphne smacks the desk.

'Oh my God, you actually like this guy, don't you? Like, really *like* like?'

'No! And that's far too many likes for one sentence. I don't even know him, he's a total stranger, and it's ridiculous.'

'It's the love story you've always wanted.' She clasps her hands together and holds them to her chest.

'It's not what I've always wanted—'

'It's just like *Sliding Doors* but with hopefully less dying. It's why you broke up with "poor Andrew" for no good reason—'

'It wasn't for no good reason.'

'It's why you refuse every date I find for you. Because you've subconsciously known that something better was coming. Because you've been waiting for this. For *Nathan*.' She waggles her eyebrows and my face betrays me by smiling at the mention of his name.

Daphne's face suddenly straightens. 'You actually want to go, don't you? To Pearlholme? You want to follow this complete stranger halfway across the country, and you're telling me that you *don't* like him?'

'Of course I don't! I'm not going all the way up to North Yorkshire to return his phone. I'll do exactly what I thought from the start – post it to him. Problem solved. End of story.' I reach over the desk and try to grab his phone from Daph's hand but she pulls it out of my reach. 'Give it here, I'll text him for his address now.'

'Oh no, you won't.' Zinnia appears in the doorway of Daphne's office, sounding so much like a pantomime villain that I half-expect her to follow up with a rousing 'it's behind you'. How long has she been standing there *again*? Is her entire job description to lurk outside doorways and eavesdrop on the staff? How does a woman in four-inch heels move so silently?

'What?' Daphne and I say in unison. I absolutely do not feel that little flutter in my chest again.

'Viral.' Zinnia shoves her iPad into my hands. 'Eighteen thousand views and counting. This is wonderful, Vanessa. Even better than I expected.'

My eyes scan the screen, unable to believe what I'm seeing. The page of statistics in front of me is a jumble of numbers and graphs, but sure enough, on the page views line, it says 18,267. That can't be right.

'This is an amazing story,' Zinnia says. 'I was telling my husband about it and even he was interested, and the most romantic thing he does is plunge the sink when it's blocked. I couldn't stop thinking about it while I was lying in bed last night, and our readers are obviously thinking the same. Look at the comments.'

I tap the screen to close the statistics and go back to the article, which I spent most of yesterday afternoon looking at when I was supposed to be fact-checking – surely most of these views are me? The social media sharing buttons along the bottom of the article have numbers showing the amount of times it's been shared, and they're all well into the thousands. There are a couple of hundred comments as well. Too many to take in. They're all saying things like 'OMG, don't leave it there!' and 'I HAVE to know what happens next!'

This is unreal. Even Daphne's articles don't get this kind of response. This is what I've always dreamed about, but my dreams have never included writing something with even *half* this amount of comments and shares. I can't believe this is happening.

'I told you, didn't I?' Zinnia says excitedly.

Daphne and I share a wary glance. Zinnia getting excited is generally a sign of an impending apocalypse or something equally welcome. Even the Botox gives way to a slight forehead wrinkle.

'This whole thing is like something from a film. It's exactly the sort of feel-good story that everyone needs. And it's only getting better. Now we've got the perfect phone call in which you discover you've got so many things in common, an adorable vintage carousel – carousels are romantic without even trying

'– and the invite to this idyllic little village …'

'He didn't invite me; it was a joke. He doesn't actually want me to go.' I feel like I'm repeating myself. 'I'm just going to put the phone in the post—'

'You're going to Pearlholme.' Zinnia doesn't let me finish the sentence. 'Yesterday I was planning on getting Daphne to write the second part, documenting your first meeting with the mysterious Train Man, but I didn't expect this incredible response. People want the second part of your article and they want it *now*. Daphne's too pregnant to be sending to some obscure little village in the back end of beyond. This is your story, Vanessa, and you've done well with the first part. You've captured the public's imagination and I believe in rewarding good work where it's due. It's only right that you should be the one to write the rest of it.'

'What's the rest of it?' I ask. I've got butterflies again for an altogether different reason now. This is amazing. Writing something that people connect with is what I've always wanted.

'We're going to run a massive campaign to find Train Man.' The Botox makes Zinnia's smile look more like a grimace.

'He's in Pearlholme,' I say. 'I'm sure it won't be too difficult.'

'Oh, we don't worry about a little detail like that.' She waves a dismissive hand. 'Over the course of a few issues, we're going to run a real-time crusade to find the mystery man. It guarantees repeat readers coming back for the next part. You've already started the ball rolling with that fantastic closing line, so in part two, we'll publish some key clues to his identity and get our readers involved in discovering who he is. I'm picturing big, flashy "have you seen this man?" headlines. We'll ask for their help in finding him. Of course, you'll have already been to Pearlholme and found him by then, but we won't tell them that. Now, I'll have the shopping list and that photo of a carousel horse with his foot in it. They'll make excellent titbits on the trail of breadcrumbs we're starting, and I'm going to get the art department to mock up some "wanted" posters that we can start splashing

42

all over social media.'

'You can't use his photos, you need permission.' I know that because triple-checking photograph permissions is one of my most mind-numbingly boring jobs.

'We'll blur the photograph and change a few items on the shopping list. No one will ever know ...' She moves on without taking a breath. 'You can write about how you've been hunting for him every morning on the train but haven't seen him since, and then in part three you can tell all about this darling little village and meeting up with the gorgeous Train Man, and then for the final part, you can write about falling in love with him and living happily ever after, and we'll end with a lovely photograph of you two together on the carousel as we finally reveal the identity of this mysterious carousel reconstructor and end with a perfect balance of old-time nostalgia and a modern feel-good happily-ever-after.'

'What if I get there and he says, "Thanks for the phone. Have you met my wife?"'

'He won't,' Daphne says. 'Don't forget, if he bought a pay-as-you-go phone then he paid for that call.'

I go to deny it, but it's a nice thought. We *did* chat for ages last night, and it never occurred to me that he must've been paying for it by the minute.

'You're doing that smile thing again,' Daphne says. 'I can't remember the last time I saw a smile like that on you. He must be really special.'

I force the corners of my mouth to turn downwards, which is harder than it looks. 'My smile has nothing to do with him.' I wave the iPad towards her, even though the screen has turned itself off by now. 'And speaking of Nathan, what about him? He might not agree.'

'Oh, we don't worry about that either,' Zinnia says. 'Who cares whether he agrees or not? He's just fodder for the article. You'll keep him anonymous until the very last moment, by which time you'll have made him like you enough to agree to the final unmasking.'

'I'm not very good at making people like me.'

'Well, I didn't like you very much, Vanessa, but this wonderful story has certainly changed my opinion of you. But don't you dare start worrying about him and what he wants. This is about you and what *you* want. You want a career writing features for us here at *Maîtresse*, don't you?'

'Of course.'

'Then this has nothing to do with Nathan. You use him to get what you want. Keep him anonymous so it won't affect him in any way. If the absolute worst comes to the absolute worst then we'll hire a model who matches his description.' She casts a critical eye over me from my frizzy hair to the scuffed toes of my shoes. 'On second thoughts, maybe *two* models would be ideal to play the parts of Vanessa and Nathan, and then we won't have to worry about your hair, that outbreak of blackheads on the side of your nose, or what he wants or doesn't want. But we'll cross that bridge when we come to it. The point is that we're selling a story here. You've given us a great starting point, but it's our duty now to make that story the best it can be. If we have to embellish a bit, then so be it.'

I nod along but something about the callous way she talks doesn't sit right with me. If she's going to make it up anyway, what's the point in me going to Pearlholme at all? I could just invent the whole thing, and it sounds like that's what I'll end up doing anyway, because there is no chance at all that this is going to go how Zinnia expects it to. I'm going to go there, hand him his phone, and that will be that. He's not going to fall in love with me. I'm not going to fall in love with him. Love doesn't happen like that unless you're reading a movie script.

'Do this well, Vanessa, and it's the start of a new career for you. And I don't just mean while Daphne's on maternity leave. People are falling in love with this story. They're going to keep

44

coming back to see how it pans out. When it ends, they're going to want to read what you write next. This will be the start of great things for you here at *Maîtresse*. At your age, and with your lack of experience, you won't get a better opportunity than this, so don't mess it up, okay?'

She makes me feel like I'm ninety-four rather than thirty-four, but I know she's right too. I was a temp before I started here. I have no experience of writing for magazines and that's my dream job. I'm never going to get a better chance than this. 'What about my job now? If I'm going to Pearlholme, I won't be here.' I excel at stating the obvious. 'How much time do I get there?'

'Take your laptop. You can do your usual work remotely. I'll make sure every article is emailed to you, and as long as you can drag yourself away from gorgeous men and golden sands long enough to work from there ...' She thinks for a moment. 'Take three weeks. Allow yourself to really feel something with this guy. Readers will see through it if you just make things up. You have to start with something real. You have to see if the connection on the real train *really* meant anything. Not just for yourself and Train Man, but for the thousands of readers following your story now.'

I gulp. No pressure then. I obviously don't look grateful enough to Zinnia because she whisks her iPad back out of my hand and points the corner of it at me threateningly. 'I'm doing you a huge favour here, and taking an enormous risk on someone who I've only ever seen one article from. The next parts had better be as good as the first. Not only do you get a chance to see if a flirtation means anything, but you also get a chance at the career you've always wanted in the process. Most people would be overjoyed to be given this chance. You can thank me for being an amazing, wonderful, understanding boss anytime now.'

She's probably joking but the unnaturally smooth face doesn't give me enough of a hint.

'Thank you, Zinnia,' I chorus dutifully, trying for my best

45

overjoyed face. I probably look more like I'm about to sneeze.

'This is amazing!' Daphne squeaks. She's still got Nathan's phone in her hand and is going through it, bluetoothing his photos of carousel horses to her computer.

'Forward those to both of us,' Zinnia says. 'And have a look through for anything else that can be used in the article – and, Vanessa? I'll go over our publishing schedule and email you the deadlines for each part. Good luck.' She salutes me as she glides out the door, leaving me wondering how much luck I'll need. Zinnia doesn't believe in luck, which makes me wonder about quite how bad an idea this might actually be.

'This is a fantastic opportunity,' Daphne says when she's gone. 'I often write about real-life couples who met in weird and wonderful ways, and now you're one of them. It's so exciting!'

It *is* exciting, but I'm terrified too. That phone call last night made me feel fluttery and excited, something that I've seen on TV but never thought could actually happen to real people … What if I get to Pearlholme and discover that it all meant nothing? What if Nathan's nothing like I think he is?

'I'm proud of you, Ness,' Daphne says.

'I haven't written anything yet.'

'Not about the article. That'll be fab, no matter what you do with it. I meant about actually doing this – *wanting* to do this – you're really putting yourself out there and taking a risk. I'm always saying that you need to do more of that—'

'And I'm always telling you to shut up.'

She grins. 'I know. And you're about to prove that I was right all along. You will throw yourself into this, won't you?'

I go to answer but she cuts me off.

'Don't find excuses not to do stuff. If he asks you out, go. What have you got to lose?'

I shake my head, because I know she's right but she'll probably explode if I admit it. I've not wanted another relationship since I broke up with 'poor Andrew', and I've had an excuse for every potential date Daphne has tried to find me even if they looked promising. I've hidden away and pretended to be happy when I'm sad. I've told people I enjoy my own company when I'm lonely. I work late every night so I have fewer hours to stare at the damp-stained walls in my flat.

But things felt different with Nathan. Even in one phone call, I didn't feel the need to pretend to be something I wasn't. I didn't pretend to be okay. I even told him I was eating a microwave meal and I never tell anyone that in case my mother finds out and immediately starts marching down the M1 with a stack of Tupperware containers under each arm.

I can't ignore the fizzle of excitement. And it's not just because people have read my story and now I've got a chance to make a real career here. It's because of Nathan. This is so out of character for me, but there's something about him that makes me want to find out whether months of eye contact and smiles on the train really did mean anything, because for just a moment when I spoke to him last night, it felt like they did.

# Chapter 5

In London, the June weather is so muggy that every breath feels like hard work and the skies are overcast and dull, but as I sit in the window seat of a refreshingly empty carriage on a train that's trundling north, the clouds outside the window turn from grey to white and the sky brightens until it's blue.

I went to bed early last night because I knew I couldn't miss getting the earlier train than usual, and I left Nathan's phone on the kitchen unit overnight because if it was any nearer then I'd never be able to resist the temptation of constantly checking to see if he'd rung. When I got up this morning, there was a missed call from his pay-as-you-go number, followed by a text message.

*I tried to call but either I missed you or I bored you silly last night and now you're avoiding me – completely understandable! xx*

Another two kisses. Daphne's waters would probably break with excitement.

I want to reply because seeing that message this morning made the butterflies start doing bungee jumps again, but I still haven't summoned the courage to, because I'm too nervous to tell him I'm on my way to Pearlholme. He *must* have been joking when he said it, but how can I tell him I've taken him seriously without sounding deranged?

48

The nearest station to Pearlholme is not like any train station I've seen before. It looks like a quaint little bungalow, but with sliding glass double doors and a railway sign outside. The air is clear and there's a warm breeze that makes me inhale deeply and I don't feel like I'm going to choke on exhaust fumes.

There's a tiny car park outside the station and a couple of bus stops on the opposite side. I remember Nathan saying he got the bus so I wander across to them, dragging my suitcase behind me. I'm staring at the timetable, running a finger down the list of place names I don't recognise, wondering if I'm even in the right place, when I spot a man selling newspapers standing on the corner of the car park.

'Excuse me?' I walk over to him, thinking of Nathan's joke about asking strangers for directions. 'Do you know if I'm in the right place to get the bus to Pearlholme? I can't see it listed on any of the timetables.'

He gives me a toothy grin. 'Pearlholme's much too small for that, love. It's on the route but it's an unnamed stop that'll take you to the edge of the village. It's the number five bus you want, and you'll need to get off outside a pub called The Sun & Sand.'

'Brilliant, thank you.'

'You've not long missed the bus though. It went through about twenty minutes ago, and they're only every two hours.'

'Oh, great.' The journey has gone well so far; something had to go wrong at some point.

'It's only about half an hour on foot and it's a lovely walk.'

I glance in the direction he points, wondering how lost I could manage to get on this walk because the chances are pretty good that I'll never be seen again. But the weather is gorgeous and I have been sat on a train for the past three hours, and the station behind me looks like you'd struggle to occupy five minutes in it, let alone an hour and forty of them.

'You're Pearlholme's second tourist this week,' the man says. 'They must be doing something right.'

I can't resist asking. 'Was the other one a tall guy with dark hair?'

'Indeed he was. If you're looking for him, he'll be on the beach doing up the old carousel that's been found. From The Sun & Sand, you can either take the back road into the village or the front road along the promenade and the beachfront. You can't miss the carousel from there.'

Wow. Nathan was right, they really do know everyone around here. 'Thanks.' I give him a smile because of how much he reminds me of where I grew up, where you couldn't walk up the road without someone asking where you were going and why you were going there.

'It's beautiful at this time of year,' he says. 'Gets a bit busy once the summer holidays begin, but this time of year is ideal. You're not staying at The Shell Hotel, are you?'

'I managed to get a room there at the last minute,' I say, smiling again.

The man visibly cringes and I feel my face fall. 'Why?'

'Oh, nothing, nothing. I'm sure it'll be lovely.' He gives me a smile that looks completely false.

'That question did not have an "I'm sure it'll be lovely" tone to it ...'

He huffs and his shoulders slump. 'The village itself is exquisite, but the hotel ... not so much. I best not say more than that, love, I don't want to put you off.'

'All the cottage rentals were full. I thought I was lucky to get a room at the hotel.'

'Yes,' he says. 'Lucky.'

He doesn't sound like he means lucky. Or like he's going to enlighten me any further.

I thank him for his time and buy a newspaper because it seems like the polite thing to do, and set off in the direction he points me in, after assuring me that it's a straightforward road.

I feel like I'm cutting school as I drag my suitcase down the wide pavement, like when you used to go on an errand for your teacher and walk through the empty school grounds when everyone was in lessons. It always felt a little bit naughty and a little bit thrilling, and it always made you feel a little bit more grown up than everyone else.

The road gradually shifts from residential houses to a tree-lined country lane, branches heavy with white flowers hanging across the pavement, hedgerows spilling over with pink wild roses, and the odd pretty cottage dotted among them. There's hardly any traffic, and the occasional car that does pass is pootling along so slowly that I can overtake them on foot. I'm enjoying the walk so much that I'm surprised how quickly the time has passed as the pub comes into view.

I stop and read the blue lettering on a sand-coloured board above the door. The Sun & Sand. Even the name makes it sound nice. There are tables and chairs outside, a wide green lawn, and two huge but neatly trimmed trees on either side, weighed down with not-yet-ripe green cherries. It looks like the kind of image you'd see on the front cover of a romance book about a woman who moves to a tiny village to run a pub and falls for the handsome builder who comes to mend the roof.

It would be so easy to take the front road and walk along the seafront and find the carousel and Nathan, but I decide to be sensible and head to the hotel first. It's not even two p.m. yet. There's plenty of time for that when I've had a quick wash and change after travelling all day.

There's a woman trimming the hedge outside The Sun & Sand who calls over as I go to walk away. 'Where are you looking for, love?'

'The Shell Hotel?' I say, not used to this number of people keen to help you find your way around.

She makes the same face the newspaper man made. 'Are you an inspector come to shut them down?'

'No, just a guest.'

51

'Oh, lovely.' She sounds just as false as the newspaper man. What is it about this hotel?

'It's that way.' She points down the second road that clearly heads into the village. 'It's right on the other end of the village, just follow this road and go downwards when you come to the fork. You can't miss it.'

'Thanks.' I set off before the idea of this hotel sends me running straight back to the train station.

'Come back anytime,' she calls after me. 'We do the best chips in Pearlholme! The fish and chip shop on the seafront will tell you otherwise, but we all know which one of us is right!'

It makes me smile as I wheel my suitcase behind me, through a narrow, cobbled street that seems barely wide enough to allow even the smallest of cars. This street must be the main residential street, and its rows of brick cottages fit perfectly with the uneven cobbles of the road. Each cottage looks like it could tumble down at any moment, but they all have perfectly neat front gardens, separated from the cobbled street by a haphazard brick wall covered in trailing purple aubrietia flowers. Each one has a path of stepping stones up to their door, a neatly trimmed lawn, and borders full of flowers. Even the birdhouses on tall stands at the end of each garden are miniature replicas of cottages, and birds who are happily pecking at seed inside their tiny bird cottages fly off in groups as I walk past, my suitcase bouncing along the cobbles behind me.

There's one house on the street that's a bit different. This one still has a freshly mowed lawn and the scent of cut grass is strong in the air, but in the window is a 'Post Office' sign, and instead of flowers in borders, there's a bright red postbox outside, a chalkboard advertising fresh milk and bread, a newspaper board with today's local headline, which is blank, and I wonder if that's indicative of how quiet it is around here. Zinnia would've told them to make up a story about someone being mauled by a starfish to sell more copies.

Even from what Nathan said on the phone the other night, I didn't realise quite how picturesque it would be. Every house has window boxes brimming with a rainbow of flowers and trailing hanging baskets on either side of their bright-painted front doors. It's like a picture-perfect film set, the kind of village that you see artists painting in watercolour.

At the end of the main row of houses, the road forks – the left fork curves down towards a battered-looking old barn, and the right twists up a shallow slope towards green hills and a handful of little cottages that must overlook the beach. I'd rather take that road, but the woman outside the pub did say to go downwards, didn't she? And I'm sure there's something written on that old barn ...

As I walk towards it, only the side is facing me, peering above rusty black railings. The back garden is hidden behind over-hanging trees that have overhung so far they've gone for a scramble through the blackberry bushes behind the building. It looks more like an overgrown graveyard than any kind of hotel, but as I cautiously walk round the front, I realise that's exactly what it is. The Shell Hotel is in big letters across the front of the building, but the S has gone wonky and dropped down, looking like it's hanging on by a thread.

This does not look like a hotel. It looks like somewhere you'd expect Lurch to open the door.

I suddenly understand why everyone I've spoken to so far has made the same face at the mere mention of this place.

* * *

The hotel is not *that* bad. If you like broom cupboards with no view. There only seems to be one elderly man working here, and the only other guest I've seen is a man I passed in the corridor with an easel under one arm, making me think I wasn't far wrong about artists painting such a picturesque village.

And I suppose I *was* lucky to get a room here at such short notice, in June, in a gorgeous little seaside village, and it doesn't matter how small my room is or how uncomfortable and stained the bed looks, because I'm *here*, and I've done something unusual for me; I've 'put myself out there' as Daphne would say, and now I'm walking up the other fork of the cobbled road, towards the cottages, and hopefully the carousel on the beach.

At the peak of the hill, I stop and take in the view. From here, to my left, are the green hills of the cliffs overlooking the beach, and they're spotted with little cottages, all with pretty gardens stretching out behind them. In front of me is the most perfect beach I've ever seen. Miles of unblemished sand stretches out into the ocean. The tide is out and the waves are lapping in the distance.

To the right is the seafront, and my reason for coming here. I walk down the lower road towards what is obviously the promenade. A blue-painted iron railing springs up along the grassy edge as I head towards a row of colourful beach huts along one side of the road, opposite a wide set of steps and a long ramp leading down to the beach. Just beyond them, is the tip of a marquee tent. It must be the carousel. It's exactly where the newspaper man described.

The road has changed from cobblestone to smooth tarmac now, which I notice because my knees are shaking as I walk, and while I could convince myself it was because of the cobbles before, now I have to admit that it's nerves. What the hell am I doing here? Coming halfway across the country to meet a man I smiled at on a train a few times? He's going to think I'm a nutter. Maybe I *am* a nutter.

If I left now, I could probably make it back to London by tonight. I could at least stay somewhere near the station and get the first train out tomorrow morning. He would never know I was here. We could meet like normal, sensible, sane people in a neutral place in London where I can hand his phone over like a normal, sensible, sane person, and not stalk him two hundred and fifty miles across the country. In six weeks' time. When he gets back … Six weeks is a hell of a long time. And I'm here now, aren't I? I can just drop by the carousel and hand over his phone like it's not a big deal … Maybe I could tell him I'm visiting family in the area? That's a reasonable excuse, right?

My legs have carried on walking without me realising, and I'm suddenly on the liveliest part of the promenade, right next to one of the sets of steps leading onto the sand, and mere metres from the marquee surrounding the carousel. He must be in there. It's too near, this is too weird, everything about it from the train to the phone to the article … and the lovely-sounding guy who phoned me, who I talked to unreservedly the night before last, who voluntarily rang again last night and then texted when I didn't answer, and I still haven't responded to.

I examine the row of beach huts on the opposite side of the promenade to delay having to approach the carousel and somehow make myself sound rational while explaining that I've stalked him halfway across the country.

They're all painted in bright colours, each one different from orange to purple, graduated so they form a rainbow along the street. All have signs above their doors and sandwich boards outside advertising their goods. There's the fish and chip shop I've already heard about, an old-fashioned arcade, an art shop showcasing paintings by local artists, a shop selling all kinds of beach goods from dinghies, windbreakers, and inflatable whales to buckets and spades and snorkels, and there's an ice cream parlour … Oh, now there's an idea.

The sign outside advertises a 99 cone that still costs 99p, something that's probably as rare in Britain nowadays as when a Freddo used to cost 10p, and I can't remember the last time I had one. I go into the little red hut and buy two. Turning up with ice cream makes this much less weird, right?

There are four rows of wide concrete steps leading down to

the beach and sandy ramps side on, so I walk down one of them, holding an ice cream in each hand.

A wooden walkway has been installed in the sand surrounding the carousel, and a temporary metal fence about six-foot high has been put up around it, stopping anyone getting any closer.

As I cross the sand towards it, I try to work out what on earth I'm going to say. Shall I knock? If I can even get in, how do you knock on a tent? Rattle the fence? Call his name?

Just as I'm thinking the best thing to do would be to run away and eat both the 99s as I go, he steps out from around the side of the tent and I freeze because it's suddenly real. He's actually here. I'm actually here. I actually did something so completely out of character for me, and maybe that's not an entirely bad thing, even if it is about to go down in flames.

He's wearing a black T-shirt and a pair of dungarees, which are covered in paint and oil stains and ripped at the knees, and he's rubbing a manky-looking cloth over something, looking out towards the sea. He looks completely entranced by the ocean and hasn't even glanced in my direction, and I wonder how long I could stand here admiring him if these ice creams weren't melting.

'Nathan?' I finally pluck up the courage to speak and it comes out barely above a whisper. I'm sure he won't have heard but he jumps at the sound of something other than the squawking of seagulls and swivels towards me.

'Ness?' He physically does a double take and squints in the sunlight.

At least he recognises me. That's something.

'Ness!' he says again, his voice going high. 'You actually came?'

Suddenly he's moving, pushing aside one of the metal fence panels and striding towards me, his mouth turning into a grin that lights up his whole face and makes the laughter lines around his eyes crinkle up. He doesn't look like someone who thinks I'm a deranged stalker.

What's weird is that as soon as I see him, the moment I see

that smile spread across his face and the dimples I haven't been able to get out of my head since the first time I saw him, all of my nerves melt away.

He looks … overjoyed. No, it can't be overjoyed. Maybe constipation? I don't think anyone has ever looked that happy to see me before.

'You made it sound so perfect.' I have to wet my lips and swallow a couple of times to make my voice sound stable.

'I can't believe you came!'

'And I brought ice cream.' I hold one of the cones out towards him.

He goes to take it but his hand stops in midair and we both look at it because he's covered in black grease. He pulls it back quickly and tries to wipe it on the cloth he was using to clean the thing he's just shoved into the pocket of his dungarees. 'Look at the state of me. I don't usually get into this much of a mess.'

He plunges a hand into the dungaree pocket again and pulls out a mini packet of wet wipes, covering it in the black grime as he struggles to open it and pull one out, and I stand there with two ice creams melting in my hands, wondering when dungarees became so sexy. I've always thought of them as a work uniform for builders, but on Nathan, they look like something from a Calvin Klein aftershave advert. Even with the rips and stains, one rip in particular shows a delicious sliver of thigh, and …

I've been here for all of two minutes and I already can't stop perving on the man. I can't remember the last time I looked at a guy and fancied him this much, no matter how much Daphne tries to make me. Fancying men and how sexy they might or might not be hasn't been on my priority list for a long time now, and yet I already want to slide a finger into that tear in the faded denim and … I force myself to think of something else.

'I'm so sorry.' Nathan's scrubbing at his messy hands with a wet wipe, which looks about as effective as a chocolate teapot. 'Talk about a good first impression. This is a boiling hot water, exfoliating handwash, and a scrubbing brush job, and I'm nowhere near any of them.'

He seems nervous, maybe even more nervous than I was, and it's completely and utterly endearing.

'Do you need a hand?' I say, wishing I could kick myself before I've even finished the sentence. *Who* makes terrible puns like that in front of a gorgeous man they wouldn't be opposed to impressing? What is wrong with me? I don't know why I bother hunting for excuses not to go out with any of the men Daphne tries to set me up with. I should go and let them be instantly put off by my terrible sense of humour. She'd soon stop trying.

At least he's polite enough to laugh and make it sound genuine, his eyes crinkling up again as he grins at me, and I find myself staring at him. His hair is so dark brown that it's almost black and his brown eyes reflect the colour of the sand and the sun, making them look golden in certain slants of light. I always thought he was gorgeous by the washed-out light of an underground train, but in natural daylight, he's glorious.

'You couldn't, er, feed it to me, could you?'

I let out an undignified snort and cover it with a nervous giggle, sounding like a pig that's had a nappy accident, if pigs wore nappies and were perceptive enough to be aware of soiling themselves. Maybe those nerves aren't so far away after all. 'Well, that's one way to break the ice.'

I try to ignore the way my stomach flips as he groans and goes to smack himself on the forehead but stops just in time to avoid a greasy handprint across his face. 'Oh God, that wasn't meant to sound as bad as it did. I meant in a completely non-erotic way, obviously. Just hold it in my general direction and I'll lick it like a dog.'

'I'd be happy to,' I say, wishing I could think up a clever, witty response to make up for the 'do you need a hand' fiasco.

'My nefarious plan for getting pretty girls to feed me ice cream is almost complete. Next step, world domination.' He steeples grease-covered fingers in an evil overlord way, making me giggle again. 'I'm going to stop making an idiot of myself anytime now.' He gestures towards the gap in the metal fence. 'Come in and sit on my wood.'

I laugh, but mainly at how fiercely red his cheeks have gone.

'I meant my wooden decking, obviously.' He points towards the edge of the platform in the sand surrounding the tent. 'I told you I'm crap at talking to people.'

'Well, I asked you if you needed a hand, so I think we're fairly even on that front. And these are melting.'

He smiles as he sits down and I perch on the wooden pathway next to him, not close enough to touch, but close enough to hold his ice cream to my right.

He leans forward and licks it. 'You have full permission to poke me in the nose with it if you want.'

I'm trying eat mine daintily without ending up in a *Beauty and the Beast*-style porridge scene and it makes me laugh so much that I nearly take my own eye out with the Flake. 'I was *just* thinking about how easy it would be to do that. Are you some sort of mind reader or what?'

He laughs too. 'I think there's an innate part of every human being that makes that connection when there's a pointy ice cream and a nose around.'

I give him a sideways glance, appreciating the way his tongue runs up that smooth ice cream. His chin is so close to my hand as he moves, near enough that I can almost feel the drag of his stubble, and it's probably a really weird thing to sit here and feed ice cream to a complete stranger but it doesn't feel as weird as it should.

'I can't believe you came. I didn't think you would and I was really hoping …' He shakes his head without finishing the sentence. 'And I can't believe you brought me ice cream. I probably shouldn't tell you this, but …' His voice drops to a whisper and I naturally lean a bit nearer to hear him. 'I've already had two of these today.'

I laugh like it's a terrible secret. 'Isn't there an unwritten British law that says you have to have a 99 when within a five-mile radius of a beach?'

'Oh, definitely, but I don't think they mean to prescribe them like Paracetamol, you know, one every four hours until your liver packs in from sugar overload. I had one when I got here this morning and then I couldn't resist running back across the road for another one after lunch. I foresee that working across the street from an ice cream parlour is going to be *very* bad for me.'

'I can't think of a nicer place to work.' I nod towards the sea in an attempt to take my mind off his tongue and how close it is to my hand. 'The ice creams are just a bonus.'

'I can't believe you came,' he says again. 'I was really hoping you would. I got the impression on the phone that you'd love it here, and I thought I'd probably scared you off and I'd never hear from you again, and I just …' He swallows and leans over until his shoulder knocks gently into mine before sitting upright again. 'I'm chuffed you're here.'

It makes the sun warming my skin feel like it's warming the whole of me from the inside out. He's so … uninhibited is the word that springs to mind. Either he's overcompensating because he thinks I'm a deranged stalker and is biding his time until he can run away, or he's genuinely pleased to see me, and instead of trying to hide it and invent excuses like I am, he's not afraid to say it. I'm still wondering if he'd believe that I have family in the area and I happen to be visiting them mere days after he told me where he was and I conveniently forgot to mention it the other night. 'You made Pearlholme sound so perfect and I liked talking to you,' I say, trying to be a bit more forthright with my answer. 'I couldn't resist seeing the village and the carousel.' *And the guy restoring it.* Well, maybe not that forthright.

'Did you get my text last night? I thought I'd better check to make sure I hadn't bored you into a coma the night before.'

'Yeah. Sorry, I'd gone to bed because I knew I'd have to get up early for the train, and I got your text this morning, but I didn't answer because ...' Right, forthright. 'I didn't know how to say I was on my way here without sounding like I was stalking you.'

'Well, I wasn't joking when I asked you. I tried to pretend I was because it's a bit weird to talk complete strangers into holidaying with you ... I mean, not *with* me but in the same place I am ...' He twists one blackened finger around the other. 'When I said I was going to stop making an idiot of myself earlier, I clearly meant now, not then. *Now* I'm going to stop making an idiot of myself. Just as soon as I finish the ice cream you've been forced to feed to me because I can't get my hands clean.'

I giggle again, and I really am going to have to stop all this nervous giggling, I'm even annoying myself, but the thought that he actually wanted me to come ... that it wasn't a joke ... It's making me feel all fluttery and light, like in the movies when you see the heroine twirling down the street in a floaty pink dress after a wonderful romantic date with a handsome man who's too good to be true.

I look over at Nathan again and his eyes meet mine and we both smile at the same time. Until he takes a bite out of the cornet and sends crumbs fluttering everywhere.

'So, is "will you feed it to me" the worst chat-up line you've ever heard? Not that it was a chat-up line or anything – I am *not* interested in that kind of thing – I just meant it sounds like something a leery drunk in a pub would think was a clever chat-up line, doesn't it?'

'I don't know, but "hold it and I'll lick it like a dog" is right up there.'

He laughs and groans at the same time. 'Oh God, I hadn't even thought of that one. See? I'm terrible at having conversations with people. I'm not even trying to chat you up and I've tried out the worst chat-up line you've ever heard in your life.'

'Nah … A bloke outside the tube station told me he'd like to eat my ovaries once. Not quite sure what he expected the outcome to be.'

Nathan puts a non-greasy wrist to his forehead and pretends to swoon. 'Oh, finally, your prince has been found?'

'Exactly. Now that's setting the bar high for bad chat-up lines.' I laugh. 'I always wonder how many women he tried it on and if any of them ever said, "Oh, lovely, that sounds like a jolly good way to spend an afternoon."'

He dissolves into a fit of laughter and the fact that he's nervous and giggly too makes me feel a bit more normal.

'So what's the worst chat-up line you've ever had then? It's not some girl turning up on a beach and ramming an ice cream down your throat, is it?'

'Are you kidding?' He meets my eyes and raises both dark eyebrows. 'This is the highlight of my day. No, my month. Although that's a bit unfair because we're only a week into June and I doubt anything will beat a beautiful girl feeding me a 99 this side of Christmas.'

I blush because he called me beautiful. I've never been called that before. Daphne is beautiful. I'm just plain and ordinary, the kind of person who would never stand out in a crowd.

He seems to realise his slip-up because he continues quickly. 'I mean, no, I've never been chatted up.'

'You've *never* been chatted up?' I ask in disbelief. I know I don't know him at all, but on face value, I can't imagine why anyone *wouldn't* chat him up.

'I think I put out a bit of a "not interested" vibe. I'm quite boring and I'm not looking for a relationship so I don't go out and meet people. I generally just work and spend my evenings collapsed on the sofa in front of Netflix.'

He doesn't put out a 'not interested' vibe to me. He seems warm, and friendly, and so approachable that I nearly broke the unwritten rule of London transport and spoke to a stranger on the tube.

'Ditto. On *all* things.' I make a point to emphasise the 'all' just in case he gets the mistaken impression that I *am* looking for a relationship because I most definitely am not. 'And hooray for Netflix – my evenings would be empty without it.'

'I would offer you a hooray for Netflix high five, but ...' He wiggles his greasy fingers in front of us. 'I also fear a high five might give away how desperately uncool I am. No one high fives anymore, right?'

I grin at his self-deprecating humour. In person, he's even funnier than he was on the phone and just as easy to talk to, but I'm more self-conscious because I can't hide how much he's making me laugh, and I'm all too aware of vanilla ice cream slowly dripping down my fingers because I'm not eating my own ice cream fast enough, and I can't remember the last time a man was more interesting than an ice cream. That just doesn't happen, right?

He uses his teeth to take the bottom of the cone out of my hand in one go, and I can tell he's making an effort not to touch me, but this time his barely there stubble does brush against my fingers, making me shiver despite the warm sun.

Somehow, he manages to fit the whole thing in his mouth at once even though it's so big he can barely chew it.

'Impressive,' I say, unable to take my eyes off him.

He laughs despite the mouthful and nearly chokes.

'Why, thank you.' He pretends to bow when he can finally speak again. 'My ability to feed myself is second to none.' He pauses for a second. 'I say while someone else feeds me.'

It makes me giggle again. I've got to stop this – the giggling is getting ridiculous.

'Did you find the place all right?' He says while I try to furtively lick melted ice cream off my fingers after finishing my own cornet.

'Not really, but I thought I'd have the full Pearlholme experience and ask a stranger for directions. The bloke selling newspapers outside the train station?'

'Yep, I asked him as well.'

'So he said. You weren't joking when you said everyone knows everything around here, were you?'

'Told ya.' He winks at me. 'Where are you staying? It's not The Shell Hotel, is it?'

I roll my eyes. 'Oh, come on. Why are you the third person to say that to me today?'

He looks worried. 'I take it you are?'

'Of course I am. I'm starting to wonder if they've changed the standard greeting in Pearlholme from "hello" to "you're not staying at The Shell Hotel, are you?" in a sinister voice. Let me guess, the newspaper guy and a woman outside the pub asked you the same thing?'

'Actually, it was the newspaper guy and an old gent who started talking to me on the bus when I went into the next town.'

'Oh, great. It's a real county-wide thing then? That's comforting.' I glance at him. 'It can't be that bad, can it?'

'I don't know. I gave it a quick peek from the corner when I was looking around the village but I didn't want to get too close. It looked like the kind of place you might walk into and never be seen again.'

'Thanks, that's even more comforting.' I know he's only joking but I narrow my eyes when he grins again. 'Not all of us are lucky enough to get a perfect little cottage with a landlady who makes us mac and cheese, you know.'

'It was an amazing mac and cheese too. I'd ask her for the recipe but I doubt I'd get further than getting the cheese out of the fridge without burning the cottage down so it's safer if I don't.'

'I'd say your inability to cook is endearing but I'm even worse. I doubt I could get further than a bowl of uncooked macaroni and a block of cheese. Sounds good, right?'

'If you ever want to cook for me, that's the cottage.' He leans

64

forward and reaches his arm past me so I can see where he's pointing. I follow his grease-covered finger towards the first cottage on the cliff, the closest one to the road where I stopped on the way down here, a delightful little picture-worthy stone building with a grey slate roof, surrounded by a lot of greenery and a garden hidden behind a rhododendron hedge. Even from this distance, I can see that it's just as perfect as I'd pictured it, although it's difficult to concentrate with his arm so near, and the movement has sent a wave of his tropical shower gel towards me, along with the sexy scent of oil on skin and an undercurrent of sea air.

'I mean it, you know?' He suddenly turns serious. 'You're welcome to come over anytime. If your hotel is anywhere near as bad as it looks from the outside, or if you want a nice view or a bit of company or something …'

'Thanks, Nathan.' I cut him off because I'm surprised that he's offered, that he genuinely seems keen to see me, and that he doesn't think I'm a nutter for coming here. I should probably say something else but I'm a tad flustered.

He looks like he wants to say something else too, but he doesn't. 'How long are you staying?'

'A couple of weeks,' I say, deciding it's best to keep it vague. 'It's kind of a working holiday. As long as I've got a laptop and an internet connection, I can work anywhere. My boss probably only gives me a cubicle in the office so she can check I'm not slacking off. She's let me bring my work with me. She was really understanding about the whole phone thing. She thought I should get it back to you as quickly as possible.'

'Nice boss.'

How can I tell him? He's just told me he's not interested in a relationship, and I'm definitely not, so what am I going to say? I'm here to write an article about whether you're going to fall in love with me or not? The answer is already a resounding 'not', so what am I here for? To make up an article about us falling in love? Neither option makes me sound any less off my rocker.

'Well, it's my own fault for being so careless.' It takes me a moment to realise he means the phone when he looks at me. 'Or so distracted.'

I go red for no reason.

'To be honest, I'm kind of enjoying being without it. Pearlholme is the kind of place you come to disconnect, and this little old thing …' he pats the pocket of his dungarees '… is perfect for that. It can phone, it can text, it can take an awful picture, and it's got no internet, which is a welcome break to be honest. Do you know, I actually slept soundly last night rather than tossing and turning for ages over something I'd just read on Twitter or watched on Facebook.'

'You don't have the apps on your phone.'

'So you went through my apps but you didn't go through my browsing history? You'd make a terrible investigator, do you know that?'

He's smiling as he says it and he doesn't seem annoyed with me. 'I didn't even think of that. I didn't want to invade your privacy too much.'

'You didn't want to open my browser and find I was into unicorn porn or something like that?'

I raise an eyebrow. 'Is that a thing?'

He laughs. 'I have no idea. I promise I'm not into anything weird. If you had opened my browser, you'd have found Google News and searches for how to make a Pot Noodle more interesting.'

'*Can* you make a Pot Noodle more interesting?'

'It's really a case of with or without the sauce packet. Some bloke on YouTube tried putting it in a sandwich, which just looked … ick. And I'm always being careful not to strain something with my adventurous cooking.'

Surely it's not normal to just sit here and smile at someone? Everything about him makes me smile. I feel comfortable sitting with him, and I'm suddenly so, so glad I came. I *know* it won't lead to anything more, and I don't want it to, but I'm just glad to have met him. He feels like someone special.

I shake myself. I have to stop it. I'm here to further my career, nothing more. 'So, are you okay? You said on the phone that you felt better than you had for months. Had you been feeling bad?'

He gives me a sideways glance and his dark eyes turn soft. 'I can't believe you heard that. Or cared.' He looks out at the sea again. 'Yeah, I hate London. My last job was restoring an Edwardian organ in the basement of a London museum. I felt like I hadn't seen daylight in months. I couldn't have asked for a better job at a better time than this.'

I glance at the giant tent behind me. There's not much of the carousel to see. He hasn't opened the tent from this side, so all that's on show is the greyish white canvas of the marquee covering and enough space for Nathan to work around it. 'Do you get many jobs like this?'

'It's been a while since I was sent anywhere quite as perfect as this, but yeah, I go out to fix things in situ if I can. Our workshop is on the outskirts of London, so we get stuff brought in there or shipped to us, or we go out to jobs like this one. There's six of us there and we all have different specialities. My boss is one of the leading antique restorers in the country, so people go to him with whatever they need doing and he decides which of us is best suited to the job. I'm lucky that I mainly fix big old things because I'm more likely to get to go out to jobs. I'm probably sixty per cent away and forty per cent in the workshop. The guys who fix up furniture and small easily moveable things are almost always in the workshop.'

Which explains his absence on the train for weeks at a time. It's easy to tell how much he likes being outside. It's something I'd never really thought about until I wandered through Pearlholme, but I don't get much fresh air either. I'd always thought I got enough on the walk from my flat to the tube station every day and the lunchtime walks to the nearest sandwich shop, but there's a difference between London fresh air and *real* fresh air.

I can't help looking at his hands again as he leans down to draw mindless patterns in the sand at his feet. 'Do you know they've invented these really clever hand coverings for people who do messy jobs … called gloves?'

Instead of being offended like I feared he might, he laughs, a warm sound that shakes the wood we're sitting on. 'I need to be able to feel what I'm doing. See this?' He reaches into his pocket and pulls out the small metal thing he was rubbing earlier. 'They're the bearings that allow the carousel to turn, and because it's so old, they've got gunk all around them where it isn't supposed to be. I've got to be able to feel if they're damaged – if there are any chips or splits it'll affect the movement – and the best tool I've got for clearing these little ridges out is my thumbnail.'

He rubs the metal thing with his thumb and then runs his nail along one of the grooves in it, a tiny noodle of grease appearing in its wake.

He wipes it on the cloth. 'We've got fantastic gloves that are like a second skin, but nowt's as good as actually feeling something this old with your fingers. I think you can almost feel the years that have passed.' He rubs the bearing with the cloth and then shoves it quickly back into his pocket, suddenly seeming embarrassed. 'Sorry, I'm sure you're not even vaguely interested in my metal bits.'

'No, I am, it's fascinating. I love carousels but I've never thought about how they work, and I've definitely never met anyone who does something so interesting before.'

'Ah, me and the word "interesting" don't belong in a sentence together. You just don't know me well enough yet.'

There's that 'yet' again. The butterflies that haven't left my stomach since the train the other morning take off in another storm of fluttering.

'And I am sorry about the mess.' He holds his hands out in front of him and wiggles his fingers again. 'Modern grease tends to come off with wet wipes. The old stuff that's in this is like tar – they don't make it like this anymore.'

I look behind us at the tent. 'How old is it then?'

'Oh, I wish I knew.' His face lights up, making laughter lines crinkle around his eyes again. 'Usually they're emblazoned with the name of the maker and the date, but this one isn't. I can vaguely date it because the horses are solid wood, anything from the 1930s or Forties would've been aluminium, and it changed to fibreglass in the Fifties, but only pre-1930 would've been made solely of wood, so it's definitely at least that old, but from the style, the trappings and just the way it's carved … I'd say it's older than that, the late 1800s to the turn of the century. It matches what you would've seen at that time, but it's nothing like a commercial carousel, and it's definitely never had commercial use— Sorry, I'm rambling. Simple answer: late Victorian era.'

'Oh, please, ramble away, it's fascinating.'

'You have no idea how many times I've heard that, but fascinating is code for, "When will the boring bastard shut up? Oh God, is he still going? Kill me now", usually accompanied by the distorted facial expressions of trying to hide a yawn.'

It makes me laugh even though it probably shouldn't. He gives me a smile when I meet his eyes, but I get the feeling that it covers something deeper. 'I used to love going on these when I was little. There was one on the seafront where we went every summer and I always went on the same horse. Mum used to call it "my" horse.'

'Me too. My nan and granddad used to take my brother and me for days out by the seaside when I was young and the carousel was the only thing my nan was brave enough to go on. Maybe that's why I was drawn to fixing them … but seriously, everyone in my life knows better than to ask me questions about work because I get overexcited talking about it.'

I tuck a leg under my thigh and turn towards him, trying to figure out why anyone would want him to shut up. 'Do you know the film *Carousel*?'

'The old Rodgers and Hammerstein musical from before *The Sound of Music*? The one that "You'll Never Walk Alone" comes from and no one knows that?'

I'm smiling again as I nod. 'It's one of my favourite films.'

He screws his face up. 'It's about a dead guy who hits his wife and then gets a chance to go back to earth and make amends so he hits his daughter instead.'

'It's about a man who died before he could bring himself to tell his wife that he loved her because he thought she deserved better than him, when all she really wanted was for him to realise that he was good enough and always had been.'

He hums the chorus of 'If I Loved You'. 'I've got about six copies on DVD. When you work on carousels, it's a go-to present every Christmas and birthday regardless of the fact someone "goes to" it every year. It's not exactly my favourite film but it has a certain charm.'

'My best friend thinks I'm nuts for loving it.'

'I like it because films were magical back then. Every movie meant something; they weren't the action-packed blockbusters that are just like every other one of the hundred action-packed blockbusters that come out each week. They were a real experience to go and see. I love watching old films because they're such a snapshot of times gone by.'

I grin at him again and wave towards the giant structure behind me. 'I couldn't believe it when I saw all those photos of wooden horses on your phone. I mean, what are the chances?'

When he smiles this time, I can see the tension drain from his shoulders. 'Do you want to have a look? It's mostly in pieces and a total mess, but if you wanted ...'

'I'd love to,' I say, loving the way the lip he was biting as he asked spreads instantly into a wide smile.

He jumps to his feet and holds a hand out to pull me up and I'm just about to slip mine into it when I look up and realise what I'm doing. 'Better not, thanks.'

He groans and rips his hand away, swiftly hiding them both behind his back. 'I don't know what's got into me today. I keep wanting to explain that I'm not usually this much of an idiot, but I've needed to say it about ten times so far and every time just proves the point.'

'You're great,' I say and then blush furiously. There's forthright and there's *forthright*. 'I mean, this whole place is great, the beach, the carousel, the ice cream. I'm glad I came.' I pretend to focus on getting to my feet and pulling the legs of my capri trousers down where they've ridden up my thick calves so I don't have to look at his gorgeous face.

My sandals tap on the wooden walkway as I follow him around the side of the tent and through a gap where the material is pulled aside.

'Welcome to my humble abode,' he says, and I smile at the way he drops the 'h'. I love a Yorkshire accent.

'Wow.' I can't help the intake of breath as I look around, even though it's no more than the skeleton of a carousel at the moment. There's a tall, thick pole in the centre, supported by diagonal posts, with rods extending out from the top of it like the arms of an umbrella. A rusty-looking engine is next to it, and an old pipe organ, but all the horses are stacked on the floor, and there are metal bars lying all over the place, and various piles of metal bits like the one Nathan showed me. 'You did all this by yourself?'

'What, took it apart?' He continues when I nod. 'That's my job. I mean, the owner got the platform built and the tent's been up for protection since he bought it, but my job is to strip carousels, fix them, and rebuild them. You can get them apart in half a day if you know what you're doing.'

'Where did it come from?'

'That's the most interesting part. No one knows. The guy who

71

owns the fish and chip shop on the promenade is some millionaire fish and chip mogul. He won it in a blind auction and got planning permission to install it on the beach. Apparently he's going to do free rides for everyone who buys food there or something.'

'A millionaire fish and chip shop mogul … It's not Ian Beale, is it?'

'An *EastEnders* fan,' he says with a laugh.

'Not really, but my mum insists on telling me every plot point in minute detail. The more I protest, the more I hear about it.' I'm sure he didn't want to know that. 'Can you find out anything else about it?'

'When I collected the fence keys from the chip shop, the girl serving said it was found in an abandoned house or something. I'm hoping that stripping it down will give me more clues about its origin.'

'What do you think?' I ask because I get the impression he wants to say more.

His face lights up again. 'It's definitely not been outside because it doesn't have the wear, so an abandoned house would make sense. Must've been a massive house though – can you imagine getting something this big into one of our crappy one-bedroom flats?'

I shake my head, looking up at the spire on top. It really is humungous.

'There's a dent in the top and damage to the rounding boards, and the top bars are bent, so that suggests something fell on it. From the scratches and debris, I'd guess a roof or ceiling came down on it, but at the same time, I'd guess that whatever it was also gave it some kind of protection. This is in incredible condition for the age of it, it must've been well cared for back in the day, and although it's obviously been let go since then, it doesn't have anywhere near the damage you'd expect.'

The tent smells of aged wood and the grease that Nathan's

hands are covered in, and I wander around the circular area, stepping over the metal posts that he's carefully laid out. I run my fingers down one of the support poles suspended from the bars above, carved into a twist and covered in tarnished gold paint, which comes off in flakes when I touch it. 'Did you say that this was all carved by one person?'

'I reckon so, yeah. I think this was a personal project, something never intended for public use. It doesn't have the glitz of a fairground ride, but it has a personal touch in every bit of carving. There are the same quirks in every part. I can't see how it could've been the work of a workshop where you've got different carvers working on each bit. It doesn't feel like that.'

'It must've taken forever.' I look around in awe as I crouch down and run my fingers over what I assume is one of the rounding boards he mentioned, a lavishly carved but battered frame surrounding cracked mirror glass, one of many stacked against each other on the floor. They look like they belong on a castle wall with an evil queen peering in and asking who's the fairest of them all. The intricacy of one simple panel is incredible, and it's unimaginable that one person could've done all of this by hand, but Nathan really seems to know what he's talking about.

'This is such a massive find. Original steam-powered gallopers from that era are so rare. There are only about seventy in the world and this isn't one that's registered. It's also the most complete one I've ever come across and in as near to original condition as possible. It's incredible. Look at this.' His long legs step over a tangle of metal poles as he walks towards one of the wooden horses lined up at the edge of the tent. 'These have only ever been painted once. That's unheard of for something of this age. Usually when I go to restore carousel animals, the biggest job is stripping back layers and layers of paint where someone's thought they were preserving it by slapping on another coat every few years. This is the original lead-based enamel that's been out of existence for decades now … Why are you smiling?'

I blush and try to rearrange my face because I hadn't realised I was. It doesn't work. I can't stop myself smiling at his enthusiasm. 'Because you know so much.'

It makes him smile too but he shakes his head. 'This is new territory for me. Usually I work on family-owned travelling carousels or museum jobs where you've got a full written history and a log of every repair and fault it's had over the years. This is such an incredible discovery, it's unreal, and … look at this.' He goes to pat one of the horses but stops himself before he puts black grease all over that too. Instead he points at it and I go over for a closer look. 'This is the lead horse, it would *always* have the manufacturer's signature on it, but this one doesn't. It's another thing that suggests this was the work of just one person and that it was never intended for public use.'

'What's a lead horse?'

'It's grander than the others and it's always behind the chariot so it leads the rows of horses. One of my jobs is to make a couple of extra chariots to make it more accessible for everyone.'

'Wow. You can do that?'

'Of course. It means it's not quite a complete restoration – if it was up to me then I'd preserve it exactly as it was – but I get the impression that it's more about money-making for the guy who owns it, so it's got to be brought up to date and made all flashy and light-y.' He laughs. 'By light-y, I mean I've got to install a load more lights. Sorry, I forget how to speak English some days.'

I grin at him. 'Same.'

The sun is warm as we step out of the tent and back onto the beach again. 'I'm so glad you came,' Nathan says quietly. 'And I'm sorry, I don't usually get so overexcited about the arrival of complete strangers. You must think I'm a right loon.'

'Well, I did have ice cream.'

His smile is so wide that I'm physically incapable of not smiling in return and we stand there smiling at each other for a few moments, and I tell myself that the sun is what's heating up my cheeks and not anything else. It's definitely not the way his forearms flex as he moves.

We're back to smiling at each other for no reason, and I know I'm delaying leaving. I've been here for a couple of hours and he hasn't got any work done in that time, but I don't want the afternoon to end yet. I haven't even given him— 'Oh, I totally forgot about your phone! Here!' I go to pull it out of my pocket but he holds up a blackened hand.

'I can't take it, I'll ruin it.'

'I could put it in your …' I nod towards the pocket of his dungarees, which he keeps putting things into and producing things from. The only thing he's missing is a baby kangaroo.

'Actually, I'd rather you keep it.'

'Why?' I stop with it halfway out of my pocket.

'Because if you give it back, you haven't got an excuse to come and see me again.' He's blushing furiously as he says it and it makes my stomach flip over in the most exhilarating way possible.

He ducks his head, dark eyelashes touching his red cheeks. 'I'm sorry, I think the sun's gone to my head.'

'Or maybe all the ice cream,' I say, trying not to think about what it means that he wants me to come and see him again, or how much I want to.

'Exactly.' He looks up and meets my eyes with that wide grin and there we go just standing there smiling at each other again.

I shake myself. This cannot be real. He doesn't want a relationship and neither do I, and I'm standing here imagining what it would be like to kiss him. 'Okay, I should go. I guess I'll see you around?'

'Yeah, of course.' He goes to fiddle with his short hair but stops himself just in time as he walks me back along the wooden path to the base of the ramp I came down. I take a few steps up it, trying to convince myself not to run across the road for another ice cream each just to delay leaving a bit longer. This is silly. Not only have I not mentioned the article, I haven't even *thought* about it myself since I set foot on the sand earlier.

'Wait, Ness?'

When I turn back, he looks like he's psyching himself up to say something, and the words all spill out in such a rush that it takes me a few moments to translate them. 'Will you come for a drink with me this evening?' He actually seems like he needs to catch his breath. 'Not as a date or anything. You came all this way to bring my phone back; the least I can do is buy you a drink. I promise to be a bit more composed and to have washed my hands and—'

'I'd love to,' I say, wondering why he seems so nervous. He's sweet and funny and absolutely gorgeous. I can't imagine there are many women likely to turn him down, date or not.

He lets out a long breath and I wonder if I'm imagining that it was a sigh of relief. It makes something flutter inside me again. Am I just projecting the feelings flapping around inside me onto him? *I'm* the one feeling relief because I didn't want this afternoon to end and now we've got an extension.

'Not that there are many options around here, but what do you think about giving The Sun & Sand a try? It looks pretty from the outside.'

'Sounds perfect.'

'Around seven?'

'I'll meet you there.'

'Okay.'

'Okay.' I nod, still holding his gaze and smiling at him.

I still don't want to walk away even though I'm going to see him again in a couple of hours.

Oh, come on, Ness. This is ridiculous. I force myself to give him a proper wave and walk back up the ramp to the promenade, feeling like I've got lead boots on my feet. I'm positive I can feel his eyes on my back, and when I get to the top, I turn around and he's still there. He holds up a greasy hand and gives me a smile, and I do the same, waiting until he turns away and goes back towards the carousel, pulling the bearing out of his pocket and rubbing at it again.

I force myself to walk back along the promenade rather than skipping like a joyous lead actress in a romance film, and I can't remember the last time I felt this fluttery and excited.

# Chapter 6

Being early is not one of my strong suits in life, and judging by the train rush the other morning, neither is it one of Nathan's, but when I get to The Sun & Sand at quarter to seven, he's waiting outside.

He stands up from the bench he was perched on when he sees me walking down the road, and my heart starts thudding harder in my chest at the sight of the smile that brightens his face.

If I thought he looked gorgeous earlier, he's off-the-scale gorgeous now. Dark jeans that make his legs look even longer, a plain black shirt that's got just enough buttons undone to show a hint of tanned skin, and sleeves done up round his elbows, showcasing those *seriously* sexy forearms.

He waves as I get nearer, making said forearms flex, and I stumble over my own feet with the distraction. I give the smooth pavement a frown like it was the tarmac's fault. There aren't even cobblestones in this part of the village.

'Hello.' He elongates the word so it sounds all warm and sexy. 'You're early.'

'So are you,' I say as I get close enough to smell his aftershave. A far cry from the grease and sea air of earlier, now he smells like the sexiest man on the planet. Something peppery and coconutty, a dark tropical aftershave. I want to press my nose into his neck and inhale.

But that would be weird, obviously.

'Ah, I've been ready for ages. Figured I'd be better off sitting out here in the fresh air than wearing a hole in the cottage carpet with my nervous pacing.' He scratches at the back of his neck. 'I mean, not that I would be nervous or anything – I don't know why I said that. It's perfectly normal for two friends to meet for a drink on a summer evening, right?'

'Right.' I feel a little flutter at the idea that he was nervous too, and I don't tell him that I've been ready for ages and I sat in the hotel room watching the clock until I could justify leaving without being ridiculously early.

He shifts from one foot to the other again, and I get the feeling he's trying to work out how we should greet each other, which is exactly what I'm doing too. A handshake is too formal, a hug is not formal enough, and would a kiss on the cheek be too weird even if I wasn't so short that I doubt I could reach his cheek without a struggle anyway?

We both decide on something at the exact same moment, except he goes for a cheek kiss and I go for a hug and I end up headbutting him in the chest.

He steps back with a nervous chuckle. 'Sorry, I'm too tall for my own good.'

I smile up at him for trying to take the blame, even though it was my fault for being so nervous of making a wrong move.

'Well, there are sparrows taller than me.' I nod to one of the little brown birds chirruping from the hedgerow.

'Aw, you're the perfect height.'

'Yeah, for a footstool.'

He laughs and then looks guilty. 'I feel like I should apologise for laughing at that but I don't know how to without digging myself in deeper. I'm laughing because you're funny, not because it's true, and now I'm laughing even more because of how awkward I've made this situation, and I think this whole conversation would've gone a lot better if I'd just kept my mouth shut.'

I giggle again because he's so adorably awkward and tongue-tied, and it makes me feel better that he might be even half as nervous as I am.

'Oh, and look.' He holds his hands out to me, turning them over and back, showing them off like someone doing an advert for hand cream.

I slip my fingers around his and hold one of his hands up to the light, pretending to examine it. What I'm really concentrating on is how warm his rough skin is, how long his slim fingers are, and how right it feels when they curl around mine and my thumb rubs against his so softly.

I have to swallow a couple of times to get my words out. 'Impressive hand-washing skills.'

He lets out another laugh. 'You'd think that most men want to be told that they look good, or they smell nice, or they're good in bed, but what every guy *really* wants a woman to notice about him is that he's good at washing his hands.'

It makes me laugh too and I force myself to let go of his perfectly clean hand, which admittedly *is* the subject of seriously impressive hand-washing skills. After this afternoon, I doubted his hands would ever look clean again.

Inside, we find a perfect little country pub, with mahogany tables and chairs, old red-brick walls, and stained-glass lampshades hanging from exposed beams in the ceiling.

'What can I get you?' Nathan asks as we walk up to the bar.

'Just a beer, please.'

'Same.' He nods, and while he stands there reading the food menu above the bar, I'm standing a little bit behind him and I can't resist a quick perv. His jeans fit like a glove, framing a perfectly pert bum; the shirt makes his waist look slim and his shoulders broad; and his hair is different to how it was on the beach earlier. This afternoon, it was windblown and unstyled, but tonight, it's softly spiked at the front and he's used some kind of texturising, touchable wax, which is having absolutely the desired effect.

'Have you eaten?' He turns around and catches me mid-stare. 'Do you want something? I keep hearing about the fish and chips here …'

'Well, I'm a vegetarian so I don't eat fish …'

'Oh my God, me too!' He looks at me in surprise.

'I did not know that, what completely brand-new information,' I say a bit too squeakily, one step away from a complete *Friends* re-enactment of Phoebe and Joey when Ross tells them about Rachel's pregnancy. I can't tell him that Daphne and I have already discovered that from his phone.

'Aw, that's amazing. Most people in my life just think I'm being a fussy weirdo when I say that.' He edges nearer to me until my shoulder touches his arm. 'Do you want to share some chips or something? I was too nervous … er, busy … to eat, so I'm famished.'

'I'd love to,' I say, because I haven't had anything since the ice cream earlier. No way could I fit anything in my stomach with all the butterflies fluttering around in there.

His smile doesn't seem like it could get any wider but he somehow manages it, and seeing those dimples so close makes my knees feel weak. 'Do you want to grab a table while I order?'

To be honest, I'm quite happy just standing here with his arm touching mine, but I spot an empty table tucked into a corner and I get the feeling it's exactly the one he'd go for, slightly away from the other tables and with just enough space for the two of us. I nudge my bare arm against his forearm, feeling the rough smattering of fine dark hair against my skin, and point to where I'm going, before I leave him standing at the bar and make a beeline for it, surprised when people sitting at other tables smile and say hello as I pass them. In what kind of non-London world do you greet other diners in pubs?

I slide onto the red cushion covering the wooden bench that curves around the corner table and look around. I want to look at Nathan again but he keeps looking over at me with a smile and being caught ogling his bum once is enough for one evening.

There are wooden anchors and fishing nets displayed across the wall, framed photos of unknown fishermen holding large fish aloft, and shelves displaying giant seashells – the kind that you'd need both hands to hold, and I wonder if they were found on Pearlholme beach and what kind of gigantic mutant mollusks live here if that's the case. Is the carousel being installed for human or crustacean use?

Despite being determined not to look at Nathan, I can't take my eyes off him as he gets two bottles of beer from the bar and makes his way across the pub, only taking his eyes off mine to greet people who say hello to him as he passes.

'People are so friendly here.' He slides onto the bench on the opposite side of the table and hands me one of the beer bottles. 'Chips will be over when they're done. Cheers.' He taps the neck of his bottle against mine.

'When was the last time you walked into a pub and people greeted you?' I ask to get my mind off the way his smile makes every inch of his face brighten.

'I wouldn't know, I don't go out much.' His eyes flick to mine. 'And there I go making myself sound all lively and exciting again. I mean that I go out every night raving and getting completely rat-arsed, obviously.'

I grin because he seems exciting to me exactly as he is. 'So rat-arsed that you don't even remember doing it?'

'Exactly.' He laughs and when his eyes meet mine this time, they're twinkling in the warm light of the pub. I've never thought that brown eyes could be twinkly before – when you think of twinkly eyes you generally think of blue ones – but his seem to reflect the lights around us and the smile on his face. 'I think I'm showing my age by talking about raves anyway. Do they still exist anymore?'

'I wouldn't know, I don't go out much either. Only when my best friend stops accepting my excuses and drags me from the flat by my ear, but she's been pregnant for the past few months so I've been enjoying the reprieve.'

'What a pair we make.' He looks over his shoulder at the pub behind him. 'We fit right in here. You know how they usually ID you in pubs to make sure you're over eighteen?'

I nod and he leans forward and whispers. 'Do you think in this one they get ID'd to make sure they're over seventy?'

I let out a laugh so loud that several of the aforementioned pensioners turn to look at us.

'Careful, we're yobs disturbing the peace. I keep expecting a policeman to appear behind us and say they don't want our sort of "yoof" around here.'

'It's your fault for making me laugh,' I say, eternally grateful that I hadn't just had a sip of beer because it would've ended up all over the table.

'All right, Nath? How's the carousel coming along?' one of the elderly men at a nearby table calls over to him.

'It's great, thanks, Frank. How's that bunion doing today?'

This time I do choke on a sip of beer because I'm trying so hard to contain another laugh. I'm pretty sure the first rule of The Sun & Sand would be not to laugh at the mention of ailments.

'It's marvellous. My daughter ordered a fancy foam plaster online for me and that's helped. What an attentive young man you are,' Frank says, before turning to me and raising his glass. 'You've got a good one there, lass.'

I fear that trying to reply may result in a burst of laughter that I'll never recover from, so I just smile and nod along.

Nathan waves to a couple of other people sat at tables around the room before turning back to me.

'Well, if talking about bunions across the pub doesn't endear you to the locals then nothing will.'

'Ah, he was nosing round the carousel yesterday. Started telling me about his latest doctor's visit. I thought they put up that security fence to keep me and my carousel bits in, but I'm starting to wonder if it was actually to keep chatty pensioners out.'

'You must be doing something right if they're shortening your name already.'

'I think they've mistaken me for one of their own,' he whispers. 'Either that or Frank has pimped me out as a cure for insomnia.'

He's cheery on the surface, but it feels like there's something much deeper behind his diffident sense of humour.

'Nice to see our two tourists found each other.' The woman who gave me directions to The Shell Hotel earlier comes over and plonks a massive bowl of steaming hot chips on the table between us.

'I'm sure we're not your only two tourists.' Nathan looks up and gives her a dashing smile that makes me glad I'm sitting down even though it wasn't directed at me.

'Of course not, the cottage lets are full and there's a few people at the hotel – you two just seemed like you should find each other.'

How could she possibly know that? I only said a couple of sentences to her and none of them involved him or the carousel.

'Did you find your way to the hotel all right?' she asks me.

'Yes, thanks.' Surely she would've noticed me walking in circles around the village if I hadn't?

'And I'm pleased to see you found your way out of it too,' she says. 'Rumour has it that some people haven't been so lucky.'

Nathan snorts and I look at her in horror. 'Seriously?'

She keeps a straight face for a disconcerting amount of time before she lets out a peal of laughter. 'I'm pulling your leg, of course. But that S isn't wonky for no reason …'

'The Hell Hotel?' Nathan says.

'That's what we call it round here.' She pats the table and goes to walk away. 'Enjoy your chips. Don't forget, they're much better than the ones you'll get on the promenade!'

'We're going to have to test that theory.' Nathan turns back to me when she leaves, and I nod probably a bit too enthusiastically at the idea that he means we'll have to test it *together*.

'Is the hotel as bad as everyone says?' He takes a chip and nudges the bowl nearer to me.

I shrug. 'I only checked in this afternoon, I haven't spent enough time there to judge it. But it's a bit … dark and overgrown, and the inside looks like it could do with a good clean and a few lightbulbs changing, and the room is tiny and the bathroom's down the hall and had someone else's pubic hair in the shower tray.'

'Oh no!' Nathan looks like it's his turn to stifle a giggle. 'I don't mean to laugh, but …'

'If you can't laugh about someone else's pubic hair, what can you laugh about?' I say, laughing as he lets out a guffaw. Somehow, laughing about it with him makes it all worthwhile. Even the pubic hair.

'In all fairness, the guy on reception looked about a hundred. I doubt he could make it up the stairs to the bathroom, let alone clean it.'

'Come up to the cottage anytime. Seriously. I've never described a building as cute before, but the cottage embodies cuteness, and the bathroom's spotless. You're welcome anytime you want.'

'Thank you.' I take a chip and shove it in my mouth to avoid having to come up with an excuse, no matter how much I want to jump at the chance. Of course, the chip is approximately the temperature of lava, and I then have to style it out and breezily answer him with a burning mouthful of boiling potato. 'To be honest, it could be a cow shed and it would still be better than my flat in London.'

'It does look like it might've actually once been a cow shed.'

'I'll let you know if I hear mooing in the night. I didn't fancy exploring much but it did look like there were a few corners that hadn't been disturbed this side of the Seventies. There could still be cows roaming around in there.' I think about it for a moment. 'Although, in all fairness, if the cows are still in there, it does smell like they probably died in the Eighties at the latest.'

'Maybe they've been dead since the Eighties *and* they're still roaming around in there.' His whole face lights up. 'Zombie cows!'

I start laughing again because he seems like the only person in the world who could make zombie cows seem like a completely normal topic of conversation *and* something to get excited about. Daphne would *kill* me if she could overhear this.

'Still better than London?'

I take another chip and blow on it this time. 'I've only been here a few hours and I can already tell that Pearlholme has a way of making everything seem better.'

'Even their chips,' he says, holding one up. 'It makes me realise how much I hate London. Some people can live there and thrive, but I am *not* one of them. I would be so happy to live somewhere like this.'

'Couldn't you? You move around for jobs anyway.'

'The workshop's in London. I travel to jobs quite often, but so much of our work comes through there first. I often assess things from there before I go to them; all of our tools are there, spare parts, lists of suppliers, colleagues to consult for their expertise. It's a good thing not to be too far away from that base.'

'Your job is so interesting. Carousels are such an ingrained part of our history but I've never met anyone who restores them before. How did you get into that in the first place?'

'I ran away to join the circus.'

I snort a laugh but he doesn't. 'Oh wow, you're serious?' He nods and I continue. 'Sorry, I thought that was just a saying, like an old wives' tale or something. I didn't realise people actually do that.'

'When your family's like mine, the circus is tame in comparison.' He shakes himself. 'Yeah, when I was seventeen, the circus

86

was in town over the summer and I hid out there all the time. I got to know the owner, he let me hang out behind the scenes and I made friends with the crew, and at the end of the season when they were packing up to leave, I asked what I'd have to do to join them, and I think they took pity on me and let me go with them. A winter season in Skegness, just what every young lad dreams about.' He gives me a smile that doesn't look like he finds anything amusing.

It makes me wonder one thing: what was he running away from?

'I was supposed to be working on an act, but I was crap at everything. I'm not a performer and I'd just go to bits whenever I had to do something in front of people. I thought I might be onto something with the aerial hoop ...'

I instantly picture the 'Rewrite the Stars' scene from *The Greatest Showman* and how impressed I am must show on my face because he lifts a hand to stop me. 'Not based on talent, solely from a humour perspective. Let me put it this way – at seventeen, I was even more gangly than I am now. I'm not a massive fan of heights so my face was always pale with fear, and I wore a lot of black. I basically looked like Jack Skellington humping an embroidery hoop.'

I close my eyes, trying not to dissolve into giggles at the mental image.

'I realised I was rubbish at every act I tried, but I didn't want to leave so I had to make myself useful in any way I could, from making tea to selling popcorn and manning the ticket booth, and one thing I found out I could do was fix things. There was always something or other breaking, and I ended up going to have a look whenever something broke down, from broken rides to holes in the tents to backed-up candyfloss machines. It became an unofficial apprenticeship. I didn't have any qualifications so a proper electrician would have to follow me around and certify everything, and the circus owner eventually got in touch with a friend in London and he offered me a proper apprenticeship at his workshop, and that was eighteen years ago and he's still my boss today.'

'Have you been doing carousels all that time?'

'No, I had an accident five years ago and couldn't do my normal work. Carousels became my speciality then.'

'What happened?' I ask, feeling irrationally worried at the thought of him being hurt.

'I fell off a Ferris wheel and wrecked my shoulder. Here, feel.' He takes my hand and pulls it across the table, pulling the collar of his shirt away from his neck as his fingers take mine under the shirt and press them against the skin of his collarbone. 'Feel that dent in the bone?'

I nod, my fingertips rubbing the warm skin of his shoulder, feeling a big indentation under my touch.

'One of the many places I chipped the bone. Snapped my shoulder joint clean in half, shattered everything else surrounding it. Totally my own fault for ignoring safety regulations. We're not supposed to repair things like that without full scaffolding, and the scaffolding guy hadn't turned up for the third day in a row, and my colleague had called in sick, and I couldn't do anything else without the top part being fixed, and I thought I could just put up a ladder and do it myself, and … well, I couldn't.'

'I'm sorry,' I murmur. I think I've short-circuited at the sudden closeness. The roughness of his fingers is still against mine, his thumb brushing my hand as my fingers rub his skin gently.

'I didn't think I'd be able to work for months, but my boss was brilliant, gave me all the time I needed, let me go for physio appointments every few days and hospital appointments whenever they came up. We'd just had a carousel in for repair, and I discovered that one thing I could do was sit and repaint carousel horses with one hand. I'd worked on carousels before, and was always enchanted by them, and it felt like exactly the thing I needed at exactly the right moment. It's a long and fiddly job, and by the time it was done, I'd recovered enough to start easing back into my regular work, and the next time a carousel repair came up, my boss sent me, and I've done every one since.'

His words have faded into the background because all I can think about is how good his warm shoulder feels and the way I can feel the edges of my nails dragging against his skin.

He suddenly seems to realise we're sitting in a pub and my hand's under his shirt because he sits back so fast that my hand falls away and I need lightning-fast reflexes to stop it clonking on the table. Which I don't have.

'I'm sorry,' Nathan says. 'I don't usually pick up complete strangers' hands and shove them down my top. I shouldn't have done that. I didn't mean to overstep the mark.'

'No mark.' I shake my head because he seems so apologetic and it really isn't like he did anything wrong. In fact, if we could spend the rest of the evening with my hand under his shirt, that would be fine with me.

We look at each other in silence across the table for a moment before he looks down and starts fiddling with a beer mat. 'I've never told anyone that before,' he says without looking up. 'I mean, people ask and I tell them about the circus and the apprenticeship, but I've never mentioned the injury.'

'Does it still hurt?'

He shakes his head. 'It aches sometimes, if it's cold or if the weather's been wet for too long. It did for a long time, but it's old now, it doesn't bother me. I don't know why I told you.'

'You sure it's not your way of gaining sympathy when you chat up all the girls?'

His eyes flash with amusement. 'You think I need sympathy when I've got "hold it and I'll lick it like a dog"?'

The laugh eases the awkwardness and he relaxes again. 'What about you? What painful accident got you into fact-checking? Or are you going to tell me that most people don't start their careers based on life-changing injuries?' He sounds light-hearted but I get the feeling there's more to it.

'No injuries, just a break-up and sympathy from my best friend. I was living with someone and struggling by on temp work, spending more hours commuting around London to various jobs than actually doing the jobs. We broke up and my friend persuaded me to move further into the city, nearer to her. She's a features writer for *Maîtresse* magazine and she somehow managed to persuade her firm to take me on as a fact-checker. I would've been stupid to turn down a permanent job, so I slept on her sofa while I found the crappiest flat in the whole UK.'

'I take your crappiest flat and raise you a crap flat with a door that didn't lock properly, and when I bought and installed my own locks, my landlord fined me for damaging the property and took my deposit.'

My eyes widen. 'You're kidding?'

'I wish. Living in London's great, innit?' His voice is deadpan and I smile at his sarcasm.

'Have you got an unidentified leak too?'

'Oh, always. I think they come as standard on tenant agreements.'

I take another chip and try to hide my smile behind it. It's not normal to smile this much at someone.

'Is fact-checking as interesting as it sounds? It sounds fun but from what you've said, I get the impression that it's not?'

He is attentive, just like Bunion Frank said. 'Honestly, it's just dull. I painstakingly go through every article that's going to be published and make sure that every single sentence doesn't mention something that's incorrect. I spend most of my day phoning around to confirm quotes that people have given the journalists and getting permission to cite sources and use pictures, and the rest of my day on Google. I find answers to things you didn't even know were questions. My internet search history could get me arrested.'

'Mine would get Weight Watchers on the phone to find out

how one person can eat so much crap,' he says with a laugh. 'Do you write?'

'I'd like to. I think I could, but ...' This is a perfect opportunity to broach the subject of the article and tell him about the first part going viral and what Zinnia's got planned, but I don't know how to say it. It's ludicrous to have sent me here to find the real Train Man and see if we're going to fall in love. How can I say it to him? It'll change things between us, and I'm enjoying his company. I don't want it to end yet. I'll leave it for tonight. There'll be plenty of time to talk about it tomorrow. Definitely tomorrow.

'Daphne is so good at what she does. She has the ability to see a story in anything and get people to tell it to her. Even if they're reluctant, she can tease it out of them like an old friend. I don't know if I could do that. I'm hoping my boss will give me the chance to find out.' I feel awkward talking about work with him. I should be telling him. I *should* have told him the moment I arrived on the beach. There's an article online that thousands of people have read, and it's about *him*, and he doesn't know. 'What's the dream in carousel repair?'

'Honestly? This is it.'

I cock my head to one side as he continues.

'A Victorian carousel that has never been discovered before, and having enough trust to be the only person restoring it ... However that carousel turns out will be because of me and me alone. I dreamt of this kind of responsibility when I started out.' He ducks his head and then looks up and gives me a wink. 'Unless it turns out to be an abject failure, of course. That won't be because of me, that'll be because of someone else.'

He's trying to be funny but I'm taken aback by the genuine emotion in his voice. 'This is something really special?'

'Yeah,' he says slowly, nodding. 'I think it is—'

'Mr Musgrove, you didn't tell me you had a friend staying in town!'

He's cut off by an elderly lady doddering towards our table, a glass of fizzy water trembling in her hand.

Nathan jumps up from his seat and goes to help her, relieving her of the glass and offering his arm to help her across the pub, while I wonder if it's normal to even like someone's surname. That's the first time I've heard it and it's just as sexy as the rest of him. 'Train Man' did not do him justice. Surely Zinnia won't expect me to reveal his *real* name in the final part of the article? Surely we can make something up? In the few hours I've spent with him so far, he seems quiet and shy, and not like he'd appreciate having his name splashed all over a national magazine.

'Oh, thank you, dear, you are a nice young man. My husband's not far behind. He's just had to run to the little boys' room. Well, running is probably not the right description at our age. More a sort of limping hobble on a good day.'

She leans on the table as Nathan sets her glass down for her. 'You don't mind if a couple of old fogies join you young folks for a minute, do you?' She looks between me and him with a smile. 'I've been looking for an excuse to get to know this lovely chap a bit better.'

Nathan's eyes widen. He was clearly not expecting this, but we can't exactly say no, can we?

'It would be a pleasure,' he says, smoothly hiding his surprise. He gestures towards the bench he was just sitting on. 'Go on, you slide in.'

'Oh no, you go in first, dear. I wouldn't like to break up you and your girlfriend.'

'Oh, we're not …' we both say in unison.

'I like to be on the end in case of little girls' room emergencies. You're both too young to understand but when you get to our age, you always need to be near a bathroom. My bladder isn't what it used to be.'

And on that note, my date with a gorgeous sexy man takes a turn towards the urinary tract. Which is probably not the best choice for seducing gorgeous men.

# Chapter 7

Nathan slides onto the bench and glides nearer to me, making room for her on the end, and lets her grip his hand as she lowers herself into the seat.

'Here comes my husband,' she says, and I look up to see the man from the hotel hobbling across the pub, leaning on a walking stick and holding a glass in his other hand.

'Ey up,' he says. 'You wouldn't believe I went two minutes before we left the house, would you? My bladder must have shrunk to the size of a pea.'

I've known them two minutes and I already know their favourite topic of conversation.

'Hello, love,' he says when he sees me, recognising me from the hotel. 'You found your way to the best pub in the village, I see.'

No one mentions that it is, of course, the *only* pub in the village.

'Budge up.' He plonks himself down on my edge of the bench without looking at how much space he's got and I have to shift closer to Nathan to avoid being sat on.

'This is my landlady, Camilla.' Nathan introduces her to me.

'And this is my landlord from the hotel,' I say. 'Sorry, I didn't catch your name this afternoon?'

'Charles,' the old gent says.

'Charles and Camilla?' I say.

Nathan looks at me with a raised eyebrow and I have to hold back a snort of laughter.

'Pearlholme's own royal couple,' Camilla says. 'It's brilliant, isn't it? We were so thrilled when they finally got married as we've been Charles and Camilla for sixty years now. I wouldn't mind getting some of the red carpet treatment they get though. Charles barely opens a door for me these days as he's too busy running through them to get to the loo.'

'Sometimes I can't wait for the amount of time it takes you to shuffle across a room. I'd have wet myself by then, and that would give you something else to moan about.'

They smile at each other across the table, big toothy grins that probably once had a few more teeth than they currently have, and I get the feeling that this good-natured teasing is commonplace.

Charles makes himself more comfortable, hiking his trousers up and spreading his legs before pulling his walking stick inside the bench and standing it between me and him so it doesn't trip anyone up. It forces me to shift closer to Nathan again, and Camilla puts her handbag on the seat between her and Nathan, forcing him to squash closer to me too. I wonder if they realise this is a table for two?

I glance up at him beside me, now so close that our arms are pressed together from shoulder to elbow and our thighs are touching on the bench. Other than the hint of lavender from Camilla and cough sweets from Charles, all I can smell is the fresh scent of Nathan's hair putty and his aftershave, and his neck is now only a few inches away, reminding me of my desire to bury my face in it earlier. I am really not complaining that this is supposedly a table for two.

'Can I get either of you anything?' Nathan asks, making me

think how sweet he is. And that if they say yes, he's got no hope of getting out of his seat short of vaulting across the table.

'Oh, you are a lovely young man.' Camilla taps her glass, making fizzy water spill over and splosh onto the table. 'No, we're all set here, thank you, dear.'

'Only sparkling water?' He nods towards their glasses. 'You're being good, aren't you?'

'I'm far too doddery for anything else these days. People wouldn't know if I was losing my marbles or pissed as a fart. I'd wake up with a hangover the morning after a bender and find this one had stuck me in a nursing home.' She gestures towards Charles.

'Anything for a bit of peace,' he says, grinning at her as he helps himself to a chip and pops it in his mouth.

The idea of this sweet old woman on a bender is too much and I can feel Nathan's muscular upper arm shaking against my shoulder as we both try not to laugh.

'How are you finding Pearlholme?' Charles asks us both. 'You're both from the big smoke, aren't you? I bet it's quite a change.'

'I think I've died and gone to heaven,' Nathan says, and I'm almost positive I can feel tension drain from him as he says it.

'It's so beautiful. And everyone is so friendly. The Wi-Fi leaves a bit to be desired, mind.' I turn to Charles. When I phoned the hotel to book and asked if they had internet, he replied, 'Yes, and it's only forty-five minutes away by bus but you'll have to change before Scarborough.' I thought he'd misheard me, but since trying to check my work emails earlier and not finding a signal, I've started to wonder.

'We have Wi-Fi.' He helps himself to another chip. 'Sometimes.'

'It conveniently didn't mention that part online,' I say, wondering quite what I expected from a hotel that didn't even accept online bookings, and had no hint of a computer on the reception desk.

'That's probably why all your reviews are so bad.' Camilla pokes her tongue out at him.

'I wouldn't know, I haven't got a computer to read them on and that's just the way I like it.' He takes another chip and points it at her. 'She gets her mate's granddaughter to read them just so she can rub it in my face how much better her cottage is doing. I don't care about all that *newfandangled* nonsense from The Online.'

Nathan meets my eyes and I know he's dying not to laugh at 'The Online'.

'People still come. We fill up in the summer because it's such a beautiful beach and there are no other options to stay nearby once the cottages are full—'

'And they fill up *super* quickly,' Camilla interjects. 'Mine is booked for months in advance.'

'But we're generally pretty quiet in the off-season, which is why you were able to have a room on such short notice, Ness,' Charles carries on oblivious to Camilla's teasing. 'We rely on people who haven't read the reviews, or people like you who are desperate to find somewhere to stay here.'

'I wouldn't say I was desperate,' I say quickly before he has a chance to elaborate.

'When I spoke to you on the phone yesterday you said, and I quote, "I *urgently* need a room because I *have* to get to Pearlholme as quickly as possible. *Please* tell me you have something available tomorrow."'

I'm sitting so close to Nathan that he must be able to feel the heat emanating from my burning cheeks. I daren't glance at him. He wasn't supposed to know *quite* how relieved I was when Charles said there was an empty room at The Shell Hotel. Although 'room' might be pushing it a bit with that description.

'I had to order bits for the carousel online earlier. I've got a strong Wi-Fi signal at the cottage,' Nathan says, like he can sense how awkward I'm feeling and is purposely steering the conversation away from my level of desperateness.

'The access point is up there somewhere.' Camilla waves a hand in the general direction of the cottages. 'We had a nice engineer explain it to us but I didn't understand a word. I just made him a cup of tea and ogled his thighs. It covers the whole village, but the signal is weak as you get further away. Personally I think all of Charles's overgrown trees block it from the hotel.'

Great. I hope the weather stays nice because I'm supposed to be working while I'm here and I'm clearly going to have to scramble up some cliffs or something to get an internet signal.

'Come up to the cottage,' Nathan says like he can hear my thoughts. 'You can't fault the signal there. You said you had work to do, and you'll have peace and quiet while I'm down at the carousel, and the sofa's really comfortable. Fetch your laptop up and stay as long as you want.'

I go to protest but he sounds so sincere, his head pulled back so he can catch my eyes, and it's not a bad idea really. I'm not here on holiday. Apart from the article I'm supposed to be writing, I have my real job to do as well. Zinnia's making sure all articles are emailed to me to check, and that's not going to work without the internet.

'Oh, yes, love, do that!' Camilla exclaims. 'My cottage is much better than his crummy hotel. You spend as much time as you need there with your strong internet signal. And look at him.' She points at Nathan. 'Look at how much he wants you there.'

'I don't think …' I trail off as I do look at Nathan. His cheeks have gone adorably red, but he doesn't deny it, and any excuse to spend a bit more time with him is not an unwelcome one. 'I suppose I could pop in while you're working. I wouldn't want to get in your way.'

'You wouldn't be in his way at all,' Camilla answers for him. 'My cottage is lovely and spacious – there's plenty of room for you both. You go there whenever you like, love.'

'I think that might be up to Nathan,' I say, even though she's turned around to wave at a friend across the room and is clearly not listening.

'You come up whenever you like, love,' he murmurs in my ear, taking off her accent perfectly.

I look up at him, his eyes dark and smiley, and I can't stop myself tilting my head closer to whisper a thank you.

We hold each other's gaze for too long, pushed so close by our table guests that it wouldn't take much of a movement to kiss him. His stubble is so close that I could press my nose against his jaw, his neck, his Adam's apple bobbing as he swallows, making me swallow too. I can't remember the last time I wanted to kiss someone this much.

And then Charles chokes on a chip, and we jump apart like our grandparents have walked in on a sex session, except we haven't got the space to move away from each other so we just turn our heads very deliberately in the opposite direction.

'Speaking of choking on food,' Camilla says when Charles has stopped glugging water to root out the errant chip. 'Did you try that mac and cheese? I do wish you'd told me you had a friend staying, I'd have made an extra large one for you both.'

'Camilla's greatest pleasure in life is feeding the cottage guests,' Charles says.

Nathan looks between them. 'It was lovely, thank you. And I'm afraid I'd scoffed the lot before Ness got here.'

She claps her hands together so hard that she jogs the table and sends the fizzy water flying again. 'I'll make another one big enough for you both seeing as you'll be spending so much time at the cottage with your boyfriend for the Wi-Fi.' She pronounces it 'wee-fee', and raises a thinning grey eyebrow that suggests all manner of naughty things that have nothing to do with the Wi-Fi.

'Oh, we're not … He's not …'

'I'm hoping she'll be my carousel assistant,' Nathan says.

'Yeah. I'll hold his ice cream while he does the work. And we've got a lot of practice in so far.' I look up at him and we grin at each other.

I can sense Charles and Camilla's eyes are on us, but looking away from Nathan proves surprisingly difficult.

'Well, I think you're a lovely couple to do up the phantom carousel,' Camilla announces. 'It deserves that after so many years of being unloved.'

'The phantom carousel?' Nathan's head swivels towards her and I can almost see his ears prick up.

'Surely you've heard the stories?' Charles says.

Nathan sits up straighter and leans forward. 'No. What stories?'

Camilla clasps her hands together. 'Oh, it's such a lovely story! They say that a man built it to win the heart of the woman he loved. He didn't have much money, he didn't have a good job and he wasn't from a rich family, and she was a well-to-do girl and had lots of suitors, but she didn't want any of them. She only wanted him, but he had nothing to offer her, so he decided to make this big, elaborate gift because he knew how much she loved riding on carousels. They say it took him years. He had no money so he couldn't afford to buy fancy parts. He harvested the wood himself and carved each piece by hand, and through all the years he was building it, she waited for him. She had countless other marriage proposals from wealthy men, but she only had eyes for one, and even though she was ridiculed by society and cast out as an unmarried spinster, she still waited. Finally it was finished and he presented it to her on the day he asked her to marry him ...'

Camilla pauses for a contemplative sigh.

'And they lived happily ever after?' I offer.

'He disappeared off the face of the earth.'

'What?' Nathan and I say together. I didn't expect the story to end like that.

'They had mere weeks of happiness, and then he vanished. He put all of that work into the carousel and then he went out one day and never returned. Tragic, isn't it?'

'When was this?' Nathan asks.

'Oh, God knows, dear. Yonks ago. Might not even have been in this century.'

'By this century, she means the twentieth century which Pearlholme is still living in,' Charles clarifies.

'So why the phantom carousel?' I ask.

'Oh! That's the best part of the story!' She claps her hands together again. 'They say that if you walk on the beach on warm summer nights, you can hear the music as the carousel turns because her ghost rides it for all eternity, waiting for him to come home.'

Nathan looks sceptical. 'I hate to break it to you but it's been a long time since anyone's been able to ride that carousel, living, dead, or otherwise.'

'No, no, it's true,' she says. 'I remember hearing the music float down the cliffs to Pearlholme when I was a little girl. They lived in a house on the cliff top. You can still see the ruins of it when the tide's low, and they say she spent the rest of her life going around and around on the carousel, just watching the sea, expecting him to come home. She died up there, still waiting, and even in the afterlife, her ghost still goes around and around, waiting for her one true love to finally come back to her. Isn't it romantic?'

'I could think of a few words …' Nathan raises an eyebrow. 'This place on the cliff top – is that where it was found?'

'I don't know, dear. I assume so. It doesn't look like the sort of thing you'd move around much.'

'I *was* told it was found in the ruins of a house …'

'See?' She squeals at such a pitch that several species of fish in the sea outside have probably just swum off in fright. 'It's true. Walk down to the shore at low tide with some binoculars – there's a pair in the kitchen drawer – and look towards the cliffs past the cottages. You'll see. And always listen for the organ music late at night. They say if you're really quiet, you can hear it all the way up and down the coast.'

'I think that's highly unlikely …' Nathan starts.

'Oh, Mr Musgrove,' Camilla says suddenly, seeming to completely forget all about phantom carousels. 'Did you find the birdseed in the kitchen?'

'I did,' he says, 'I take it I'm meant to put some out every day? I put a handful in the feeder at the end of the garden this morning.'

'Oh, you are a nice man. The little dickies will appreciate it.'

I glance up at Nathan and he looks back with a raised eyebrow at the name.

'We make a real effort for the garden birds here in Pearlholme,' Camilla continues. 'The seagulls are such big bullies, the poor little dickies would never get any food if we didn't do something. Every resident has feeders in their garden that are too small for the nasty gulls to get into, and we all put out seeds every day, and nuts and suet blocks in the winter, although you shouldn't feed birds nuts in the summer because they can choke the little baby dickies.'

'I didn't know that.' I can hear the restraint in his voice as he tries not to laugh. His arm is shaking against mine as he holds it back, and how much he wants to giggle makes me want to giggle. 'Dickies and choking in one sentence is a bit much for me.'

It's no good. I hold my breath to try to stem the laughter, but I can't contain it. I let out a howling burst and it sets Nathan off too until we're both crying with laughter, shaking so much that we're jogging the table, leaning against each other, and every time I glance at him, he tries to straighten his face, and the attempt starts us both up again.

He turns his head towards me, so close that I can feel his hair against mine, his breath against my skin where's he's panting as he tries to get himself under control.

He's got tears running down his face and I've given myself hiccups, and I can't help thinking that wouldn't have been even remotely funny without him.

Camilla looks pointedly between Nathan and the half-empty beer bottle on the table, clearly thinking it's not his first.

I hiccup.

'I'm sorry,' he says eventually, taking a deep breath and sliding a hand down his face, still struggling to keep it straight. 'It's her fault.' He nudges me with his elbow. 'Everything seems funnier when she's around.'

Camilla looks across the table at Charles. 'I know that feeling.'

I let out another hiccup and Nathan bursts out laughing again. 'How strong are these beers?' he says in my ear. 'I've only had half a bottle but I haven't laughed this much in years.'

'Tell me—' hiccup '—about it.'

'It's the sea air,' Camilla says.

'It's definitely something.' His eyes are crinkled up with laughter as he turns back to Camilla. 'I'm sorry. Tell me more about the dickies and the choking?'

I take a deep breath and hold it, trying to stop myself laughing at the earnestness in his voice and get rid of the hiccups at the same time.

'I think I'd better not.' She shakes her head, looking between us with an affectionate look on her face. 'I remember laughing with him like that when we first met. It certainly set us up for a good marriage.'

'I don't know how you found your way to the feeder given how much of a mess that cottage garden is in,' Charles says, a teasing tone in his voice.

Camilla gasps in mock outrage. 'Says the man whose garden is going for a year-round Halloween theme.'

'All right, it's a little overgrown,' he says to her, and I get the feeling they've forgotten we're here.

'*Overgrown*? There are parts of the grass that haven't been seen since 1968!'

'We used to compete in Pearlholme's annual flower garden festival,' Charles explains. 'The Prettiest Pearlholme Patch, or PPP for short.'

'But he gave up because I always won,' Camilla finishes for him.

'And now I get my payback because she's too old to do hers anymore. You shouldn't enjoy your wife getting old but at least she can't be so smug about her garden now.' He winks at her as he says it.

I glance at Nathan and he's smiling at them fondly. They seem to have such a lovely relationship.

'The Sun & Sand always win now. There's a lovely trophy for the winners to display outside all year, a big pearl for Pearlholme, but I haven't got my hands on it for years now.' She sighs. 'He makes fun but he knows I'm devastated.'

'When's the festival?'

'First of July,' Charles says. 'Same every year. It's the ideal time for flowers.'

'I'll still be here then. What needs doing?' Nathan says. 'I'm rubbish at flowers but I can mow the grass and trim the hedges …'

'And my mum loves gardening – I used to help with her flower beds at home,' I say without thinking. 'I could do some flowers.'

Camilla squeals in delight, attracting the attention of every other human in the pub and a black Labrador that's asleep under one of the tables. 'Did you hear that, everybody?' she announces. 'I'm going to win the PPP again this year!'

Nathan looks at me with wide eyes. 'That wasn't quite what I—'

'Ooh, I'm so pleased.' She wiggles her fingers in excitement as she turns back to us. 'Now, when can you get started? It's only three weeks away! Why don't you go up to the cottage in the morning, Ness? You can use his *wee-fee* signal, and you can help him feed the little dickies – I never trust a man to do these things properly – and you can both get a good look at the garden too.'

'Yeah, men aren't good with little dickies,' Nathan says, and I thought I couldn't possibly laugh any more tonight but it makes me snort again, despite the fact that the idea of garden designs and winning competitions sets my heart racing. The gardens I've walked past in Pearlholme are all absolutely immaculate, and at least this explains why. I didn't know they were all in competition with each other to be the Prettiest Pearlholme Patch. It's a bit more involved than popping down the garden centre and bunging in a few flowers as I'd imagined.

'Come up for breakfast,' Nathan blurts out. He goes to bump his arm against my shoulder but we're still pressed so closely together that all he can really do is press his arm against mine a bit harder. 'We'll have a look at the garden, and then you can stay and work for as long as you want while I head down to the carousel.'

I smile up at him because he's so sweet, and thoughtful, and he sounds so nervous, like he expects me to say no.

Charles shoves another chip into his mouth and talks while he chews it. 'I'd advise it, actually. There's a kitchen where you can make your own breakfast at The Shell but the kettle broke down last night. The chap who runs the shop has ordered a new one for me but it won't be here 'til next week.'

'Next *week*?' I try to contemplate going that long without a cup of tea.

Charles shrugs, seeming completely unperturbed by the idea of having a hotel with no kettle. I definitely *should* have read the reviews before I booked a room, no matter how eager I was to get here.

'You know that we're British, right?' Nathan says to him. 'Your guests will be rioting in the streets by daybreak.'

'I take my hearing aids out when I go to bed. I won't hear them.'

I raise an eyebrow even though I'm not sure if he's joking or not.

'There are plenty of people around here who'll make you a

lovely cup of tea. Charles and I are in the house on the corner of the main street, right next to the fork towards the hotel. I'd say you can give us a knock if you need anything but we're both old and deaf and it takes us half an hour to totter down the hallway to the door. You'd be better off giving him a knock if you need anything.' Camilla points at Nathan.

'I have absolutely no problem with that,' he says with a wide grin directed at me. He drops his voice to a low, sexy whisper, so close to my ear that I can feel his breath moving my hair. 'And I don't mean to sound too seductive, but I've got Coco Pops.'

I burst out laughing. 'My favourites!'

'Is that some sort of infectious disease?' Charles asks, making us both laugh again. 'Should you see a doctor?'

Camilla shushes him before we have another never-ending fit of giggles. 'The post office does fresh pastries but you'll have to get there early, they get snaffled up quicker than they can be made.'

I look up at Nathan. 'I don't think there's ever been a better breakfast than Coco Pops.'

He beams. 'You can't say I don't know how to treat a lady. Free "wee-fee" and Coco Pops.'

'If anyone ever asks what Prince Charming was missing in the Disney films, it was definitely Coco Pops,' I say, loving the way he starts laughing again.

* * *

'I can't believe it's dark already,' Nathan says as we leave the pub. 'Where did the evening go?'

I'm thinking something about time flying and having fun but decide not to put the two phrases together in a cheesy sentence, unlike the 'do you need a hand' debacle this afternoon.

We stop and look at the pearl trophy on the way out, a big bronze flower with an iridescent pearl perched on top, displayed

106

at the front of the pub garden. 'I'm sorry about the garden thing. I didn't mean to get us both in over our heads.'

'No worries, it'll be fun.' By the skin of my teeth, I stop myself adding *to spend more time with you.*

'Let me walk you back to the hotel?' he says, even though he's going in the same direction towards the cottage anyway. 'I'm kind of curious to see if it's as bad as it sounds.'

'I'm starting to fear it may be *worse* than it sounds.'

'Come up to me anytime you want,' he says again as we start wandering down the main street, past the post-office-slash-tiny-shop, and rows of perfect gardens lit up by solar lights along their paving stone paths. 'Whether you want a cup of tea, chocolatey cereal, or a shower *sans* pubic hair.'

'Thanks,' I murmur, wondering how many excuses I can find to do just that.

We're both walking really slowly. I tell myself it's because I don't want to trip over the cobblestones in the dark, but really it's because I don't want this night to end yet.

'So that's your mac-and-cheese-making landlady?'

'Yeah, bless her. I'm hoping I never have to find out what happens if I call her out to fix a leaky tap or something. She can't carry a glass of water across the pub; she's not going to be lying upside down on her back fixing the boiler in the middle of winter, is she?'

He's got a knack for creating the most absurd mental images, and it makes me grin again.

His arm is next to mine as we walk, and I can feel his fingers almost-brushing mine as our arms swing, and it makes me want to edge just a little bit nearer. 'What do you think of this ghost story then?' I ask to distract myself.

He laughs. 'Well, I like the story but I suspect the ghost part is bollocks. You grew up in a small village – you know how these stories go. They're started by children sitting around campfires and passed down through the generations with an extra flourish added every time they're told, like a giant game of Chinese Whispers, and if my guess at the date of the carousel is anywhere near accurate then this one's got over a hundred years behind it.' He shrugs. 'It's a romantic old story and I'm not one for romance. Some parts of it are plausible, but it doesn't help with proving who built it or when. Although if any lonely old ghost wants to ride it tonight, she'll have a bit of a job on her hands considering it's in bits in the tent.'

We come to the fork in the road and Nathan walks down towards the hotel with me. He looks up at the lettering with a grimace when we stop outside the door. 'I think we should jump up and remove that "S" entirely. *Who* runs a hotel in Britain without a back-up kettle?'

'I know, right? And they've been doing this for years. They must know that kettles don't last forever.'

'Camilla's probably got four spare kettles and just won't let him have one so her cottage will be better.'

It makes me laugh again and I wonder how I can find someone so easily funny.

'And he ate most of our chips,' he continues. 'They were good chips too, but we still need to compare them to the ones on the promenade. Next time, we're going to find a secluded corner of the beach where only seagulls are likely to nick them.'

It makes me ridiculously happy that he seems to be suggesting another chip-testing date … or not-date. Preferably with no elderly gatecrashers.

'I don't like leaving you here.' He glances up at the darkened hotel. 'There's not even a light on.'

'It's fine,' I say, trying not to think about it. 'I was lucky to get somewhere on such short notice, and Pearlholme had to have a fault somewhere. It would be the most perfect place in the country if it didn't have a rubbish hotel.'

'I'm serious when I say come up anytime. I got plenty of food when I went into the next town the other day; there's always hot water, a clean bathroom, a strong *wee-fee* signal … and I promise not to natter about carousels and bore you to death.'

'I love your nattering about carousels,' I say. 'This carousel is the most interesting thing I've heard about for years. I'd love to know if Camilla's story is true and where it really came from.'

He makes a noise of disbelief and his smile doesn't reach his eyes, and I'm suddenly desperate to know who has ever told him carousels are boring, and why he's ever believed them.

It's coming to the point where we can't find any excuses to linger much longer, and we're just standing in the street looking at each other.

'Thank you for a brilliant night,' he says. 'With and without the gatecrashers.'

'It was fun.' I want to add something about it being fun *because* of him, because of his sense of humour and the way the same things make us both laugh, but I can't think of how to word it without sounding like even more of a crazed stalker. *I followed you halfway across the country and now I think you're the best thing since sliced bread if sliced bread was tall, dark, handsome, charmingly awkward, and hilarious.*

'How does eight sound for breakfast?'

'I'll be there.'

He beams in a way that makes me feel so important, but he still seems reluctant to walk away. Maybe he's trying to work out the politest way to say goodnight, like I am. Saying goodbye to a gorgeous man is just as complicated as saying hello. There should be a rulebook or something.

'Okay, I should …' He reaches out to take my hand but seems to reconsider and his fingers end up touching mine once before he pulls back. 'I had a great time tonight.'

'Me too,' I say. I reach out to touch his hand too but he turns towards me at the wrong moment and I end up accidentally punching him in the stomach. I suppose I should be glad it wasn't anything lower.

'See? Too tall,' he says, trying to take the blame again. 'Okay, I should go or I'll still be asleep at eight o'clock in the morning. You have my number if you need anything, right? I mean, if you hear the undead mooing of zombie cows or anything, call me on this little flip phone. I'm only five minutes up the road if you need protecting.'

'Oh, I have your phone in my room. Shall I run and get it?'

'Nah.' He shakes his head. 'Some other time.'

It gives me a little shiver again that he might've meant what he said on the beach earlier, about having an excuse to see him again, and that's the exact reason I didn't bring his phone out with me tonight. I could've handed it to him the moment I saw him outside the pub and that would've been it, but then I wouldn't have had an excuse to go and see him again, even though I'm starting to wonder if I don't need an excuse.

'I hope you bought the big box of Coco Pops and not the small one.'

He looks offended. 'What do you think I am, some kind of heathen? Of *course* I bought the big box. I know how to impress the ladies.'

His waggling eyebrows make me dissolve into giggles again as he turns around and walks up the street. I stay outside and watch him until he stops at the top and turns back. Even in the darkness, I can see the smile lighting up his face as he gives me another wave and disappears over the hill towards the cottages.

I can't stop smiling as I let myself into my box of a hotel room, feeling like I'm in my very own chick-flick film, but with a guy who could give even the hottest of leading men a run for their money.

# Chapter 8

'Quarter to eight and you tourists have almost cleared me out of goodies already,' the lady in the shop says as I peer into the glass counter of baked goods and try to decide what Nathan might like for breakfast. Coco Pops are one thing but I can't turn up at the cottage empty-handed, can I?

The display case is tiny and the selections are limited to fruit pies, blueberry muffins, cinnamon swirls, and maple pecan twists. Nathan doesn't strike me as someone who'd appreciate fruit for breakfast so I choose two cinnamon swirls and watch as she bags them up.

The shop itself is even tinier than it looks from the outside. There are only two aisles with the absolute barebones essentials of survival – milk, bread, eggs, tinned vegetables, flour, sugar, a tiny refrigerated stand with some cheese and a packet of bacon, newspapers, and chocolate bars. Next to the bakery display case is a stand of bubble wrap envelopes and parcel tape, and there's a picture of a postage stamp on the wall behind the counter, and along with the postbox outside, I think that might be the extent of Pearlholme's post office.

'It's going to be another beautiful day,' she says as she pushes buttons on the till, giving it a wary look like it's about to bite. 'Are you doing anything nice?'

'Work,' I say as I hand her a two-pound coin. Things are certainly cheap around here. 'I'm borrowing a Wi-Fi signal from one of the cottages and checking the emails that I couldn't check yesterday.'

'Aww.' She makes a disappointed noise. 'I thought you might go down to the beach again and see that lovely tall chap working there. He's been in this morning and had two maple pecan twists. I was sure one must be for you.'

Is there *anything* they don't know about us around here? Even so, I love the idea that Nathan's had the same idea as me about pastries ... or is really greedy ... but I don't want to confirm her suspicions or encourage *more* village gossip. 'Guess I made the right choice with the cinnamon swirls then.' I give her a smile that hides my desire to get out of there as quickly as possible. 'Thanks, have a good day!'

'That's exactly what he said,' she calls after me. 'He is a polite young chap! No wedding ring either!'

How do they know so much? I know it's a small village, but have I got my daily to-do list printed on my forehead or something?

I stop at the hotel on the way back to grab my laptop and Nathan's phone before I head up the hill towards the cottages. It's impossible not to pause at the top and take in the view. This early in the morning, there's still mist across the sea, but the sun is burning it off quickly, and the breeze is warm. Hazy sky stretches for miles in front of me, until you can't see the point where it meets sparkling blue water. The beach itself is empty apart from the odd dog walker, the tide is halfway out, and the smell of the seaweed left behind is strong in the air.

Nathan's cottage has two brick steps up to a daffodil-yellow front door. It's built of the same higgledy-piggledy stone that makes the houses on the main street look so quaint, and up close, I can see how unkempt the rhododendron hedge is around the back.

I knock on the door and hear a clunk from inside and he swears under his breath, and then there are footsteps on stairs and the click of a lock.

'I'm not late. I intended to answer the door with shaving foam all over my face.' He pulls the door open to reveal the lower half of his face covered in white mousse and a smile showing through it.

I can't help but smile back at the sight. It shouldn't be sexy, but he's got on a plain black T-shirt that fits in all the right places and another pair of dungarees that are ripped in different places to yesterday's ones and have different colours of paint all over them, and these ones are undone to his waist with the top part hanging down over his legs, and when I breathe in, I can smell the clean, masculine scent of the shaving foam. 'Is your toe okay?'

He pulls the door back and looks behind it. 'Is there a peephole in this thing that I don't know about?'

'I have much experience of stubbing toes in a rush to answer the door. Or phone. Or anything really. I'm quite capable of stubbing toes even when I'm not in a rush.'

'I'm always tripping over myself. I think my toes have grown an armoured coating by now.' He steps back from the door and gestures to the hallway. 'Come in. I'm going to wash this gunk off my face. You seem to have a knack for turning up when I'm covered in something I'm not meant to be covered in.'

'Plenty worse things you could be covered in,' I say. It's probably a good thing he doesn't realise quite how sexy the shaving foam looks.

'Can't deny that.' He laughs and points to two open doorways. 'Kitchen, living room, spectacular view that way. Make yourself at home, I'll just be a second.'

He disappears up the stairs and I wander into the living room in the direction of the view. It's a spacious room with pale grey carpet and cream walls, a stone fireplace, two squishy charcoal-coloured armchairs and matching sofa, all facing a flatscreen TV mounted on the wall, and it smells vaguely of lavender from a reed diffuser on the hearth. At the far end, there's a wide bay window and it pulls me over like a magnet. I dump my laptop bag next to the nearest armchair and go to stand in front of it, unable to stop an audible gasp at the view.

It's like what you can see from the road outside but better. Below the window is a dishevelled garden. I can see that it was neat once but hasn't been maintained for a while now. There are plenty of plants, but most of them have outgrown their containers and are flowering willy-nilly and scrambling across the lawn, which is made up of more daisies and dandelions than grass now.

But beyond the garden is what must be the best view of the beach in the village. Miles of empty sand winds in both directions, and the cottage feels like it's directly above it on the cliff edge. To the sides is the greenery of the cliff tops, and the edges of fence surrounding the other nearby cottage gardens, but in front of me is nothing but the beach. Sun, sand, sea so big that it stretches over the horizon until it joins the sky, and if I lean forward and press my face to the glass, I can even see the tip of the tent covering the carousel.

'There are no words for how incredible this view is,' I say when Nathan comes back in.

He walks over and stands beside me at the bay window. 'I've done very little apart from stand here looking out since I arrived. I think I'd sleep here if the window ledge was a bit longer.'

All I can think about is the warmth from his bare arm where he's standing so close and the lingering smell of shaving foam and deodorant. His hair is still damp from a shower, thick at the back of his neck and even darker than the soft, spiky top, looking like he's just rubbed it dry.

'Look at all the *dickies* waiting to be fed.' I nod towards a row of birds lined up along the hedgerow next to the feeder at the end of the garden.

'Yeah, I'll get on that if you want to get something to eat.' He gestures towards the doorway behind us, separating the kitchen from this room. 'The kettle's full, and I know I promised Coco Pops but I figured that you deserved a choice. I popped down the shop earlier and got—'

'Two maple pecan twists?'

He raises an eyebrow. 'Okay, I get the toe-stubbing but if you really are psychic, can you tell me next week's lottery numbers?'

'The woman in the shop told me.' I hold up my bag. 'And I got cinnamon swirls so we've got a choice.'

'I nearly got those as well, but then I thought if I just got one thing, I'd have an excuse to make you come over for breakfast another day so we can try something different.'

Bugger. I should've gone for the maple pecan twists too.

Just past the living room, there's a little foyer area with a doormat and row of coat hooks on the wall, and Nathan picks up a bag of birdseed from beside the door and goes outside to put a handful in the cottage-shaped bird feeder. There's a path curving through the overgrown lawn, but the concrete is stained and there are weeds growing from every crack in it. It's only when he turns back and waves at me that I realise I'm just standing in the window staring at him.

I hurry off to the kitchen and push the kettle switch down as I start opening and closing cupboards on the hunt for teabags, mugs, and plates. The kitchen has cheery yellow walls and deep red tiles on the floor. Red gingham curtains and red appliances complete the modern but charmingly retro look. It's the kind of kitchen that makes me wish I knew how to cook something more complicated than three-minute noodles.

'How'd you sleep?' he asks when he comes back in. 'No zombie cows?'

We sit on the window seat in the living room and watch the *dickies* having a feeding frenzy in the garden, although our pastries are so good that we're both ripping them apart and making noises of pleasure that are so uncivilised it makes the squawking and flapping outside look positively refined. 'I'd have been happier with the zombie cows than the giant spider that ran across the floor in the middle of the night. So big that I actually *heard* it.'

He cringes, and I don't tell him that my poor sleep had very little to do with crappy hotel rooms, zombie cows, ancient ghost stories, or even the giant spider, and quite a bit to do with the way I couldn't stop picturing his mouth, his voice, and the crinkles around his eyes every time I closed mine.

'How about you? No carousel ghosts kept you awake all night?' I ask to distract myself from how everything feels so easy and comfortable with him. He doesn't seem like someone I met a few days ago, he seems like someone I've known for years. Maybe it really is the sea air and the spectacular view. The view has a way of making everything seem better than it is.

'Not a chance. I've been sleeping more soundly than I have for years since I got here. Hence why I was still shaving when you knocked.'

Which I am definitely not complaining about. Nathan shaving could probably be sold as porn.

He snorts, making me *really* hope I didn't say that out loud.

\* \* \*

After Nathan has left for the carousel, I've just sat down in one of the armchairs and opened my laptop when my phone rings and Daphne's work number flashes up.

'I'm going to assume the reason you haven't texted me since yesterday afternoon is because you had the most amazing first date and are now busily falling in love, and not because he's murdered you and dumped your body in a ditch,' she says before I have a chance to say hello.

I hadn't even thought about texting Daph. I let her know that I'd got here safely, and then I texted to say I was meeting Nathan at the pub last night, but it was so late by the time I got back to the hotel that I didn't bother to text, and I haven't been able to think of anything but him yet this morning. It was the shaving foam that did it.

'Hello to you too,' I say. 'And you don't have to worry, I'm ninety-five per cent sure he's not a murderer. He was just outside feeding the birds. Murderers don't feed birds.'

'I suppose they don't have dimples either?' she says with a laugh. 'Come on then, are you head over heels in love with him yet?'

'Of course I'm not. I've spent two days with the man – you don't fall in love that quickly.'

'No, but you haven't got the first train back to London, which is a promising sign. I half-expected you to turn up for work this morning.'

I don't tell her that I seriously considered it … before I actually met him.

'What's he like then?'

I sigh and snuggle further back in the squishy armchair. 'He's so lovely, Daph. He's restoring this old carousel on the beach and he's *so* knowledgeable about it. He makes me feel more intelligent just by talking to him. He's thoughtful and kind and he's got this sense of humour that's just so cheesy but somehow it makes him even funnier. If you heard his jokes, you'd go "what is *wrong* with this guy?" but I can't stop laughing at him. Every time I think I can hold it together, he's got this look that starts me off again …' I realise I've gone on a bit too much and stop myself before she starts phoning around wedding venues.

'Glad to know your judgement of men is based on how much I'd hate them.'

'He likes all the things that you laugh at me for liking. He even buys Coco Pops, and you say no one over the age of five eats them.'

She snorts. 'Sounds like all you want in a guy.'

'Say what you want but it works for him. He's adorable and

so flipping gorgeous. His eyes dance when you talk to him and they look different colours in different lights, and he—' I stop myself when I realise I've gone off on one again. I'll be gibbering on about his nose hair next. Not that he has nose hair … well, he probably does, everyone does, don't they? I clearly need to spend more time looking up his nose. 'He's really kind too. He went out to get us breakfast this morning even though he was running late, and I'm at the cottage now while he's—'

'You spent the night with him already?' Zinnia squeals, making me jump because I didn't realise she was there.

'You're on speakerphone?' I squeak. I would never have been that open if I'd realised my boss was listening.

'Oh, there are no secrets between us,' Zinnia says. I can hear her perfectly manicured hand swooshing through the air. 'Besides, you're writing about this man for me. You *are* writing about him, aren't you? Taking notes of all these things you're falling in love with?'

'I'm not falling in love with anything. He's just a nice guy.' I decide it's best not to mention my lack of note-taking or any vague idea of what exactly I'm going to write about Nathan in part two.

'I think there's a bit more to it than that, don't you, Vanessa? And you've already spent the night with him. That's moving very quickly for you, considering you do work-related things at the pace of a supremely slow snail.'

'I haven't spent the night with him.' I ignore the insult. She's not exactly wrong. 'I came up this morning to have breakfast and borrow his Wi-Fi. The signal is terrible at the hotel.'

'Oh my God, that's genius,' Daphne says. 'What a great excuse – I bet he didn't suspect for a minute.'

'It's not an excuse. The signal really is—'

'I wish I'd have thought of that one when I was still dating. I'll have to save it in the unlikely event that Gavin and I ever break up. Ooh, maybe I can share it with our readers in an article about secret ways to get closer to a guy ...'

'How did the first meeting go?' Zinnia asks. They're both completely convinced that I'm some kind of femme fatale expert at underhanded seduction techniques. The only thing I've managed to seduce lately is a bag of crisps. 'Was he pleased to see you? Ooh, I bet it was deliciously awkward! I can't wait to read about it in your first draft. Do play up the awkwardness, won't you?'

'It was kind of awkward,' I say, even though it was less awkward than I'd spent the train journey imagining it might be. 'I was nervous and he was nervous and I ended up feeding him an ice cream.'

By the squeal on the other end of the line, I know the words were a mistake as soon as they leave my mouth.

'You *fed* him an ice cream! Bloody hell, I've been with Gavin for years and I've never fed him anything! That's so sexy!'

'Our readers are going to *love* this!'

'No, no, no,' I say, realising I can't pull this back now. 'His hands were mucky. There was absolutely nothing sexual about—'

'Put that in part three of the article, won't you?' Zinnia says. 'That'll give our readers a real sense of the awkwardness. They'll be *right there* in it with you!'

'Actually it was surprisingly unawkward,' I say, hoping my boss doesn't realise that isn't a word. Using non-words is not exactly a great start for my writing career, is it?

'Oooooooh,' they both chorus.

'Not in that way,' I try to protest again, knowing this conversation isn't going to go my way no matter how many different ways I try to get the point across. 'He's someone I could be friends with, but it's not going any further. He's not looking for a relationship and neither am I.'

'Everyone says that until they meet "The One",' Daphne says.

'I said that until I met my husband,' Zinnia says.

'And of all people, *you* know how much I'd sworn off men

until I met Gavin,' Daphne adds. 'No matter what he says, *he* invited you to the pub last night, and he obviously fell for the Wi-Fi excuse, and he wanted to have breakfast with you this morning, and—'

She's cut off by the ringtone of Nathan's phone, which I've left on the coffee table in front of me. I peer over my laptop at it and make a noise of surprise. 'That's him.'

I realise I should've been a bit more restrained when Daphne squeals. 'I can't remember the last time I heard a noise like that come out of your mouth. Reminds me of a toad's mating call.'

'And on that compliment, I'm going to see what he wants. Bye, ladies.'

'Wait, is that his phone? Why have you still got his phone, Ness?' Daphne shouts as I hang up on her.

I'm almost out of breath by the time I pick his phone up. 'Hi, this is Nathaniel's phone,' I say in a throwback to our first conversation.

His familiar laugh echoes down the line. 'Hi, this is Nathaniel, but please don't call me that. I might start thinking you don't like me.'

I'm pretty sure that's unlikely to happen. 'All right, Nath,' I say instead, channelling Bunion Frank from the pub last night.

I can hear the smile in his voice when he speaks. 'I don't mind Nath. Anything but my full three syllables is fine.'

It makes me wonder again what that's all about. I don't particularly like being called Vanessa but I don't think people who use it dislike me. Except for Zinnia, it's safe to say that she doesn't like me, no matter what name she calls me by. 'What's up? Phoning to check I haven't raided the place and given all your valuables to a passing seagull?'

He laughs again. 'Actually, I've just been reliably informed that the tide is almost at its lowest point and is about to turn. I was wondering if you wanted to walk down to the shore and see if we can spot the house that Camilla mentioned?'

'Where the ghost lives?'

'I don't think "ghost" and "lives" really go together, but yeah, why not?'

I get the feeling I could see him if I went outside, so I get up with the phone still pressed to my ear as I open the bright yellow door and step down the two stone steps.

Nathan's standing on the wooden staging next to the carousel tent, looking up at the cottage, and even from this distance, I can see the smile spread across his face as I come outside. He waves and I wave back, my smile matching his.

'And someone just happened to inform you of that?'

'The bloke who works in the beach shop across the promenade. He said he overheard our conversation in the pub last night, but I suspect that Camilla went around ordering everyone to tell us after we left. I knew it was a mistake to leave her unsupervised.'

I laugh, keeping my eyes on him down on the sand. Nothing sounds better than a walk along the beach. 'I'd love to.'

I give him another wave and go back inside. I close my laptop down, and remember to grab the binoculars Camilla mentioned from the kitchen. There's an empty flask on the draining board that I guess Nathan didn't have time to make up this morning, so I make a flask of tea and put it and the two cinnamon swirls we didn't have for breakfast in a bag. If nothing else, it'll give me an excuse to avoid work for a bit longer. The conversation with Zinnia has done nothing to boost my confidence in my ability to write this article, and now I've mentioned anecdotes that she's going to expect to see in it, and I haven't even told Nathan what I'm supposed to be doing yet.

I should probably leave his phone here – at least I'd have given it back to him then – but I like him phoning me on it. I like always having an excuse to see him and I *love* that we're both using it as an excuse. I slip it into my jeans pocket alongside mine. It's not right to just leave it here. Someone could break in and steal it, or there could be an earthquake and the cottage could collapse on it, or a fire, an alien landing perhaps, and we are right near the beach so there could definitely be a tidal wave, or a crowd of light-fingered giant squid could rear up from the depths. Better safe than sorry. I slip it into my jeans pocket alongside mine and lock up behind me.

# Chapter 9

It's a beautiful day, endless golden sand and blue sky filled with banks of white cloud, and the beach is almost empty apart from a couple having a picnic, and a couple building sandcastles with their toddler.

The sand is smooth under our shoes, warm and dry at the top of the beach but getting wetter as we head towards the water. Our feet are sinking and seawater instantly refills every deep footprint, and I've rolled my jeans up to my knees but I'm regretting not taking my ballet flats off further up the beach. The wind from the sea is not just the gentle breeze it is near the promenade, but a full sea gale that is flapping my hair around and making me wonder why I didn't bring a band to tie it up with.

The bracing wind and the salty air has filled my lungs, and the tide is so far out that everything looks small, even the tent covering the carousel and blue metal railing between the beach and the rainbow of huts on the promenade. It doesn't feel like we've walked that far, but from down here, the cottages dotting the cliff side look like pretty doll's houses and the sheep on the hillsides above them look like white ants.

'Is that it?' Nathan points at a speck of stone on the peak of a hill at the top of a cliff, past Pearlholme and probably past the next beach over as well.

I squint in the direction he points. 'Well, she did say it was a ruin …'

'It looks old enough,' he says. 'And there's nowt else around that fits the description.'

'It doesn't look very spectacular,' I say. 'Given the size of the carousel, I was expecting a castle or something.'

'I don't know, Camilla seemed to think the guy who built it didn't have much money. Maybe he built his own house too.'

He fishes the binoculars out of his dungaree pocket where he stashed them and offers them to me, and I hold them up to my eyes and fiddle with them until the random piles of stone come into focus and I can tell they're vaguely house-shaped piles of stone. Unless you knew the story, you probably wouldn't even realise it had once been a house.

'Let's have a— Argh!' Nathan shouts and I squeal as a wave breaks against my legs, soaking me up to the calves and making me jump so much with the sudden coldness that I nearly fall over.

He stumbles too and his strong arms slide around my waist, pulling me to him and somehow managing to keep us both on our feet. He's laughing as he finds his footing in the wet sand.

Neither of us have been paying attention to the tide and it's obviously turned while we've been looking at the cliffs and is now swiftly on its way back up the beach. More cold water pools around my ankles as I cling on to Nathan's sun-warmed arms, which has very little to do with overbalancing and quite a lot to do with having a sexy bloke's arms around my waist.

It's not funny but his proximity is making me all giggly, that combination of shower gel and dark coconut aftershave, fresh salty air, and the underlying grease he's been removing this morning is too near, filling my senses.

'You okay?' he murmurs when it becomes obvious that neither of us are likely to fall over now, and I'm just sort of swaying in his arms.

'Mmm hmm.' I force myself to stand upright and push away from him. 'Just the shock.'

'Yes, I'm always surprised when I walk on the edge of the sea and get wet.'

'You screamed just as loud as me.'

'I did not!' He's unable to keep a straight face as he says it. 'I'm *so* glad I didn't take my only work boots off further up the beach when I thought they might get wet and then thought, "nah, that'll never happen" though.'

I look down at our feet as we stand facing each other. We're both up to our shins in seawater, our shoes disappearing into the sand as more waves lap against our legs one after the other. After the initial shock, the water isn't too cold and it's actually quite pleasant on such a warm day, it just would've been nice if the sea had given us a choice.

'Too late now,' Nathan says with a shrug, looking positively joyful at this turn of events. He stomps about a bit, splashing further up my jeans and I shriek and pull one of my feet up with a sucking squelchy noise as the sand releases its grip. I go to kick water at him, but my other foot comes loose and I nearly over-balance, squealing again, glad the beach is still empty so there aren't many people to scare off. All I can think about are the two phones in my pocket. They will not be happy with an unexpected dip in the sea and one of them isn't even mine.

His arms are around my waist again, holding me upright while I find my own footing and water washes around my knees. It's still only reached his calves, the tall bugger.

'Well, that was fun,' he says as I hold on to his arms for a moment longer. Dodgy Wi-Fi may not have been an excuse, but overbalancing in the surf definitely is.

'Your definition of fun is …' I go to tell him that the fumes of old carousel paint must've been addling his brain, but I realise I haven't stopped grinning since the first splash of water and I'm feeling positively giddy '… fun,' I finish eventually. I can't remember the last time I laughed like that.

He grins as he drops his arms from around me and takes a step back, looking down at his wet legs. 'May as well enjoy it now. See how much wetter we can get.'

We wander along in the surf, both having given up on trying to rescue our shoes or trouser legs, gradually veering sideways as the tide comes further in, keeping the water level below our knees.

'Might get a better view of the ruins from further along the beach.' There's something about his smile that's so easy and unguarded. His eyes are dancing with mischief in the sunlight, and it only ends when another wave crashes against our legs, soaking me to the thighs this time.

I look away and we carry on walking, close enough that our hands brush deliciously together. It would be so easy to reach out and curl my fingers around his but I stop myself, enjoying the little thrill each time my hand touches his for the briefest of moments. I keep expecting him to move away but he doesn't, so I don't either.

I force myself to keep my eyes on the horizon, focusing on two little fishing boats out at sea instead of the smile in his eyes or the way they look lighter brown today, reflecting the brightness of the sky.

'So, how's work?'

I can't hide the groan. 'Very, er, fact-checky. Lots of colleagues surprisingly annoyed that I'm not in the office. And you can tell I couldn't get a signal yesterday, I heard my inbox audibly groan when I opened it.'

He shakes his head. 'I couldn't do an office job. Not many things have gone right in my life but my job is one thing I'm so lucky with. Whatever luck we get, I think my job inhaled my full share and left everything else to fall apart.'

It makes me want to ask him endless questions about his life and what exactly has fallen apart in it, but I feel like I'm under-handedly trying to glean information that Zinnia will like.

I know I should talk to him about the article, but it sounds so stupid. My boss thinks that you being friendly and polite every time we catch each other's eye on the train and then dropping your phone means something, and now I've got the chance to make a career for myself by running a campaign in which we pretend to find you, share private details of your life, fall in love, and live happily ever after. He's not looking for a relationship, he doesn't believe in romance or ghosts, he's not going to take Daphne's *Sliding Doors*-esque view that we're souls destined to find each other and the universe regularly puts us on the same train for that very purpose, is he?

He suddenly stops and leans down, bending gracefully to retrieve a shell that was half-buried in the sodden sand. He holds it in the waves to wash it off and then lifts it up to the light for me to see as well, seawater running in droplets down his bare arm.

'That's so pretty.' I look at the conch shell his long fingers are holding. It's white with pink lines on it, a perfectly formed swirl that fits in his huge palm.

'Isn't nature amazing?' he murmurs.

I look at him looking at the shell and get the feeling he's miles away. We've stopped walking so his hand has stopped moving, the side of it pressing against mine, and I stay stock still, because I don't want to break that connection, and I wish had the courage to reach over and slide my other hand onto his shoulder.

And then I wonder why I'm not just doing it. Why am I looking for excuses not to do something as simple as touching him?

I slip my hand onto his left shoulder and give it a gentle squeeze. If he thinks about it, it'll just seem like I'm trying to get a better look at the shell, but really I just want to acknowledge what he told me last night about his injury.

His breath hitches and I suddenly want to know everything there is to know about him. There's something that runs deep under his smile and self-deprecating humour, from the running away to join the circus thing to the certainty that he's boring me with carousel talk. Someone has really done a number on him in the past and I probably shouldn't be this determined to find out who.

Another wave crashes around our legs and seems to jolt him back to reality. 'Here you go, for you.' His finger hooks into mine where our hands are touching and he lifts my hand and presses the shell into it, using his elegant fingers to close mine around it. 'A reminder of your time in Pearlholme.'

'Thank you.' I rub my thumb over the shell as his hand drops from mine, and he grins, his smile looking lighter than it did just now.

I hold the shell to my ear, which is probably what every other person in the world does when holding a conch shell. 'I can hear the sea!'

'You can hear the sea because you're standing in it!' He laughs, and I blush because I genuinely hadn't thought of that, and usually I'd be embarrassed about making such an idiot of myself, but his smile is kind and his laugh is one of solidarity rather than making fun of me.

'Don't worry, I once asked someone what *Snakes on a Plane* was about.' He pauses. 'Wait, why did I tell you that? I meant that I'm completely sophisticated at all times, obviously. I never say anything daft.'

We're both giggling again and he holds his hand out for the binoculars. 'Gimme those before I say something I can't recover from.'

I hand them over and can't resist looking at him while he's distracted. The sea has made the dark denim of his dungarees even darker and the wet material is clinging to his legs at the thighs and flaring out below the knee with the flow of the water we're still standing in. One of his T-shirt sleeves has ridden slightly up his bicep and I can see the tan line where he's been in the sun, and it's ridiculous how much I want to touch that smooth skin and run my hands over the muscle that flexes as he holds the binoculars up and twists the focus knob.

'Do you think we could get there?'

Okay, I take it all back. He's a lunatic. It's a pile of stone halfway up a cliff and he wants to *get there*? That's something extreme sports fanatics do, not normal, fun, sensible people like I thought Nathan was. 'Get there?' I say, going for breezy, coming across as gale-force. No way did he hear the gulp of apprehension.

'Yeah, look, there's a path.' He hands the binoculars over and I hold them up to my eyes.

He's insane. 'No, there's not.'

'Yeah, look. Between all those brambles and gorse.'

Oh, joy. That sounds fun. I squint through the binoculars again but all I can make out is indistinct greenery.

He's suddenly behind me, his arm around me, his hand on top of mine where I'm holding the binoculars. He bends and lowers his head until his chin is resting on my shoulder and his head is level with mine. His other arm comes out and his finger traces a line where I should be looking.

'That is *not* a path,' I murmur, too distracted by how close he is to think straight. I have no idea if there's a path or not.

'Yeah, it is.' His hand touches my shoulder to turn me slightly to the left and points again. 'Look, there are dunes underneath and you can see a sandy path winding up to the ruin.'

'They're not sand dunes, that's where the cliff has collapsed with subsidence.'

He chuckles, the movement making his chin press against my shoulder. 'I reckon if we go up past the cottages in Pearlholme and along to the next beach, we're going to come across a load of dunes, and somewhere there'll be an opening to that path ...'

I can still smell his lingering shaving foam, feel the side of his face smooth against mine, and it's making my brain completely malfunction. That's the only explanation as I say, 'I suppose it could be.'

'Will you come?'

'What, now?' I glance down at my feet in the water. 'I'm a bit wet.'

He laughs as he steps back and stands up straight, grunting as he stretches his back out, making me realise how tall he is and how short I feel next to him. And I wish I could just grab him and sort of hold him against me for a bit longer. 'No, some other day. Maybe the weekend? When we're both dry and we can set out a lot earlier than this. It looks like it might be a bit of a walk.'

A *bit* of a walk? To me, it looks like you'd need a set of those walking pole things, an oxygen tank on your back, a few base camps on the way up, and a couple of machetes to cut down whatever it is that's grown over that sorry excuse for a path. If it even is a path. I think he's hallucinating. To be honest, jumping out of a helicopter from the top looks like an easier way to access it. Sans parachute.

'What do you say? We can take a picnic. I'll even make sandwiches …'

I'm having an out-of-body experience. I must be because I can hear myself saying, 'I'd love to, that sounds like fun,' but I'm pretty sure that such words would never come out of my mouth.

'Yes!' He punches the air. 'Thank you, I was a bit scared to go on my own.'

Oh, great. That's comforting. What good does he think I'll be to him up there? The hill between the main street and the cottages is too much of a climb for me and a village of ninety-year-olds do it every day.

He clears his throat. 'By that, I mean I'm completely brave and macho and not at all scared that the ghost is going to get me.'

His adorableness makes everything inside of me melt. Honestly, another excuse to spend time with him is more than welcome, even if it is climbing a flipping mountain. And I *am* intrigued by Camilla's story and would love to find out if there's any truth to the romantic legend and see where the carousel came from.

What's left of it, anyway. I give the pile of stones on the cliff another doubtful glance and then look back at Nathan, who's still smiling with that wide, unguarded grin and that lightness in his eyes makes everything else fade away. This means a lot to him. It's worth it.

Even if we die on the way.

'Wait, *you'll* make sandwiches?' I say, wondering if I should be concerned that that thought occurred immediately after thinking about certain death. 'I thought your cookery skills ended at Pot Noodles.'

We start heading back the way we came, still walking in the surf but further up the beach now the tide is coming in, and he grins an unmistakeable 'I know something you don't know' grin. 'Ah, I have a secret weapon sandwich recipe that I think you'll love.'

'What is it?'

'I can't tell you that. Not until you've tried it anyway, hence the "secret" part of "secret weapon sandwich recipe".'

'Weapon as in it's a good sandwich or weapon as in it's liable to kill people?'

He laughs. 'Oh, come on. Do you trust me?'

It's the moment Princess Jasmine steps off the balcony onto Aladdin's magic carpet.

But with sandwiches, not flying rugs, obviously.

He holds his hand out just like Aladdin does and I'm helpless to resist slipping mine into it.

'Of course,' I whisper as his fingers close around mine.

He smiles and doesn't let go as our hands drop back to our sides and we paddle back along the beach.

# Chapter 10

'Got time for that cinnamon swirl and a cuppa?' he asks when we get back to the carousel.

'I'd love to.' I force myself to tear my eyes away from his forearms as he leans on the security fence and pulls off one boot and then the other with a wet plop and holds them upside down to tip the water out. I sit on the wooden staging and remove my dripping ballet flats, which now have sand glued all over them. I bang them together to remove the loose clumps, poke my sodden footlet socks inside, and lay them on the wooden staging surrounding the carousel to dry out in the sun. I do the same with Nathan's boots while he goes into the tent and pulls the sides back, revealing the pieces of carousel laid out in an order that probably makes sense to him.

Even in pieces, it's an impressive sight. The top finial and strong centre pole is metres above our head, the top of the tent far above that, piles of long metal bars that support the animals, and the wooden horses themselves, still in rows in one corner of the tent.

I pad barefoot across the smooth staging that the completed carousel will sit on in all its glory one day. It looks like a phenomenal amount of work to get this age-battered thing running again, but Nathan doesn't seem fazed in the slightest.

After we've had a cuppa from the flask and pulled apart a cinnamon swirl each, he gets back to work but I can't tear myself away yet. I watch him in the middle of the carousel, doing something that looks complicated to the engine. 'What are you doing?'

'Just cleaning it before I flush it out and see if I can get it back working again. Nothing seems damaged and there's no obvious reason for it not to be going, I think it's more a case of how long it's stood unused, although even this is not in as bad a condition as you'd expect for something over a hundred years old. A bit rusty but that can be sorted easily enough.'

I glance at what looks like a mangle of metal that he's currently got his hands underneath. It's never crossed my mind what's inside a carousel before, and nothing about it looks easy to me.

I wander around the tent instead, letting my hands trail across a stack of decorative curved panels that would usually form a circle around the engine to hide it, battered wooden boards that once held paintings of striking landscapes but are now too damaged to make out what landscapes they might've been. Each panel is expertly carved into a curve at the top, with scrollwork and fancy ivy leaves surrounding the paintings. 'Do you really think a guy without much money could've built all this from scratch by himself?'

Nathan looks up with a shrug. 'Sure. It wouldn't have been a quick job, but yeah, this is a labour of love, not expense. He must've been experienced in wood carving, and if he collected the wood and dried it himself, he could've made or bought the metal poles, and the engine was definitely scrap from something else. See here?' He pulls a cloth from his pocket and rubs a patch of the complicated-looking metal contraption. It's just a jumble of wheels, cylinders, and pulleys to me, and I'm impressed that anyone could understand how it works, let alone fix it. I step across to see what he's looking at. 'See the scratches showing the green underneath?'

I nod, peering at the red metal he's pointing to.

'Means it's been painted. He wouldn't have bothered if it was new.'

I can't help smiling at him. 'You're very good at this.'

He ducks his head, and I move away again, running my hand down one of the once-gilded posts that support the carousel and touching the pile of wooden sweeps that he's marked up for light installation.

I look out the open tent side towards the sea, sparkling in the sun as it gradually comes nearer, the empty sand free of everyone except a dog yapping at the waves as his owner throws a stick into the water for him to fetch. 'He must've really loved her.'

'Or had too much time on his hands.'

'Aw, that's not very romantic.'

'I don't believe in ghost stories and starry-eyed fairy tales handed down through generations. This is an amazing carousel – the craftsmanship is astounding even over a century later – but I don't care why it was carved, I just want to know who by and when.'

'But you want to visit the place it was found. You believe the villagers enough to think it's worth going up there.' I look towards the cliff even though the house isn't visible from this high up the beach. '*All* the way up there.'

'That's different. The age of the building may give us some clues about the exact age of the carousel. I think it's worth having a look from a factual point of view. Not because we might run into a ghost.'

'But we might.' I flash my eyebrows at him and he grins.

'That's why I'm taking you for protection.'

'I don't know, I keep hearing about this secret weapon sandwich of yours. If you brandish that at any ghosts, they'll probably run a mile. Well, float a mile. Ghosts don't really run, do they?'

He laughs, the warm sound filling the tent, and I can't help watching the way his shoulders shake, his black T-shirt clinging to muscle, the denim straps of the dungarees over them.

'Do you want some help?' I say without thinking.

'I'm already dragging you up to the ruins at the weekend.'

I fear he doesn't understand how literal that 'dragging' might be. Also, possibly carrying, lugging, hauling, phoning for an air ambulance, et cetera. 'I meant now. With the carousel.'

'Don't you have work to do?'

I think about my overflowing inbox, which is undoubtedly getting fuller by the minute with journalists sending over articles to be checked. I should have gone back to the cottage an hour ago and made a start on the backlog from yesterday before creating even more of a backlog today, and that's without part two of the article, which Zinnia wants by Monday, but I don't want to leave Nathan yet. This carousel steeped in history, the beautiful beach I'm standing on, laughing with this gorgeous man ... I feel more alive than I have in years. I don't want to go back to the reality of work, even if it does come with a slightly better view than usual.

'If anyone asks, I could call it research. Someone's bound to want some carousel facts checking sometime, I'm doing pre-emptive research.'

'I like your style, Ness.' He grins again and then shakes his head. 'You sure? This is long, boring, repetitive work. Most people don't find this interesting.'

I nod. 'I have no idea what I'm doing – you'll have to give me something easy.'

'You can make a start on cleaning up the horses, if you want?' He gets up and goes to one of his toolbags, coming back with a packet of wet wipes. 'I feel a bit sexist for giving a woman a cleaning job, but I need to get the engine and then the organ sorted before I can even think about the superficial stuff.'

I take the packet of wet wipes from his hand enthusiastically.

'Just give them a surface wipe – I'll get a brush on the deeper grooves later – and don't worry about the amount of paint that peels, it's all got to come off anyway.'

I go over to the first horse in one of the rows at the edge of the tent and crouch down beside it. It's the lead horse that Nathan showed me yesterday. It's an impressive thing with brown glass eyes and intricately carved trappings, ivy leaves curving around the edges of its saddle, with wooden rosettes pinning engraved ribbons along its side, and a pattern of more ivy leaves engraved in its mane.

One side is more impressive than the other, which is mostly plain.

'That's the romance side,' Nathan explains. 'In Europe, carousels turn clockwise, and in America they turn anti-clockwise. The side that faces away from the public is never as intricate – that's how you can easily tell where a carousel originates from.'

'The saddle's really worn on this one.'

'Maybe that's the one the ghost has been riding for all eternity.' He looks over at me with a raised eyebrow.

'You laugh but I'm going to stand outside the cottage playing a recording of carousel music at midnight tonight – you won't find it so funny then.'

He laughs. 'Ah, but now I'll know it's you. I'll come downstairs and, believe me, catching sight of me in the middle of the night will give you more of a fright than any ghost.'

I quite fancy catching sight of him in the middle of the night, actually. I bet he's adorable.

He glances at me with a soft look on his face making me wonder if I said that out loud.

I go back to concentrating on the wooden horse. Like every other part of the carousel, it's buried under a century's worth of grime, and I set about rubbing it off, pleased when the industrial-strength wet wipes glide through it and reveal cracked but bright paint underneath. The horse was white once, with decorations in various shades of blue, a navy saddle with five-petal flowers painted in baby blue, a carved blonde mane and tail, and feet of royal blue with silver hooves. I can't quite get my head around the fact that this is *so* old. Apart from a bit of dirt, it's amazing that something so elaborate can have survived for so long.

I look at the other horses standing nearby, all with different designs and colours, but none quite as fancy as this one. Even though they're all in the same mucky condition, there really is something different about the saddle on this one. As I clean it off, I can see the blue paint is worn through to white undercoat and back to the original wood in some places, and the wear is in the exact shape of someone sitting on it. None of the others have the same problem. It makes me think about Camilla's story, minus the ghost part. Maybe someone really did sit on this horse for years on end, going round in constant circles waiting for the love of their life to return. It's a sad story, especially knowing he never did. It's a far cry from the joyfulness that you usually associate with carousels.

I shake myself because it's far too beautiful a day, a beach, and a carousel to feel this sad. 'So what's your next step with these after they're clean?'

'Firstly check for damage. Any breaks, any cracks, any missing pieces. I can already see a few ears that need replacing, so I'll have to make replacements and glue them in place.' He shows no sign of being annoyed by my questions, even though I'm pretty sure he's used to working by himself. 'Then I need to find as close as possible colour matches to all the paintwork, sand the whole lot down, basecoat and repaint.'

'You make it sound so easy.'

He shrugs. 'I love my job. This doesn't feel like work to me. If I could do anything I wanted, I'd *choose* to be restoring a Victorian carousel on a beach. I feel like the luckiest guy in the world to get paid for doing this.'

I smile at the way he smiles without even realising it as he talks. I have never felt like that about a job in my life. 'And what's your biggest challenge? What's the biggest problem that you're going to have to fix here?'

He thinks for a moment. 'If I start up this engine and discover it doesn't work. They don't make 'em like this anymore, and the chances of finding a new one would be slim-to-impossible. Secondly, the organ, although that's not such a big deal. If I can't get that working, there's still a firm in Blackpool that will make them on commission. The owner would have no chance of getting one before the summer holidays, but even that can be solved with any sort of modern-day music player, although it wouldn't give it the true carousel sound, and my brief says he wants to retain that as much as possible with a few modern updates ... Sorry, I'm rambling again. You should know better than to ask me questions about carousels by now. I don't shut up once I start.'

I bite my lip as I watch the way he goes back to twisting something on the engine like it needs as much concentration as landing a space shuttle. I want to go over and give him a hug, but it's a line I don't feel like I can cross yet. 'What other problems are there, Nath?'

He looks up at me and raises that gorgeous eyebrow again. 'You're going with the Nath thing then?'

'I figure that if you think using your full name equates as someone disliking you, then shortening it as much as possible equates as liking you *and* your carousel knowledge,' I say. 'And if Bunion Frank can get away with it, so can I.'

He laughs, an unrestrained cackle that makes him throw his head back and tears form in the corners of his eyes. I feel the atmosphere slip away as he goes back to talking about how worn the scenic panels that disguise the engine are and how he's got to make two more chariots to make the carousel fully accessible.

It's the sort of thing that sounds impossible to me, and leaves me in awe of his talent and how easy he makes it sound, and how excited he is about it.

I concentrate on rubbing a wet wipe over the underside of the horse and getting my fingers inside the hole where the pole goes through, while Nathan shifts the engine and makes a noise of surprise. He suddenly leans forward and runs a hand over the inside of one of the wood panels in front of him. 'Oh, wow. Ness, come and have a look at this.'

The wooden base is warm under my feet as I walk over to where he's kneeling.

'I hate to admit it, but I think there might be something in your romantic old ghost story,' he says as I crouch down beside him and he points at the inside wall of the panel.

*Ivy* is carved into the wood, with a scroll and some ivy leaves around it, and underneath in carving so neat it could almost be handwritten are the words *I will love you until the carousel stops turning.*

The atmosphere in the tent changes again. Everything feels suddenly intense, like we've just seen magic for the very first time. The hair on the back of my neck stands on end, like a ghost has just walked by.

I nearly overbalance and grab Nathan's shoulder for support as I reach out to touch the words too. My little finger brushes against his as we both feel the intricate carving.

'This is hidden right in the heart of the carousel,' Nathan whispers, because it would feel wrong to talk in normal voices. 'This panel protects the engine. Without the engine, the carousel doesn't turn.'

'Ivy must be who the carousel was built for. The name of the ghost.'

'The lead horse is called Ivy,' Nathan murmurs. 'Usually they have individual names painted on their necks, but these ones don't. Only the lead horse has "Ivy" carved in the traditional place.'

'And there are ivy leaves everywhere.'

He looks around in surprise. 'Of course there are. I hadn't made that connection. I thought they were just a decorative theme, but maybe they mean something.'

'And the lead horse is more worn,' I say. 'Do you think that was her horse? That was where she sat, day after day, waiting for the love of her life to come back?'

He looks over at the horse I've just been cleaning. 'You're good at this too, you know that? I'd noticed the wear but hadn't read anything into it.' He looks at my hand still resting on his shoulder and then looks up and meets my eyes, but he doesn't seem to mind it there, so I give it a squeeze, determined not to let go yet even though I don't need the support.

I reach out and run my fingers over the lettering again. 'Maybe this is why the ghost still rides it – so it doesn't stop turning. She can still believe there's hope of him finding her again for as long as it turns.'

'I hate to be the unromantic voice of reason here, but it's been *many* decades since this thing turned, let alone played ghostly music in the dead of night.'

'I know, but … even without the ghost bit. All those years ago. If there's any truth in the story, she sat here for years, watching and waiting for someone who never came.'

'Well, that's love for you, isn't it? Always a let-down.'

I glance at him but he's still intently focused on the words in front of us and his face doesn't give anything away. 'And now it's stopped turning. She must have thought he stopped loving her.'

'Aw, don't worry, Ness.' He reaches up and pats the hand on his shoulder and then jumps up abruptly, making it drop. 'We'll get it back working for ol' Ivy. I wouldn't mind knowing a name and date in exchange though. Do you think our ghostly friend will share that with me?'

'No, but there must be some locals who know more than Camilla does … We could ask around.'

'Are we going to get anything but ghost stories though? I don't want romanticised old tales, I want to know his name, when he made this, when he lived, when he died, if he made anything else. Fact not fiction.'

'I want to know what happened to him,' I say. 'They were madly in love. He must've spent years making this for her. He wouldn't have just disappeared after that, would he?'

'Probably realised love was a load of bollocks.'

'Aww,' I mutter as he goes back to his engine, and I follow his cue and get up and return to cleaning the lead horse, wondering if she'll provide any more clues about her namesake, listening to the roll of the waves as they come closer and the distant chatter of passersby.

'I think you're right,' he says after a while. 'I think he loved her.'

'Are you saying you believe a romantic old ghost story?'

'You know I said I like to feel the things I work on?' he says after a long hesitation. 'You can feel it. This whole carousel is a strange thing. It's carved beautifully, but not efficiently. It's incredible to look at but it's so big and bulky that it's not practical. This isn't someone trying to make money or better the work of what's already out there. Every inch of it is made with love and that comes across, even all these years later. The story reinforces what I can tell from the carousel and the carousel reinforces the story. It shows me why there are all these little touches, like the ivy leaves everywhere, that don't serve any purpose and actually make it bigger and bulkier than it already was. Generally carousel makers wouldn't do that – they need to make them as streamlined as possible.'

I love listening to him talk about this. I could sit here and listen to him all day, and not just because of the soft lilt of his Yorkshire accent.

'At least you're here to fix it. It will turn again for Ivy and her missing love.'

He snorts as he undoes something on the engine. 'Not like me to be fixing love.'

I pause mid-horse-leg and look over at him. There's something so sharp in his voice that I can't stop myself pursuing it. 'How come you're so anti-love?'

'I'm not anti-love, I'm just anti-*me*-in-love. I'm sure it's great for other people – Ivy and her missing man for instance, Charles and Camilla, probably the Pearlholme couple *and* the royal couple – it's just not something that works for me, but good on anyone who's found it.'

'Why?'

'Because I genuinely like other people being happy.'

I throw him such a glare that he actually recoils. 'You know full well I meant you. Why doesn't love work for you?'

He's silent for so long that I'm sure he's decided to ignore me.

'I'm divorced,' he says eventually, so quiet that I can barely hear him.

When I look over, his head is bowed and he looks like it's such a shameful secret that I wonder if there's a hidden meaning I'm missing. 'Regular divorced or, like, just got out of prison for divorcing your wife's head from her body?'

He laughs and it eases the tension I can see in him. Instead of crouching next to the engine, he sits on his knees and looks at me. 'Just regular divorced. And there's no kids or messy exes or owt like that. I just thought I'd met someone to share the rest of my life with … Turns out I was wrong. We married at twenty-three and I was thirty-one when we got divorced.'

'Five years ago?'

He nods.

'Like your shoulder injury?'

He nods again. 'Yeah, it was a *great* year.'

'That's a long time to be married to someone.'

He nods yet again.

'What went wrong?' I ask, wondering if I'm pushing him too far when I can clearly see that he doesn't want to talk about it.

'Everything and nothing,' he says with a shrug. 'I was too young and too head-over-heels. I thought love worked like you see in the movies – you fall in love, you get married, and you live happily ever after. I had no concept of the idea that it might not work out.'

'At least you gave it your all,' I say, thinking about how much I hold myself back with everything I do, no matter how much I want to throw caution to the wind and jump in headfirst. 'I don't think it's a bad thing to have committed to someone you loved, even if it didn't end up working out. You know what they say – it's better to have loved and lost ...'

'Why do you have a way of making everything sound better than it is?' he says, looking at me with a soft smile. 'And why do you make me want to tell you everything that's ever happened in my life? I start talking to you and I just don't stop.'

'I don't mind that,' I say, without adding that 'don't mind' is quite possibly the understatement of the century.

'And no, it is definitely not better to have loved and lost. Load of old bollocks. Almost as much rubbish as carousel ghost stories. If I could meet my twenty-three-year-old self, I'd whack him round the head with a wooden horse leg.' He nods to a broken one lying on the floor nearby. 'Anything to stop him making such a stupid mistake.'

He sounds so bitter and hurt, even so many years later, but there's no heat behind his words. They sound like a well-practised front that he's used to hiding behind, and the urge to go over and hug him returns. But it doesn't seem right. Even though I feel like I've known him for years, I have to keep reminding myself that it's only been a few days. It's not right to feel this close to someone in such a short amount of time, and he's obviously shy and reserved, and so am I usually. I don't know what's got into me lately.

'Better than me,' I say instead, because I don't think he's going to share anything else and it might make him feel better to know he's not the only one with a disastrous love life. 'I tried to force a relationship that was clearly going nowhere. The "perfect on paper" guy who my mum loved. My friends had already chosen

143

the colours of their bridesmaids' dresses. I convinced myself that all relationships were as devoid of love and affection as ours was. We shared a flat and, honestly, I was more excited to see my neighbour's dog when we passed in the stairwell than I was when he came home after work.'

'How long?' he asks, looking like he's grabbing the chance to talk about something other than his own love life.

'We were together for three years but the relationship was over for at least two of them.'

He makes a pained face. 'Ouch. You broke it off?'

'Yeah, and my friends and family still haven't forgiven me. He was thereafter forever renamed "poor Andrew". My mum joined Facebook solely so she could keep in touch with him. She still phones weekly to tell me about the pictures he's posted of him and his new girlfriend travelling around Thailand. Apparently he's much fitter now but he always looked so much happier with me. But that's the point. We weren't happy, we were making each other miserable. And everyone kept telling me that he was perfect for me, and rather than trusting myself, I kept thinking they must be seeing something that I wasn't, but eventually, you just ...'

'... have to give up,' he finishes for me, sounding like he understands.

I nod and give him a grateful smile and he smiles back.

'When'd you break up?' he says quickly, almost like he's aware the conversation has shifted back to him and he doesn't want to give me a chance to ask any more questions.

'Two years ago now. All my friends and family think I'm some kind of heartless cow for breaking it off out of nowhere ... well, what they thought was out of nowhere. And my best friend's been on a mission to find me someone else ever since.'

'The pregnant one who hates *Carousel*?' I nod and he continues. 'And she's never succeeded?'

I wrinkle my nose and make the face I always make when Daphne's talking about guys she wants me to go on a date with,

144

the face that annoys her no end. It makes Nathan smile. 'I met "poor Andrew" through online dating. Daphne and I made a pact to try it together and we both met nice guys around the same time, and hers was her now-husband, and mine was … very much not. I felt like I'd tried too hard to find someone, like I'd been too desperate for something to work and tried to make it something it wasn't. I don't want to make the same mistake again. I don't want to force something, and going on blind dates with guys she's interviewed for some weird article like "how to live with an extremely long penis" feels a bit too … force-y,' I say, knowing Zinnia would be impressed with my butchering of the English language.

'I bet people on the other end of the long penis say the same thing,' he quips, and it takes us both a while to recover from the laughter.

'I know what you mean,' he continues. 'Well, not about the long penis. Wait, I shouldn't say that. I should say something flirtatious like "maybe, but you'd have to find out for yourself," shouldn't I?'

'Oh my God, Nath,' I say, struggling to speak because I'm laughing so much, more at the horrified look on his face than anything else.

'Please, please continue this conversation from before any mention of penises arose. And arose and penises aren't words you want in the same sentence, are they? Oh God, I'm making it worse. Can we go back to before the penises and pretend the interim never happened. Please, Ness, I beg of you before I embarrass myself any more.'

I grin at him because he's so adorable. He tries to be flirty but it just doesn't work, and that's part of the charm. 'Okay, let's forget all about the penises. There are no penises here … although is the plural penises or penii? No one wants grammar mistakes when it comes to penises.'

He can't answer because he's busy dying of laughter. Or embarrassment. I am too, but seeing him laugh so much somehow makes it worth it.

'I just thought if I was ever going to have another relationship, it should happen naturally,' I say when we can both breathe again. 'I'd bump into someone somewhere and there'd be a click and butterflies and I'd just *know*, and maybe it would have more chance of succeeding if it had started organically … and if it never happens, then it's still better than what I had before.' I realise I've never said that out loud. I've been so busy thinking up excuses for not going on any of Daphne's dates that I've never actually told her that one simple truth. I don't want another 'poor Andrew'. I want something real or nothing at all. I would rather live alone and adopt seventy-nine cats – as she always tells me I'll end up doing if I don't try harder to find love – than have another loveless relationship. 'What about you?'

'No clicks, no butterflies, no looking.' He drops the unused tool in his hand onto the wooden floor and walks across to the side of the tent nearest me. 'I don't ever want to go through that again. It was such a mess that it'll never be worth the risk.'

'Ever? Doesn't the story of Ivy and her mystery carousel maker inspire you to believe that there's real, true, enduring love out there?'

He looks at me like I've lost the plot. 'Yeah, and look where it got her. A lifetime of sadness, riding a merry-go-round day after day, so distraught that apparently even death wasn't enough to stop her misery. If anything, this carousel proves that even with the best of intentions, love isn't worth the pain.'

I abandon my wet wipes and go over to stand next to him, looking out at the bay in front of us. The tide is far up the beach now. It's reached the highest point and started to go back out again, leaving layers of wet sand in its wake, and it makes me wonder how the afternoon has gone so quickly. I haven't even noticed the time passing.

'Yeah, exactly,' I say, swallowing hard. 'It's not worth the misery it'll undoubtedly bring.'

He lifts his left arm and drops it around my shoulders, squeezing me in to his side. 'What a pair we make, huh? Here we are at the most romantic carousel in the world and its sentiment is lost on us.'

I reach up and put my hand on his injured shoulder and give it a gentle squeeze. 'Yeah, completely lost.'

He sighs and rests his head against mine for just a moment, then he starts humming 'If I Loved You' from *Carousel*, and we stand and look out at the ocean, glistening blue under the bright summer sun, and I can't help thinking the romance of this gorgeous old thing might not be quite so lost after all.

# Chapter 11

'I am going to die.'

'You can't die, you have to be alive to call an ambulance when I keel over,' Nathan pants, making me feel slightly better about my lack of fitness because he's struggling just as much as I am with this climb.

'Did you at least tell someone where we were going so they know where to send a search party before vultures tear all the remaining flesh from our rotting carcasses?'

'I don't think we have vultures in Britain.'

There's an ominous squawk of a gull overhead and we both look up at the sky, then back down at each other and chuckle nervously.

'All right, maybe they're not vultures but there could definitely be unknown species never before seen by humans this far up. There are probably a few bears, wolves, and yetis having a tea party, safe in the knowledge that no idiot with half a brain would be daft enough to come up here.'

'You said yes,' he says with a grin.

'I believe my exact words were, "You're insane, but I can't let you die up there, cold and alone, on this ridiculous pursuit."'

'Actually, your exact words were, "I'd love to, that sounds like fun." I remember them because I doubted my own sanity in suggesting it and I was touched that you had so much faith in me.'

'I'm starting to think that was misplaced,' I mutter as I stop and bend over with my hands on my knees, trying to get air into my screaming lungs.

We're not even halfway up the cliff where the ruins of the house stand. It seemed like it might be doable at first, as we walked up past the cottages of Pearlholme and along gently sloping grassy paths, then it got a bit more hilly, then we hit monstrous sand dunes, and it only got worse from there on out. We're now on the bit that, from the beach, I thought was the cliff collapsing with subsidence, and now up close, I see that I was right. These are not just sand dunes, they were once solid grassy cliff face that has fallen away over time, which is always a comforting thought when you're standing on it. We're not even anywhere near what looked like the hard part, and I can't describe how much I'm looking forward to reaching that. If we make it there alive.

'Here.' Nathan presses my water bottle into my hand and stands up to take a long glug from his, and I can't help but watch the way his glistening Adam's apple bobs as he swallows and swipes a forearm across his forehead and shakes sweat from it. Which, again, makes me feel better about how hot I look. And not in the attractive way. I'm wearing a plain T-shirt and three-quarter-length black trousers, but it could be a bikini and I'd still be too hot, and that would put Nathan right off his sandwiches too.

Not that he's told me what his mysterious secret sandwich is yet.

He's quite the gentleman, actually. He's made lunch for both of us, been to the shop and got fresh pastries, borrowed water bottles from the cottage, and carried the whole lot in the rucksack over his shoulders to save me having to carry anything.

I look down the dune we've just clambered up. 'If we lose our footing for even a moment, gravity will slide us straight back down to the bottom again.'

'Bloody gravity. It wasn't even a good film.'

I nod my agreement because I'm too out of breath for unnecessary speaking.

'Something else we can agree on,' he says. 'Overhyped films and the joys of toaster pizzas.'

'There's such a thing as toaster pizzas?' I say in surprise.

'Oh, what a sheltered life you lead.' He puts on an American accent. 'Stick with me, grasshopper, I'll teach you everything there is to know about junk food.'

I hand my water bottle back to him and watch as he pushes it into his backpack and swings it onto his shoulders. 'Should you be carrying that?'

'What? With the injury?' He looks over at me and I nod. 'Ness, it was five years ago. It's not a problem now.'

He sounds offhand about it, but there's something in his face whenever he mentions it that makes me think there's more to tell.

'But thank you,' he says, quieter now. 'No one's ever asked me that before. It was my own fault. I didn't deserve any sympathy, and I never told anyone at work how much pain I was in, and when I started getting on with things again, everyone assumed it was completely recovered, and I didn't correct them.'

I go to say something else but he interrupts before I have a chance.

'We should get a move on – it's nearly ten and we're nowhere near that path up to the ruins yet, and it might take a bit of chopping down, and—'

I find superhuman strength from somewhere and leap across the sand between us and throw my arms around him. It's the wobble in his voice when he interrupted me, the look of surprise on his face when he says something without thinking and then his brain catches up moments later, and mainly it's how much something so small says about him. I suddenly feel like I can't *not* hug him, and whether it's the sun, the exertion, or the genuine possibility of impending death on this mountain, for once I stop making excuses and just go for it.

I expect him to pull away in horror at the sweaty body suddenly clinging to his sweaty body, but his arms come up and wrap around me too, pulling me closer for a long moment, his chin resting against my damp hair, his shoulders dropping as he exhales and the straps of the bag slip down.

'What's this for?' he murmurs, making no attempt to pull away, even though we're both hot and sweaty and being so close to another hot, sweaty person is doing nothing to help the situation. There are ideal times for hugs, and this is not one of them.

I shake my head and squeeze him a bit tighter.

'Note to self: old injuries make good chat-up lines.' I feel tension shoot through his body. 'Not that I was trying—'

'I know.' I reach up and pat the shoulder in question and then slide the strap of the rucksack back up as I pull away. 'What were you saying about finding that path?'

I can feel his eyes on me as I step back, and my foot slides further down the dune than I intended it to and I end up doing a demented impression of the splits until I manage to get both feet back together again. Hazards of walking up dunes with gorgeous men should be taught in schools or something.

'Er, yeah.' He points above us to where the cliff face turns from open dunes to a covered mangle of greenery. We've even lost sight of the ruins that we could see from the bottom now. We've walked so much that we might not even be on the same cliff anymore. To be honest, we might not even be in Yorkshire anymore. 'See those brambles creeping in? There was definitely a part of this dune that continued up through them.'

It's the 'through them' part that I don't like. When thinking of enjoyable things to walk through, brambles are right near the bottom of the list, just behind things like hot coals, broken glass, stinging nettles, and snake pits. All of which could well be lurking in there.

We keep walking up, although it's more of a slow trudge than any form of walk. The hill is so steep and the sand is so thick that every time you put your foot down, it slides back at least half the length of the step you've just taken, making slow progress feel even slower with the morning sun burning down on us. We're both experimenting with anything from tiny shuffles to long strides. Nathan was even brave enough to try a sprint, which was quite cartoon-ish in how quickly he slid back down even lower than where he was when he started.

I can feel him looking at me as we trudge upwards in a way that he wasn't before the hug. He keeps looking behind – because, let's face it, I'm usually the one of us lagging behind – and either he wants to say something or he's monitoring me for signs of an impending heart attack. Maybe he's trying to work out quite how *that* much sweat can come out of one person's body and figure out the best way to sell me to science.

'Look, this has got to be it.'

He's managed to stand still on the steep dunes and he's staring intently at a kind of opening in the brambles. It's not really an opening. I suppose it could've been once, but now it's just sand disappearing into the undergrowth at a slightly higher level than the rest of the sand that turns into grassy banks of prickly weeds. We're too close to see what we saw from the beach. We just have to hope we're in the right place and forge ahead into unknown territory. Like Neil Armstrong walking on the moon. It feels like the moon might actually be nearer than the house ruins at the moment. And probably a lot more fun to get to.

Nathan pushes a bramble aside and instantly pulls his hand back when he gets scratched. He slips the bag off his shoulder and crouches down to root around in it.

'I've got secateurs.' He holds the tiny garden tool aloft in victory.

'Great,' I say, trying not to compare them in size to the bram-

152

bles wrapped around gorse bushes that are taller than even Nathan.

There's not even a way around them – they're too dense, creeping in on either side from the surrounding cliffs. I suddenly wish we could've seen it as it was back in Ivy and the carousel maker's day. It couldn't have looked like this. It couldn't have been this steep or this eroded, and there must have been an access road somewhere. I look around. Those days are gone. Unfortunately. I could just do with a nice flat road. And a shower. And a glass of wine.

There's a plink as the secateurs snap together and Nathan uses them to remove the bramble he's just cut because he hasn't got gloves. Make that several glasses of wine.

'There was a machete in Camilla's garden storage box but I didn't bring it,' he says. 'I thought it might be a bit weird for you to go to a remote location with a stranger and a machete. Not that we're strangers now but you know what I mean? I thought it might be less murder-y to stay away from machetes in general.'

'Do you think the machete's actually for gardening or for use on Charles when he steps out of line?'

'Oh, definitely for Charles. Probably for us too if we don't win the PPP, which is not looking likely considering this is the extent of my gardening ability.'

I watch as he parts cut brambles and edges forward, using his bare arms to push them aside. I like how dedicated he is to getting up here. From the moment he saw the ruin from the beach, he decided to go there, and nothing has put him off. It would be admirable if we weren't halfway up a sheer cliff face and forging our way through a narrow, spiky, prickly, painful path, but a path nonetheless.

I look at Nathan's back in front of me. The nape of his neck is red with exertion or sunburn and there are sweat patches around the edges of his black T-shirt. He cuts brambles and holds them back until I get past too, using his boots to stamp them down underneath our feet and create a walkway bit by bit, until scraggly grass takes over from the brambles, the gorse bushes become more sparse, and we emerge from the undergrowth onto another open dune before the cliff side flattens out and disappears over a hill, which I'm fairly sure is where the ruins are standing. Unless we really have taken a wrong turn and ended up in Belgium.

When we emerge from the brambles, we stop for another drink and to get our breath back, and I'm surprised to see over an hour has passed since the last stop. Nathan's determination really is admirable.

'Nearly there.' He holds his water bottle up in a toast gesture and grins, his forehead glistening with sweat in a way that somehow looks sexy. Sweat on most people just looks sweaty. It's not just the sweat though. It's the achievement that's making him look so happy. He doesn't mention it, but I don't think he was half as assured about getting up here as he sounded, but he did it anyway.

I'm suddenly really glad I came. Despite how much I'm convinced that my pounding heart is about to literally explode and how I can't hear anything other than the blood thundering through my ears and the rasp of my oxygen-deprived lungs. I grin over at him as he holds the cold water bottle against his forehead, taking in gasps of air. He's resplendent as he grins back. There's sweat beading in his short hair that was styled this morning but has blown out into a spiky mess by now, but his eyes are light, the blue sky making them look closer to a deep grey than the usual dark brown, and his arms are covered in raised pink scratches from the bramble bushes, whereas I barely have a mark on me because he's such a gentleman.

I stand up straight and shake my shoulders out, re-do my ponytail, which has gradually fallen down and is clinging to my sweaty neck, and flap the bottom of my T-shirt around me. I can feel his eyes on me and he smiles when I look up and it makes something inside of me flutter again. Which is no easy task considering that *every* part of my body is currently gasping for breath and has no business fluttering when death is probably imminent.

'You ready?' he asks when the sweat has started to dry and our breath has got back to semi-normal rather than the panting rasps of earlier. 'It looks steeper here until it levels off.'

Oh, joy. I look up at the wide dune ahead of me, the sand so clean that it looks almost white, probably because no human has ventured up here in years. It does look a bit steep, but it can't be that bad now we've come this far, can it?

\* \* \*

Famous last words. At least, they would be if I could think about anything other than my burning thighs and screaming calves. Sand always looks so nice in pictures, but trying to climb up an almost vertical cliff face knee-deep in it is not so much fun.

'We're there!' Nathan calls from above me. 'I can see stone and grass!'

He's ahead of me – of course he's ahead of me, his legs are about two foot longer than mine – but I'm so focused on remembering how to breathe that I've lost track of where he is. It's probably the first time all day that I've managed to take my eyes off the curves of his shoulder muscles in that tight T-shirt or the flex of his forearms as he's been cutting down brambles.

One step at a time. Shuffle, shuffle, slide back down a bit, another shuffle, a longer slide back down, one foot in front of the other. Will it ever end? I think I've been shuffling up this mountain since 2010.

When I look up, Nathan's reached the peak of the hill and shrugged the bag off his shoulders, and I'm so close to solid, flat ground I can taste it. Unless that's the sand I've inhaled.

'C'mere, I'll pull you up.' He reaches a hand out and I slip mine into it, and at exactly the same time as he hauls me up with an almighty pull, I go for a final sprint to make it easier on him, and the momentum is just too much. I go careening into him with so much force that he lands on his back in the sand and lets out an 'oof' as I land on top of him.

'Oh my God,' I say, bracing my hands on either side of his head to stop us sliding right back down where we came from.

He's laughing so much he can barely speak. 'You know when you envision doing the gentlemanly thing and charmingly helping a lady up? That is *not* how it was supposed to go.'

Him having the giggles sets me off and we're both lying there on an almost sheer sand dune laughing over nothing.

'I wish someone had caught that on camera. We couldn't have done that if we'd tried.' He throws his head back in the sand, his crow's feet crinkling up, tears of laughter pooling in his eyes.

'Sorry, Nath,' I pant, trying to get the giggles under control, but every time I look at him, I laugh at how much he's laughing.

I'm lying on him from top to toe, his hands have come up to either side of my waist to stop me sliding off, and his sandy denim-clad leg is hooked around one of mine.

'Why is this so funny?' He looks up at me with his eyes shining and his forehead glistening with sweat.

I can feel his chest heaving, although that could be more to do with the fact he's got my weight on top of him than the struggle of getting up here. I feel weirdly close to him, like we've known each other forever, and laughing with him feels so natural.

'Why aren't we getting up?' I lower my forehead to his and try to remember how to breathe.

'I don't know how to,' he murmurs, so close to my ear that his breath stirs the wisps of hair that have come loose again.

'Good point.' It sets us both off again and I realise we're just lying here in the sand clinging to each other, and we're both so hot and sweaty that we need an ice bath, but neither of us have made any attempt to move.

'You okay?' I say, suddenly realising he could've actually hurt himself, falling over like that and cushioning my fall.

He looks up and meets my eyes, and all the laughter stops, and his eyes are dark and serious again. 'Never been better.'

I swallow at the sudden intensity as I realise this is the perfect position for kissing. My mouth is level with his for what is probably the first time due to our usual height difference. My boobs are pressed against his chest. I can feel every breath he takes as they turn quicker and more ragged. Every inch of his muscular body is pressed tight against mine and his hands tighten on my waist.

I want to kiss him more than I've ever wanted to do anything in my life before now. I often feel like life has just moved along without my input. I sort of go with the flow and don't really push for anything; I make excuses to avoid dates and find sensible explanations for why I'm still in the same job. I don't take risks or do anything that might rock the boat, even though the boat isn't very comfortable in the first place, but with him underneath me, I suddenly want to steer the boat. I want to wrap both hands in his hair and crush his lips against mine.

I wet my lips and his breath catches, his eyes blown almost-black with desire. His head lifts as mine lowers, and we're so close …

And then sweat drips from my forehead onto his cheek, a bit like Rapunzel's tear at the end of *Tangled*, but not quite as romantic, obviously. It ruins the moment a bit, to be honest.

He bursts out laughing again and any hint of desire is gone. *So* long gone, it's probably in the Outer Hebrides by now.

'Oh God, I'm so sorry.' I didn't think I could get any redder, what with the desire to kiss him, the giggling, and the exercise, but my traitorous body somehow manages to add even more redness from embarrassment to my already flushed face.

'Don't worry about it, I'm dripping with sweat too,' he says, struggling to breathe through the laughter again. Maybe it's the

157

relief of stopping before we did something stupid. No matter how much I wanted to in that moment, I can't kiss him. I barely know him, and then there's the article I'm supposed to be writing about him. This is complicated enough without adding kissing to the mix. And I definitely didn't want to stop at kissing.

I automatically reach out and go to wipe his cheek but my hand was obviously one of our only anchors because the movement dislodges us and we're suddenly sliding down the dune again.

I squeal and Nathan shrieks and our arms tighten around each other as we go flying through the sand and come to a screeching halt just moments away from the forest of blackberry.

Nathan rests his forehead against mine again and tries to get his breath back. 'Well, that was fun. I was just thinking how much I'd like to walk up that steep hill again. Like my thighs aren't on fire.'

We both dissolve into laughter again.

It shouldn't be funny. That last stretch of sand dune has nearly killed me once already, but somehow I can't stop laughing because he's laughing. And we're not dead yet. If we've made it this far without dying, surely we're on the home stretch now.

'I thought the burning thighs was just me,' I say when I can breathe again.

'Are you kidding? My thighs are killing me. I'm aching in places I didn't know I had. I had shins once but I haven't felt them for at least two hours. You'll have to come up to the cottage for breakfast again tomorrow morning because I might need you to haul me out of bed and tip me down the stairs.'

Any excuse to do something with Nathan in bed, even if it *is* hauling him out of it. And another excuse to have breakfast with him, like every other morning this week. 'If I can walk tomorrow. At the moment, it's looking doubtful.'

He laughs. 'At least we can creak around the village together with all the ninety-year-olds. Maybe someone will be kind enough to lend us a Zimmer frame.'

I grin down at him. 'My best friend is eight months pregnant and she moves faster than me. Your level of fitness makes me feel normal.'

'I wouldn't know what the inside of a gym looked like if a treadmill smacked me in the face, but I had a couple of years of physio that taught me a lot and made me stronger than I was before. I rely on my job for fitness because I'm active with that.'

A couple of *years*? His injury must've been much worse than he makes out. But at least it explains why he feels so good, I think as his sinewy thigh presses against my flabby one. I've watched him working on the carousel in the past week. He almost never stops moving; he's constantly back and forth to grab different parts or tools.

'Speaking of active …' His big hand is spread open on my back, supporting me as I roll off him and struggle onto my knees even as they're sliding underneath me in the sand. I sit on them and look up the hill we've just climbed once. It was hard enough the first time.

He gets onto his knees too and looks over at me, and I know he's thinking the exact same thing. 'This might be the best way up actually.'

'What, crawl?'

He grins. 'Yup. Come on, hands and knees, I'll race ya. Go!'

'Nath!' I squeak as he takes off, scrambling up the dune, arms and legs everywhere, like a giant spider. He makes it look easy.

I barely have time to consider how undignified it is as I rush after him, not managing it quite as elegantly as he did, and glad that he's too busy with winning to look back and see the state I'm in. When he gets to the grassy edge, he holds a hand out to pull me up to the safety of the green flat bit.

'Because it went so well last time?' I pant.

'Well, it wasn't entirely unenjoyable. I'm willing to risk it again if you are.'

I can't resist the cheeky glint in his eyes. I slide my sand-covered hand into his and let him pull me up, and this time I crash into him on the ground, his arms wrap around me to stop us falling, but we start sliding down the shallow grassy bank on the other side anyway.

He's already out of breath from the climb and now he's laughing again, so I'm laughing again, and I'm not sure if I'm laughing because it's funny or because of how absolutely jubilant he seems. 'Are we the clumsiest people on the planet or does this hill not want us up here?'

'I think you're just really terrible at helping people up hills.'

'Ah, but you like my hand-washing skills so I'm still winning.'

'I'm too knackered to laugh this much, Nath,' I say, still laughing.

We're both lying upside down on the grass in a tangle of limbs, trying to catch our breath. I close my eyes and try not to think about how close he is, or how I can feel his chest heaving where my forearm is squashed against him, how after all that climbing and sweating, I can still smell his cologne, and feel the scratch of his stubble where his chin is brushing my bare upper arm with every ragged breath as we both try to calm ourselves down.

When I open my eyes, the old grey stone that we could see from the beach is looming above, and Nathan disentangles his arm from underneath me as we sit up.

I bite my lip as he holds my gaze for a long moment, until he hastily looks away, getting to his feet with surprising ease. My legs are literally shaking with exhaustion.

He holds a hand out and pulls me up again, and somehow, this time we both manage to stay upright as we turn to look at the ruins of the house. I've had so much fun getting up here with him that I'd forgotten we were coming here for a reason. It's easy to see from here that the piles of stone were once a house. Now it's just a few crumbling walls and half-formed doorways. You can see a bit of the foundations and a couple of what used to be rooms, but whatever was left of the roof and most of the walls have fallen in.

'You're covered in sand,' I say as Nathan reaches over to collect his rucksack from where it landed on the grass.

'Brush me off, will you?'

It's a tough job but someone's got to do it. It's weirdly intimate as I brush his back down with my hand. I linger a bit too long on his left shoulder and carry on down his back, loving the feeling of solid muscles under the soft black material of his T-shirt, warm from the sunlight, stopping myself before I reach his bum, then I make him bend down so I can brush it out of his hair. I'm sure he could manage that bit himself, but he doesn't seem to be minding the closeness.

'You're glowing,' he says when he stands back up and gets the water bottles out again.

'That's a nice way of saying I look like I'm about to spontaneously combust.'

'I *am* about to spontaneously combust, if it makes you feel better.'

I turn to look at the view as I desperately suck water from the bottle, trying to wash away some of the sand I've definitely swallowed, and it takes my breath away in a completely different way.

'Wow,' Nathan murmurs.

It's been over four hours since we left the cottage at eight o'clock this morning, and for the view alone, it's been worth it. From up here, you can see right the way along the coastline as it stretches out either side from Pearlholme. The sea goes on forever, glittering in the mid-afternoon sun and disappearing into the sky where it meets the horizon. We're too close to see the village, but Nathan points out the spot on the beach where we must've stood with the binoculars.

'Do you want to do the *Titanic* thing?'

It makes me grin because it *had* crossed my mind and I love that he's thought about it too.

He's standing behind me before I can even say I think it'd be wrong not to. His arms hold my wrists and spread my arms out wide.

'I'm flying!' I shout into the distance and we sway about on the hilltop for a moment.

It really does feel like flying, kind of. Well, if flying feels like standing still in a strong breeze. Unfortunately we don't end it with a kiss like Leo and Kate do in *Titanic*.

'Your turn,' I say, moving to stand behind him as he takes up the position on the crest of the hill.

'I'm the king of the world!' he shouts, howling like a wolf a couple of times. 'Well, Pearlholme anyway! Not quite the world!'

'I wonder how long it's been since anyone's been here.' I say as we both step back, lest another sliding-down-dune disaster befall us.

'A while, I think. It looks completely undisturbed.' He glances at the fresh trenches in the sand. 'Well, it did.'

'It's like our little secret place.'

'Just for us.' He meets my eyes again. 'Maybe it was like that for Ivy and the mystery carousel maker too. Isolated up here, together.'

'Until she was alone.' I look back out at the amazing view.

'Waiting for someone who would never come …' He shakes his head. 'I'm even making myself sad now. Come on, shall we have a look?'

We head towards the ruins of the house, and go through one of the crumbling doorways into what was probably an entrance room of some kind. There's only two parts that you can clearly see were once rooms, the rest of it is barely more than walls that have fallen down to knee height, and arches where everything but the arch itself has collapsed around it. I stop as Nathan goes over to a wall and starts poking at it, and I assume he's trying to guess at a date for the property.

I turn around and look back at the view, because stone walls aren't very interesting but that view is something that will never get old. I run my hand down the side of a stone arch, brushing away white lichen as I lean against it because I'm still recovering from the climb but I don't want him to know quite how shaky my limbs are. And I'm not sure it's just from the exertion.

Everything feels different here. I feel different. Barely a week has gone by since that morning on the train, but it feels like a different lifetime. You can get lost in Pearlholme, in vintage carousels and sea air and gossipy old villagers. I can't imagine ever not being here, ever not knowing Nathan, and yet a week ago, I'd never met him or heard of this place.

I stay in the archway and watch as he goes through another empty doorway into a roofless room, made up of nothing more than four walls demolished down to varying heights. It was obviously a huge room once, bigger than my entire flat at home, but now every wall and ceiling that was once above it is in debris on the ground, and what's left of the concrete floor has been taken over by grass and weeds. Even some gorse bushes have crept in.

Nathan pokes around among the rubble, picking up things and examining them, pocketing the odd one or two and tossing anything else back where it came from. 'I think this is where the carousel stood.'

'Really?' I can hear the excitement in his voice and I feel it rubbing off on me too as I walk across the clumps of Marram grass and stand in the broken doorway watching him.

'This is a horse's ear.' He holds up a lump of wood, pointed at one end, a few specks of red paint still remaining on it. 'I know exactly the one that's missing it. And this is the rounded edge of an ivy leaf,' he says as he rolls another unidentifiable piece of wood between his fingers. 'And the roof's on the floor. I thought a roof had caved in on it. And look at that view.'

I make my way across the rubble-filled room to where he's standing and look out of the wide hole in the broken wall he points to.

'Wow.' It really is the best view in the house. It's directly above the path we came up, and gives the widest, almost-panoramic view right the way along the coastline. You can see every inch of beach in both directions from Pearlholme, until it rounds a jagged cliff to the north and disappears around a bend in the seashore to the south. The sparkling sea seems to go on forever. You could sit at this window for fifty years and you'd never get tired of that view. If the stories are true, maybe that's exactly what Ivy did.

'There's no other spot in the house with a view like that. The room would definitely have been big enough and, if you look at the way these walls join, I think it was the Victorian equivalent of building an extension.'

'You think he built a room especially for the carousel?' I ask, impressed that he can tell that.

He nods. 'It was what I couldn't work out. Camilla said he didn't have much money, but he had a house big enough for something so huge – it didn't make sense. But getting up here and actually seeing it … the stones aren't as aged and you can tell they're laid differently. Again, it's just a guess, I'd need documentation to prove it and God knows how you'd find that from so long ago.'

'So he didn't just build her a carousel, he built her an actual extension on his house to keep it in? Wow.' I shake my head, unable to comprehend how much he must've loved her.

'Nothing's too much trouble for a man in love,' Nathan whispers.

I don't know why he's whispering but it feels like a sacred spot, like some kind of hallowed ground that we shouldn't disturb. There's a feeling of magic dancing just below the surface, like I could reach out and touch it if we just stayed here long enough. I lean close to him so he can hear me. 'This is really special, isn't it?'

He drops his head to rest against mine for just a moment. 'I thought it was just me.'

*I think you might be really special too.* 'I understand why you like touching the things you work on. Just standing here, you can feel it.' I suddenly feel like I should move away from him before the ghosts of lovers past make me do something stupid. I step across a pile of stone to put some space between us. 'You can sense the history of the place. The love that's come and ... gone.'

I step back out the doorway and go round to the window from the outside, peering in as he goes back to moving his foot through the debris on the floor. 'What are you looking for?'

'I don't know. Anything that tells me something about it. This is where the carousel came from. I just wanted there to be *something*. Something solid rather than guesswork, assumptions, and ghost stories.'

I should be looking at the view, but I can't tear my eyes away from him as he crouches down to examine something before discarding it with a disappointed huff, all the while humming 'If I Loved You' under his breath. 'Are you humming that because you'd usually hum it or because you know I like it?'

He looks up with a grin, his eyes closing against the sun behind me. 'Let's just say it's been in my head lately.'

Something inside me flutters even more than it was fluttering in the first place. I lose track of time as I stand there listening to his humming and watching him move around the room, half-heartedly kicking at fragments, clearly not expecting to find anything worthwhile.

He uses his foot to push a large stone aside and crouches down to poke at something sticking out of the ground.

'Ness, look at this!' When he stands back up, he's got a flat piece of metal in his hand, which he blows on and then rubs his thumb over, trying to clean it up as he reads it out loud. 'For Ivy. 1896 to 1901. Carved by ... no! No, no, no, you can't corrode there.'

'What is it?'

'A nameplate. There are two little holes in one of the panels

165

of the carousel where I thought one must have been, but I never in a million years expected to find it up here. God, that's amazing. Even if I can't read his name.'

I lean in the window hole and take it when he holds it out. It's a little metal plaque with the inscription engraved on it. It's started to rust and is covered in scratches, but you can still make out the first part of the words, the dedication and date, but the part where his name was is worn away and blackened by corrosion. 'Any way of getting it back?'

He shakes his head. 'It's gone beyond that. The dampness from the soil has destroyed the part that was underground. It's disintegrated entirely. There's nothing I can do with that. So after all this, we still don't know his name.'

'We know more than we did before.' I lean in the window to hand the nameplate back to him, and he pauses in the middle of taking it to look up at me, his little finger touching the side of mine as he holds my gaze.

'So it was worth all the climbing?'

'Definitely.'

He winks at me. 'And you haven't had one of my sandwiches yet. Believe me, *that's* definitely worth it.'

I can't help grinning at how excited he is about these sandwiches, because so far they're a bigger mystery than anything to do with Ivy and the missing carousel maker.

# Chapter 12

'Close your eyes.'

'What the hell is in this sandwich, Nath? I'm getting a bit worried now if I can't even eat it with open eyes.'

'You just have to taste it first. It's good, I promise, but if I tell you what it is, you're going to go, "Urgh, that doesn't go at all." You have to try it with an open mind and then you can judge it. Go on, trust me, I think I know you well enough by now to know you'll love it.'

I narrow my eyes at him but he grins and I can't resist his cheeky smile, so I close them and let him open a Tupperware container and place it on my lap. His hands close gently around my wrists and direct them to either side of a soft-bread sandwich.

It's so tempting to open my eyes as I lift the sandwich and try to aim for my mouth, but I decide to let him have his fun. He directs my hands until I'm nearly there, then he lets them go and shifts to the side, and I hear him sit down and get his own sandwich out.

I take a fortifying breath and try a bite, immediately surprised by the crunch as salt and vinegar bursts across my tongue, followed by the tang of something else, and the warm softness of the bread.

Usually when someone tells me I'll like something, I'm determined not to just to prove them wrong, but it doesn't even cross my mind with Nathan. 'Okay, crisps and …' I say with my mouth still half full.

'Marmite,' he finishes for me.

I open my eyes in surprise and look over at him. He's chewing his own sandwich and trying to swallow and beam proudly at the same time. 'Good, right?'

'Oh my God, Nath, I would never have tried that if you'd said what it was, but this is amazing. I haven't had a crisp sandwich since I was young and Mum and Dad would go out for the night and leave me to get my own tea and then come back expecting me to have eaten something healthy, and I'd tell them I'd had a sandwich, which technically wasn't a lie.'

'Food of the gods,' he says, not even trying to hide the proud smile.

'I've never thought of having anything with it though. I mean, Marmite … who would've thought? You're a genius, do you know that?'

'I didn't invent it,' he says with a laugh. 'It's an old British tradition. I've just perfected the art of making the perfect crisp sandwich over the years. There's not many things I'm good at but I would put making crisp sandwiches on my CV.'

'Don't forget your hand-washing talent. You're probably one skill away from taking over the world.'

His laughter rings out across the cliff tops, making me laugh too, even though there's definitely more than a few things he's good at.

* * *

After eating, we're both sitting on a picnic blanket stretched out on a slope in the grass in front of the ruin, looking out at the view. Nathan's got his arms wrapped around his knees and he's

168

turning the carousel nameplate over and over in his fingers.

'So why spend six years carving a carousel to show your love for someone, win the fair maiden's heart, and then disappear?' He twists it in a spiral on his palm.

'It couldn't have been deliberate. He must've been in an accident ...' I look at the sceptical expression on his face. 'Mustn't he?'

'What, and no one told our Ivy? If he was dead, why did she spend so many years waiting for him to come back? She couldn't have known, but if any part of Camilla's story is true, they lived together, they were engaged. How would she not know?'

'Maybe they didn't live together. Maybe she just visited him? Things were different in that day and age, maybe his family didn't approve and kept it from her ...'

'But she was allowed to stay in this big house, with this incredible carousel, and no one else laid claim to it? It doesn't make any sense. Six *years*, Ness. You could knock together a carousel in much less time, but not with the love and thought that he put into it. She was worth six years of incredibly hard work to show her how much she meant to him, to give her something that no other man could, this thing that is *unimaginable* to own, and for her part, he was worth the wait and the ridicule she undoubtedly suffered. If the stories are true, she waited for him *forever*. Literally.' He shakes his head. 'See? You leave me to my thoughts for two minutes and I turn the conversation back to carousels. I'm sure you don't want to hear any more about this today.'

'You've been told to shut up a lot, haven't you?'

I see tension shoot through his body and he freezes on the spot. He stops turning the nameplate, stops even breathing. The only thing about him that still moves is the wind rustling his dark hair.

The silence stretches between us for so long that I think he's not going to answer.

'No. I don't know where you got that idea from.' He crosses

169

his arms behind his head and lies down on the picnic blanket with a huff.

I'm sitting level with his waist so I can't see his face as he lies behind me, but I can see how stiff his denim-covered legs are, bent at the knees, full of the tension thrumming from him.

I must've said the wrong thing, crossed a line I didn't mean to cross, and I want to say something but I don't know what. I sit there in silence instead, pulling petals off a daisy a la *The Little Mermaid.*

'All the time,' he murmurs after I've gone through another daisy and a half, decimating the little patch on the hill next to us.

I look over my shoulder at him. He's lying taut, his arms folded behind his head, the pale underside of his biceps where the sun hasn't caught is straining against the cotton of his black T-shirt, his face is turned away from me, and his eyes are squeezed shut.

I reach back and touch his bicep, trailing my fingers down the line where untanned skin meets the golden glow of his upper arms while I try to figure out the best thing to say. 'I hate it when people have been conditioned to apologise for loving something they love,' I settle on eventually.

His breath judders and I turn to face him, shifting around on my bum until I'm sitting cross-legged, then I shuffle forwards until my knees press against his sides, determined to get him to talk to me. 'You shouldn't ever have to apologise for being yourself, Nath, and if you ever have had to, then you don't have to with me.' I let my hand trail from his bicep to his left shoulder and settle there.

He bites his lip and the lines around his eyes uncrinkle as they go from squeezed tight shut to just closed. A few long minutes pass in silence, but I don't push him. Instead, I keep my hand on his left shoulder, rubbing the sun-warmed material of his T-shirt under my fingers.

'I'm kind of the black sheep of the family,' he says, still refusing to turn in my direction.

'You?' I say in surprise. He's the kind of guy any girl would be overjoyed to take home to meet their parents. He's kind, funny, and respectful, with an interesting job and a charm that makes him impossible not to like. 'I can't imagine you being the black sheep of anything.'

'Well, let's just say you don't repair old carousels for the money or the prestige.'

I squeeze his shoulder. 'What do you mean?'

He shakes his head. 'My father was a barrister. Even now, years after he retired, he still does consulting work for big, important cases. My brother's a solicitor, owned his own firm before he was thirty, and my mother is the head of the board of governors for one of the top schools in the country. And I'm a repairman.'

'The whole world would fall apart without repairmen.'

His eyes finally open and he turns towards me, blinking in the bright afternoon sun. He gives me a grateful smile. 'Maybe so, but according to my father, they're not meant to come from my family.'

'But you love what you do.'

'Yes, I do.' He smiles like he's completely unable to stop himself. 'I really do. Until I get into a room with my family and hear yet another chorus of "when are you going to get a proper job?" and my dad asking my brother if he couldn't possibly find a position for me at his marvellous firm, my brother patiently explaining that there's nothing quite menial enough in a tone that suggests one of those monkeys that fling their own poo at other monkeys would have a better suited skillset, and my father then loudly enquiring about the latest extension my brother's built on his mansion and how those sailing lessons for the yacht are coming along.'

'Carousels are a million times more interesting than yachts and extensions.'

'Yeah, well, whenever he introduces us to someone, he spends

171

ten minutes gushing over my brother and his achievements, and then if – and only if – the person looks at me curiously, I get a perfunctory "and this is my other son, Nathaniel," like using my three-syllable name is long enough to cover any mention of my embarrassing job.'

He turns away again and closes his eyes, and I suddenly understand why he doesn't like using his full name.

My hand tightens on his shoulder, trying to resist the temptation to touch his skin again. His tanned neck is stretched out where he's turned away from me, and my thumb brushes his collarbone, running over the indentation he let me feel in the pub the other night. I let my fingers wander back to the edge of his T-shirt and graze his bicep where skin meets sleeve, when all I really want to do is lie down beside him and give him a hug.

My knees are still pressing against his sides, and I shift closer still, looking at the red scratches covering his arms from the brambles because he wouldn't let me get near them. He hasn't shaved today because he didn't have time between going to the shop for fresh supplies, making lunch for us, feeding the birds, and packing up the bag with water and sun cream and other essentials. Who could possibly care about what he does for a living? I think repairing old carousels is pretty damn special. 'You make things better for a living. You restore joy that was lost. That's an incredible job. And you love it. How could anything be more important than that?'

'You don't know my family. My father has worked every day of his life and *hated* every hour of it, but he liked the respect that such an important job got him. To me, that's no way to live. I'm so lucky to do this job because I love it, but it's never going to make me rich. In my father's world, all he cares about is what people think of him. That's more important than being happy.'

'So you trained yourself to stop talking about your job? Every time you get excited, you force yourself to stop. And sometimes you forget, and every part of you illuminates as you talk and it's inspiring to see how happy it makes you, and then suddenly you remember and cut yourself off.'

'It's boring, Ness. No one wants to hear it.' His eyes are still closed and he's facing away again, and I wish he'd look at me and *see* how much I love hearing it.

My hand tightens on his shoulder hard enough to hurt. '*Yes*, they do. And do you have any idea how heartbreaking it is to know you think that?'

He's quiet for a while. 'My brother is the golden boy. He's never done anything he regrets or made any mistakes. He's got two perfect children, a well-behaved dog, and a huge house with a white picket fence. I'm divorced, I've got no career prospects, and to be honest, even if I did have marriage and kids in mind, my father would think they were better off being raised by actual wolves. I'm an embarrassment to them, and I only make it worse when I talk about my "job", and yes, you can hear the inverted commas when they say it.'

I can feel my nose burning and my eyes starting to fill up. 'Part of being a family is loving and supporting each other, accepting your differences, and celebrating the other people's joys and successes and commiserating when things go wrong. I can't imagine ever being bored or embarrassed by someone I loved loving something.'

'Then you're lucky to have a family who behaves like a family should. Not everyone is that fortunate.'

He still won't look at me, so I nudge his side with my knee and turn around so I can lie down on the blanket beside him.

The gingham-patterned fleece is warm against my back and it feels nice even though the sun is beating down on us. There's a strong breeze up here that makes it pleasant.

I can feel his eyes on me as I wriggle around until I'm comfortable, and when I look over at him, he smiles, and the butterflies that are almost permanently twitching their wings when I'm with him get all aflutter again.

173

'You're amazingly good at what you do, Nath. You can tell so much from such little things. You can look at something and instantly see how to make it better. If they can't appreciate that, it says far more about them than it'll ever say about you. I would be *so* proud to introduce you to anyone. My parents would love you, my friends would love you, Daph would think you're kind of dorky but that's okay because I am too. You're fun to be around, and your job is fascinating, and you're just bloody lovely.'

Maybe I shouldn't have been that forthright. I crack an eye open and risk a glance towards him, and his eyes are closed again but he's smiling so widely that it makes my embarrassment slip away. He *is* bloody lovely, and he clearly needs to hear it occasionally.

My arms are by my sides on the blanket and his left hand creeps over towards my right, his fingers brushing against mine, giving me a chance to pull away if I want to. I hook my little finger over the top of his, and he moves his over my ring finger. I turn my hand over so my palm meets his, but instead of entwining his fingers with mine in the usual way, he lifts mine one at a time and runs his thumb and forefinger up and down them. It's kind of holding hands, but dorkier somehow, and it makes me smile because it's so perfectly *Nathan*. I glance towards him and he's still got his eyes closed but he's smiling too, and we just lie there listening to the rustle of the wind, playing with each other's fingers, until his are in between mine and he's drawing mindless patterns on my palm with his thumb.

I think he's got some kind of magical hand-masseuse powers or something because I'm pretty sure I'm so relaxed I could just slide back down this hill like a puddle of Fairy Liquid, and I can't remember the last time I ever felt this peaceful. I might have drifted off for a minute with my hand in his because the call of a gull makes me realise we've been lying there for far too long, not really speaking, our fingers toying with each other's. I disentangle my hand from his and sit up to try to wrestle my ponytail back into place where it's come loose, but quickly give up and pull my hairband out altogether. Nathan sits up while I've got both hands behind my head, pulling my hair back through the band and wrapping it round.

Before I even realise what's happening, his lips touch my cheek. 'Thank you,' he whispers, his skin warm against mine. 'I've never said that to anyone before.'

I freeze as his stubble burns in the sexiest way possible and the urge to drop my ponytail, grab his face and turn my lips to meet his is overwhelming. The pull of kissing him, properly kissing him, is so strong, and I get the feeling that he wouldn't mind – he didn't seem opposed to it when we nearly kissed in the sand earlier.

I feel the heat cross his skin and thankfully he scrambles to his feet before I've had a chance to do anything other than sit there like a lemon, because I can't pluck up the courage to do it. He doesn't want a relationship, and neither do I. And in the back of my mind, I know I need to talk to him about the article. It's the sole reason I'm here, and I feel like I'm hiding something from him by not mentioning it. What if he stumbles across it online? It's possible because it's still being widely shared on Twitter. My name is on it. He'd know he's Train Man.

I can't kiss him when I haven't even told him that.

* * *

At least gravity's in our favour on the return trek. Once we get past the brambles, Nathan gets the picnic blanket out of his backpack again and folds it so it's just big enough for us both to sit on.

'What are you doing?'

'We're sliding the rest of the way.'

'On that?' I raise an eyebrow.

'If it's good enough for Aladdin ...'

175

'Aladdin had a magic carpet and a cute monkey! Oh, and a genie to save his life when he inevitably crashed!'

'We've got a picnic blanket and plenty of room to brake before we go flying off the edge and end up in the sea.' He sits down on the blanket and holds his hand out. 'Come on, do you trust me?'

The fact that he's just quoted *Aladdin* again makes me soften. It's a fact that humans are physically incapable of saying no to someone who can quote *Aladdin*.

He wriggles back on the blanket and pats the empty space between his legs, looking up at me with such a childlike grin that I can't refuse. I sit in front of him like we're on a sledge about to go down a snowy hill. But warmer. And probably more dangerous.

I glance back at him. 'You know this is never going to work, don't you?'

He grins. 'It's worth trying. When I was young, I would've tried this, and you make me feel like acting like a child again.'

I think of the daft race up the dunes today, the crisp sandwich, paddling in the sea the other day, the carousel like the ones I loved riding when I was little. He makes me feel young and carefree in a way I haven't for many years too— 'Argh!' I squeal as he leans past me to lift the bottom corners of the blanket and uses his legs to push us off.

He laughs as he wraps his legs around mine and slides his arms around my waist, holding me so I don't fall off. Instead of a zooming whiz as we go flying off down the mountain in a whoosh and finish with a cartoon plop into the sea while the picnic blanket comes floating down on our heads, we start halt-ingly inching down the sandy dune, sliding occasionally, but mostly with Nathan using his foot to push off every time we stall yet again. To be honest, it would be easier and quicker just to walk down, but I'm kind of enjoying sitting between Nathan's legs with his arms around me, so I go along with it, enjoying the way his chin is against my hair and his laughter is shaking through me too, and the way he shouts in delight and holds me tighter every time we pick up enough speed to actually slide an inch or two.

It's when he starts singing 'A Whole New World' that it really does me in. I cling on to his strong thighs and try not to double over with laughter. He carries on singing even though he's giggling too, which somehow makes it even funnier, because just when I think he can't get any more painfully adorable, he proves me wrong.

We eventually come to a stop on a flat bit before the last dune down to the grassy hills that lead back towards Pearlholme, and we're both out of breath from laughing.

He clambers to his feet and holds out a hand to pull me up, and even though it's gone so well the other times we've tried it today, I'm unable to resist sliding my hand into his and letting him pull me to my feet. And I can't help watching the flex of muscle as he bends over to shake out the sandy blanket and stuff it back into his rucksack.

He shoulders it again and looks up just in time to catch me appreciating the way his biceps move and his tanned forearms flex.

I blush and he grins like he knows exactly what I was looking at.

He nod towards the bottom of the dunes, the last patch of sand we'll have to struggle through today. 'Race ya.'

'No, you won't—'

He takes off running and I shriek and take off after him, wondering how I can possibly still be moving after doing so much exercise today. I should have been at home with my aching feet in a foot spa at least eight hours ago, and yet somehow, I still find the energy to chase him down the last bit of cliff.

He wins, of course, and stands panting at the bottom while my legs are still sinking knee-deep in sand with every step as I try to half-slip, half-slide, and mostly not fall flat on my face. Sledging down on a blanket would've been more dignified than this.

I barely have time to shout a warning before I barrel straight into him, but he catches me easily. His arms wrap around my waist and he pulls me to him and lifts me up, turning us both in a circle. I loop my arms around his neck because my heart is suddenly pounding even harder than it was from the exercise, and I feel all unsteady and overheated. And it's definitely not from the running.

'Best day ever,' he says in my ear. He's stopped turning but he's still holding me against him. 'Thanks for coming, Ness. It was amazing to share that with someone.'

I squeeze him tighter, letting my hands rub across his upper back and rest on the top of his backpack. There are so many things I want to say – I want to thank him for making me feel young and excited again, for making me not afraid to be myself. I spend most of my working life constantly afraid of making a fool of myself, but it's different with him. He makes me celebrate being a clumsy idiot because he's a clumsy idiot too, but I don't know how to word it without snogging his face off, and he doesn't want that, so I settle for a squeeze of his left shoulder instead.

'Sorry, I'm all sweaty.' He puts me down and steps back, readjusting the bag on his shoulders.

'So am I.' I grin at him. Being sweaty in the presence of hot men is not usually something to smile about. Well, unless it's a certain type of sweat caused by a certain type of activity with said hot man. Thinking about that certain type of activity and this particular hot man is doing nothing to help the pounding heart and boiling red face. 'Thank you for getting us down in one piece before we died and vultures ate our corpses.'

He laughs. 'Thank you for risking death with me.'

'Ah, it was worth it.' I glance behind me up the hill we've just slid down. 'And I can't remember the last time I said exercise was worth it, not even when I ran two whole aisles of Sainsbury's to grab the last tub of Ben & Jerry's Cookie Dough.'

He lets out a moan of desire. 'Do you think the ice cream parlour on the promenade will still be open? If you're not rushing back, I think we deserve at least one ice cream to end this day.'

'Just in case both of us are aching so much that we're unable to walk tomorrow?'

He grins. 'Exactly.'

'In that case, I think we deserve two. Just in case.'

'I'd say we've walked off the calories of at least three.'

'I love the way your mind works, Nath.'

We're both giggling as we make our way back towards Pearlholme, and despite the fact my lungs are still rattling from all the exercise, I can't remember the last time I felt this happy and at ease with myself or with someone else.

# Chapter 13

'You did *what*?' Daph says in disbelief when I talk to her the next night. 'And why does every conversation we have about this man involve me sitting here with my mouth agape in shock asking questions like that?'

I hear her shifting around and trying to get more comfortable as she settles in for some gossip.

'So, let me get this straight, you did actual outdoor pursuits with this man? Like, outside? In the fresh air? That involved walking?'

'Yep.' I feel a bit smug at how surprisingly un-achy I am today. I expected to be stiff and hurting, but other than a slight burn in my thighs from the climbing, I'm fine. Maybe exercise isn't so evil after all. 'We climbed a mountain to where this carousel he's working on was found. I know they say Everest is the world's tallest mountain, but I think they've got it wrong.'

'Bloody hell, Ness. We've been best friends for, what, fifteen years? And the furthest you've ever walked with me is to the rail replacement bus service.'

'Well, you made me promise not to find excuses not to do stuff, and I promised to throw myself into this, whatever "this" is, headfirst, or more specifically feet first into a sand dune. And it was … fun. Exhausting, but things are different with him. He makes things seem different. Even outdoor pursuits.'

'Are you sure he *is* a man, and not, like, some Clark Kent-esque Superman type? Because he's got to have some kind of super-human powers to get you to do exercise.'

'You see? Usually I'd be embarrassed by that and tell you to keep your voice down, but I'll tell Nathan that tomorrow because I know he'll laugh. And probably be overjoyed to be compared to a superhero.'

I can hear her grinning. 'So you've clicked then? Are there butterflies?'

'Oh God, we've clicked like a Rubik's Cube. A Rubik's Cube in a butterfly farm. I've never known anyone who makes me smile so much. I'm not afraid to make a fool of myself in front of him, because he's probably next to me making a fool of himself too. He's sweet and kind and an absolute gentleman, and those dimples … and his eyes. His eyes actually dance when he laughs, Daph. They change colour when he smiles. Everything feels a bit better when I'm with him. And you should hear his voice. He can do an impression of anyone instantly, he's so—' I realise I've gone off on one and rein myself in. I'll be on about his nose hair again in a minute. 'I mean, yeah, we've kind of clicked …'

She's quiet for a long moment. 'Call it best friend's intuition, but why can I hear hesitation in your voice?'

I sigh. I should've known I can't hide anything from Daph. 'Because … how can it be real?'

I expect her to tell me to stop hunting for excuses and putting up barriers, but I hear her shift again and thump a cushion. I can envision her sat on her cosy sofa leaning forward to shove it behind her back. 'What do you mean?'

'You're not on speakerphone with Zinnia lurking behind you, are you?'

'It's Sunday night, Ness. I'm at home. Gavin is in the kitchen cooking and I'm sipping a glass of lemonade and pretending it's

181

wine. Zinnia's probably busy plotting how to squeeze a microgram more Botox into her face before the working week begins.'

I laugh despite myself and then sigh because I keep feeling like I'm reading more into this than is actually there. 'He's Train Man, Daph. A random guy I've occasionally smiled at on the way to work some mornings—'

'A stranger you've had a connection with,' she interrupts. 'And now he's not a stranger and you've still got a connection with him. That's brilliant. That's what you wanted.'

'No, it isn't. I just wanted to get his phone back to him. I didn't mean for anything to happen between us.'

I hear her sit forward. '*Has* something happened between you?'

'Well, no, but … up on that mountain yesterday, we kind of held hands, and we kind of almost kissed—'

'Oh my God, there's been kissage already!'

'No! And since when do you call it kissage? That sounds like something you'd need a vet to prescribe.'

'Well, that sounds like a lot of "almosts" and "kind ofs" and not many "doing ofs" to me. You obviously like him. And you haven't seen the look on your face every morning you've come into work after he's been on the tube. You've obviously liked him for a long time.'

'But I didn't know him then. He was just a handsome guy with a nice smile. But whatever this is, it started like a romantic comedy, and that doesn't happen in real life.'

'Does it matter how it started?' I can hear the tone that she usually uses when I refuse to go on any of her proffered dates creeping into her voice. 'I know he's special because this is the first time in over two years that you've even considered speaking to a guy, let alone doing physical exertion with one, even if not in the fun way. What matters is how you feel about this guy you've met. How you met isn't important. You deserve to be happy, Ness. No matter how unhappy you were with Andrew.'

'That's the first time you haven't called him "poor Andrew".'

182

I hear her shaking her head. 'You know why I always hated that you broke up with him? Because you were brave enough to do it. Even after all that time, you were brave enough to stand up and say "this isn't working, I'm not happy" even when the rest of us had already planned your hen do. You were brave enough to prefer to be single than to stay with someone who was okay. Andrew would've married you. I'd have settled for that. You were brave enough to realise you wanted more.'

'Why have you never said any of that before?'

'Because I've been thinking about it since you left. About fate and stuff. Or maybe my hormones are just completely up the spout. I cried at an advert for a donkey sanctuary yesterday – don't mind me.'

'You're going to make me cry in a minute.'

She laughs. 'I'm just saying. You can't be brave enough to end things with Andrew and then not be brave enough to start something with someone else. It's been two years, Ness. Let yourself feel something again. Don't push him away. Even if he says he doesn't want a relationship. Even if you say you don't. Why can't you just spend time with him without overanalysing it?'

I do actually get a bit choked up because she knows me too well. I bite my lip and force a smile to the empty room. 'Never mind me, how are you, pregnant lady?'

'Fat,' she mutters. 'And too flamin' hot. And sweaty. I've got sweat in places I can't even reach. I'm constantly glistening and not in a good way.'

I laugh because Daph's done nothing but moan throughout her pregnancy but I know she's overjoyed really. I've never seen her as happy as the day she made me walk down to Boots to get a pregnancy test and then sit in the bathroom at work with her while we waited for a result.

'And work? Counting down the days until your leave starts?'

'Three weeks, twelve hours, and forty-three minutes. And no, not counting at all,' she says with a laugh. 'At least you'll be back by then to take over. Zinnia is so happy about the response your article is getting. None of mine have ever had that kind of public engagement before. She really thinks you've got something special. When I come back from maternity, I'll be fact-checking for you.'

The thought makes me feel a bit sick and I'm not sure why. I'm enjoying life in Pearlholme, with Nathan, and the idea of going back to the noisy, busy, sweaty tube trains of London, without Nathan, is not as welcome as I thought it would be. 'Are you sure I'm really the right person to write this ...'

'Of course you are,' she says with such confidence that it makes me wish I could share some of it. 'You've been desperate to write for *Maîtresse* for ages. This is the job you've always wanted.'

Have I always wanted this job? I suppose when I first started at *Maîtresse*, Daphne was the one to aspire to, the one who everyone else in the office envied. I love reading her articles and have always thought I'd love to write about the kind of things she writes about – couples who have met in strange ways or triumphed over adversity, couples who broke up and found each other twenty years later and fell in love again, ones that got away who came back, interesting people with interesting stories that make you believe in love again, but it's not exactly a lifelong dream. It would just be more interesting than fact-checking, and it pays better.

I force myself to stop overthinking it. This is a brilliant opportunity. The best I'm ever going to get. A chance to start a career that will be mine for the rest of my life, after a lifetime of struggling by on minimum-wage jobs and temp work.

Thinking about my job makes me think about Nathan and how much he loves restoring carousels. I can't imagine ever feeling like that, no matter where in the office I work. Even if I get a job equivalent to Daphne's and a matching paycheque. Even if I get respect from Zinnia and my name in print every fortnight. Will it ever make me smile the way he does when he's talking about his work?

I realise I'm smiling at the thought until Daphne snaps me back down to earth.

'Zinnia's not happy, mind.'

'Why not?' I ask, wondering if Zinnia would ever be happy with anything I do.

'She thinks you're taking too long.'

'I've only been here a week! She told me to take my time!'

'Yeah, but she thinks you're not keeping in touch because you're slacking off. She wants regular updates. Part two is due tomorrow and she expected to see it on Friday.'

'It's not my fault that she can't read a calendar. Monday is Monday. I can get it done by then. Part two is meant to be short. I'm just supposed to pave the way for these "have you seen this man?" images she wants to put all over Twitter.'

Zinnia emailed me the graphics that the art department mocked up after I left – social media shareable images with a blurry stock photo of a faceless brown-haired model and big, bold headlines reading things like 'Have you seen Train Man?' and 'Where has Train Man gone?'

'What have you got so far? Pop it over to me and I'll give it a look before you send it to her if you want.'

'Well, I've, er, thought about it … quite a lot …'

'You haven't even *started* yet? Ness!'

'I know, I know,' I mumble, feeling like a naughty school kid who's done something so bad that even the nicest teacher in the school has been forced to have a word. 'But it's disingenuous to run a campaign to find him. He's five minutes up the road.'

'Get used to it. You want to write features for *Maîtresse*, the only way you get to carry on doing that is if people read the features you've written. The best way to get them to do that is social media engagement. You need something that catches the attention of people quickly scrolling through their timelines. If you have to bend the truth a little to make something eye-catching …' She sighs. 'This whole Train Man thing is great. People will follow it until they know who he is.'

'But that's the point. *I* know who he is. He's not just Train Man now. He's more than that. He isn't just fodder for an article to further my career. He deserves better than this.'

'What does he think about it all?'

I swallow.

'You haven't told him, have you?'

'I don't know how to do it, Daph,' I say eventually. 'He's sweet and shy and he wouldn't want this. I feel like I'm exploiting him. I thought I could get to know him for a bit first without the article tainting things and then write about it afterwards. I mean, he could've turned out to be a complete git and then I'd have had to make something up anyway.'

'If you're already seeing this article as a negative thing, maybe …'

She trails off but I know what she's going to say. Maybe I'm *not* cut out for this. But I don't want to think about it because without this, what have I got? Am I going to be a fact-checker forever? I bloomin' well hope not, but there's not exactly a great scope for promotion, and moving onto actual journalism is what I want. Really, it is.

'I've been keeping up with my normal job,' I say instead. I don't add how much of a struggle it's been some days, with an intermittent Wi-Fi signal and the distraction of Nathan, who somehow seems more important than any job.

'Yes, Zinnia's also noticed you've been very close to the deadline some times. Most times, actually. She was muttering yesterday that when she says five o'clock, she doesn't mean four fifty-nine.'

'That's not fair. If she says five and I get it in by five, I've still made it.'

'It doesn't say much for your enthusiasm, Ness.'

'The Wi-Fi …'

'A good excuse for staying in hot men's pretty cottages – and oh, how I wish that was a euphemism – but not such a good excuse with Zinnia. She doesn't like you working remotely. You know what she's like. She likes everyone in the office so she can keep a beady eye on them.'

'She doesn't trust me even though I haven't yet missed a deadline, no matter how finely I've cut it.' I thunk my head back against the headboard of the hotel room bed where I'm sitting and wonder why I'm trying to defend myself. I do know what Zinnia's like. I know she doesn't appreciate deadlines being hit with minutes to spare, and I know I should have done *something* towards the article that I'm supposed to send in tomorrow. The part where I have to write a little something about the mysterious vanishing of Train Man and get the public to help me find him, published alongside his shopping list and the picture of the carousel horse and his shoe. It's an invasion of his privacy, and I know he'd hate it, and I've let myself get sidetracked by Nathan and the carousel and Ivy and the mystery carver, and had to rush through the articles waiting in my inbox every evening, sitting in Nathan's garden and looking down at the beach, watching him packing up the carousel for the day and wondering why I'm so distracted.

'I'm not trying to make you feel bad,' she says. 'I just wanted to give you a heads up about Zinnia. I'm sure she'll be fine if you send it in tomorrow morning. It doesn't have to be perfect, she just needs to know that the only thing you're working on isn't your tan.'

'I'm not working on my tan—'

There's the ding of a kitchen timer in the background and Gavin calls something, which prevents me from telling her that, far from my tan, I've spent a fair few days this week working on carousel animals with Nathan, which has been infinitely more interesting than fact-checking *or* writing articles about a gorgeous guy who doesn't know I'm supposed to be writing about him.

'That's my lovely husband telling me that my lovely dinner is about to be served,' Daph says. 'I've gotta go. But for God's sake, write *something*, Ness, and see if you can't get a few articles checked with a bit of time to spare. This is a fantastic opportunity, and—'

'I know,' I say, because I *do* know, I'm just struggling to make myself care. 'Enjoy your wonderful gourmet meal with your wonderful gourmet husband.'

'Text me when you kiss the gorgeous Nathaniel! Actually kiss him, not kind of kiss him. Even that would appease a bit of Zinnia's wrath.'

Great, I think as I hang up and sit there staring at the blank screen of my phone. Nathan's phone is still on the dressing table beside the door, ready to grab whenever he wants it. He just doesn't seem to want it. And now even my boss wants updates on us locking lips. It doesn't make it feel very organic, does it? If I kiss him now, will it be because I want to kiss him or because kissing him might temporarily stop my boss from sacking me?

I drag my laptop onto my lap and start it up, glad the Wi-Fi signal at the hotel is intermittent so I haven't got the excuse of catching up online and can just open a document and get on with the article.

Except ... what on earth am I supposed to write? If I had a longer deadline, I'd put it off for longer. Daph's right. Zinnia *is* going to kill me if this isn't in her inbox tomorrow morning. She'll definitely fire me.

### The case of the missing Train Man

*By Vanessa Berton*
*From Paula Hawkins to Agatha Christie. The mystery deepens. Where has Train Man gone?*

*He got off at a stop that wasn't his usual one and he had a suitcase with him. He must've been going somewhere because I haven't seen him since. And believe me, I've been looking. Every day on the tube, I scan the carriages and feel an unnatural sense of excitement whenever I spot a tall, dark-haired man, only to be disappointed when he turns around and is, once again, not my Train Man.*

*Train Man has disappeared from London.*

*But I still have his phone.*

*Like Columbo with boobs and (marginally) better hair, I've searched every inch of his phone, and it has given up some clues to his identity. So I'm asking for help in the disappearance of Train Man. Do you know him? Do you know a tall man with dark hair and dark twinkly eyes who gets the tube some mornings? A man who buys vegetarian food and works on carousels?*

*Yes, carousels!*

*His phone is packed with pictures of his work restoring old carousels. My favourite childhood seaside ride. Vintage merry-go-rounds that evoke memories of happy times gone by and decadent romance. I can't count the number of times I've seen the film Carousel or hummed 'If I Loved You' under my breath while doing the housework. Does Train Man know my favourite musical too?*

*I'm keeping his phone charged in case he calls, but so far, nothing. Where is he? Why hasn't he tried to find out where his phone is or get in touch with the person who's got it?*

*But modern girls don't wait around for princes to find them, do they? Not if I can find him first …*

The whole thing is a fight with a blinking cursor, every word needing to be pulled from me with pliers, and I hate every one of them because none are true. And I know that Zinnia's going to try to blow this up to even bigger viral proportions than the first part. Those shareables are going to be posted *everywhere*. I'll be surprised if she doesn't plaster them all over bus stops on Oxford Street. And what about the photo of the carousel horse? It's *his* photo and she's going to use it, because he's just a story to her. It doesn't matter what he wants. It doesn't matter that anyone who knows him could see it and recognise his work.

I run my eyes back across the lines I've just written. Why am I blaming Zinnia? I'm the one writing the article. If I care so much about him, why don't I just refuse to write another part? Because never mind a career in writing, I could kiss goodbye to my fact-checking job for doing that. And she wouldn't stop. I've been too scared to look at the number of views on part one now, but it's undoubtedly a lot more than the eighteen thousand who'd read it before I came here. Even if I refuse, she'll get someone else to write part two and three, and get models to play our roles in the happily ever after of part four. At least if I write it, I can do it carefully. I can keep Nath anonymous. I can be more vague than someone else would be.

I read over the article again. It's exactly what Zinnia wants, but I wish I'd never started this. Why did I ever mention Train Man? Why did I tell Daphne so loudly about the dropped phone? Why did I ever agree to any of this?

As I hit send, Nathan's phone rings on the dresser, and if that isn't a sign from the universe then I don't know what is. I shove my laptop aside and scramble over to reach it, hoping it'll be him. He always phones me on his phone and I always phone or text him from it too. We've never even swapped our real numbers. Pearlholme is so tiny that there's barely a space where you haven't got eyes on each other, and you can pop over to say something in less time than it would take to send a text.

'Hello, this is Nathaniel's phone,' I say using my regular greeting.

He laughs down the line. 'This is Nathaniel, who doesn't find that name as much of an insult when it comes from you.'

'It's not, Nath,' I say, my fingers tightening around the phone. 'What's up?'

I can hear the smile in his voice when he speaks again. 'I know I only saw you a couple of hours ago, but it's a gorgeous evening and I'm sitting here alone thinking about you sitting there alone and it seemed wrong not to see if you wanted to wander down

190

to The Sun & Sand and get a drink or something?

'I'd love to.' I tried to pluck up the courage to ask him the very same thing when we were cleaning up carousel horses this afternoon but I thought *he'd* be glad to have a break from *me* because we've been spending so much time together.

'Brilliant!' He sounds so excited that he may as well have just landed a drone on the moon. No one has ever sounded that happy about me going for a drink with them before.

'It's all right for you. To get ready, I've got to brave the bathroom with someone else's eyebrow pluckings left in the sink … at least, I hope it was their eyebrow pluckings.' I shudder at the thought.

'Come up here,' he says instantly. 'As you can tell, I've never plucked my eyebrows in my life.'

I giggle because his dark eyebrows are unreasonably sexy whether he plucks them or not. 'It's all right, I'll meet you at the pub, if I can avoid the unidentified but extremely unpleasant-looking stain on the bathroom mat that looks like it was last washed around the same time as Ivy's lover was carving her a carousel.'

It's not that it wouldn't be easy to nip up to the cottage for a wash and change, and to get all the sand out of my hair from the windy beach today, but I've been spending so much time there that it's getting a bit ridiculous. I've only been at the hotel for sleeping on the thin mattress and rickety bed that wobbles every time you move on it.

'My door's always open if you change your mind,' he says. 'See you around seven?'

I glance at the clock on the wall that's an hour slow because no one's changed it since March when the clocks went forward. Whether it was March this year is anyone's guess. That gives me less than quarter of an hour to get ready and brave the bathroom.

I look at the laptop abandoned on the bed. Articles to fact-check are stacking up and I'd intended to crack on with them after sending off part two. I silently apologise to my inbox. 'Seven's great. Can't wait to see you.'

I instantly slap my hand over my mouth. I can't believe I just said that. I saw him literally two hours ago. Daph would tell me off for not playing it cool. Aren't you supposed to act all aloof and nondesperate?

'I can't wait to see you either,' he says. I would've thought it was impossible to tell that someone's blushing over the phone, but I can picture the way he's looking down, probably poking at the carpet awkwardly with his toe, and imagine the lopsided dimples as he tries to stop himself smiling.

I'm smiling too as I hang up and put his phone back down on the dresser. I won't take it with me, because for as long as I've got it, I've got an excuse to keep seeing him.

I shut the lid of my laptop and slip it back into the bag. Work will just have to wait. Again.

# Chapter 14

A few days later, after doing a bit of weeding in the cottage garden, I've left Nathan reshaping the rhododendron hedge and come inside to get some work done. I've just sat down in the armchair – because the window seat is too distracting and it has very little to do with the scenery – with my laptop on my lap when my phone rings.

'Mum!' I say in surprise. She usually phones me every weekend but we only texted this weekend because I didn't want to explain what I was doing halfway up a mountain with Nathan. 'Is everything okay? I didn't expect to hear from you on a Wednesday.'

'Oh yes, fine, dear. I phoned you at work and that lovely boss of yours put me onto darling Daphne and she said you were still away in this little Pearlholme place. You're not far from us, you know?'

So Zinnia's just answered one of my personal calls at work. That's totally professional, isn't it?

'I've never heard of it, but your dad and I know that area of the coast well – we used to go there for our holidays before you were born,' Mum continues. 'We didn't realise you were still there.'

'I told you I was away for work.'

'Yes, but that was ages ago. I thought you were back in London

193

by now. What on earth are you doing up there?'

'Just some research,' I say, trying to be deliberately vague. I wasn't joking when I told Zinnia that my mum would go nuts if she got wind of the guy on the train.

In the garden, the hedge trimmer Nathan was using cuts out. I push myself up on my chair to see out of the window, and he's standing there holding up two ends of the power lead, having obviously cut through the hedge trimmer itself rather than the hedge. The expression of absolute sorrow on his face makes me have to bite my lip to stop a giggle escaping.

'Why have you gone quiet?'

'I haven't,' I say as her question snaps me back to reality. This is *exactly* why I chose the armchair and not the window seat. 'I was just about to tell you why I'm here. Just a bit of fact-checking on an old carousel,' I lie. 'Zinnia thought it would be more accurate if I came to see it in person.'

In the garden, Nath swears loudly, sending the family of sparrows that were feeding on the bird table skittering into the sky as birdseed scatters everywhere. He apologises to them and I read his lips as he asks them to come back.

'I can hear you smiling. Why are you smiling, Ness? Are you alone?'

Nathan puts down the broken trimmer and collects up some of the fallen seeds and holds them skyward for the birds, like some kind of sacrificial offering, and the grin spreads across his face as the little *dickies* carefully venture back. There's something about people who care about animals that makes them seem like inherently good people, and I like watching him out there, having a one-sided conversation with a gang of birds.

'What? Oh yes, completely alone,' I say, trying to stifle another giggle as he hangs his head in shame and shuffles across the garden to unplug the broken trimmer.

'Since when do *Maîtresse* write about carousels? I read every issue. I adore the romantic tales and those real-life love stories

194

Daphne writes.'

I thank my lucky stars that she only buys the print issue and doesn't check the website or she'd know about Train Man by now. I haven't yet worked out what I'm going to tell her by the time the physical copy comes out.

'There's a love story behind the carousel.' I force myself to look away from Nathan and concentrate on Mum. I'm on thin ice here, and I've probably told her too much already.

'Oh, how lovely.' I hear her clap her hands together. 'Do tell!'

'I haven't, er, checked enough facts yet. It's nothing important, probably just an old ghost story. I'm here to find out.' It's a terrible lie, but she'll get completely obsessed if I tell her about Nathan. 'How's "poor Andrew" this week?' I say before she can ask anything else. I hate talking about my ex with her, but it's her favourite topic of conversation, and the only thing guaranteed to steer her away from carousels and love stories.

'I don't sit on Facebook waiting for his every update, you know.' She sounds quite offended that I've asked her. 'He's just on my friends list, like people from my gardening group and my book club. If you want him back, you shouldn't have to go through me. You could just tell him you made a mistake and ...'

I don't realise I've sighed so loudly until she trails off.

'Or not. If you're happy being single and alone while your best friend has a handsome husband and a beautiful baby on the way ...'

'What's going on in Daphne's life has no bearing on mine,' I start the same old line I've said to her approximately 35,389 times in the two years since I broke up with 'poor Andrew'. 'I would rather be alone than in—'

'Hey, do you want—' Nathan shouts, the back door banging behind him as he comes in from the garden. He sees me and instantly claps a hand over his mouth. 'Sorry, I didn't realise you were on the phone,' he whispers.

'Was that a man?' I can almost hear Mum's internal radar start beeping maniacally. She's like a metal detector but the only thing she detects is men within a ten-mile radius of my ovaries.

'No,' I lie, throwing Nathan a panicked look. 'It was an … um … sea lion.'

Nathan does an impression of a sea lion on cue, and no matter how hard I try, I can't contain the giggle.

'A really crap one, obviously,' I say to Mum.

She ignores me. 'Vanessa! You're not there for work at all, are you? You're skiving off to go on a naughty holiday with your new man! Why didn't you tell me you were seeing someone?'

'I'm not—'

'Ness has got a new boyfriend!' she yells out to my father.

'He's not—'

'He's not what? New? Have you been keeping him a secret, Ness?'

'No!'

'No wonder you're not interested when I try to tell you how "poor Andrew" and his new girlfriend are getting on in Thailand.'

'It's nothing to do with—' I try to protest but I get the feeling she hasn't heard a word I've said since the sound of Nathan's voice.

'What's he like? Is he handsome?'

*No, he's bloody gorgeous.* 'He's not my—'

'How long have you been seeing him?'

'I haven't!' I say loudly, trying to break through the endless stream of questions. I'm sure I can hear her rustling the pages of a catalogue as she chooses her wedding outfit. 'It's not like that, Mum. He's not my … We're just …' I meet Nathan's eyes across the room and his mouth twitches up at one side, almost like he wants me to label it. What are we? How can I tell my mum when even I don't understand it? We're definitely not going out, but I'd feel like I was cheating on him if I kissed someone else. And even if there was any chance of that happening, I wouldn't *want* to kiss anyone else. I want to kiss him.

'… friends,' I say eventually, looking down at the grey carpet. It doesn't feel like the right description.

'Put him on,' Mum demands, proving that she's ignored everything since she heard him speak.

'I'm not putting him on!'

'I want to speak to him. I know he's there. Put him on.'

'I'm not—'

Nathan holds his hand out and scrunches his fingers, and I look between the phone and his open palm. This is asking for trouble. I know that, but I stupidly hand the phone over anyway.

He puts the phone to his ear, crosses his arm over his chest and bows like he's a prince rescuing me from a dragon. Which is not much of an unfair description when my mum gets onto certain topics, like my ex and the having of grandchildren.

Maybe it's not such a bad idea, I think as he introduces himself to her. She's got so overexcited that she's not listening to a word I say. He can reiterate that we're just friends and that will be that. There's nothing to worry about.

Even though I want to go and stand next to him and press my ear against the phone so I can hear what she's saying, because translating Nathan's one-sided answers to questions I can't hear is getting a bit worrying.

'Thirty-six,' he says.

Well, that's okay. It's normal to ask someone how old they are.

'Yes, I'm sure it's a very good age to become a father.'

'Mum!' I shriek, even though her hearing seems to have become utterly selective throughout the course of this phone call.

'Yes, my intentions are honourable,' he continues. 'No, I don't think it's appropriate to discuss our sexual activity with my future mother-in-law either. Yes, I have a clean bill of health. Yes, strong gums.'

What does she think he is, a racehorse she's assessing for breeding stock?

'No, I don't want children.'

This obviously provokes Mum's must-have-grandchild emergency response system because he holds the phone away from his ear and winces.

'Yes, one woman *can* be that shrieky,' I whisper with a bit of vindictive glee. Serves him right for thinking he can charm my mother.

His eyes widen as she keeps going and I'm struggling not to laugh at the bewildered look on his face.

'I suppose I *might* reconsider if I met the right girl,' he says, looking like words are coming out of his mouth without his permission.

'She might be.' He looks at me with a cheeky glint in his eyes and waggles his eyebrows.

I'd be lying if I said it didn't make me melt. I have no intention of having children, with or without Nathan, but I love the fact that he's willing to field this call from my mother while telling her exactly what she wants to hear. This little trail of breadcrumbs could get me *months* of freedom from hearing about 'poor Andrew' and his new girlfriend.

'Yes, she did tell me you were in Nottingham. No, I didn't know that was under two hours away in the car. Yes, it would be lovely to meet you too. Yes, there's a spare room here at the cottage, and it is lovely weather we're having. It *would* be a shame to miss it.'

'Nath! No!' I shout to try to stop him. 'No, no, no!' I frantically do the 'cut' gesture, slicing my hand across my neck again and again with reckless abandon. I run at him and try to grab the phone, but he sidesteps me easily and pushes himself up on his tiptoes so I can't reach, the tall bugger.

'Yes, that's Ness getting excited at the thought.'

'Don't you dare!' I hiss.

'Oh, that'll be lovely. See you on Saturday morning!'

As he hangs up, I sink down in the armchair and bury my head in my hands. 'Please tell me you did not invite my parents to visit.'

'I don't know what just happened.' He looks a bit shellshocked as he stares at the blank screen of the phone in his hand. 'Does your mum have some kind of hypnotic, mind-bending powers? Five minutes ago, I was a completely rational man. I don't think I invited anyone. I was making polite conversation and suddenly they're coming for the weekend.'

'The weekend? The *whole* weekend?'

'I'm sorry, I panicked. I'm not good with parents – I just want them to like me.'

'You couldn't have told me that *before* I handed over the phone?'

'I was trying to help. It didn't seem to be going very well for you.'

I go to yell at him, but as I open my mouth, it strikes me how sweet that was. He *was* trying to help. He was actually lovely to my mum during that conversation, polite and patient, no matter the inappropriate questions she asked him, and none of it seemed false. Unlike 'poor Andrew' who would put on the most cringe-worthy, fake charm when talking to my mum and then slag her off as soon as her back was turned.

'Sorry,' he murmurs as he comes over and nudges my phone back into my hand. 'I didn't mean to upset you.'

I look up at him and I can't stop myself smiling at how guilty he looks. 'You haven't done anything wrong. It's my fault. I haven't coached you well enough in dealing with my mother yet. You're like Bambi learning to walk for the first time. I should've known the moment she asked to speak to you that she'd invite herself up here.'

'Maybe it's not that bad …'

'You don't know my mother, Nath. She'll have named our children by Saturday night and started building a nursery for them by Sunday. She'll probably arrive with a wedding hat and a suitcase full of Babygros.'

'Oh, come on. You said you don't see much of them.'

'I don't see much of them because my mum likes my

ex-boyfriend more than she likes me.' I tighten my ponytail with a sharp tug. 'Where are they going to stay, anyway? Charles said the hotel's full this week, and I wouldn't want to inflict that on them anyway.'

'Here. Like I said, there's a spare bedroom.'

'Here with you? Alone? They don't even know you, Nath. Isn't that a bit weird?'

'Not if you stay too.'

'Here?'

'No, on a raft in the sea with only a sea lion for company, a crap one obviously. That'll teach you for making fun of my sea lion impressions.' His eyes flash with mischief. 'Of course here, Ness.'

'You only have two small bedrooms. I'm not sharing a room with my parents. You haven't heard my dad's snoring yet.'

'They can have the spare room, you have my room, and I'll have the sofa.' He nods towards the three-seater sofa along the opposite wall of the room, facing the TV.

It makes something inside me turn to goo that he's willing to put himself out that much. 'You're six-foot-four, Nath. You're a lot longer than that sofa is.'

'I'll squash. Give me a couple of good thumps and I'll get in there.' He grins and then his face turns serious. 'I mean it, Ness. I want you to stay. And not just for the weekend. After your parents go, you can have the spare room and stay here.'

'Nathan, I can't ...' I say quickly, my usual impulsive reaction without giving myself a chance to think it through.

'All right, let me be honest about it. Your parents are just an excuse. I've been trying to figure out a way to ask you to stay here since the first time you walked onto the beach with an ice cream in each hand but I couldn't find a way to say it without it being weird. Every time I walk you back to the hotel, I walk away and kick myself for not just coming out with it. I've got an empty room and a good Wi-Fi signal, comfortable beds, a clean bathroom, and a fantastic view. And the garden to do for the PPP – how are you supposed to help with that if you're all the way down in the hotel?'

He sounds so confident that it makes me smile and my nerves diminish. Instinctively, I want to make an excuse and run away, but I force myself to stop and actually listen to him, because there's something about Nathan that makes all my old excuses seem like exactly that.

The cottage is gorgeous and I hate leaving him every night. It's one of the reasons I've got so little work done. I find as many excuses as possible to spend time with him. When I'm not with him, I'm generally thinking about him, and not in the way Zinnia intended.

His eyes are glued to the carpet, and I have the overwhelming urge to throw my arms around him. I'd *love* to stay here, and I can't quite believe that he wants me to as well. 'You just want me to protect you from carousel ghosts, don't you?'

He bursts out laughing. 'Damn it. You got me. I'm terrified that Ivy's going to come and get me in the middle of the night.' He looks up, his eyes still glinting as they catch mine. 'The spare room's yours for as long as you want it. I hate thinking of you in that crappy hotel with all the zombie cows every night. And if Ivy comes howling around with her old carousel music, she'll come and get you first and your screams will be enough warning for me to get away.'

It makes me giggle as he continues.

'I'm running low on food, so why don't we do an online shop together and make sure we've got plenty of stuff in for your parents? I know we like the same things so we'll find plenty to agree on there. Go on, it'll be fun, I promise.' The intensity in his eyes takes my breath away. 'Please stay, Ness.'

No one's ever asked me to stay before. Not like that. No one's ever made me feel as wanted as Nathan does. I bite my lip as I look at him, and I'm glad I'm already sitting down because my knees suddenly feel wobbly.

'I'd love to.' I can't contain the smile that threatens to split my face in two. Usually, I'd be hunting for excuses not to even add a man as a friend on Facebook, but everything feels different with Nathan. I can't think of anything better than spending the rest of my time in Pearlholme here, with him, not having to say goodbye every night or feeling guilty for *still* being at the cottage even though I have a hotel to go to.

His face lights up and his eyes look a lighter brown than they ever have before as his crow's feet crinkle around them and the brightness of his smile somehow manages to make my smile even wider.

'Yay!' he squeaks and then clears his throat. 'Obviously I meant that as a completely dignified, manly "jolly good, thanks".' He puts on a deep voice that doesn't work at all with the unbridled joy on his face. 'I promise to make you Marmite and crisp sarnies whenever you want them.'

'Don't say that out loud in front of my mum – she'll think it's a wedding vow.'

He laughs. 'Aw, she seemed lovely.'

'Within zero-point-two of a second, she'd started interrogating you on your future fatherhood plans.'

'At least she cares,' he says with a shrug. 'I'm looking forward to meeting her. It'll be fun.'

'Last time you said that, we ended up halfway up a mountain and I'm *still* fishing sand out of my bra. This will be an unmitigated disaster, Nath. You mark my words. There's no way they can stay here.'

# Chapter 15

'Of course they can stay!' Camilla squeals the next night in The Sun & Sand, taking a seat at the edge of our table, pushing Nathan further in towards me while we wait for Charles to come back from the loo.

I groan. She was my last hope. I was thinking there might be some health and safety landlord laws about more than the allotted number of guests staying, but she's delighted by the idea of my parents visiting for the weekend.

'And I'm so glad you're staying with him too, Ness. I gave him extra girly toiletries for the bathroom as soon as I met you, and it's taken him this blimmin' long to ask you. Men are strange creatures, aren't they? You can't trust them to do anything right.' She tuts and rolls her eyes.

'And there's me been showering every night in sweet pea and rose blossom scented shower gel.' Nathan laughs. 'Smell me.'

He bares his neck and leans towards me and I'm just about to bury my nose in it when he blushes and hides his face in his hands. 'I can't believe I just said that in public.'

'Smell him in private, love,' Camilla says. 'It's much more fun that way.'

Nathan and I are both blushing by the time Charles hobbles

across the pub towards us.

'Ooh, let me tell him,' Camilla trills as he squeezes onto the bench beside me, making me shift closer to Nathan again and sandwiching us between them.

'You've lost another one, matey! Ness is leaving your awful hotel for the cottage!'

'Finally plucked up the courage to ask you, did he?' Charles says to me before giving Nathan a toothy grin. 'Good on you, lad.'

He doesn't seem in the least bit surprised.

'I feel bad for abandoning you, Charles,' I say.

'It's all right, love. The hotel's crap. I'd go and stay with him too.' He nods at Nathan and nudges me. 'Who wouldn't? Even I fancy the pants off him.' One of his hearing aid batteries chooses that moment to give up the ghost, and he shouts the last bit like *we're* the ones who can't hear *him*, attracting the attention of several elderly couples sitting at nearby tables and the Labrador on the floor.

'Me too!' Bunion Frank shouts across the pub, raising his glass in a toast.

There are strawberries paler than Nathan right now.

I can't take my eyes off him as he sinks down against the bench. His head drops onto my shoulder and he hides his face until everyone else in the pub looks away.

'Didn't you say your mum's a gardener, Ness?' Camilla says, suddenly excited. 'Do you think she'd have a look at the garden for the PPP?'

'I hope so,' Nathan says, his cheeks still red. 'What we've discovered is that I'm absolutely *not* a gardener and Ness is brilliant.'

'All I've done is a bit of weeding.'

'All I've done is scalp your rhododendron.'

'Sounds like a fun euphemism,' Charles says. 'I think about scalping my rhododendron sometimes but then I go to the bathroom and all is fine again.'

Nath's already sunken so low in his seat that the laughter nearly makes him slip out. 'Oh God, not again. I nearly died last time you two joined us for a drink.'

'At least we haven't done anything to choke the *dickies*,' I say, and it sets him off again.

'Why do I feel like I'm drunk whenever I'm with you?' he murmurs. 'I've only had two sips of a beer.'

'Ahh, young love,' Camilla says, looking at us and clasping her hands together over her heart.

'Oh, we're not …' I wave my finger between the two of us.

'Charles and I said the same thing when we first met, and look at us now.'

I do look at them as Nathan wriggles himself back upright on the bench, his warm arm pressed against mine.

It's not a bad way to be, really. Growing old and spending the rest of my life with someone isn't something I've ever really thought about, but Charles and Camilla make me want something like that. Happiness shines from them. They have such a cheeky, teasing relationship, and they never stop smiling. Every time they look at each other, their dentures make a break for freedom.

I glance up at Nathan and he smiles back at me and I'm sure he's thinking the exact same thing.

Charles and Camilla leave us eventually to go and have a gossip with their friends sitting at another table, but Nathan doesn't move any further away now we've got some extra space, so I don't either. There's something nice about sitting so close to him, feeling our arms touching, his breath against my hair whenever he turns towards me, our thighs together. The feeling that he doesn't *want* to move away.

The woman who I saw on the first day brings our chips over and leans across the table to set the bowl neatly between us. 'About time you moved up to the cottage. I don't know how you've managed nearly two weeks in that dreadful hotel. It needs a new owner because I strongly suspect the current one has been dead since 1993.'

We both burst out laughing and risk a glance towards Charles, who's deep in conversation with another bloke a few tables over. He's still shouting because of the hearing aid battery, so we can hear every word as he shares a rundown on the best brands of incontinence pads.

Which does distract a little from *how* she could possibly know I'm going to stay at the cottage. Camilla was the first person we mentioned it to. Maybe there really are peepholes installed in all the doors?

'Glad you came back here for another date,' she says. 'There's a special offer on at the moment. If you come here for five dates, you get the sixth free.'

'You have a special offer on *dates*?' Nathan's forehead screws up in confusion. 'The fruit or actual dates?'

'Actual dates, like you two are on. Generally more fun *without* the elderly village busybodies tagging along.' She nods to Charles and Camilla again. 'But yeah, we've seen you a few times now, come a couple more and you'll get a free drink and bowl of chips. Least we can do for the couple restoring the old carousel. We're in a chip war with the owner, but it'll bring in so much tourism that we can't even begrudge him that. Cheerio!'

'Chip warfare,' Nathan says when she walks away. 'Just when you think this village can't get any weirder.'

'And free dates.'

He shakes his head fondly. 'Like when you buy ten coffees and they stamp your loyalty card so you get your eleventh free. I've never heard of free dates before, but I don't go on dates so I wouldn't know. Is that a thing?'

'I don't think so. I don't go on dates either, but lots of girls in the office do. I'm sure they would've said.'

He takes a chip and blows on it, and I love that he still hasn't moved away even though the woman who works here insinuated we're a couple. My natural reaction is to put a bit of space between

206

us so people don't get the wrong idea, but if Camilla and Charles think we're a couple, it seems a safe bet to say that the rest of the village will think so too, no matter how close we sit to share a bowl of chips.

'Do you really not date?' I can't stop myself asking him. It's impossible to believe because he's so much fun, and every time I go out with him, he's like the most perfect date you could ever wish for. I'm surprised he hasn't got a queue of women following him around.

'Like I said, I'm not interested. I don't like crowded places, I don't want to go out drinking and get off my face every weekend, I'm happier curled up on the sofa with a cup of tea and Netflix. If I do end up in crowded places, I'm generally uncomfortable so I come across as unapproachable – my mates have told me so often enough. Like that's the *only* reason I don't date.'

'Why don't you?'

He sighs. 'I did once.'

'You dated at one time or you've been on one date?' I say as a joke.

'One date.'

I feel my eyes widen in surprise. 'One date in, what, the whole five years since you got divorced?'

'Yes. And thanks for sounding as shocked as my mates do when they try to set me up and I turn 'em down. How many dates have you been on?'

'Not many. A few here and there of varying degrees of awfulness before I met "poor Andrew", but none since him.'

'Exactly. I only had one degree of awfulness and it was so far past the scale of awfulness that it straddled the line between enough to put me off for life and literally the worst night I've ever had.'

'You know you can't leave that there, don't you?' I bite the end off a chip. 'You have to tell me now.'

'Yeah, I thought I might.' He gives a hesitant laugh and takes another chip. 'I never saw the point in dating because I'll never have another relationship, but I was on a friend's stag do a couple of years ago, and I had a moment of weakness, or madness, or loneliness, or all three combined with too much to drink, and I agreed to let them set me up. Which, with hindsight, was a huge mistake.'

'How come?'

'What is it about you? Why do you always manage to get me telling you things I've never told anyone before?' He rolls his eyes and nudges his elbow against mine. 'My brother chose someone eventually, a girl who'd been trying to seduce him for ages even though he's married, which *really* should have been my first clue that it wouldn't go well. And, like I said, I'm not good with crowded places, but I met her in a crammed pub, and she refused to sit outside, so I was getting more uncomfortable and nervous, and you know me when I'm nervous, right? I ramble. And I could tell that she was getting annoyed by it, but suddenly she was all over me. Like, full-on clambered onto my lap, hands in my hair and tongue down my throat. And I was thinking I was lucky to meet someone who liked me so much they couldn't keep their hands off me, and I carried on rambling just to try to stop her kissing me in this crowded pub where people were watching, and it lasted until I happened to mention that I repaired antique fairground rides for a living, and she jumped back in surprise and said, "Don't you earn loads of money like your brother?" and when I laughed at the thought, she climbed off with a noise of disgust and said, "Urgh, I *suppose* you're expecting me to pay for half of this crap meal too?" and didn't say another word to me, not so much as a thank you when I *didn't* expect her to pay half, *and* it wasn't a crap meal.'

'Wow.'

'My entire dating life summed up in one word.' He shoves another chip in his mouth. 'I think a life of designer handbags and Louboutin shoes flashed across her eyes and that would've been worth the sacrifice of dating someone as dull as me.'

I point a chip at him threateningly. 'Don't you dare say that. I nearly choke to death on laughter every time I'm with you. You're a joy to be around. You deserve someone who appreciates that. Not every date's going to be like her.'

'Nah, not interested now. I mean, I wasn't interested before – my marriage was enough to put anyone off relationships forever – but that did make me very guarded and very aware of what people *really* want and how far they'll go to get it.' He holds his hands up and smiles. 'I told you about the trust issues, see? I'm suspicious of how easy it is to say one thing but mean another.'

I gulp. Isn't that exactly what I'm doing here? I'm supposed to be writing the third part of an article that he doesn't know I'm writing, about *him*, and inventing a story about falling in love with him, and the longer time has gone on and the better I've got to know him, the harder it's got to tell him. How can I now come out and say, 'By the way, my boss thinks we have some magical connection and has sent me here to invent a story about us living happily ever after, oh and we've borrowed some pictures from your phone so we can run a national campaign to pretend to find you'? That is straight out of the rulebook for people who say one thing but mean another. He's going to hate me if he ever finds out. He's going to think my job is what I really want and that I'm using him to get it.

'Did you really just call me a joy to be around?'

I bury my face in my hands as my cheeks flare burning red. 'No, you misheard.'

'Thought I had. I think Charles's shouting has deafened me.' He lifts his arm and drops it around my shoulder, tugging me even closer in to his side. 'Thank you,' he whispers against the shell of my ear. 'You're a joy to be around too.'

My nose burns because he sounds so genuine that it makes me want to cry. No one's ever said anything like that to me before, and I lean my head back against his arm and try to get a look at his face to see if he's just being funny, but he's holding me too close and I can't pull back far enough to see his face.

The atmosphere between us is suddenly charged. Every movement feels electric. There's warmth sparkling out from where our thighs are pressed together, my elbow is against the shirt covering his ribs, his finger drifts up and down the top of my arm, lifting the sleeve of my T-shirt with every upward stroke so his fingertips are against my skin, and if I turned my head just a little bit, I could touch his jaw and pull his head down until his lips meet mine, and I can feel the want coming from him. I *know* he wouldn't object if I kissed him ...

Apart from the fact he's *just* told me how uncomfortable he is with kissing in public. I have to stop thinking about it. I should move away from him, but that's beyond my capabilities as the moment because my brain has short-circuited from how much I want to kiss him. I want to wipe that horrible date from his mind and make him realise how lucky anybody would be to have him.

I go for a swift subject change instead. 'Mainly, I love that the thing you're most offended about from that date is that she thought the meal was crap when it wasn't.'

He dissolves into laughter, his face burning hot as he rests his head against mine again. 'No, it wasn't. It was this artichoke tart thing that was really good. And I love that that bothers you as much as it bothers me.'

He's laughing so much that his arm loosens around my shoulder and I incline my head until I can meet his eyes. 'I think good, healthy, well-balanced food is one thing we'll always agree on, Nath. Coco Pops, Nutella, those cinnamon swirls from the shop here ...'

His eyes crinkle up even more and there are tears of laughter running down his cheeks. 'God, Ness, I ...'

His eyes darken and his hand slides up my jaw. He lowers his head and I lift mine, wetting my lips in anticipation, because this is it. Our first kiss and I—

'Ouch!' we both say in unison as our foreheads crash together and the sudden seriousness of the moment is lost as we both jump apart and Nathan scrambles away from me so quickly that he nearly slides off the bench.

He groans and drops his head into his hands on the table, laughing again. 'You even make a headache fun.'

I laugh too, because there's not much else you can do in this situation. Although if there was ever a choice between a kiss and a headache, I definitely wouldn't have minded kissing him. And not *just* because it's preferable to the headache.

# Chapter 16

'You're going to hate me after this.' I pinch the bridge of my nose and shake my head. 'You don't know my mum, Nathan. She'll probably arrive with an ovulation calendar and a homemade smoothie to increase your sperm count.'

'Don't worry so much. I'm prepared for anything. I'm looking forward to meeting them.'

It's Saturday morning and I'm sitting on the doorstep of the cottage, waiting for my parents to arrive, and he's standing in the doorway behind me, his knee resting against my back. I don't know if he's doing it on purpose as a gesture of moral support or if I'm just in the way, but I like it there.

'I suppose it will be nice to see them,' I say. 'I haven't seen them since I came up for the Easter weekend.'

'There you go, then. Isn't it good that I invited them up?'

'You didn't invite them. My mum used mind-altering Uri Geller powers on you. Didn't you notice all the cutlery had started to bend after her phone call?'

He nudges his knee into my back and that simple touch makes me melt.

'She thinks we're together, Nath, and she won't take no for an answer. It took her four months to accept I'd broken up with

212

"poor Andrew" and that was only after he posted a picture of him snogging his new girlfriend. Until then, she thought we were winding her up, and that it was a cover for me being pregnant, and no, I could never make sense of where she got that idea either.'

'There are worse things I could be than your boyfriend.' Another knee nudge. '*We* know we're just friends. If it makes your mum happy to believe otherwise, well, I'm not going to perpetuate it, but where's the harm? In the most respectful way possible, she seems like the kind of woman who's not going to believe owt until she's decided it's true in her own time. I'm sure she'll see after spending the weekend with us.'

'Well, don't be surprised when she asks you for a DNA swab, and if she demands a sperm sample, for God's sake, don't give her one. She's so desperate for a grandchild that she's probably got rubber gloves and a turkey baster in the car.'

'Oh my God, I love her already.'

I look up at the fondness in his voice. He doesn't know quite what a force of nature my mother is yet, but the fact he hasn't already run screaming for the hills, and actually seems genuinely pleased at the idea of my parents coming to visit is really lovely. 'Poor Andrew' used to moan for weeks if they visited, and would deliberately book overtime at work to coincide with the dates we'd arranged to drive up to Nottingham and visit them.

All thoughts of running screaming for the hills disappear as their little orange car pootles up the promenade towards us, right on time, as always. My mum is never late.

Nathan steps across me and holds out a hand to pull me up from the step, and then he's standing on the path outside the cottage, waving more enthusiastically than anyone has ever been to see my parents before.

'Oh, Ness, isn't it lovely here?' Mum bounces out of the car in a blur of pink floral dress and floppy sunhat.

'We used to come to this area of the country for our holidays when we were courting. We're wondering how we could possibly have missed such a pretty little village, and that gorgeous beach,' Dad says, shutting the driver's side door behind him and taking a deep breath of sea air. 'Good to see you, kid. The sea air's done you good. You look better than you have in ages.' He gives me a hug while Mum squeals at Nathan.

'Oh, you're just as gorgeous as you sounded on the phone! And so tall! Ness is so short that she needs to marry a tall man or she'll never reach anything from the upper shelves. And you've got such lovely dark hair. My grandchildren will be the epitome of tall, dark, and handsome.'

I go over to try to rescue him but she sweeps me up in a hug without taking her eyes off him.

'Hi, Mum. This is Nathan. He's an axe murderer and has got a freezer full of chopped-up bodies downstairs. He was planning on using them in a casserole tonight.'

'Oh, but isn't he handsome?' she says purposefully loudly.

He's blushing as he tries to shake hands with my dad but gets yanked into a bear hug instead.

'He's just a friend, Mum.'

'Well, he can be a handsome friend, can't he?' She holds my shoulders and runs her eyes up and down me. 'Your dad's right, the sea air must agree with you. You're looking all glowy and healthy. You always look so pale when you come up to see us. You're so …' She suddenly gasps. 'Glowy! You're positively glowing! People always glow when they're expecting! You're pregnant already, aren't you?'

Nathan chokes and my dad whacks him on the back.

'Oh good lord, Mum, you're obsessed. I'm not pregnant. I barely know this poor man. You haven't been here for three minutes yet, and you're already scaring him off.'

She claps a hand over her mouth. 'You're right. Men get all jittery when the "p" word is mentioned, don't they? It'll be our little secret.'

214

'I'm not pregnant,' I say as she turns to coo at a blackbird on the grass. 'Nath's just a friend. There's no physical way possible that I could be pregnant. Are you even listening?'

The blackbird's far more interesting.

'Mum,' I say loudly to get her attention. 'I haven't had sex for over two years! *Well* over!'

Of course, she chooses that moment to stop cooing, and it coincides with a lull in the conversation between Nathan and my dad, so I announce my celibacy to all of them, plus a few guests in the nearby cottages, a couple of dog walkers on the beach, and probably half the promenade too.

Nathan meets my eyes and grins and then shouts at the top of his voice. 'Me neither!'

I love him for trying to make me feel better.

Mum drops her voice and beckons me closer. 'That's not really something you want to advertise to all the world and its husband, Ness. Oh, unless he's into the demure, virginal bride thing?'

'He's not *in* to anything. At least, he probably is, but I wouldn't know because it's not like that with us. He's just a—'

'Well, you want to find out. They like it when you indulge their fetishes—'

'A cup of tea!' I squeak before she gets any further embroiled in this conversation and starts on about her and Dad's sex life *or* Nathan's fetishes or lack thereof.

'Good idea,' Nathan says quickly. 'Our landlady, Camilla, has sent up some biscuits she baked specially for your visit.' He gestures to the open door. 'Come in, I'll get the kettle on, Marilyn.'

'Call me Mum!' she trills, following him in. 'Ooh, this is a pretty door. Ness, can you grab my bag out of the boot before your dad locks the car?'

Nath meets my eyes from the hallway of the cottage and raises an eyebrow before Mum bustles him into the kitchen, and I stand on the path outside feeling like a five-foot-tall florally dressed tornado has just gone through Pearlholme.

Bless him for taking it all in his stride though. He barely knows me and he's still willing to handle my mother with good-natured enthusiasm and politeness. She's been here for less than five minutes and she's already got into his sex life and what our children will look like. God knows what kind of damage she can do in the rest of the weekend. And yet, the smile hasn't slipped from his face once.

'She just wants to see you happy,' Dad says, pulling his own bag from the back seat.

'I'm happy in London. Not dating anyone and not having children anytime in the next decade.'

'If that was true, she'd probably leave you alone a lot more.'

It is true … isn't it? I mean, I'm happy enough, my job's okay, my flat's kind of crap but the best I can afford on my wages. I like living near Daphne. I like living in the city where everything happens … don't I? I used to, but now I feel like everything happens around me while I sit in my crappy flat wishing for something better.

I question myself as I open the boot and lift out Mum's pink, flowery suitcase, which is more than large enough and heavy enough for a two-week holiday, and her … hatbox? 'Mum! Why does this look suspiciously like a wedding hat?'

She pops her head round the kitchen door and calls out from the hallway. 'Oh, I thought you asking us to stay for the weekend might be code for something and you didn't want to say in case I got overexcited. I wanted to come prepared, just in case!'

I look at Dad. 'How does she translate inviting herself to stay for a couple of days into me possibly marrying a guy I've known for two weeks? No wonder her suitcase is so heavy,' I mutter as I heft it out of the boot and drag it inside. 'She's got enough mother-of-the-bride outfits for sixty weddings in here, hasn't she?'

'She may have gone a little overboard,' Dad says. 'Which is, of course, totally out of character for your mother. She almost never

216

goes overboard about anything.'

I laugh at his sarcasm. He's always the voice of reason.

I take her suitcase upstairs and show Dad to the spare bedroom, which we've set up with fresh line-dried bedding, the windows open and the pretty daisy-patterned curtains blowing in the breeze, and a fresh vase of flowers from Camilla, and then I quickly rush back downstairs to save Nathan from Mum's clutches.

I stick my head round the kitchen door to find her doling out vitamin powder into his tea. 'Good for the sperm count!'

How long do you get for murder these days, assuming the crime is, of course, completely justified?

Nathan holds up his hands and shrugs like he's just letting her get on with it. I mouth 'I'm sorry' to him, but he grins, genuinely looking like he doesn't mind at all. It makes me smile, because I doubt many other blokes would've managed this long in my mother's company. Daphne's husband Gavin needed a stiff drink when he met her for the first time, and she only spent a few minutes with him.

I don't realise I'm just standing there smiling at Nathan until Mum shoves a plate of Camilla's shortbread biscuits into my hands. She's definitely clocked the look between us because she suddenly looks so excited she could burst. 'Take these in and we'll all have a good catch-up! I want to know everything about this gorgeous man. You've got a good one here, Ness!'

'I haven't—'

'Ooh, what lovely décor!' she shouts from the other room, completely ignoring me.

'Thanks,' I murmur to Nathan as he picks up two cups and comes to stand next to me.

'You don't have to thank me. She's great.'

'Easy to say after five minutes. I'll ask you again on Monday morning.'

'Honestly, Ness, it's—'

'Come on, you two! I saw you undressing each other with your eyes just now! No hanky-panky with your parents in the next room! Oh, unless you're ovulating! Are you ovulating, Ness?' Mum calls out.

'No, but I might be,' Nathan shouts back and I hear a peal of laughter from the next room and the deep boom of my dad's chortle.

At least my parents find him as funny as I do.

'Never mind Monday morning, give it five more minutes and you'll be hijacking their car because even your long legs aren't quick enough to get away.'

'And miss this delightful second-hand embarrassment? Not a chance. She's already been telling me what you were like as a baby. I can't wait to hear more.' He grins and gestures for me to go through the kitchen door first.

Great. Knowing my luck she's got a box of old photos in the car, and she's not afraid to use them.

Which is marginally better than ovulation calendars and fertility-boosting vitamins.

\* \* \*

'This is such a lovely place,' Mum says as we all walk down to the beach that afternoon to show them the carousel. 'It's got such a welcoming atmosphere. Everyone's so friendly.'

'Sorry, it's a bit of a mess in here. I'm only two weeks in to a six-week project.' Nathan unlocks the security fence and lifts the heavy panel aside with ease. 'But Ness has been helping me – I don't know what I'd do without her.'

He looks over their heads at me and gives me a secret smile above their line of sight, and it makes me feel all warm inside. I've been spending a lot of time down here, cleaning and sanding the wooden horses while he works on the engine and takes the organ to bits and rebuilds it, but not one part of it has felt like work. It's been fun to spend time with him, to watch him work, to rush through the articles piled up in my inbox, and ignore the one I'm meant to be writing, and come down to the beach and breathe in the sea air and just listen to him as he talks animatedly about carousel history and what his job involves and tells me about some of the previous jobs he's done. He never gets annoyed at my endless questions and theories about Ivy and her missing carver. I've thought I was more a hindrance than a help, but that little smile makes me think he might've been enjoying it too.

I don't miss the look Mum gives us both when she catches us smiling at each other again though, and Nathan quickly drops his gaze and yanks the curtain aside to let them in so clumsily that he almost pulls the whole marquee down.

My dad lets out a low whistle as he walks into the tent. 'Wow. It's been years since I saw one of these.'

'It's nowhere near finished,' Nathan says, gesturing to the mess in the tent. There's even less of a carousel skeleton now than when I first saw it – nothing but the centre pole, engine, and organ is still in place.

He's organised and methodical in his work. I've been watching as he deals with the biggest parts first, the integral workings of the carousel like the bearings and gears around the central pole, followed by the engine and the organ, leaving the metalwork and wooden parts for later on. I'm actually quite honoured that he's let me watch him, and that he's let me get involved with cleaning and sanding the horses, because he usually works alone and I get the impression he likes it that way.

My dad crouches down and rubs his hand over the freshly sanded muzzle of one of the horses, still in such good condition that the bare wood looks like it's just been carved rather than like it's been here since Victorian times. 'This isn't the missing carousel, is it?' he says with a laugh.

I can see Nathan's ears prick up. 'What?'

'Oh yes, I remember!' Mum squeaks. 'We used to hear stories about it when we went on holiday to Scarborough, didn't we?

They always said you could hear the music of a carousel playing late at night, but no one could ever find where it was coming from.'

Nathan meets my eyes across the tent, and I know we're both thinking the same thing – if the carousel was in the house on the cliff, could the music from it have been heard that far up the coast? Could it be that the legend of the carousel stretches much further than Pearlholme?

'They always used to tell ghost stories about it,' Mum says. 'Oh! Ness, you said you were investigating a ghost story. Do you think it's the same one?'

'Was it about a guy who built the carousel for the love of his life and then disappeared off the face of the earth?'

'No.' Mum shakes her head and looks at my dad. 'Let me think. It's been so many years since we heard it. It was much more macabre than that.'

'I always used to say the big seaside resorts got fed up of tourists in the summer months and told it to put them off,' Dad says.

'Oh yes, that's right,' Mum says. 'It was said to have been built as a gesture of true love, but the love wasn't true, and the man who built it had a wandering eye. After one affair too many, his wife got so fed up that she killed him and no one ever found the body, and afterwards she went completely mad and didn't know what she'd done. Apparently she carried on looking for him and sat on the carousel waiting for him to return until the day she died.'

'No, wait a minute,' Dad says. 'Didn't they used to say that she sat there lying in wait for other unfaithful men so she could chop their willies off? The carousel was supposed to be hidden in a place popular for illicit affairs, unseen by everyone except unfaithful men, and if you ever saw it, it was already too late. It was said that every time you heard the music, she'd caught another one.'

'Now *that's* a ghost story I can get behind,' Nathan says with childlike glee. 'Not everlasting true love but murder and madness and a spot of castration. Brilliant!' He claps his hands together, and I'm mesmerised by how deep his dimples are when he's smiling so wide. I can't stop smiling at him, despite the fact I much prefer the first version of the story.

'Why do I think the husbands heard one version of that story and the wives heard another?' I say.

'Why do I think the wives added that willy part onto the original story just to scare their husbands?' Nathan grins at me, his eyes shining with delight.

'They always used to say he worked as a barker for a carousel on Scarborough seafront and one day he just disappeared and was never seen again.'

'A barker for a carousel.' I look at Nath. 'Like Billy Bigelow.'

'Who's Billy Bigelow?' Dad asks. 'Not another one of these secret boyfriends you've been hiding from your mother, Ness, is he?'

Mum slaps him. 'Ness doesn't have any other boyfriends. She only has Nathan.'

'I don't have *any* boyfriends, Mum.'

Her selective hearing kicks in again. 'He's the lead character from *Carousel*. You took me to see it when we were courting, don't you remember?' she chastises Dad instead. 'It's such a lovely old thing.'

'It's brilliant, isn't it, Marilyn?' Nathan asks, and I'm glad to see he *isn't* calling her 'Mum' as she's insisted multiple times now. 'Ness and I have been talking about it a lot lately.'

He hums 'If I Loved You' and reaches out to take my mum's hand and give her a quick twirl across to my dad, leaving her fanning a hand in front of her red face.

He grins at me, like he knows full well that he's charming the socks off them both, and I grin back at him, because he is, and I like him doing it, and I like him *wanting* to do it.

After we fill them in on our version of Ivy and the missing

man and show them the hidden message carved in the panel, Mum and I leave Nathan showing my dad the intricacies of a Victorian portable steam engine as she drags me off for a walk along the beach.

'Well, he's lovely, isn't he?' She slips her sandals off and swings them in her hand, slotting her other arm through mine and pulling me closer.

'He's all right, I guess,' I say, trying to sound nonchalant because I cannot tell Mum how much I like him.

'I'm so glad you've finally found him. He's the one!'

I choke on the sea breeze. 'You've been here for less than three hours. You can't make that judgement yet. I've only known him for a couple of weeks – *I* can't make that judgement yet. Why is he the one? Because he's good breeding stock? Because I'm so short that I have to marry someone tall so our kids have a fifty-fifty shot of making it to average height? Because you fancy dark-haired grandchildren? Because he—'

'Because he makes you happy.'

'He doesn't *make* me happy. I don't rely on men for happiness. I'm happy because it's nice to be out of London and this is a pretty village to stay in, and it's been *so* long since I went to a beach …'

'You can make all the excuses you want, but mums always know these things.' She looks over at me. 'Answer me this, Vanessa. And you know I'm serious when I use your full name. Yes, this is a lovely little village and a charming place to stay, but would it be as nice if he wasn't here?'

How can I answer her? She's got a point and I know she has. No matter how lovely Pearlholme is, it would be nothing without Nathan. *He* is what's making me enjoy my time here so much.

Conveniently, the thing with my mum is that she doesn't need any answers, she just hears whatever she wants to hear anyway, and she clearly takes my silence as an affirmative and barrels on regardless.

'At least now I see why you broke up with "poor Andrew".'

The wind drags hair out of my ponytail and flaps it into my mouth and I paw it away, wondering how long she'll let me get away with ignoring that remark. Conversations about 'poor Andrew' never end well, but I'm too curious to find out where she's going with it. 'Why?'

'You knew something better was coming. You were waiting for *him*.'

'Okay, first of all, that was two years ago. I haven't known Nathan for three weeks yet. And secondly, I broke up with the hereafter forever renamed "poor Andrew" because the relationship was ... you know that saying "as dead as a doornail"? Well, it was deader than a doornail. Deader than multiple doornails, even. If anyone knows what doornails are and why they keep dying.'

'The world works in mysterious ways,' she says, sounding like a budget version of Mystic Meg.

'I don't think it ends relationships for you on the off-chance that you might meet another man somewhere down the line. Besides, have you completely missed the fact that Nathan and I are just friends?'

'Ah, but you won't always be.'

'I'm sorry, I must've missed you unpacking your crystal ball. It didn't take up too much space in the boot, did it?'

'You can be sarcastic as much as you want. You can tell yourself that I'm a silly old romantic fool. You can make all the excuses you want, Ness, but I'm not the one who hasn't stopped smiling all morning.' She gives me one of her patented no-nonsense looks. 'Am I?'

I try to force my mouth into a frown but it doesn't work. I feel like I've barely stopped smiling since I got on that train. I don't even realise I'm doing it anymore.

'And what about him, huh?' Mum nudges her elbow into my ribs where her arm is still slotted through mine. 'He's all giggly whenever he's with you. I was talking about you while you were outside this morning and he got this dreamy, drifty, faraway expression on his face. Haven't you seen the way he looks at you?'

'He's probably wondering what I did to him to make him agree to letting my crazy parents stay,' I say, even though the thought makes me feel all warm and melty inside.

Mum's selective hearing kicks in again. 'And that song. That's how Billy and Julie say "I love you".'

'What?'

'In *Carousel*. When they sing "If I Loved You", what they're really saying is that they *do* love each other.'

'Well, yeah, but outside of the *make-believe* world of film, it's just one of the most recognisable songs from the musical. It doesn't mean anything. I was humming "The Carousel Waltz" the other day; it doesn't mean I want to jump on Nathan's back and ride him like a wooden horse.'

'Now that would be a sight for sore eyes.'

I roll mine. 'You're reading way too much into this. I don't love Nathan. Him humming a song from a film we both like while he works isn't some secret way of telling me he loves me because he doesn't. He doesn't even believe in love.'

'Everyone says that until they feel it,' she says with a shrug.

She definitely talked to Daphne for too long the other day. 'Yeah well, he was humming something by Black Sabbath the other day; it doesn't mean he's going to start biting the heads off bats. He's a vegetarian for a start. That would never work ...'

'Well, I for one am glad you broke up with "poor Andrew".'

'But you *loved* "poor Andrew".'

'Yes, I did. He was a lovely person, but he wasn't *your* person. I was waiting for you to realise that for yourself instead of making all those excuses to stay with him when you weren't happy.'

I look at her in surprise but she keeps her eyes steadfastly on the cliff in the distance. 'You couldn't have told me that before? I only stayed with him as long as I did because I thought you were all seeing something that I wasn't.'

'Your love life has nothing to do with me.'

I trip over a dead starfish and nearly die of shock, and not from the starfish. 'All you do is try to influence my love life.'

'Oh, it's just a bit of harmless meddling.' She pats my arm. 'You have excuses for everything, Ness – to always stay in your comfort zone and never do anything scary. Someone has to try to break them down. Daphne tries, but—'

'I'm going to change my number at work and forbid anyone from ever patching you through to Daph ever again. Things go wrong when you two get talking.'

'You haven't made any excuses since you got here, have you?'

'Well, I …'

'It's him.' She squeals in delight. 'He brings out the goofy, embarrassing side that you always try to hide because of your fancy job.'

I snort. 'There is nothing fancy about fact-checking. And I don't try to hide anything, I just try to be a little bit more sophisticated than I would usually be because that's what Zinnia expects. And she's not the kind of woman I want to disappoint more than I do on a daily basis anyway. She's professional and stylish and put-together, and I am not.'

The selective hearing is back. 'You always tried to be something you weren't in front of "poor Andrew". But you're not afraid to be yourself with Nathan, and look how happy it's making you.'

'I reiterate: you've been here for *three* hours.'

Mum taps her nose. 'I could tell after three minutes.'

I sigh because she isn't going to listen, no matter what I say. Thankfully she moves on to one of her book club friend's hamster's health issues and leaves me thinking about what she's just said.

I never thought I'd hear Mum say a bad word about 'poor Andrew', or that she had any clue that I was often nervous around him and afraid that he'd realise things like my legs aren't naturally hair free, I bleach my upper lip, and have stretchmarks on my thighs. And the same with Zinnia. It's hard to commute through London on a summer morning and arrive the other end looking like you've just stepped out of the pages of a glossy magazine. Zinnia manages it. I step out of the tube station looking like a frazzled poodle with the wrong shade of foundation on. I sweat, my hair frizzes if the weather forecast so much as *suggests* a drop of moisture in the air, and I often have a change of clothes in my bag to try to make myself a bit more presentable.

I haven't thought about any of that stuff with Nathan.

And it does feel good.

# Chapter 17

That night, I'm sitting up in Nathan's bed with my laptop open on my knees, trying to start the third part of the article again. The dulcet tones of my dad's snoring are reverberating through the walls like a warthog with a wind problem, and all I can think about is how small the sofa downstairs looked when Nathan threw his duvet across it and promised it was comfortable, despite the fact both his legs were hanging over the arm and his head was folded at an angle that looked akin to demon possession.

I don't think anything of it when I hear the spare room door open and footsteps move across the landing. Dad's still snoring so it's probably Mum nipping to the bathroom. I think it's a little strange when the footsteps bypass the bathroom and I hear the creak of the floorboards as she goes downstairs. She's probably gone to get a glass of water. I hope she doesn't wake Nathan up. He's probably asleep by now, like everyone else. It's gone one a.m. I'd thought I was the only one still awake, and that's not really out of choice, it's because when I did try to sleep, all I did was toss and turn because I couldn't get the thought of the article out of my head, and of how angry Zinnia will be if I just don't do it.

Part three is where I'm supposed to talk about following an

anonymous tip from a reader and coming to Pearlholme, meeting him at the carousel and retelling some of the things that actually happened, culminating in telling readers that we're falling in love with each other. I look at the in-depth email from Zinnia detailing exactly what she wants, and casually mentioning that the office is feeling a bit like *Crimewatch* headquarters with messages from readers with names we should check out and possible sightings of Train Man.

*I stare at the blank screen, the cursor blinking at the top of it, taunting me with its emptiness. Once upon a time, there was a single girl who didn't want a relationship, and she stalked a single boy who didn't want a relationship halfway across the country to a perfect little village, where they didn't have a relationship. I delete it.*

*Once upon a carousel … I delete that too.*

*Can you really make a connection with a stranger on a train? Can you know if someone is 'The One' with nothing more than a glance?* I read that line aloud, feeling a bit like Carrie Bradshaw, minus the MacBook. They're too expensive when you're not on Carrie Bradshaw's budget. Carrie Bradshaw with a scratched netbook and an F key that doesn't work. It's not quite staring out the window into the streets of New York and wistfully answering all of love's greatest questions, is it?

All thoughts of Carrie Bradshaw are forgotten when I hear movement coming up the stairs again and this time, there's a knock on my door.

I push the laptop off my legs and scramble across to answer it. 'Is everything oka—'

Mum is standing there with Nathan, who looks more asleep than awake. She's got one hand bunched in the duvet, holding it around him, and one hand behind his back propelling him forwards.

'Here you go, dear, I found a stray for you.' She pushes him towards me until he hits the doorframe and bounces off, gladly padded by the duvet.

'What? He's meant to be sleeping there, Mum – there are only two bedrooms.'

'Oh, I know, Ness, but I can't sleep with that dreadful racket your father's making and I want to watch some TV. I can't with him there.' She manoeuvres him into the doorway and gives him another little push.

My mum is even smaller than I am, and the sight of this tall man being manhandled by such a tiny woman does something to me. He really doesn't look fully awake, bless him, but she's somehow managed to bundle him all the way up here and he's obviously let her. Most guys would've told her where to go in no uncertain terms.

I step aside and let him shuffle through, putting a hand on his shoulder through the duvet to guide him in. There's a pillow crease down one cheek, his hair is all smooshed forwards, and his eyes are dark and heavy-lidded.

'Thanks, Ness. Nighty night!'

'Mum …' I say quietly so as not to wake my dad, but her selective hearing has kicked in again and she's already halfway down the stairs. I stare at the empty landing like that five-foot-tall pyjama-wearing tornado has just been through again.

Nath yawns and blinks at me. 'What just happened?'

'I don't know. What just happened?'

'I don't know! I was fast asleep on the sofa and suddenly she's got hold of my hands and pulled me to my feet.' He sinks down on the edge of the bed with the duvet still held around him, even though he's fully dressed in tracksuit bottoms and a plain T-shirt. 'She's surprisingly strong for someone so small.'

'I don't think it had anything to do with watching TV. She's slept with my dad's snoring every night for fifty years and she's never watched TV at this hour in her life. She's meddling.'

He scrubs a hand over his face and looks around, his eyes falling on the laptop. 'You're working at this hour?'

'Deadline,' I mumble, hating lying about it. Even though deadline is not exactly a lie. I do have one, I just can't tell him that he's supposed to be the subject of it.

'Sorry, I won't disturb you. I'll just sit here until she goes back to bed. Give me a poke if I fall asleep and I'll go back down.'

'I know my mum – if she's gone to the trouble of getting up at one a.m. to meddle, she's going to see it through. Just stay, Nath.'

He looks up at me and squints in the glare from the bedroom light. 'Okay, I'll take the floor.'

'No, you won't.' He's still half-asleep and pliant, so I touch his shoulder and push him gently, urging him to lie down. I yank my own duvet aside and get him onto the bed with his duvet wrapped around him, surprised that he lets me manhandle him too.

'Thanks, Ness,' he mumbles, sounding asleep again already as I flick the big light off and replace it with the bedside lamp.

'This is your room, gentle giant,' I murmur.

'No one's ever called me that before.'

For some reason, it makes me smile.

I go back round to my side of the bed and sit up against the headboard, pulling my duvet over my knees and resting my laptop on them again, but my hands touch the keyboard and go still, because if I had no idea what to write before, having Nath within touching distance is doing nothing to help.

He shifts and pulls his duvet tighter over him, his back to me, and I reach out and touch his left shoulder. I don't even know why. The dark material of his T-shirt is showing over the top of the chevron-patterned duvet cover, and I can't stop myself. I slip my hand over it and just sort of hold it gently, and he does a happy sigh from deep within his chest and snuggles into the bed. His fingers come up to cover mine and he gives them a soft squeeze, and I watch the curve of his spine straighten out under the duvet as he relaxes, and his hand doesn't drop away until he falls asleep.

Usually I get fed up of my mother's meddling, but this is one time I don't mind letting her get away with it.

* * *

If I'd have thought about it, I'd have thought it might be weird to share a bed with Nathan, but luckily I didn't think about it, so I didn't worry or make excuses not to, and it turned out to be the best night's sleep I've had since I got here.

When I wake up, he's lying on his back and I've turned over to face him, and somehow my hand is still on his left shoulder.

He opens his eyes when I move and smiles at me, looking soft and sleep-tousled. 'Good morning.'

His voice has got that deep not-quite-awake rasp to it and it sends a little shiver down my spine and my fingers rub over the material of his T-shirt rather than removing my hand from his shoulder like I should do. 'Morning.'

'I didn't snore, did I?'

I shake my head.

'Drool? Fart? Other things you generally wouldn't want a guy to do in front of you?'

I pat my fingers on his shoulder. 'You were a perfect gentleman in sleep.'

'Makes up for it in wakefulness then,' he says with a laugh.

It makes me snort because I'm pretty sure we both know he's the personification of a gentleman, conscious or unconscious.

He closes his eyes. 'Why do you always touch that?'

His voice is quieter than a whisper and I'm not sure I've heard him right, but I look at my hand on his shoulder, and then up at his neck, how he turns away and refuses to look at me, just like he did at the ruin the other day.

'Because I think there's more to it than you've ever let on. You talk about it nonchalantly, but no one has *years* of physio for something that's healed and back to normal within a couple of

231

months. It must have been a traumatic injury.'

He shrugs and I feel the muscles bunch up under my hand. 'Well, yeah, but it wasn't just the shoulder. It wasn't a great time in my life. But it doesn't matter now. I got over it. It made me stronger, physically and mentally. Before, I'd spent my whole life trying to run away from my family, but it made me realise that I didn't need their approval. I was better off alone in all senses of the word.'

'They're why you ran away with the circus in the first place?' I let my fingers keep gently brushing his shoulder, hoping he might answer in his own time, like he did before.

'My father is very … academic. Like I said, both my parents had important, powerful jobs, and I was coached to follow in their footsteps, and that's just not me. I *hated* school. I hated people telling me what to do and being stuck inside all day. I hated being expected to be something I wasn't. So in my infinite wisdom as a teenager who thought he understood the world better than he actually did, I decided to prove to my father that I wasn't cut out for a career in academia by deliberately failing my GCSEs. I thought it would make him leave me alone.'

'Did it work?'

He does a soft snort. 'What do you think? 'Course it didn't. It made him go nuclear. I had to retake the exams, and he actually took time off work to stand over me and make sure I wasn't slacking off in my studies, and I couldn't take it. Having someone who unashamedly hates you breathing down your neck all day is soul crushing. The circus was in town that summer – it's one of those travelling fairs that moves to a different town every season so it's in place for a couple of months before it moves on again – and I took refuge there. He'd be driving around in his flashy car looking for me, shouting my name and showing people a picture of me like I was a missing pet. The owner of the fair had seen me a few times by that point, noticed the extra bruises after my father had inevitably caught up with me, and he let me hide.'

My fingers tighten on his shoulder so much that it might actually start hurting him, so I slide my hand across his chest to his other shoulder, trying to give him a one-armed hug with quite a bit of space and two duvets between us.

His hand comes up and covers mine. 'You don't have to worry about the shoulder. Honestly, Ness, it was five years ago – you'd never know there was anything wrong with it now.'

Instead of pushing my hand away, his fingers intertwine with mine and he holds it there. He throws his left arm wide across the pillow towards me and inclines his head, a clear invitation, and I shift over until I can rest my head on his upper arm, and his arm goes around my back and pulls me in to his side. I nestle my head against his left shoulder, and his hand comes up and strokes through my hair, flattening out the smooshed-up parts where it's been pressed against the pillow, his fingers playing in the split ends.

And it takes all I have not to let out a sob, partly because of how much he's just opened up, and partly because of how special he makes me feel. No one has ever touched me with the gentle, almost reverent touch he's got. No one has ever got me the way he does. No one has ever seen me first thing in the morning and not recoiled in horror.

I look up at him and he looks so peaceful, his eyes closed, his fingers stroking up and down my fingers where they're resting on his right shoulder, his other hand still playing in my hair. It's probably the most relaxed I've ever seen him, because he always seems to be aware of protecting himself, just slightly on edge, hiding behind the trust issues he's mentioned a few times, and I think about that remark on the way up the cliff the other day. 'You never told anyone how much pain you were in.'

He glances down at me with a raised eyebrow. 'I think you've got the same mind-bending powers your mum has got. I've never, ever told anyone any of that before, but I think you touch my shoulder and put me into a trance or something.' His eyes drift shut as he exhales slowly. 'I was broken in all the ways you can imagine. But being able to get back to work within a couple of weeks, being able to sit and paint horses and put my headphones in and blast music out loud enough to drown out my own thoughts … that carousel saved me. That's why they mean so much to me now.'

I squeeze his other shoulder again and his arm tightens around me, pulling me closer even though we've still got two duvets between us.

'The accident was my own fault. I knew health and safety regulations and I went against them. Apart from physically being able to work again, I wasn't sure I'd still have a job to go back to, but my boss was brilliant. He should have given me at least a formal warning but he let it go because he knew I'd learnt my lesson. It might sound strange but it changed my life for the better. Obviously I didn't think that at the time, but I see it now. It knocked my confidence a lot at first. I couldn't do any of the things I usually did at work. I started to hate being out in crowds. I was on a packed train once while it was still healing and I got shoved and it tore something else and put the healing back by a couple more months. I still hate crowded places.'

He's turned away and his eyes are shut again. 'I was held together by pins, bruised for months, right the way down my arm and across my chest. Every breath hurt because it moves the chest wall and that shifts the fractures. Even now, I don't like taking my shirt off because you can still see the surgery scars and my shoulder looks all weird and misshapen.'

It makes me want to rip his shirt off and tell him he's the most gorgeous man I've ever seen, and it has nothing to do with his scars. I settle for turning my head and pressing a kiss to his shoulder, letting my lips linger against his T-shirt for longer than strictly necessary.

His breath hitches and my arm automatically tightens across his chest. I let my hand drift up until I can run my finger down his jaw, urging him to turn his head towards me, and he lets me manoeuvre him, but his eyes stay shut.

'Why don't you ever open your eyes when you're talking about something that hurts you? It's like you're trying to shut old ghosts out or something,' I whisper, wondering if this'll be the one question that pushes him too far.

His eyelids lift and he looks me directly in the eyes. 'Because I've never talked to someone the way I talk to you. You touch a part of me that's been closed off for many years. You make me feel so comfortable, so unafraid to be myself, and if you believe honesty is the best policy, then I'm afraid of falling for you.'

It takes a few moments for the weight of those words to sink in, but when they do, I'm barely even aware of the huge smile creeping across my face. 'I've always been afraid of falling too, but I'm not with you.'

'Because you find me so hideously unattractive that there's no possibility you could ever like me?'

I grin and smack his chest. 'Because it doesn't seem scary with you.'

He smiles and pulls back a bit before twisting around and lowering his head, and I lift mine, not even feeling self-conscious that our first kiss will be when my hair's all matted at the back and there's a pillow crease across my cheek.

Well, maybe a bit self-conscious.

I push myself up on an elbow and his forehead rests against mine, and I wet my lips and pray that my morning breath isn't too bad. This kissing in the morning thing is *nothing* like it is in the movies, when people wake up looking perfect with a full face of make-up and minty-fresh teeth.

He breathes a contented sigh as his lips lower to mine, and I've gone from relaxed in his arms to my heart hammering at ninety miles per hour, and I can feel the scratch of his stubble, the warmth of his breath, the heat coming from his lips as they're just a breath away from mine …

235

'Coo-ee! Only me!' Mum opens the door without knocking and we jump apart like naughty schoolchildren.

I drop my head back against Nathan's arm and sigh in frustration, my heart thumping with adrenaline from the shock of my mum walking in rather than from the prospect of kissing Nathan, which seems increasingly destined not to happen. 'Mum!'

'What? I heard voices – you were obviously awake.'

'We could have been having sex for all you knew!'

'I heard voices, not moaning. Besides, Daphne said it's been so long for Ness that the creaking would've been audible. How about you, Nathan?'

He gives her his most charming smile. 'It had been a while for me until I ravished your daughter last night. Many ravishings, actually. Probably won't be able to walk straight this morning.'

'Nath!' I protest, wondering which one of them is worse.

Most mums would probably be embarrassed by this, but mine nods approvingly. 'Good good. Have you checked your cycle, Ness? Are you ovulating? I must pop out and buy a pregnancy test, just in case!'

I throw a pillow at her and she giggles, already backing out the door. 'I only came up to say breakfast's ready. You get back to whatever you were doing!'

I don't think there's much chance of that, unfortunately. My sixty-eight-year-old mum bursting in mid-kiss kills the atmosphere a bit.

'Sorry.' I bury my face in Nathan's shoulder when I'm certain she's out of earshot, having conveniently left the door wide open so picking up where we left off is out of the question.

'Don't worry, she's great. I wish I had a mum like her.'

'What's your mum like?'

He closes his eyes again and he's quiet for so long that I think he might be trying to go back to sleep and ignore me.

'Cold,' he says eventually.

'That's an interesting choice of words,' I murmur, mainly

because of how long it took him to settle on that one.

'She's … a professional.' His voice is low and right next to my ear. 'When she was married to my dad, she walked a strange line between trophy wife and her massively successful school governor job. She was all about never doing anything to get her designer dresses dirty, nothing that might break a nail extension or leave a pristinely styled hair out of place, and I was the kid who went looking for puddles to jump in, frogs to catch in swamps, and stagnant ponds to fall in, so we weren't exactly a match made in heaven. Now she's remarried to Alan, she's exactly the same, but when I fall in ponds these days, I don't rely on her to clean me up.'

'Do you fall in a lot of ponds?' I say with a giggle.

'A surprising amount. It's an unexpected hazard of adult life.' He laughs too. 'I think your mum's just about adopted me anyway. She asked if there was any laundry she could do for me yesterday, then she tried to mend the holes in my work dungarees, and she's obviously made us breakfast this morning.'

'She's probably caught sight of the Coco Pops in the cupboard and started worrying they might affect your fertility.'

He laughs but I want him to keep talking. 'So that's who Alan is.'

'Yeah, and I admire your restraint in not asking before now. And no, we don't get on. She divorced my father a few years ago and basically married a younger version three months later.'

'Do you still see much of your parents?'

'Yeah, of course, they're my parents. I don't hold anything against them. I see them at family gatherings and stuff. Christmas, birthdays, weddings, funerals, the usual. Mum sends a round-robin email once a month listing all their achievements. But I'm under no illusions. Their love is conditional and I don't meet their requirements.'

The words hit me like a punch in the gut. No child should ever feel like that, and I'm suddenly incredibly grateful for my

237

meddling, interfering, frustrating mum who's got nothing but good intentions really. My mum, who keeps a copy of every issue of *Maîtresse* just because I work there, who constantly nags on the phone to see if I'm eating right, drinking enough water, and getting enough sleep, who phones to see if I'm okay every time she sees something bad about London on the news, who I should appreciate much more than I currently let her know I do.

He suddenly jumps upright and bolts from the bed. 'Sorry, I shouldn't have said all that.'

His feet tangle in the duvet and he stumbles into the wall. 'Breakfast! Our bathroom will be getting cold! Er ... did I say that the wrong way round?'

He chucks the duvet back towards the bed but I dodge it and scramble after him. 'Wait!'

I'm not that coordinated first thing in the morning, so I fall into him and end up crashing us both against the wall, but I get my arms around him and pull him tight to me, no duvets between us now, only old holey pyjamas. Which, really, would've been a bit sexier if I'd have known I'd be sharing a bed with a gorgeous man.

I wasn't sure how he'd react to being forcibly hugged, but I had to do it because it's not right for someone to talk so openly about something that's clearly affected him so much, and *not* have a hug afterwards, but his arms come up and wrap around me too.

'What's this for?' he murmurs, his chin resting on the top of my head.

'Because *no one* should ever, ever feel like that, Nath. You do a job that makes you happy. Nothing else should matter.'

'I didn't say any of that because I want you to feel sorry for me. For some reason, I just want you to understand why I'm like I am, and I've never felt like that before.'

I squeeze him impossibly tighter, trying to find the words to tell him how much that little bit of trust in me means, but Mum yells from downstairs about breakfast getting cold, and I reluctantly pull away, and watch as he disappears into the depths of the landing. I wish I had the courage to say what's in my head. *I think you're quite possibly the best person I've ever met.* If you were the hero in a romantic movie, I'd laugh at how unrealistic you were. Me and Daph would poke fun because men like you don't actually exist, and yet, here you are, standing right in front of me.

# Chapter 18

As with most things, Mum gets overexcited about Pearlholme's gardening competition, and she drags me outside to have a look, sending a flurry of birds scattering from the feeding table.

The shell Nathan picked up for me on the beach is sitting in the centre of the garden picnic table, and I explain my idea of using it as inspiration and digging Camilla's flower patch into a circular shell shape and planting flowers in rounded lines of pink and white to recreate the pattern. Nathan's going to cut the hedge into a wave shape, and we're going to fill the edge borders with blue flowers to represent the sea. He's even suggested laying something beige across the grass to make it look like sand, but neither of us have come up with what to use yet.

'I know exactly what flowers you need!' Mum squeals. 'Garden Pinks in white and pink, and blue petunias, and meconopsis poppies! You get your dad and your boyfriend; I'll get the car! The garden centre awaits!'

'He's not my—'

'Yes, I was there when you were conceived, he's definitely your dad!'

'I didn't mean him, Mum,' I say, knowing she knows full well who I meant and what he isn't.

'Oh, joy,' Dad says when I find him trying to hide in the broom cupboard. 'An afternoon at the garden centre, where every other person in the universe will have also chosen to spend their sunny summer Sunday.'

'Nice alliteration,' Nath says, actually looking thrilled at the idea of going out with my parents.

'At least if we all go, we triple our chances of finding your mother again. Last time we got near a garden centre on a weekend, she was MIA until the Wednesday.'

Nathan laughs like he thinks Dad's joking. He really doesn't know my mum well enough.

* * *

'Don't forget I'm cooking tonight,' Mum says when we get in. 'I thought it'd be nice if we all sat down and had a meal together. Camilla's given me a lovely recipe for a pasta bake that I can't wait to try.'

'When have you spoken to Camilla?'

'I was out and about exploring the village while you two lazybones were still in bed this morning.' Mum waggles her eyebrows at the implied suggestion. 'I had a lovely chat with her and Charles, and that darling woman who works in the shop, and the lady from the pub. They were very *informative*.'

Three guesses what they were informative about. I get the feeling she's got an hour-by-hour spreadsheet of mine and Nathan's movements in the past two weeks. He catches my eyes across the hallway and raises both eyebrows and it makes me grin because he's clearly thinking the same thing.

Nathan and I unload the plants from the car, while Dad settles himself in front of the Sunday afternoon sport on the telly, and Mum commandeers the kitchen and shoos us all out.

It's gone six p.m. before she lets us back in and the place smells of herbs and spices, the sink is piled high with saucepans, and there's veggie sausages in a tomato sauce bubbling away in the oven, the cheese on top just starting to brown off.

'Now you sit there.' Mum physically manhandles Nath into a chair at the four-seater kitchen table and pushes me down opposite him. She lights a candle between us and opens a bottle of wine, filling two glasses to the brim and setting them in front of us, before she starts dishing up.

Just as she puts the second plate down, my dad appears at the bottom of the stairs, looking smartly dressed. 'Ready?' He asks Mum.

I look at him in confusion. 'Ready for what?'

'We're off to the pub with Charles and Camilla,' Mum says. 'Oh, if my book club friends could hear me saying that, they'd wet themselves. When we get home, I might not tell them it wasn't the real Charles and Camilla just for a giggle.'

'But I thought you were cooking for all of us?'

'No, dear. Camilla invited us this morning, didn't I tell you?' She tries to do the exaggerated wink thing like this is a secret we're in on together.

'No, *mother dearest*, you didn't. As you know because you've spent all afternoon saying how nice it will be for the *four* of us to sit down together and have a family meal.'

The selective hearing kicks in again as Mum whips off her apron. 'Cheerio! There's plenty more if you want seconds. And I've hidden ice cream in the freezer for afters. Why don't you two polish off this wine and have an early night? Don't wait up for us old fogies!'

She flips the kitchen light off, leaving us with only the flame of the candle, and within a matter of seconds, they've disappeared out the door and down the street.

'What just happened?' I say, feeling the tailwind of that passing tornado again. 'And why has this become such a common question since my mum arrived?'

'I hope they're well up on bladder functions. If they're not, they soon will be,' Nath says, making me laugh. 'Do you think she's spent all afternoon planning that?'

'Like a military operation. She would put actual military commanders to shame.'

'We wouldn't want to ruin her planning, would we? Cheers.' His eyes are twinkling in the candlelight as he smiles. 'Here's to meddling mums.'

'Cheers.' We clink glasses and start eating. 'And you can complain about the meddling, you know. I love her to death but she gets a bit much sometimes.'

He laughs. 'I don't mind. I've never had anyone who wanted to meddle in my life. I'm quite happy to sit back and let her get on with it.'

I bite my lip as I watch him shovelling pasta into his mouth. 'You're so good with her. I mean, you let her manhandle you and push you around as much as she wants. I was with "poor Andrew" for three years and he barely allowed her to shake his hand. On special occasions, she wrangled a one-sided hug out of him while he stood there like a statue questioning where his life had gone so wrong.'

'Are you kidding? Oh, bless her. It's not like she's doing any harm, is it? She's made me feel all special now, like I'm worthy of manhandling.'

'Even when she drags you out of bed at one in the morning?'

'Well, sharing a bed with you didn't turn out to be the *worst* way I've spent a Saturday night.' He grins. 'Seriously, Ness, I love her. When this is over ...' He suddenly stops and looks at the table and I watch his Adam's apple bob as he swallows.

And I can see the dread on his face because I feel it too. I don't want this to be over. This holiday, this visit to Pearlholme, this carousel, this ... whatever this is with Nathan. I don't know how to go back to real life after this.

'When this is over and we're both back in London, we'll still be ... friends, right?' he finishes the sentence.

'Of course. I can't imagine …' *ever letting you go.*

'Me neither,' he says, like he knows exactly what I'm thinking. He shakes his head. 'We have to be because I can't never see your mum again. Especially when she cooks like this. This is *goo-ood.*'

'She's an amazing cook. She'd probably kill me if she saw the kind of food in my fridge.'

'She must have gone through the kitchen here thinking we were a pair of barbarians. Crisps, Marmite, peanut butter.'

'At least the Marmite and the peanut butter don't go together.'

'Yes they do.'

'Oh come on, you're having a laugh now. I trusted you on the Marmite and crisp sandwich thing but …'

'Marmite and peanut butter on toast. It's good, I promise. I'll make you breakfast after your parents leave and prove it. Your mum might kill me if she catches me feeding you such uncivilised recipes.'

'To be honest, you're male and you're within a five-mile radius of my uterus. She's probably taken out an insurance policy to make sure you don't get damaged. She's definitely not going to kill you.'

He laughs until he almost chokes on his pasta. When he looks up at me, his eyes are watering and the shadow of the candle flame flickers across his face. Like he can tell exactly what I'm thinking, he grins. 'This is a bit too formal for me. What d'ya say we relocate to the sofa and see what mindless rubbish is on TV on a Sunday evening?'

'I was hoping you were going to say that.'

He beams. 'And you wonder why we get on so well.'

I turn the light on in the living room and he blows out the candle as we take our wine glasses and bowls through and sit on the squishy sofa.

'So what do you think of this new version of our ghost story?' I say, pulling my legs up underneath me and turning towards him as I take another bite of pasta.

'Ghost stories don't get much better than that kind of vengeful murder and mayhem, do they? I can imagine kids sitting around campfires with torches under their chins.' He puts on the voice of Freddy Krueger. 'Stay faithful or dear old ghostly Ivy lies in wait to chop your willy off.' He laughs and shakes his head. 'I love it but I don't believe a word.'

I look up in surprise. 'Really? I thought you'd be all over that.'

'Nah, you don't spend all those years building a carousel full of so much love and attention to detail if you're constantly looking around for the next affair. That wasn't carved by a guy on the lookout for a quick thrill. He loved Ivy, and nothing will ever convince me otherwise.' He gives me a cheeky wink. 'Or maybe you're just turning me into a sad old romantic, Ness.'

I smile at the thought.

'Just goes to show you can never trust a ghost story though. I guarantee that you could go to any other town up and down this coastline and they'd have a different version to tell.'

He's surely got a point there. So far we've heard two stories from two different places and neither version could be more different.

'I also have this weird theory that it might not be such a ghost story after all,' he says quietly, sounding cautious.

I narrow my eyes at him.

'Think about it, right? I don't know how old Ivy was when he built the carousel for her, but people married young in those days and Camilla said something about Ivy having lots of suitors but choosing to wait for him. Chances are, she was only twenty or thereabouts at the turn of the century. She could easily have lived another fifty-odd years, until roughly the 1950s. Camilla must have been born in the 1940s. So …'

'When she says she heard ghostly carousel music as a child, you think she heard actual carousel music? Ivy was still up there in the house before it became a ruin?'

'It doesn't seem that far-fetched to me. Like your mum said,

245

people could hear this music but never knew where it came from, hence a ghost story is born.'

'That's brilliant! That makes it so much more real.'

'Right?' His whole face lights up. 'I could be completely wrong. I have no evidence, although I think the carousel has enough wear to have been in use for about that long. It just makes more logical sense than a 120-year-old ghost story. It had to originate somewhere.'

'I love that you've been giving this so much thought,' I say, because I have no doubt he's completely right.

'I want to know. And not just because I need a history of the carousel for work records. I want to know why someone goes to so much effort to show their love only to disappear afterwards. I want to know if something did happen to prevent him coming back or if he just threw it all away for something better. I want to believe that love existed back then, that it's our modern world that's somehow spoilt it, not that it's always been a myth. I want to believe that the carousel maker really did love Ivy *that* much. If anything can make you believe in love again, it's old ghost stories.' He stretches and leans over to put his empty plate on the coffee table and his T-shirt rides up just enough to show a hint of skin, and it takes all I have not to reach out and touch it.

He glances at me as he sits back and pulls his top down self-consciously like he knows exactly what I was looking at. 'Never mind all that, did your mum say something about ice cream?'

* * *

'I am never eating again.' He folds his arms behind his head and leans back on the sofa. 'Unless your mum makes breakfast in the morning, then I could be persuaded.'

I'd forgotten how much I'd missed my mum's cooking, and watching Nathan enjoy it so much has made me realise how lucky I am. Mum's getting a massive hug when she comes in tonight, despite the meddling, and I'm going to start coming up to see them more often. I didn't realise how much I miss them until I realised I'll actually be sad to see them go home tomorrow, and that's something I never would have imagined forty-eight hours ago.

'I know she bought us Ben & Jerry's and cooked us an amazing pasta bake but do you want to play your mum at her own game?'

'What did you have in mind?' I feel an eyebrow quirk up. I'm already on board, no matter what he suggests.

'I'm too bloated to move, you'll have to come to me.' He pats the space beside him and I lie back too, my arm pressed against his, our thighs touching.

'When they come in, why don't we lie here and pretend to have fallen asleep together? Let them walk in and find us. Let your mum think that plying us with ice cream and wine was successful.'

I love the way his mind works. 'I think we might have to get a bit closer than this.'

He grins, his dark eyes glinting with mischief. 'Yeah, I think we might too.'

'Well, she is very meddling, isn't she? She deserves to be meddled with for a change …'

'A taste of her own medicine.'

'Or village gossip for tomorrow morning.'

He shrugs. 'Half the village think we're together anyway. I don't care if we add a bit more fuel to their fire, do you?'

I grin at him. 'Not at all.'

He lies back so he's in the corner of the wide sofa and pulls his long legs up, caging me in, and I stretch out along his side. I nestle my head against his chest and slide my arm under his back. His arm drops around my shoulder and pulls me tighter against his side, and his chin comes to rest on my head.

His body is warm and he smells ridiculously sexy, that peppery coconut aftershave again, and I let out a deep breath and relax against him.

'And just pretend to be asleep when they come in?'

He nods silently against my hair.

'She'll love that.'

'Mmm.' He does that happy sigh thing again and snuggles further down into the cushions, holding me even tighter against him. I think she might not be the only one.

'Don't think she won't come over and lift your eyelids to make sure you really are asleep. She has no concept of personal space.'

He laughs and it reverberates through me as well, making me smile against his chest.

I should probably get up and sit normally until they come back. Now we've tested the position, we can just dive back into it when we need to, but I glance up at him and his eyes are closed. He looks so relaxed, and I watch the smile spread across his face when he feels me looking at him.

'What?' he murmurs.

'Just thinking we should get up and only reassume the position when we hear them at the door. They might not be back for ages yet.'

'Yeah, we should.' Instead of making any attempt to move, his arm tightens around me, holding me closer and he nudges his knee underneath mine. 'But if we do, we might not get back into position quickly enough, and they'll never believe we've fallen asleep together if we're all red and puffing and sweaty in the rush to get back into place in time.'

'They might be even happier to come in and find us all red and sweaty and puffing with exertion, but I doubt sleeping will be their first assumption.'

I love how red his cheeks go.

Instead of moving, I make up excuses for all the reasons he's right and we should definitely stay cuddled up here for the foreseeable future. Daphne would think I'd been replaced by a pod person if she could see me now. Usually I only think up excuses to avoid meeting men, now I'm doing everything in my power to persuade myself that convincing my mum I'm having a relationship with this man who I'm not having a relationship with is a good plan. That sentence doesn't even make sense to me, and yet, I can't remember the last time I was happier than I am now.

I've never understood the term 'falling' when it comes to love before. I'd thought I was in love with 'poor Andrew' at first, but there was definitely no falling involved. I never felt the butterflies that I've felt from the first moment I saw Nath. I never felt relaxed around him like I do with Nath. I never looked for reasons to spend more time with him, and yet, I've been doing everything I can to help Nath at the carousel because I like being near him – to the point where I'm slacking off in my own job. I know I've been lax and rushed with fact-checking, and the article is a disaster. Part three is due at the end of the week and I haven't even got a first line I'm happy with yet.

But as I rest my chin on his chest and look up at him, his dark lashes resting on smiling cheeks, stubble darkening his jaw, I can't think of anything that describes it better than falling. I smile every time I look at him, I laugh whenever he opens his mouth, and every time he touches me, no matter how small the touch, I just want to cling on and hold him closer.

I've been trying to hold back because of the article, and the smiles on a train that led to it. I've tried to convince myself that he isn't special, that you can't make eye contact with a stranger, and then meet them and fall in love, but the more time I spend with him, I know it's just another excuse. He *is* special, and I am falling in love with him.

And I don't know what to do about it, because as he's mentioned tonight, this *will* end. We won't always be living in a sandy bubble in Pearlholme, and even though I know he's opened up to me, and I get the sense that he likes me too, he's never suggested we're anything more than friends.

I know above all things that I don't want to write about him. I don't want to be part of a false campaign to find him. I don't want to share personal pictures from his phone, including one of a carousel horse that clearly links back to him, because he wouldn't want that. He's shy, quiet, and private. He'd hate the idea of anyone using him like this.

And above all, I don't want to share this with anyone. Something's happened here in Pearlholme, something that's better than any romantic movie I've ever seen, and it's personal, between me and Nathan, not something I want to use to further my career, and I have no idea what to do about it, because Zinnia is not going to let me off without firing me.

'I can hear your mind whirring,' he says without opening his eyes.

*I open my mouth to tell him the truth. I talked about you in work every time you smiled at me, and when you dropped your phone, I made the mistake of telling my boss, and she thought the universe had spun on its axis to put us in the right place at the right time, and now there's this little matter of an article that thousands of people have read …*

'Tell me about your ex?' I say instead. How can I tell him? If there was ever a time, it was the evening I spoke to him on the phone, or the first day I arrived here at a push. The longer I've left it, the worse it seems.

'There isn't much to tell. It was a crappy relationship that made me very keen never to venture into one again.' His voice sends a low vibration through my chest as he speaks.

'You were married for eight years?'

He pulls his head back and looks down at me with narrowed eyes, but he's got that soft smile on his face like he knows I'm wheedling for information but he knows he's going to tell me anyway. 'I was down on the Kent coast when I had the accident. I was staying there in the week and only going home at weekends.' He lets out a long breath, closes his eyes and settles back again. 'I was only in hospital for one night, and I'd killed my phone in the fall so I couldn't get in touch with my wife. Obviously the nurses offered to call her but I knew she wouldn't answer an unrecognised number, and I thought it was best not to worry her. I thought if I just went home the next day and she saw me and knew I was okay, it would be better than making a big fuss. My boss came down to drive me home and dropped me off at our flat, and it was a Thursday afternoon. I wasn't due home until the Friday night ...'

My fingers clench in the material of his T-shirt because it doesn't take a genius to work out where this is going.

'I walked in and she was curled up on the sofa watching a film. With another guy.'

I unclench my fingers and smooth out the creases I've made in his T-shirt, using it as an excuse to keep stroking his chest even after the soft material looks like it's been freshly ironed.

'I think it would have been easier if I'd walked in on them having sex. It was how cosy and comfortable they looked that got me. It had been years since she and I had sat together and watched anything, and I'd never seen her look as happy as she did with that bloke. Turned out that every time I'd been away for work, she'd been going to stay with him or he'd been coming to our flat. It had been going on for years and I'd never had a clue.'

'What about the injury?'

'Never told her. I mean, she knew something had happened – my face was cut and bruised and there was barely an inch of me that wasn't screaming in agony. It must have shown, but she was too busy telling me how in love she was and how I must've known our marriage had been over for years and how she was only sticking with me because one day my father would kick the bucket and leave us all his lovely money.' He shakes his head. 'I've long been disinherited, but at least it explained why she was always so pushy for me to get a "real" job and reunite with my family.'

'Bloody hell,' I murmur, tightening my arms around him until

251

it gets difficult to breathe. 'I'm so sorry, Nath.'

'Like I said, the accident did me a favour in the long run. If I hadn't got home at the wrong time, how much longer would it have gone on without me knowing? It'd probably still be going on now.'

'You really didn't know?'

'Not a clue. I mean, I knew we'd been distant for a while. Most of our time together was spent on our phones, and most of our conversations revolved around when I was going to get my brother to give me a proper job so we could all be a big, happy, rich family. My hours can be unpredictable, and she worked late all the time – and I only then realised that no one does *that* much overtime – so we didn't see much of each other, but I trusted her completely. I still thought she loved me. I didn't think there would ever be a version of the world where we would split up.'

I tilt my head until I can see his face and watch the way his teeth pull his lower lip into his mouth. I can't stop myself reaching up and stroking through his hair, and the butterflies take off in my stomach again when he turns in to the touch.

I should stop, I know that, but he closes his eyes again and a blissful smile crosses his face, and I just keep letting the strands of his dark hair slide through my fingers, brushing it back, enjoying the way he seems to be enjoying it.

'You let that put you off for life?' I say eventually. 'You don't trust anyone now?'

'No. And I would never, ever make myself that vulnerable again. Love never lasts, no matter how much you think it will. When we got married, I was *so* in love. I thought we loved each other enough to overcome anything life threw at us. How would I ever know that I wasn't making the same mistake again?'

'Older and wiser now?'

He laughs. 'Definitely older, not sure about wiser. As evidenced by the fact I'm lying here in a very precarious position with you.'

'Sorry.' I pull my hand away from his hair but his eyes shoot

252

open and he reaches up and catches it, curling his fingers around mine and lifting it to his mouth to press a kiss to them, and it's a good job I'm lying down because my knees would've definitely threatened to buckle at the intensity in his eyes.

'Please don't stop,' he murmurs against my fingers. 'I was just trying to explain that I thought love was enough, but it wasn't. I can't take that risk again because it won't be next time either.'

'Yeah.' I bite my lip. 'Me neither.'

'God, we're a pair, aren't we?' He gives a thick laugh that doesn't sound remotely genuine.

I squeeze his fingers where his hand is still around mine, and when he lets go, I reach up and slide my fingers through his hair one more time and let them trail down and come to rest on his chest.

'Do you want to really get your mum going and put it underneath my T-shirt? Or would that be crossing a line?' He hesitates. 'And I've just realised that makes me sound like a creep trying to get a free grope, and I'm really not, and if I'm having to reassure you that I'm not a creep then something has gone seriously wrong in my life and I probably am a creep. Non-creeps don't have to tell people they aren't creeps.'

I dissolve into giggles at his flustered rambling. 'Well, as subject changes go …'

He laughs – for real this time – and the tension eases.

'It's a tough job but someone's got to do it,' I say, because there are really far worse places to put your hands. I lift his black T-shirt and carefully slide my hand under the hem, letting my fingers rest on his stomach, and laying my arm carefully across his lap to ensure Mum won't miss the rare sight. I can't remember the last time I had my hand under a man's T-shirt, but there's definitely been a blue moon since then. Several blue moons, probably.

It should be weird to do something so intimate with a guy I'm not dating, but it feels ridiculously natural.

'I feel like this isn't as weird as it should be,' he says, putting my thoughts into words.

The thing with his warm skin underneath my fingers is that there's a natural instinct to touch it, and I'm powerless to stop my fingertips gently brushing up and down, feeling his muscles rippling with every breath. 'This isn't weird at all,' I say, and the irony makes us both laugh, the movement making my fingers slip even further across his skin.

He stretches and exhales, letting his body relax as he melts into the sofa and lets out that sigh from deep within his chest again, the one that I've only ever heard as he was falling asleep last night.

His arm tightens around me and he reaches up to tangle his fingers in my hair like he did in bed this morning, playing with the split ends that suddenly don't seem like such a big deal in Pearlholme. Two strangers have even told me they like my hair since I got here, like it was intentional and not the best way to disguise a budget highlights disaster.

'You're making me realise how much I need to go to the gym,' he whispers, sounding groggy.

'No, you don't. You're perfect.' I suddenly realise what I've said and go bright red. I duck my head against his chest to hide my blush, even though I'm pretty sure he'll be able to feel the heat from my face through his T-shirt. 'Er, I mean …'

'Don't correct yourself just yet. Let me have that for one moment. No one's ever called me that before. Just let it linger for a bit and then correct yourself. Please.'

He might not have a six-pack, but he's muscular, solid, and gorgeous, and more importantly, kind and caring. I slot my hand around his ribs and give him a gentle squeeze. 'I'm not going to correct myself. You're perfect.'

I can't see his face but he can definitely feel mine burning. I'm never usually that honest about things and I've gone so red that probably even my fingertips are on fire and he can feel that as I go back to stroking his stomach.

Thankfully, I hear the click-clack of Mum's shoes on the road outside, and the rattle of wood as they undo the door.

'So are you.' He leans forward to press a kiss into my hair and quickly lies back down again.

It's just the adrenaline of hearing the door open, I tell myself. It doesn't mean anything. He couldn't have made it any clearer that he doesn't want a relationship, and no amount of little affectionate touches changes that.

His other arm comes up and wraps around me too, his rough fingertips resting against my upper arm in the nick of time as we hear the front door click shut and the voices of my parents in the hallway.

Thankfully, they distract me from how much I want to kiss him as I hear Mum come to a halt in the living room doorway and the 'oof' as Dad barrels straight into her. You can't think about kissing someone when every fibre of your being is focused on trying not to giggle at the ridiculousness of this situation.

My breathing is shallow and I don't realise I've forgotten to breathe through my mouth until I'm panting for breath and have to furtively part my lips without being noticed.

His toes curl against my calf and I know he's done exactly the same thing.

'Aww,' Mum whispers, elongating the word. There's a soft clap as she clasps her hands together.

I chew the inside of my cheek to stop myself laughing.

Dad grunts as she obviously elbows him. 'What did I tell you?'

I can feel the shake in Nath's chest as he tries to suppress laughter, and knowing that we're both doing the same thing makes it even funnier.

'I've never seen Ness so happy.'

It surprises me because it's Dad saying it. Mum would say anything if she thought it might lead to a grandchild, but when Dad says something, I believe him.

255

'They're such a lovely couple, aren't they? They bring out the best in each other.'

Dad murmurs his agreement, and I suddenly don't feel like laughing anymore. I can feel the extra tension in Nathan too and the way his heartbeat has sped up underneath my ear.

Mum shushes Dad as his footsteps go back into the hallway and I hear her pad across the living room carpet. She wouldn't really check we actually are asleep, would she?

All she does is turn the main light off and tiptoe back out and I feel incredibly grateful to have such lovely parents.

We don't move as we listen to the floorboards creak as they go upstairs and across the landing, one to the bedroom and one to the bathroom.

After a few minutes, Nath's fingers start drawing mindless patterns on my arm and I let mine trail up and down his ribs again.

The floorboards are old enough that you can hear almost every step from downstairs, and we can easily make out when they cross the landing again and swap places between the bathroom and bedroom.

When it seems relatively safe from either of them venturing back down, Nathan starts humming 'If I Loved You' as quietly as a breath, his mouth moving gently against my hair, as we wait until the floorboards stop creaking when they both get into bed.

It's probably fine to move anytime now, but neither of us do. After 'If I Loved You', he moves on to 'Soliloquy' and 'When the Children Are Asleep', and I know he's doing it for me because I love *Carousel*. Although if my mum catches him singing about children, being caught out in our ruse will be the least of our worries.

And I lie there enjoying his closeness, surrounded by his body heat and the fruity aftershave that reminds me of sun-warmed driftwood on tropical beaches. I love that he's silly enough to think this would work. I love knowing that if I was to try explaining this moment to Daph, she'd think I'd lost the plot more than when I put up a fight for Coco Pops being a legitimate breakfast for an adult, but it makes sense with him.

Eventually, it seems stupid just to lie here. There hasn't been a noise upstairs for ages, and even if my parents are still awake, it's quite reasonable that we'd have woken up by now. I reluctantly peel myself away from him and sit up, pushing one of his legs down so I can get my feet back on solid carpet and regain some control of this situation.

'*Are* you happy?'

I glance back at him where he's still lying against the sofa arm. 'I guess,' I say, because I don't know how to tell him that I *am* happy but I think a large part of it is to do with him. 'Everything seems a bit nicer in Pearlholme.'

He makes a noise of agreement.

'Are you? I know you like it here.'

'I don't ever want to leave. Camilla was saying her next booking has cancelled so I could have the cottage for longer if the job overruns, but ...' He swallows hard and trails off.

I can tell what he's thinking. *It's not enough.* I know he hates London, and I know he's in his element here. He wants more than an extra week or two. So do I. And I also know that Zinnia gave me three weeks and I've had two of them. I'm going to be on a train back to London by this time next week.

'It's getting late. We should head for bed.'

He groans as he stretches and I watch his body arch and then collapse back against the sofa. 'I'll stay here.'

I've still got one of his legs across my lap and I rub his navy jeans. 'You know she'll be down in a few hours to drag you upstairs again, don't you? If you could give my mum an award for anything, it would be persistence.'

'Are you asking me to share a bed with you, Miss Berton?' He puts a hand on his chest and does a scandalised gasp of mock indignation.

It makes me laugh and eases what could've been an awkward moment. 'No, but the alternative is to be dragged out of bed by a surprisingly strong pensioner and bundled up there anyway, and you didn't look like you enjoyed it much last night.'

'You make a compelling argument. One that is obviously the *only* reason for us to share a bed.'

I giggle. 'Obviously.'

'I don't know why you complain about your mum's meddling. I've enjoyed everything she's meddled in so far.' He thinks for a moment. 'Well, maybe not the sperm-count boosting vitamin powder – that tasted like something you'd put down the plughole of a blocked sink.'

I don't tell him I'm thinking exactly the same thing. Well, maybe not about the sperm-boosting protein powder, but I dread the day she finds one for making ovaries more productive.

* * *

'I'm so glad you came,' I say as I hug Mum goodbye on the doorstep the next morning.

'I know, dear, quite surprising after how annoyed you were at first.'

'I wasn't—'

'I'm a meddling old fogey, Ness. I know you don't like me interfering in your life, but I just want to see you happy.' She glances at Nathan. 'And I don't think you have been until recently.'

I go to protest but she moves on to him.

'Now you will come for Christmas, won't you?' She pinches his cheeks in a move usually reserved for people under the age of five, and he doesn't even pull away.

'Mum! It's not even July yet!'

'Yes, but he's coming, aren't you, pet?' She gives him her most beseeching smile. 'I want to book him early in case he gets a better offer.'

'He's not a children's party clown, Mum. You can't arrange someone's Christmas for them—'

'Oh, Marilyn, there couldn't possibly *be* a better offer. I'd love to spend Christmas with you three.'

I'm pretty sure most blokes would be *terrified* by my mum, but Nath just hugs her and tells her she can't make him wait until Christmas to see her again, and she blushes and flaps a hand in front of her face as Dad hugs me goodbye and then they both get in the car.

I don't realise I'm crying until Nathan puts his arm around me and pulls me in to his side.

'I've never been good at goodbyes. Sorry, I know I'm a daft sod.' I sniffle and scrub my hands over my face, then paste on a smile and give them a wave as they pull out of the grassy verge beside the cottage and pootle off down the promenade. They toot as they go and some passing villagers wave, and I'm not sure if Mum's made friends with them or if people are just that friendly around here. 'Thank you for inviting them.'

'I didn't, but I don't mind taking credit for it.' He squeezes me again. 'Thank you for letting me see how parents are supposed to act. It's eye-opening.'

I look up at him but his eyes stay firmly fixed on the retreating orange car and he doesn't look like he's going to expand on it.

'So were you just telling her what she wants to hear? Because she *will* hunt you down on Christmas Eve if you don't turn up.'

'No, I'd love to.' His arm drops away from my shoulders and he kicks at the pavement. 'I just want an excuse to see you, Ness. I don't want to lose touch when we get home. We live on opposite sides of London, and we're busy. You're always up against a deadline and I'm often away for weeks at a time. I don't want to lose what we've found in Pearlholme. And I don't want to scare you off by being too honest about it—'

'I feel exactly the same way,' I say quickly before I can chicken out.

I feel better just knowing that he feels it too. Even though I'm not quite sure what *it* is. We've had a few near-miss kisses, but no actual kisses. He's still steadfast about not wanting a relationship, but I can't imagine him not being a part of my life from now on, even if that's all it is.

His eyes are lighter than usual, reflecting the grey stone under our feet, and his gaze is intense as he looks up from the pavement and a smile spreads slowly across his face. 'So we're both on the same page. You know what the answer to that is, don't you?'

'I didn't realise it was a question,' I say, knowing exactly what the cheeky glint in his dark eyes means.

'It wasn't, but the answer is always ice cream.'

It makes me laugh as he locks the front door behind us and offers me his arm, and I slot mine through it as we walk down towards the ice cream parlour on the promenade, and then lean on the blue railings and look out across the beach, the squawk of gulls overhead and the splash of waves rolling further down the sand as the tide comes in. I watch him breaking off tiny pieces of his cornet and tossing them to a seagull that's pecking around the pavement, and I think about the first time I saw him on the train, the surprise of making eye contact with another human being and the complete shock when not only did he *not* look away but he actually smiled as well. The way I nearly missed my stop because I couldn't take my eyes off his dimples.

Maybe the question of the dropped phone and coincidence and fate doesn't have an answer, just like I don't always need an excuse not to do the things I really want to do. I just need the courage to throw caution to the wind and say yes, and it's always so much more difficult to find that than an excuse to stay in my comfort zone ...

Or maybe the answer is always ice cream, which is something we will both always agree on.

# Chapter 19

'Hello, this is Nathaniel's phone,' I say a few mornings later, smiling automatically when his number comes up on the display.

'Do you know how much I've always hated being called that, and yet, I look forward to hearing it every time you answer my phone?'

As if my smile could get any wider. 'Yeah, you do know I still have your phone, right?'

'Well, since you moved into the cottage, it's not exactly a mile away, is it? I'm still enjoying the break from it. Pearlholme isn't the place for technology.'

He's absolutely right on that. 'So, what's up?' I'm unable to resist poking my head out the back door to see if I can see him at the tent, and sure enough, he's standing outside it and looking up at the cottage. I grin and wave, and I hear the smile change his voice when he sees me too.

'I'm about to have a make-or-break moment in the restoration of the carousel. I could do with my lucky charm …'

'Sure, I'll fetch it down. Where is it?' I step back inside and look around for something charm-like, wondering where he's managed to leave it.

He laughs. 'It's you, Ness.'

'Oh!' I giggle, snort, and choke at the same time, glad he wasn't here to witness such an undignified display. It's bad enough that he had to hear it.

'Sorry, that was so corny.' He sounds flustered. 'Do people even use the word corny anymore? Am I corny for saying corny?'

'That's too many "cornies" to keep up with.' I step back outside into the sunshine.

'I know you're on a deadline. I don't want to disturb you if you're working.'

I glance in through the door at my laptop on the coffee table. I expect it to start screaming in despair, if it's not too busy groaning under the weight of the unanswered emails in my inbox, but it does nothing more than blink its green Wi-Fi light at me. Even an inanimate object has recognised the sound of my deadlines whooshing past and has given up on me.

'I'd love to,' I say without a second thought.

Zinnia told me to give myself time. Daph told me to throw myself headfirst into things. Surely there's some work-related spin I could put on this, because not only have I not started the next part of the article, but I'm now behind on my fact-checking work too. If Zinnia thinks 4.59 p.m. is too late for a five o'clock deadline, she's going to *love* the story I've just started checking that was due at eight a.m yesterday morning. All those missed calls on my phone are probably Zinnia calling to say how impressed she is with my initiative. Most likely.

He whoops and I love that he doesn't hide his excitement when he's happy about something, especially when that something is me.

When I get to the promenade, I stop in the beach hut and buy us a 99 each and make my way down the sandy steps towards the carousel. Inside the tent, he's kneeling beside the engine with his forehead furrowed in concentration but he looks up when he hears me and the brightest grin spreads across his face when his eyes fall on the ice creams in my hands.

'For luck.' I hold one out to him. 'I don't think I'm very good at being a lucky charm so I thought I'd better have something else as a back-up plan.'

He gets to his feet and wipes his hands with a cloth as he comes over to take one from me. 'Thank you, and thanks for coming down. I probably shouldn't have called because I don't want you to see me fail if it goes badly, but things tend to go better when you're around so I think you must be my lucky charm.' His eyes are on the engine as he licks his ice cream. 'This is where it all could go horribly wrong. I've finished cleaning the engine and got the organ back together, and I'm just about to start it up. If either of these things fail, this job is much bigger than I anticipated and unlikely to be finished before the summer holidays.'

'It'll work. You know what you're doing.'

He meets my eyes. 'Thanks, Ness.'

There's something so deep in his eyes, darker brown than usual today, and I feel like the air is zinging between us, waiting for something to happen.

Then I misjudge a bite of my cornet and get ice cream up my nose instead.

Nath laughs. 'At least it's not just me who struggles with feeding myself.'

I decide to let him have that one. I've made enough of a wally of myself in front of Nathan that even ice cream up the nose is normal now.

We finish our ice creams and he beckons me over to where he was working. The engine is clean and shiny and all the wheels and pulleys he'd taken apart are back in place, and the organ is nearby, also back in one piece.

'Cross every crossable thing you've got and think lucky thoughts,' he says. 'I estimated the length and cost of the job based on this. If it doesn't work, I'm in trouble.'

I hold up crossed fingers on both hands, and when he crouches down by the engine, I step across and slide my hand over his left shoulder, and he tips his head down until his ear touches the back of my hand in gentle acknowledgement.

He puts his hands on the wheel and turns, slowly at first, obviously a struggle after it's been still for so long. There's a jarring screech of metal on metal until it starts to turn easier. The engine lets out a burst of steam, and after a few tense moments, starts chugging away.

He breathes a sigh of relief and we wait with bated breath for the organ to follow suit, until it finally makes a few jarring, untuned noises.

Nathan sags so much with relief that he nearly overbalances and only my legs behind him are holding him upright.

'Thanks for coming down. It would've felt wrong to start it up without you,' he says as he gets to his feet without dislodging my hand.

'I would've hated to miss such an important occasion,' I say, genuinely touched that he wanted me here. I love that he's let me get so involved in the carousel. It's something so special, and I'm humbled that he's let someone as clumsy as me anywhere near it. My hand tightens on his shoulder because I don't think he lets people into his work very often.

The organ thrums into life, that tinny, old-fashioned gramophone sound that you don't hear these days, and I recognise the music immediately. 'That's "The Carousel Waltz" from the film.'

He grins. 'Thought you'd like it.'

'Did you program that?'

'I might have.' He meets my eyes. 'I mean, not just because of *Carousel*. It's such a beautiful piece of music, a real nostalgic carousel sound; there's nothing more fitting really, is there?'

'And you thought I'd like it?' I ask, feeling flushed and shy.

He reaches up and slots his fingers between mine where they're still resting on his shoulder and nods almost imperceptibly.

It's such a soft, sweet gesture that it makes me go all weak at

264

the knees as we stand there waiting for the carousel to start turning, his hand not letting go of mine. I know he did it because he knows how much I love *Carousel*, just like he always hums 'If I Loved You' because he knows I like it.

I don't have a chance to think about it any further because slowly but surely, the bearings at the top of the central pole start to turn and the relief on Nathan's face is palpable. Even I know that the whole carousel revolves around that one thing, the bars that hold the horses up and turn to simulate the feeling of jumping are suspended from the top of it. Even the platform that riders will stand on is hung from that pole, and seeing Nath looking so relieved makes me realise how important this is to him.

'It'll be a bit more impressive when it's finished,' he whispers, like speaking in a normal voice will break the spell.

'This is impressive enough,' I say, because it feels like something magical is happening, even though all we're doing is standing in a tent on the beach watching the mechanical turning of bits of metal.

My fingers tighten around his where my hand is still on his shoulder, and his close around mine in return and he turns around without letting go. His eyes are damp and how much I want to kiss him takes my breath away. He is so raw and open, and I'm sure this is a moment he's never shared with anyone before, and I'm floored that he's letting me see such a vulnerability in him.

He lifts my other hand to his mouth and presses a kiss there, his eyes not leaving mine, as he holds one hand against his chest and uses the other to push me away, starting a waltz to the tune of the carousel.

'Nath!' I squeak. 'Only you could start waltzing to "The Carousel Waltz"!'

He grins and treads on my toes, but I realise I'm laughing as I follow his lead, the emotion of a few moments ago being replaced by joy as he's back to being the silly, uninhibited Nathan that I don't think many people ever get to see.

He's laughing as I fall against him, both of us tripping over ourselves yet again. I've always thought I had two left feet, but I think he's got at least six of them, and probably a few right feet as well, because it's like dancing with a giant spider, in the nicest way possible. If spiders were six-foot-four, gorgeous, and smelt of pink pepper and dusky coconut aftershave.

The song comes to an end and halts for a few moments while the engine continues chugging, puffing steam into the tent because the chimney to route it outside isn't fitted yet, before it finally starts up again from the beginning. His eyes fill with delight.

'We did it!' The smile on his face is obscenely wide and his arms slide around my waist and he lifts me up, holding me against his body and spinning us in a circle.

I wrap my arms around his neck and squeeze him so tightly that it must start to hurt.

'We?' I say in his ear. 'I didn't have anything to do with this. All I've done is sand a bit of paint off wooden horses. That organ terrifies me. It looks like something that would be running an evil robot factory in a horror film.'

He nuzzles his face into my neck and I can feel his smile against my skin even though he makes no move to put me down. 'Don't you understand how much difference it makes to have you here? Listening, asking questions, getting involved, helping, talking. Caring. I'm not even halfway through and this is the best job I've ever been on because of you, Ness.'

It makes my breath catch in my throat and my arms tighten around him. 'I hate that anyone's ever made you feel inferior for doing something you love,' I say against his ear.

He sets my feet back on the wooden flooring but doesn't step away, and I pull back until I can make eye contact, because he needs to hear this.

I reach up and brush my fingers through his hair. 'You're

incredible, Nath. Do you have any idea how much I've enjoyed spending time with you? Any idea how amazing your stories are? How fascinating it is to talk to you? I'm behind on my own work because I don't want to be anywhere else. Your enthusiasm has captured me. Other than loving the film, I didn't know the first thing about carousels until a couple of weeks ago. I didn't know how they worked or the stories behind them. You've made me care. You've made me interested. I will never look at a carousel the same way again because of you. How much you love your job makes me want to chuck mine in and find something I love. You're inspirational like that.'

I'm still brushing his hair back and his face has turned in to my hand as I've been speaking and his eyes are closed. 'Where have you been all my life?' His words are muffled against my palm. 'Can I keep you? Just, like, have you in my pocket all day to pop out and say nice things when I need to hear them?'

I reach my other hand out and jiggle the denim edge of the pocket of his dungarees. 'Well, you do seem to keep everything in there.'

'I mean it, Ness.' His eyes are serious when they open. 'Well, maybe not about the pocket thing, that would just be weird, but … I don't know how to go back to before I met you—'

I use my grip on his hair to pull his head down, push myself up on my tiptoes, and smash my mouth against his. No false starts. No drips of sweat, forehead clashes, or parents walking in. A kiss that I've wanted since I saw the dimples dent his cheeks on that train.

He kisses me back like a drowning man. His hands come up and cup the back of my head, his fingers tangling in my hair, fingertips brushing my skin so gently and the way he touches me makes me feel precious. The way he kisses is so careful and hesitant, like he isn't sure it's real either, and my fingers tighten in his hair, pulling him impossibly closer, letting him know I want this too, and he gets the hint. He moans against my mouth as

267

the kiss gets stronger, and my knees go weak until I'm hanging on to him and I squeak into it as his hands slide down, around my waist, under my thighs and he lifts me, our lips not leaving each other's as my legs wrap around him. He carries me across the tent and sits me on something wooden and curved, a carousel horse, as he keeps kissing me, and I pull him closer again. I hear the grunt as he nearly overbalances, and I never, ever want this to end. Nothing beyond him and me exists in this moment.

We're both gasping for air when he eventually pulls back and I've gone all light-headed.

Now *that* is throwing yourself in with both feet and not making excuses to avoid the things you really want to do. Daphne would be so proud.

'I didn't pull back because I wanted to stop kissing you but because I'm going to black out from lack of oxygen any second,' he pants.

'Same,' I wheeze, wondering if I look as dazed as he does.

That's the kind of kiss I've only ever seen in movies. So breathtaking that it takes me a while to get my bearings. I'm sitting on the saddle of Ivy's horse, which is sanded down and ready for priming like most of the others now, and he's leaning against it, looking like he can barely hold himself up, one arm behind me, one in front, holding me on because he's so caring.

'You have *no* idea how desperate I've been to do that.' He rests his forehead against mine, still breathing heavily.

'Me too.' I grin at him, loving the sight of the smile he can't seem to get off his face. 'I thought you didn't want a relationship.'

'I didn't until I met you. The only reason I keep saying it is because I'm trying to convince myself it's still true, when it isn't.'

I grin and he leans down to press his lips against mine again, just a peck this time, but it makes my heart start pounding again.

'I don't know how to be without you. I don't even know how to explain it. I feel like a part of me is missing whenever I'm not with you. And I know we haven't known each other for three weeks yet, and I don't … I didn't think I even believed in love, and I definitely don't believe in love at first sight, but I don't know how to explain what's been happening between us on the train, because something has, hasn't it?'

I nod silently, blown away by his words.

'You calm me every time I see you. I *hate* travelling and I *hate* crowded trains, and I focus on something on my phone to prevent a full-blown panic attack whenever I have to get one, but a sense of peace settles over me whenever I see you. And that morning when we were much closer than usual to each other, I seriously considered missing my connection just to talk to you, which is so flipping out of character for me, and then you answered the phone that night and I *knew* it was you. What was that, Ness?'

'The same thing that made me want to come up here and meet you in person? The same thing that's made this very odd situation seem completely normal? I basically stalked you halfway up the country. I thought you'd run a mile.'

'I've literally never been happier to see someone than when you walked onto the beach with two ice creams. I thought I was hallucinating. I'd spent the whole day trying to figure out how soon I could afford a weekend off from the carousel and come back to London with the excuse of getting the phone, but really because I didn't know how to wait until I was due back at the end of July to meet you. And you know me, London is not somewhere I voluntarily return to.'

He kisses me again and I melt into his arms for a long few minutes, before common sense takes over. I *have* to tell him about the article. 'Listen, Nath, there's something I—'

I'm cut off by the sound of the engine coming to a very grindy halt, as the organ comes to a screechy stop, and bearings on the metal pole creak into stillness.

Nathan swears and kisses my cheek quickly. 'Hold that thought.'

Because it wouldn't be a kiss without some form of unmitigated disaster, would it?

'Is everything okay?' I jump off the horse and follow him across the tent.

He mutters something about a water injector and does something to the engine, and I wait, barely daring to breathe as he turns the wheel again and it chugs back into life, the bearings start turning, and 'The Carousel Waltz' kicks in where it left off.

He stands up and wraps his arms around me from behind, pulling me against his chest and pressing a kiss to my hair. He holds me tight and we just stand there and listen to the music, the old organ making the tune sound exactly the same as it does when Billy invites Julie onto the carousel in the opening scene of the film.

'Will it always play this?' I ask after a few minutes of just enjoying the feeling of his strong arms around me, my fingers trailing up and down his muscular forearms where he's holding me tight.

'I don't know, that'll be the decision of the carousel operator.'

'God, that would be an amazing job, wouldn't it? Can you imagine getting to stand here and operate it all day? A modern-day barker, like Billy Bigelow. Taking the money, helping people on, starting the engine … Watching the joy on little faces as the horses start to move. I'd love that.'

I feel him smile against my hair. 'I'm happy fixing them, but you should go for it. You could stay here then. We both could … Sorry, I shouldn't be saying that, you're happy in your own job, aren't you? I know you don't *love* it, but …'

'I used to think I did. I thought it was just a stepping stone to something better but I don't even know if I want the something better. I meant what I said just now. Seeing how much you love what you do has made me realise how much I don't.'

'So find something else. Even if it's scary. Even if it's a massive risk.'

'It sounds so easy when I'm here with you, but back in London, job-hunting is tough and not being able to pay the rent is tougher.

And I have no idea what kind of job I'd be looking for anyway. I'm rubbish at everything.'

'You're good at restoring vintage carousels.'

'Hah.' I snort at his well-meaning but misguided words. 'All I've done is clean up some horses and sand some old paint off them. I can't even mend the ones that are broken. They're all waiting over there for you to do.'

'I could show you.'

'It's a lovely idea, Nath, but it's not a permanent solution, is it? I'd *love* a couple more weeks of helping you out here, but then reality kicks in and I have rent and bills to pay.'

'Yeah, I guess so.' His sigh sounds as disheartened as I feel.

'Will you ever come back here after the job is finished to see the carousel up and running?'

'I don't usually – my job ends when the restoration ends, but this one feels a bit more special than any other job. I think this one will stay with me for a long while after it's finished.' I hear him swallow hard. 'I've been trying to pluck up the courage to ask if you'll come for a holiday here next year, just you and me if we can get a week off work at the same time, book the cottage …'

'Next year? I don't want to leave it that long before coming back to Pearlholme.'

'I don't want to leave Pearlholme,' he whispers. 'I can't imagine not coming back. And it would be amazing to see the carousel in full swing.'

'It feels a little bit magical.'

'It found me you,' he says into my neck. 'Maybe Ivy never found her missing carousel maker, but the love for her that he put into this spills over and draws people in. Maybe she's not lying in wait to castrate cheating blokes but to spread the love she lost …'

'You're sounding like an old romantic, Nath,' I whisper, barely getting the words out before he kisses me again.

When we eventually stop kissing because the engine grinds to a halt again, we step outside the tent for a breath of fresh air, only to be greeted by a crowd of onlookers standing on the promenade.

'We heard the music and came to see!' Camilla calls, leaning on the blue railing with Charles's arm around her.

'It sounds beautiful, just like I remember it!' the lady from the shop calls.

Bunion Frank, the black Labrador, and the woman from the pub are there too, and a few of the other residents.

'I hope it's going to look as good as it sounds,' Charles says and Camilla smacks him.

'Seems like the magic of the carousel is still alive after all these years!' she shouts, the expression on her face leaving no doubt that they all know exactly what we were doing inside that marquee, if the swollen lips and holding hands weren't enough of a clue.

To my surprise, Nathan pulls me closer and bends down to kiss me on the lips. 'Seems it is,' he calls back.

Camilla whoops with delight and the other residents cheer.

'Took you long enough!' Charles shouts.

'I thought you didn't like kissing in public,' I say to Nath.

'Ah, they're not public, they're our mates now whether we like it or not. Besides, we've got a few more weeks here. They're going to have to get used to it because I want to kiss you a *lot*.'

I smile but it doesn't reach my eyes and I know he can tell. I *don't* have a few more weeks here. I have seventeen missed calls from Zinnia and several missed deadlines, and no idea of how I'm going to get out of it. Where's a good excuse when you need one?

# Chapter 20

'It looks spectacular.' Camilla's nearly bursting with joy as she stands outside the back door and looks around the garden. 'We're certain to win. Ooh, it'll be my first time in years, and it's all because of you two.'

I glance in the living room window and I can see straight through to the kitchen where Nathan's making her a cup of tea.

'I've never seen anyone put sand on the grass before.'

'It was Nath's idea,' I say. 'I was trying to figure out if we could cover the grass with brown cloth or something, but he suggested dumping actual sand from the beach onto the lawn and then vacuuming it up afterwards and putting it back. Only Nathan could've thought of hoovering the grass and make it sound like a sensible suggestion.'

'It's such a clever idea. The wind blows enough sand from the dunes into the garden anyway, and I bet no one else in Pearlholme will have done it. Ooh, I can't wait for the judging on Saturday!'

'Me neither,' I say, because no matter how much I try not to get excited about winning the PPP, a thrill goes through me every time I look out the window and see our little cottage garden. The pink and white flowers planted in the shape of a shell, the blue flowers around the edges, and I've fitted pots of trailing blue lobelia along the hedgerow, spilling out to complement the wave shape that Nath's cut it into.

'Are you sure you can't stay? You both look so much happier and healthier since you came here and we're all going to miss you terribly. You're by far my favourite guests I've had in the cottage.'

I have to laugh at her bluntness. 'I wish we could.'

'Charles could use some help with the hotel, and the carousel will be looking for a barker. Is that what they still call them these days?'

'They just have operators now, and this carousel will have no competition, so it's not like it will need a barker trying to draw people away from other attractions.'

'And if we win the PPP, I suspect your garden design skills will be in demand,' she continues like I haven't spoken. 'And I'm getting far too old for the upkeep of the cottage, you could help me out with that, and we're not very good at "The Online" advertising, you could do that for us ...'

I don't pay much attention to the low thrum of a fast engine speeding up the promenade, my mind drifting while she talks. It's nice that she wants us to stay, that she's willing to offer odd jobs that she probably doesn't really need help with to try to tempt me, but you can't live on thirty quid here and there for trimming someone's hedge or writing a bit of advertising copy about a hotel that could only be advertised honestly to spiders looking for a holiday home.

The engine noise gets louder as a sleek black car approaches the cottage.

'Probably lost,' Camilla says. 'We don't get many fancy cars like that here.'

I can't see much from the back garden, but I hear it come to a stop and the slam of a door as someone gets out, and I don't know why but it makes a stone of dread settle inside my stomach. I know someone who's got a black sports car, but there's *no way* she'd be in Pearlholme. It must just be a coincidence. Probably a guest in one of the other cottages.

A few moments pass and I don't hear anything else. I try to get my breathing back under control. There is more than one black car in the world. I'm just imagining things because I know how far behind I am on my deadlines.

'Hey, Ness?' Nathan sticks his head out the back door. 'Your, er …'

'Zinnia,' says a voice from the living room.

'Your Zinnia is here,' he says, glancing back towards her and then at me again and making a face.

It should make me smile but it doesn't. I knew I'd be in trouble, but Zinnia is one of these people who thinks life only exists within the M25 and would never deign to travel north of it. If she's come all the way up to Pearlholme, I'm in something much deeper than trouble.

Camilla starts walking towards the living room, and I need to follow her, but my feet are rooted to the spot.

'I say, dear, you've gone white. Are you okay?' Camilla takes my hand and pulls me in the back door. 'Let's get you sat down. You'd better have my tea.'

She pushes me down on the sofa and a cup of tea appears in my hand. I stare at it because I can't bring myself to look at my boss, who I never in a million years imagined would be here.

You could cut the tension in the room with a knife.

'Well, I was going to stay, but I can see it's not the best time. Maybe I'll see you in the pub later?' Camilla pats my shoulder, making tea slosh around in the mug.

Nathan helps her into her coat as she introduces herself to Zinnia, who doesn't say a word in response. Camilla obviously senses the barely contained contempt because she stops and peers at Zinnia's face as she passes. 'Oh dear. Have you been in a dreadful accident? Did you have a fight with a plastic surgeon? They have solicitors who specialise in medical negligence, you know.'

I can't prevent the laugh bursting out. Nathan hurries Camilla to the door and sees her out, but I can hear how much he's laughing too, and it makes it even funnier somehow. I know I shouldn't laugh. I risk a glance up at Zinnia and she is definitely *not* laughing, but Nath reappears in the living room doorway, his whole body shaking so much with the effort of holding it back that he's grasping the doorframe to keep himself upright.

'I'm so sorry,' he says in Zinnia's direction, so determined not to laugh that he can barely get his words out. 'Camilla's harmless. She didn't mean anything by it, she's just lost her filter to old age.'

Zinnia uncrosses and recrosses her arms, her top lip curling into as much of a sneer as the fillers will allow.

She taps the toe of her stiletto on the carpet. 'If you've quite finished …'

Nath puts a hand over his mouth. 'I'll make you a cup of tea.'

'Green tea.'

'Er, we only have normal tea.'

'No, thank you.' She looks him up and down. 'I'm not staying. I didn't realise places quite so provincial as this still existed.'

'Would you like to sit down?'

She scans the sofa like she might catch something from it and brushes her black dress down in case the germs have hurled themselves across the gap. 'I'll stand.'

'Okay, I'll leave you to it.' He looks at me with a questioning look on his face and I nod. 'You know where I am if you need me.'

'Stay,' Zinnia demands. 'You're part of this too. At least, I assume this *is* the mystery man, Vanessa.'

I nod and she looks at him like something found floating in a public toilet. Not that I expect Zinnia has ever used a public toilet in her very posh life. 'The blurry photo on the phone was much better-looking.'

He should be insulted, but Nathan puts on his most dashing smile. 'I do look better blurry.'

The insult annoys me. I put my cup down on the coffee table with a resounding thud to let her know I mean business. He might laugh at inappropriate moments, but she doesn't get to insult his looks. 'What are you doing here?'

'Why haven't you answered your phone for the last week, Vanessa? Why has every email been ignored? Where are the fact-checked articles that were due Monday? Yesterday? Last week? And where's the rest of my article about finding *him*?' She jabs a finger in Nathan's direction. 'This is the big one, Vanessa. People are dying to know what happens when you finally meet Train Man. Do you know how many tweets we've had from people saying they can't wait for it? We've been teasing it all week. It *has* to go live on Friday morning. I've been emailing and phoning to get your first draft so we can make it perfect together. We can't afford to miss any delicious little details in this one, but I haven't even seen a line of it yet. Daphne keeps saying that you won't let me down but it's getting increasingly difficult to believe her.'

'So you came all the way up here?'

'Believe me, this is a *last* resort. I phoned the hotel where you *said* you were staying and some old bloke started talking about his bathroom habits. I couldn't get a word of sense from him. I phoned the local pub but they'd never heard of a Vanessa Berton. This article is one of the biggest *Maîtresse* has ever had, no matter how useless the writer I sent to write it has proved herself to be. The amount of readers we're gaining offsets the inconvenience of driving up here in person, but I certainly couldn't trust anyone else to do it, and time is of the essence. I don't like being ignored, Vanessa.'

'I wasn't ignoring you …' It's not exactly a lie. I *haven't* been ignoring her – I've been looking at the growing number of missed calls and emails and worrying myself sick over what to do about them and trying to pluck up the courage to email her and say I can't do it. I didn't expect her to turn up here before I managed it though.

'I suspected that I knew exactly what you were doing, lazing around on the beach all day, so I thought I'd catch you in the act, so to speak, and judging by your tan, I'd say that *is* the only thing you've been working on, no matter how many times Daphne has tried to tell me otherwise. I come up here and find you nattering away in the garden with some old woman.'

*'I wasn't nattering, I was talking about the ...'* annual village gardening competition, which I've got involved in instead of working.

'I don't want to know. I didn't send you up here for a holiday.'

'And I haven't been taking one.'

'She's been working all the time,' Nathan says. 'She's up until all hours. She's always got her computer on her lap.'

It's so sweet of him to try to stick up for me, and yet he must be wondering what all this is about by now.

'Okay, great. Where are the fact-checked articles that were due last week? You can transfer them to me now and at least we'll have some chance of getting back on schedule.'

'I'm behind, okay? I'm trying to catch up but there are only so many hours in a day.'

'When you're busy lying around on the beach?'

'I haven't been—'

'Your tan says otherwise, Vanessa.'

'Oh, that's my fault. She's been helping me with the carousel. I've made her take the horses onto the beach to sand them down to disperse the dust. The tan is from working outside. I'm the same – look at my arms.' He lifts the sleeve of his T-shirt to show her the tan line around his bicep, which is enough to make me go giddy, but Zinnia looks at him like he's a caterpillar she's just plucked from her Harrods broccoli and avocado salad.

He doesn't realise that Zinnia is not a normal person. Most people would have at *least* one hot flush at the sight of Nath's arms.

Zinnia smiles but it's not really a smile at all. 'Well, I'm glad the carousel is more important than your own job.'

'It's not that.'

'What is it then? An excuse to get to know him? If it's all for the article, where *is* the article?'

'I don't …'

'Do you know you made several mistakes last week? You're letting down the journalists who work hard on these stories. We've printed things that are incorrect and readers have called us out on Twitter. I've had to issue retractions. As you would know if you'd answered your phone. I've always been pleased with your work in the office because you're so thorough, but suddenly you come up here and your pride in your work goes to hell in a handbasket. Now I have to hire another fact-checker to fact-check you, do I?'

I shake my head because I don't know what to say. I have messed up and I know it. I've kept telling myself I can still write the article I promised her, without realising how quickly my time is running out. I should have come clean and told her I didn't know how to write about meeting Nathan as soon as I realised I couldn't do it. I didn't know I'd made mistakes in the stories I've fact-checked since I got here, but I do know I've been rushing through my work because all I've wanted to do is spend time at the carousel. It shouldn't have become more important than my real job, but it has. I love it, and I don't love my real job.

I hold my hands up. 'I don't have any excuse to make. I'm sorry, Zinnia. I've screwed up. It won't happen again.'

'You're bloody well right it won't.' She throws her hands up and lets out a huff of air to rival a horse digging around in its chaff bag. 'I don't understand what you've been doing here, Vanessa, because it's certainly not work, is it? What have you spent the past three weeks doing?'

*Falling in love.*

I can see Nath chewing on his lower lip out of the corner of my eye but I can't bring myself to look at him. I can't bring myself to look at Zinnia either. I'm ashamed because I don't know how I ever thought I'd get out of this.

'How about you?' She turns to Nathan. 'What do you think of the article? *Are* you in love with her yet?'

'Er …' His face shows his confusion. 'I think I might be,' he says carefully, clearly thrown by the question.

'Yes!' She raises a fist in a victory gesture and turns back to me. 'I assume that *that* is what you've been waiting for and now you're going to turn in part three tomorrow, fully formed, proof-read, fact-checked, and ready to go online?' She holds her hand out like I'm going to pull the story out of my armpit and hand it to her right now.

I shake my head.

'What article? What's it got to do with me?' I can hear a tone of frustration edging into Nath's voice. I know he's getting worried, and I know it's way past time I explained myself. 'I didn't even know you wrote articles, Ness.'

Zinnia doesn't hide the gasp of surprise. 'You haven't even *told* him? What the hell are you playing at, Vanessa?'

'I don't know,' I say honestly. 'It was never the right time …' It's just another excuse and I know it. I *should* have told Nathan by now. I should have told him on the first day. I should have told him any other time between then and now. He would've understood. At the very least, we could've talked about it in private. It wouldn't have been sprung on him by my very put-together, quite scary boss turning up unannounced.

'You're Train Man.' My voice barely squeezes out of my tight throat.

He looks even more confused than he did before. 'What? Who's Train Man?'

Zinnia whisks her tablet out of her handbag, touches the screen a few times and hands it to him.

'He's the subject of an article that's gone viral online.' I can't bear to watch his face go from amused to serious as his fingers scroll down the screen, so I watch the way his hands move, and see the exact moment he clicks the link at the bottom of part one that leads to the second part. 'I wrote it on the day you dropped your phone.'

'These are my photos.' He doesn't hide the surprise in his voice. 'That's *me*. How the hell did you get this? You can't use these without my permission, can you?' He looks exasperated as he holds up the iPad so Zinnia and I can both see what's onscreen.

I've never seen part two of the article. I sent it and tried not to think about it. I didn't want to see what a show Zinnia had made of it with her wanted posters and photos from his phone, but instead of the shopping list that I expected published with the article, she's used not just the picture of a wooden horse with his shoe in it, but the actual picture of him standing on a carousel in the distance, the one we all pored over in the office when I'd just found his phone.

Zinnia waves the screen away. 'We blurred it out more than enough. No one will recognise you.'

Everyone will recognise him. He doesn't even need to say it. It's a distant photo but it's a photo of him. 'I didn't agree to letting you use that one.'

'You were there when I told Daphne to transfer everything that might be useful. After the success of part one, it turned out to be very useful indeed. Readers were dying to see this man, the real thing, not just the faceless model in my graphics. Have you seen how many hits it's had?'

Nathan goes back to the screen and his face visibly pales. 'Twenty-seven thousand on the first one, twenty-one on the second.' He sinks down to sit on the sofa, but his eyes don't leave the screen in his hand. 'Please tell me you didn't do this, Ness. You wrote about me?'

'I didn't know you. It was just meant to be a fun little story. I didn't mean for it to get the reaction it's had.' I drop my head into my hands and then look up again because the very least Nathan deserves is eye contact. 'You were meant to be anonymous.

There was going to be a model in your place. We were never going to use that photo.'

'So, let me get this straight …' He taps the screen and goes back to the first part of the story. 'You thought we had a connection and that you picking up my phone was a sign from the universe, so you … thought it was in the national interest to make sure *everyone* knew about it?'

'It wasn't like that. I wanted to send the phone in the post, but Zinnia thought … and when we talked that night, I felt like we had a connection, and I wanted to meet you, and—'

'You'd already written this by then!' He touches the screen again and goes back to part two. 'And this was written last week. *Last week,* Ness! It's dated last Sunday, the day after we climbed up that cliff. The day after I told you stuff I've never told anyone in my life before. And you still wrote this.'

'It wasn't meant to be like this. I didn't know anything about that picture. I didn't want to write it, Nath, but I was going to lose my job if I didn't.'

'What job? I thought you were a fact-checker.' He shakes his head. 'Well, you said you were hoping your boss would let you write articles one day, and I was the perfect foot in the door, was I?'

'This story was her big break,' Zinnia intervenes. 'You said you love her, surely you're happy to help her get what she wants in life.'

'Oh, I've helped a few people get what they want in life over the years. It's a shame that no one has *ever* been interested in helping me and what I might want. I thought Ness was different.' He gets up from the sofa and hands the iPad back to Zinnia. 'Thanks for that, it's been very enlightening.'

'It wasn't like that,' I say again. 'We talked that first night and I loved talking to you, and—'

'So, what, you went and told your boss about it? Pitched it as the next big idea?'

282

'I told my best friend and Zinnia overheard,' I say, despite the fact she's still in the room. 'I never pitched it. I never wanted to write it.'

'I *knew* that no boss would let you have three weeks off in Pearlholme just to return my phone.' He lets out a groan and shoves a hand through his hair as he leans forward, tension clear in his taut shoulders. I can see the cogs turning in his mind. '*Are you in love with her yet?*' He repeats Zinnia's earlier question in her accent and I can see the moment it dawns on him. 'You didn't come here to return my phone. You didn't come here to meet me, or because you thought there was something between us. You came here to further your career, no matter who or what you had to use to do it.'

'No! It was never about that—'

'Right, I'm not going to stand here and watch you two have a domestic,' Zinnia announces. 'Vanessa, if you're not back in the office at nine o'clock tomorrow morning, and I don't have a finished copy of part three and a good chunk of part four on my desk by ten, you're fired. You can already forget being given any more features, *ever*, and covering Daphne's maternity leave is long gone. You've done nothing but prove yourself unreliable and incapable of following instructions. The sea air is obviously getting to me because I haven't fired you from fact-checking yet. I'm going home, but first I'm going to hope that dreadful-looking little pub serves a very large gin.'

I should see her out but I can't make myself get up. I can't make myself leave Nathan.

We sit there in silence as we listen to her car door slam and the engine start up as she pulls away and zooms down the promenade.

The rumble of the engine is a distant memory before either of us plucks up the courage to speak again.

'So all those times we've smiled at each other over the months … were you already planning to exploit me then, or was it only when you saw my phone?'

'Nath, it was nothing like that. I smiled at you because I got bloody butterflies every time you looked at me. We had a connection—'

'No, we didn't. The butterflies and whatever the *hell* I thought I felt with you … they were all part of your story.' I can see him closing himself down. The light in his eyes goes out. They're so dark brown that they're almost black now. There's no cheeky glint, no smile, no mischievous raised eyebrow, no laughter lines playing around his mouth that make him look like he's permanently about to burst into giggles. He looks tired and drawn and like he is one hundred per cent *done* with this conversation. And with me.

'This all sounds so much worse than it is, Nath,' I try again. 'I didn't mean to lie to you. I was supposed to be writing an article but I couldn't do it once I got to know you.'

'And yet, conveniently, your boss doesn't know that.'

'Only because I was too much of a coward to tell her.'

He laughs, a sharp and bitter sound that's nothing like his usual laugh. 'Oh, come off it, Ness. Everything has been in aid of your article. You're not interested in me, not in the carousel, nothing. You must've been bored to bloody death listening to me prattle on for weeks. You've earned your promotion just from having to suffer through that.'

'That's not true. Nathan, please, I've loved every second I've spent with you. I'm in trouble with my own work *because* I love spending time with you so much.' I reach over to touch his knee but he jumps away so fast that he nearly falls off the sofa.

I pull my hand back, surprised at his reaction, but as I sit there holding my fingers like he's the one who's burnt me, I wonder why I'm surprised. Of course he's hurt. I knew he would be, that's exactly why it was so difficult to tell him, and it got harder the longer it went on.

I can feel him slipping away. I can feel the coldness coming from him, like a big security fence has just sprung up across the living room, separating me and him. I know he's been hurt before, and I know how much it took for him to let me in, and now he thinks I was just using him.

I swallow hard and wet my lips a few times to make the words come out. 'Please let me explain.' I feel sick and my hands are shaking, but he's silent so I grab the opportunity. 'Nothing I've said to you has been a lie. Everything I've felt for you is true.'

'I've heard that before.'

'I'm not your ex, Nath. I'm not using you. This only got as messy as it did because I was trying *not* to hurt you.'

'You lied to me point blank. I asked you why you were here, what you were doing, I've asked you about the stories you're working on, the facts you've had to check, and not once have you said that you're writing an article about me falling in love with you!' His voice breaks and he gets to his feet and paces across the living room.

I watch him face the wall and take a few deep breaths.

'Everything we've shared has been because you needed an ending for your story.'

'No, it hasn't.' I feel my lip wobble. People always say that your bottom lip wobbles when you're about to cry but I've always thought it was a myth until now.

'And I was stupid enough to give you one. I was stupid enough to fall for it.' He shakes his head, seeming more annoyed at himself than at me. 'I thought I was different now. I thought I was strong enough to never trust anyone again. I shut myself down on that day – that day I told you about, the one where I vowed I'd never feel anything for anyone ever again, the worst time of my life that I've never shared with anyone until this week – and you got inside my walls and all my emotions came back and I felt like you'd woken me up for the first time in years, and it was all for this. You were just using me to get what you want—'

'I'm head over heels in love with you, Nath.'

He spins around and the hard set of his jaw, the red under his eyes, the rawness in them is so heartbreaking that it makes another wave of tears threaten to pull me under because he looks so broken that he's almost a different person to the smiley, funny guy I've got to know.

'No, you're not. You're head over heels in love with a promotion.'

'No, I'm no—'.

'You came here to make a story out of something that doesn't exist. You came to make Train Man fall in love with you. Well, congratulations, it worked.' He takes a deep breath and strides across the room, plucks his phone from the coffee table and shoves it into his pocket. 'Thanks for bringing my phone back. You can see yourself out.'

I sob as the front door slams behind him.

I don't know how long I sit there for. Long enough for the sun to move across the sky over the beach behind me, casting shadows that are different than the ones that were here when he left. I don't even know why I'm still sitting here. Hoping he'll come back willing to listen, or that I'll suddenly think of the perfect, magical thing to say to make him realise I didn't want to hurt him and this all got way out of hand and I'll run down to the carousel and tell him and he'll take me in his arms and we'll kiss again.

The reality is that I'm sure he's staying away until he knows for certain that I've left, and what good am I doing by staying? What else can I say that I didn't try to say earlier? I could go back to the hotel and hope he calms down enough to listen, but I know it won't make any difference. He wasn't angry. He doesn't even blame me – he blames himself. Trying to force him to listen to me, telling him to trust me when I've spent the last three weeks lying to him, repeating that nothing I felt for him had anything to do with what I was supposed to be writing … all of that would only make him hate me more.

286

I haul myself off the sofa and start gathering up my things. I shut down my laptop and shove it back in its bag. I go round the side of the house to collect my washing off the line, back upstairs to grab my suitcase from Nathan's bedroom, which I kind of didn't move out of after my parents left …

I sob as I think about last weekend. Mum is going to *kill* me for hurting him. Things have gone so wrong in the few days since we waved them off. It's my own fault, and I have no idea how to fix it.

And I would do anything to make this better, because what I felt for Nath was *so* much better than anything I've ever seen in any romantic movie. It was the kind of love I've always dreamed about but convinced myself doesn't exist in real life.

Maybe it's easier to believe that. I scrub my hands over my face and throw my last few belongings into my suitcase. There's no such thing as love, or romantic, fated coincidences, or magical connections, or butterflies. Those things are fictional and should stay in the movies, where they belong. I'm no Gwyneth Paltrow. I didn't split in two on a tube train while one part of me stayed in my dull, boring existence and the other part of me followed Nathan to Pearlholme and found happiness. We're not two souls destined to meet each other through every lifetime. We're just two strangers on a train who should've stayed that way.

# Chapter 21

'What the hell am I going to do?' I'm sitting at Daph's computer in her office because my cubicle has been taken over by the freelancer Zinnia has hired in my place, while she's lying on the executive two-seater sofa with her feet up, fanning last week's issue of *Maîtresse* in front of her face. She's got a few days left before her maternity leave starts, as she keeps reminding me. I think she's under some mistaken impression that if I nail this article and have it on Zinnia's desk by ten o'clock, I'll still get to take over her job when she leaves.

I don't even know how I managed to drag myself here this morning, let alone back from the North Yorkshire coast on the only train yesterday afternoon. I don't remember the journey back; it was like it was happening without me. I don't think I woke up from the nightmare until I burst into tears on the tube this morning because the last time I got that train, Nathan was on it.

But with Daph's encouragement, and patient phone calls late into the night, I've decided that the only thing I can try to salvage from this is my fact-checking job, which will obviously never be anything more, and that's okay. I'm clearly not cut out for feature writing.

It's now quarter past nine, and the first line problem is back with a vengeance. I have forty-five minutes to write the most anticipated story *Maîtresse* will publish this year, a story about falling in love with someone who will never speak to me again. If it seemed impossible in Pearlholme, it's even more impossible now. I try to find some emotional distance, to write it as if I was writing a novel, a fictional story about characters who don't actually exist, but it doesn't work. I'm still picturing Nathan's smiling eyes and ever-present grin, and I don't even realise that my eyes have started watering again until Daph shouts at me.

'Ness! For God's sake, read out your first line and we'll go from there.'

'Once upon a time …'

'That's it?' She groans and increases the magazine flapping.

I pick up one of the print-outs of the first two parts of the article that are strewn across the desk. Thankfully the article hasn't made it into the print edition yet. 'How did I ever get into this? From the word go, I knew I'd be exploiting him. Even if I could've kept him anonymous, I was still using him for my own personal gain. I should have just invented a Train Man and used a model to play him. No one would've been hurt then.'

'I shouldn't have encouraged you,' she says. 'It was just an excuse to get you to go because you liked him, and I haven't seen you like a guy, *really* like a guy, in years. And with the dropped phone and everything, and then Zinnia came in, and you talked to him that night and you clearly wanted to go. And the coincidences, the food on his shopping list, the carousel pictures and your love of that film … That sort of thing doesn't just happen, right? I thought it was a genuine *Sliding Doors* moment. You deserved the chance to chase it up and find out.'

She fans *Maîtresse* in front of her face again, and I get up and take the battery-operated fan on her desk over to her.

'You can't hit me, I might go into labour.'

I laugh as I take the magazine from her hand and replace it

with the fan. 'Don't blame yourself. I didn't go to Pearlholme because of the article, I went because I *loved* the conversation we had on the phone. I didn't feel butterflies because of the article, I felt them because of *him*. This is my mess because I should have walked up to him and told him exactly what I was doing there, and I didn't, and now he thinks that nothing I've said in the past few weeks is true and I was just using him to get a story.' I go back and throw myself down into Daph's desk chair with a huff, annoyed at myself because I could see exactly how this was going to turn out, and I still didn't do anything to change it.

'I thought you might hate me because I pushed you into it as much as Zinnia did.'

'How could I ever hate you? You've been my best friend for fifteen years.'

'And you're not going to withhold babysitting services?'

I spin around in the desk chair twice, coming to a stop and staring at the wall behind me. 'As if. I can't wait to be a best-friend aunty.' I spin the chair back around and lean over the desk, the print-out of 'The case of the missing Train Man' staring back at me. I run my fingers across the blurry picture of Nathan in the distance on a carousel, the one that was never supposed to be used. Blurred out or not, he's recognisable. Anyone who knew him would put two and two together and know who he was.

'I should never have transferred that photo,' Daph says. 'I've worked with Zinnia for years now, I should've known she'd use it.'

'I'm the one who hurt him.' I put the page down and stare at the blank screen again. 'I let him open up to me, and I knew how he'd feel when he found out about the article, and I still didn't have the courage to tell him. I didn't even have the courage to tell Zinnia where she could shove her article.'

'For what it's worth, I never agreed with writing about a pretend search for a man you'd already found. Our readers aren't that stupid. But you've got to admit it was a great story. It really captured the public imagination. No wonder people are waiting for the next part.'

'Yeah, well, at the rate I'm going, they're never going to get it.' I stare at the cursor blinking on the blank screen in front of me, a familiar sight lately. 'I can't do it to him. There aren't that many carousel restorers in the country. Everyone will know who he is, no matter how much I fictionalise this article. He's quiet and he keeps to himself. He hates crowds and he hates people looking at him. No matter how far removed I can make it, it will hurt him even more. It's not worth it.'

I realise then and there that it's really not. I don't even like this job, I certainly don't want to hurt Nathan even more to save it.

We're silent for a while. My eyes are on the carousel horse in the picture with his foot on one of the printed pages, and Daph's watching the clock, waiting for ten o'clock to roll around when Zinnia will inevitably come in and fire me, and undoubtedly get someone else to continue the fictional story anyway. She's not going to give up those page views without a fight.

'You're in love with him, aren't you?' Daph says quietly. 'Like, really *truly* all-consuming, ridiculous, inconvenient love?'

Tears fill my eyes again, blurring the photo even more. I don't need to answer her.

She nods. 'You were happy up there. Happier than you've ever been. Isn't that worth fighting for?'

I nod again, and this time, she starts crying too, and it makes me smile through the tears. 'Why are you crying?'

'Because I'm pregnant – I've been an emotional wreck for months.' She laughs despite the tears. 'And because I don't want you to move out of London, and if you go and win him back, you're obviously going to stay there, and it's so far away.'

I shake my head. 'You don't know him. You don't realise how hurt he was. How can I win him— That's it!'

'What's it?' She sits up straight. 'You've got ten minutes left before Zinnia fires you.'

I leap out of the chair. 'Stall her, Daph! You owe me one for transferring that photo! I'll repay you in babysittings!'

'She's never going to let you keep your—'

'I don't care about the job! I don't want this job! I just want her to publish the conclusion of this article for me! I have to do something for Nath. I have to show him that I care about that carousel as much as he does!'

'What are you going to do?'

I grab my bag and run out of the office. 'I'm going to write an article about finding a man!'

# Chapter 22

The following Wednesday, I squash my way onto the early morning train to *Maîtresse*, although Daph won't tell me why, considering I don't work there anymore. As I stand crammed against a rail with the corner of someone's handbag digging into my back, I wonder why she was so insistent that I get this train. It's not like I have to be there by nine o'clock now, surely I could've come later when it's less crowded.

The tube smells like Satan's unwashed scrotum, and I lean my head against the rail I'm holding on to and close my eyes, picturing the tranquillity of the cottage garden in Pearlholme instead of the sweaty armpit against the side of my face.

June has moved into July now. The PPP would've been judged last weekend, and I keep wondering if we won. Everyone kept saying we would, and Nath deserved it for the amount of work he put in. Thinking about that makes me think about Charles and Camilla and the other villagers, all of whom have undoubtedly heard about what happened between us by now.

I keep telling myself not to lose hope. When the final part of the article is published, I'm going to print it out and send it to the cottage, and hopefully he'll read it and realise that I did care. It won't be enough to make up for how I treated him, I know that, but I also know that I can't leave things as they are. Nathan deserves better than that.

The person with the handbag in my back steps backwards, jabbing it into my ribs instead, and my eyes spring open, blinking in the bright artificial light as they lock on to a man at the other end of the carriage. He's standing up and holding on to a rail like I am, his attention on the phone in his hand, but it's *him*. Just like it was before.

Train Man.

*Nathan.*

I feel like time has stopped. Or like I'm hallucinating. What would he be doing in London? It can't be him. But his height makes him stand out above the people surrounding him, and the way his eyes crinkle as he squints down at his phone ... that's the kind of thing you don't hallucinate.

The noisy tube train, the sniffing and clearing of throats, the ringtones of phones, the beeps, the conversations ... it all fades away as I push myself upright, my heart suddenly pounding fast, at odds with the way the world turns to slow motion as he lifts his head, almost like he can feel my eyes on him, and his eyes lock on to mine too.

I expect him to turn away at the sight of me, but he suddenly stands up straight and his mouth curves up a tiny bit at each side, and it's impossible to look away.

The now-familiar butterflies start flapping in my stomach, except they don't feel like butterflies anymore, they feel like hummingbirds with their wings fluttering eighty times per second.

His face slowly spreads into a smile as he looks at me, and I feel myself smiling back, unable as always not to return Nathan's smile whenever it's directed at me. The dimples appear and he starts making his way towards me.

Never mind *Sliding Doors*, maybe I've ventured into *Groundhog Day* and gone back to the start of the day we were last on this train together until I have a chance to fix what went wrong. Bill Murray is sure to pop out at any second.

I don't even realise I'm moving until someone barks an angry 'ouch' in my direction when I accidentally tread on their toes. I turn to apologise and half-expect the illusion of Nathan will have disappeared by the time I look back.

He's still there, manoeuvring his way through the packed carriage towards me. He tilts his head like he's trying to hold my gaze, and it makes that now-familiar feeling of nervousness and excitement twist in my belly.

It seems like a lifetime until we've edged our way across the train to each other.

'Hi,' I say nervously, my body pressed against his because there's barely room to breathe on this train, not that I'm complaining about that, but the last time I saw him, he definitely didn't seem like he'd want my body anywhere near him ever again.

*'Hi.' He grins like his smile is too wide for his face to contain and looks down at his phone again. 'I recently went looking for a missing man, a man of mystery, a man who had never been found before. He isn't the man I set out looking for, but he's the one I want to talk about today.' He reads the first line of my article in a funny accent.*

'Is that supposed to be me?' I ask instead of the eleventy-billion other more appropriate questions I could ask him.

*His teeth pull his lower lip into his mouth and his eyes are dancing again. 'Abraham Elwood was a barker for a carousel on Scarborough seafront. In 1896, at nineteen years old, he began carving a carousel of his own, the most gorgeous, intricate carousel that he'd probably be proud to know hasn't lost any of its charm in the century since he finished it. The carousel was a gift to show his love for a lady who had waited six years for him to finish it, but was unfortunately destined to wait for him forever, because that's exactly what she did when he went missing just months after finishing the carousel. He was declared dead in 1901. Lost at sea.'*

He lowers his head so I can hear him. 'This answers every question we had about the carousel. Ivy knew he was dead, but his body was never found, so she always had hope that he would come back to her. That the carousel music from the cliff top would guide him home. She knew that he would love her for as long as the carousel kept turning. She was keeping him alive in the only way she could.'

I look up at him, still trying to convince myself that he's really here and that he doesn't hate me as much as he did the last time I saw him. 'She was waiting for a miracle that never came.'

'But she believed in their love so strongly that she never gave up.' He smiles that secret smile that makes me feel like I'm the only one who's ever seen it. 'It's quite romantic when you think about it, isn't it?'

'You don't believe in romantic old stories, Nath.' I fight the urge to reach up and brush his hair back. It's so tempting this close, with the way his aftershave has blocked out the other smells around me, the way his voice blocks out all other sounds.

'This isn't just a story though, is it? This is fact. You found all this because you knew I needed to know.' He taps his phone and turns it to show me, and I love that he's so excited that he's sharing it with me like I've never seen it before. 'This is a copy of the actual newspaper report about his boat sinking. He was going to get material for her wedding dress, Ness. This is so much more than history to me now – I feel like we actually know these people. Look at this. You even found their death certificates. *Ivy Loren. Died 1956, aged eighty-two, heart failure.* How did you get all this?'

Another tube stop is announced and people flock past us, and I like the way his arm slides around me and pulls me tighter against him, holding me steady.

'Until last Friday, I was a fact-checker. For my last trick, I decided to check some facts,' I say after one set of people have swarmed off and another have swarmed on. 'We knew where he lived, we knew his occupation, we knew Ivy's name, and the date of the carousel. There was a census taken every ten years back then. It wasn't that hard to narrow down in the end. Once I had a name, I could search through the national archives and build on what we already knew.'

'You really quit your job?'

I nod. 'I know you don't believe me, but I wasn't using you to further my career. I used my job as an excuse to come to Pearlholme and find you. That's why it kept going so wrong – because I didn't need an excuse. As soon as I met you, I knew I was exactly where I was supposed to be.'

'You solved the mystery. You found out who he was. For me.'

I reach out and slip my fingers around his. 'For me too. I care about that carousel, Nath. And I care about you, and I wanted to show you that you were right. I wanted you to know that even when you doubt yourself, I don't.'

'I liked the bit about the carousel restorer.' He's blushing as he speaks.

'*Ah, you mean the paragraph I agonised over for hours to try to make it sound casual and detached?' I take the phone out of his hand and scroll down until I find the words, even though I know them off by heart anyway. 'And then there's the man I did set out to find. A beautiful carousel restorer who can look at things and instantly see how to make them better. A man who's inspired me to want something more out of life. A man who's made me realise there's a difference between being happy and being distracted from how sad you are. A man who knows that if there's something missing in your life, it is generally always an ice cream.'*

The train jolts and I fall against him, and his arms encircle me again, but not just because he's holding me up this time. He pulls me in tight and drops his head to rest on mine, his mouth moving against my ear. 'I'm sorry about the other day. It took me back in time and I shut down rather than listening to you. I *knew* I knew you better than that, I *knew* that nothing between us had been pretend, and I just … I don't know … I'm so damaged—'

'You're perfect.'

'So are you.' His lips press into my cheek, and I giggle because he makes the loudest 'mwah' sound and several people turn to look at us, and I wait for him to start blushing with embarrassment, but he doesn't.

'How do you have that, anyway? It hasn't been published yet. Zinnia refused to put it online until next week when she's done some damage control.' I push his phone back into his hand, even though I strongly suspect I know exactly how Daph's been spending her last week before maternity leave.

'Daphne emailed it to me.'

'How does Daph have your email address? *I* don't even have your email address. I wanted to call you but …'

'We never swapped numbers. I know. It's ridiculous when you think about it, right? I only ever called you on my phone. I didn't expect things to end like that …' He shakes his head. 'And her email said something about using her journalistic powers that us mere mortals mustn't question to track me down, but what she actually did was phone The Sun & Sand, who phoned Camilla, who got it from my booking form, and couldn't wait to tell me about the trail of espionage. I think her and Charles are applying to join MI5 next week.'

'That sounds like Daph all right,' I say fondly. I know she felt bad about the Train Man articles, but that's going above and beyond, even for her.

I look up at him and his eyes are smiling, the crow's feet crinkling up around them, and it's never been more difficult to resist kissing someone in my life.

'What are you doing back in London?' I force myself to think about something else. 'And on a train? You hate travelling and crowded places.'

'Not as much as I hated losing you last week. I'm on my way

to *Maîtresse* to try to win you back.'

'*I'm* on *my* way to *Maîtresse*. Daphne did tell you I don't work there anymore, didn't she?'

'She did, but she also said you'd be in this morning if I wanted to catch you. And if you don't work there anymore, why are you going?'

'I don't know. Daph told me to. She said she had a surprise for me, something that was too heavy for her to carry while pregnant …' I trail off as I fall in. 'And I've just met it. *You're* the surprise. She was making sure we'd meet again.'

'Well, I'm definitely too heavy to carry.'

'She could've just given you my address, I wouldn't have minded.' I glance up at him. 'She always writes about couples who meet in unusual ways – she probably wants an article out of this.'

'I don't mind that. I just want you, Ness.' His finger slides along my jaw and he tilts my head up to look at him. 'I've been alone for so long, I hadn't realised how much had been missing from my life until I met you. You made me feel loved in a way I didn't think existed. I've tried so hard to convince myself I don't want a relationship, but now I don't know how to be without you. If you'll give me another chance?'

I don't realise I'm crying until he wraps his arms around me and pulls me against his chest. 'I'm so sorry about the articles, Nath. It wasn't meant to go as far as it did,' I say into his T-shirt. 'I was so scared last week. I know we haven't known each other long but I can't imagine my life without you in it.'

'Maybe there's a little magic in that old carousel after all …' He waggles his eyebrows when I look up at him. 'All I know is that I look forward to finding out.'

I can feel my pulse thrumming in my lips, all over my body, as he lowers his head to mine, and everything stops. The whole world stills and every noise fades away to nothing but Nathan, the scent of his aftershave, the feel of his mouth against mine,

299

his hand in my hair, and the complete relief that nearly knocks me off my feet as I cling on to him. I hadn't realised until this moment how scared I was that I'd never get to kiss him again.

My hand automatically goes to his shoulder and he pulls me impossibly closer, having seemingly forgotten that we're in the middle of a *very* packed train, and somewhere in the recesses of my mind, I'm sure the announcement for our stop came three stations ago.

I let myself get lost in his kiss, swept away by him, and let go of all the excuses I've built my life around in the past few years. This kiss, and a future with him, is worth every risk I've always been too scared to take.

When we pull apart, there's a round of applause, cheering, and whistling from the rest of the carriage, and this time he does blush, resting his forehead in my hair and turning his face away.

I'm blushing too, but I don't care. 'You hate kissing in public.'

'Again, not as much as I hate losing you. Besides, I'm not planning on staying in London. I don't give a toss what these people think.'

'You wouldn't be planning on going back to Pearlholme, would you?'

'You have to come back, Ness. We won the PPP but they wouldn't give me the trophy because that whole garden was you, your idea, your creativity, and you're not there. People keep saying they want you to do theirs next year because no one's garden looked as good as ours.' He swallows. 'And it *is* ours. If we want it. Camilla keeps saying she's getting too old to do holiday lets, and she knows how much I love it there. She asked if I wanted to rent the cottage on a more permanent basis and be a proper tenant, but I can't imagine living there without you.'

I know my face has lit up because I see the joy reflected in his eyes. 'What about work?'

'We'll figure it out. I can't live in London anymore, and I don't think you can either. Most of my jobs are out-of-office anyway, but when I'm needed in the workshop, it would be easier to commute *to* it and live somewhere that makes me happy the rest of the time. And Camilla's list of work she wants you to do is growing by the day. If she gives up the cottage, she's going to get involved with the hotel instead. She wants you to oversee it. She's determined to make it the best hotel in the north, rather than the one thing that lets Pearlholme down. She's already been out with her machete chopping branches off overgrown trees. Charles is positively overjoyed, as you can imagine.'

The sarcasm makes me laugh. I grin at him, my face genuinely aching from smiling so much, a smile that's barely faded since the last time I saw him across a crowded train carriage, on a morning that feels like it might have been just a little bit magical after all.

# Chapter 23

The sun is shining down on us as we gather at the beach where Nathan and I have spent the past three weeks restoring the carousel. I've sanded and painted the horses and learned how to fix broken wooden limbs and reattach lost ears, while he's painstakingly checked and repaired every part of the carousel and rebuilt it one piece at a time. We've been to every DIY shop in Yorkshire to match the original paint colours, we got a local artist to repaint the decorative panels with scenes from the area, and found a haberdasher online who still manufactured the pink and yellow ribbons used for the canopy all those years ago.

'It was worth the trip up,' Daphne says, pushing baby Ivy in her pram with Gavin by her side.

'And I promised we wouldn't wait until Christmas to see you again, didn't I?' Mum says, patting Nathan's arm, who looks genuinely overjoyed to see my parents, despite the fact he probably didn't bank on seeing them again *quite* so soon.

All the villagers are here too: Bunion Frank and his Labrador, the woman from The Sun & Sand and the woman who works in the shop, old couples who keep coming over and asking how much I charge for garden design services. There are parents with children who have come for a day on the beach and stumbled across the opening of the carousel, and others who have heard about it and come specifically to have a first ride on the historic merry-go-round, and of course, Pearlholme's very own royal couple, Charles and Camilla, are cutting the ribbon.

Camilla claps to get everyone's attention. 'Thank you all for coming. This carousel has been at the heart of a mystery that's haunted Pearlholme for many years, and I'm pleased to say that this restoration puts some old ghosts to rest.'

'And lets many men sleep easier in their beds!' Charles guffaws.

Camilla wallops him before he can explain any further with children present, and points to an engraved plaque beside the carousel that tells the story of Abraham and Ivy, sharing their love with a new generation.

Nathan has turned around the panel that hid Abraham's message to Ivy. It's now in the centre of the carousel for all to see so their love will live on, until the next time the carousel stops turning, which won't be for many years with Nathan around.

Camilla and Charles hold a pair of oversized scissors and cut the ribbon between them, and the crowd on the beach whoops and cheers as everyone starts lining up for a ride.

Charles delays letting anyone on until Nath and I have stepped onto the suspended wooden platform and have first choice of the horses, and he pulls me across to a certain one. It's not the lead horse – that's still Ivy's – but there's something about this horse that I've been taken with. It had a missing ear, chips out of its trimmings, and two broken legs, and it's the one I've been practising on while I learnt the techniques Nath has showed me. It's white with a pale pink mane and turquoise trappings, a fuchsia saddle with sparkling gems embedded around the edge, and a bridle made of tiny carved daisies. It still has a few scars, but they give it character, and I hope that some little girl will choose it as a favourite and always ride this one whenever they come here, just like I did with my favourite when I was young.

Nathan helps me up onto it, and places my hand very specifically on its neck.

'What is that?' I ask him as my fingers rub over lines that were definitely not there the last time I saw this horse. I lean over for a better look, only to see my name carved at the side of the neck, exactly the same place as Ivy is carved on the lead horse.

'You named it Ness,' I say, glad he's still standing beside me because it's probably the sweetest thing anyone's ever done for me and I quite literally melt against him as he hugs me.

'The owner is going to run a competition for children to name the other horses. Until now, Ivy was the only one that had a name.'

'Thank you.'

I feel his smile against my skin. 'Thank *you*. I couldn't have done this without you, Ness. This is the best job I've ever done. Next time I have a carousel to work on, you're coming with me.'

'I could get used to that.'

He doesn't move away, just stands beside the horse I'm sitting on, holding on to the pole, with one arm around me and his head against mine.

When all the horses have got a rider, and there's still a crowd waiting on the beach, Charles starts the engine, and it feels like there's magic in the air as the carousel begins turning for the first time in full splendour, the lights twinkling, the bright paint gleaming, the sparkling horses galloping up and down as the bearings at the top of the central pole turn, twisting the bars that hold them, giving them the feeling of jumping as the speed picks up, and children squeal with excitement.

The old organ strikes up, and I recognise the first notes immediately. I look up at Nathan in surprise and he smiles back at me, because the organ is playing 'If I Loved You'.

It's nothing like a traditional carousel tune, but I know he's done it because he knew how much I'd love it. And it's overwhelming as I sit there, letting myself feel it all, the gentle motion of the horse, his arm around me and his head still against mine, the smell of sea air and fresh paint, sand between my bare toes when I scrunch them, and the beautiful old organ playing one of my favourite songs.

He only speaks when the ride is coming to an end. 'I do, you know. Love you.'

I pull back and grin up at him. 'Me too.'

Mum is on the horse behind us and she squeaks with joy. 'I told you what that song meant!'

Even Camilla is riding side-saddle on one of the horses, and she calls over to Charles. 'You need to up your romance game, matey!'

Our friends on the surrounding horses cheer as Nathan kisses me, echoed by the crowd still watching from the sand, and I'm not sure which one of us is blushing more when we pull away as the ride stops and everyone around us starts to dismount.

'Do you think Ivy would be happy?' I ask him, not ready to get off yet.

He looks out towards the ocean and then back to me. 'I think she would. She kept her own love alive for as long as she could. I think she'd be glad to see the carousel with a new lease of life, ready to share the love that was put into it with a new generation.'

I look around me at the beautiful old thing, breathtaking now, unimaginable compared to the pile of debris it was when I arrived six weeks ago. 'It worked for us.'

'It did.' He smiles and kisses me again. 'And I can't wait to spend every day in our little cottage, watching it bring magic to everyone else who comes here too.'

After a couple more rides, Nath and I wander a little way down the beach by ourselves. His arms are around me, his chin resting on my head, as we stand in the warm summer sun and watch the delighted faces of children and adults alike enjoying a truly vintage ride by the sea, and I realise that, for the first time, real life is better than any romantic movie.

Maybe there is just a little magic in the air whenever an old carousel turns.

# Acknowledgements

Mum, this line is always the same because you're always there for me. Thank you for the constant patience, support, encouragement, and for always believing in me. Love you lots!

Bill, Toby, Cathie – thank you for always being supportive and enthusiastic!

An extra special thank you to Bev for being so caring, kind, encouraging, and always writing such lovely letters!

Special thanks to two talented authors, great friends, and supportive cheerleaders – Charlotte McFall and Marie Landry!

The lovely and talented fellow HQ authors – I don't know what I'd do without all of you!

All the lovely authors and bloggers I know on Twitter. You've all been so supportive since the very first book, and I want to mention you all by name, but I know I'll forget someone and I don't want to leave anyone out, so to everyone I chat to on Twitter or Facebook – thank you.

The little writing group that doesn't have a name – Sharon Sant, Sharon Atkinson, Dan Thompson, Jack Croxall, Holly Martin, Jane Yates. I can always turn to you guys!

Thank you to Aaron for making me watch *Carousel* despite my insistence that I would hate it. I loved it, and it turned out to be the final puzzle piece that made this story whole!

Thank you to the team at HQ and especially my fantastic editor, Charlotte Mursell, for all the hard work and support, and for always being there to answer my every question!

And finally, a massive thank you to *you* for reading!

Turn the page for an exclusive extract from another enchanting novel from Jaimie Admans, *It's a Wonderful Night* …

Turn the page for an exclusive extract from another enchanting novel from Jaimie Admans: *It's a Wonderful Night*.

# Chapter 1

I'm in the cupboard under the stairs trying to wrangle a naked mannequin up the narrow steps to the back room when I hear the phone ringing. I groan. It's only going to be a telemarketer, isn't it? It's eleven o'clock on a November night and I'm working overtime because, as the manager of the One Light charity shop, it's my responsibility to get the Christmas window display finished before morning. I don't have time for discussing 'an accident I've had recently that wasn't my fault', mis-sold PPI, or my solar panel needs. Don't they even stick to normal working hours now?

I'll ignore it. I take a defiant bite of the fun-size Crunchie I've just found a bag of in the cupboard under the stairs. Who put chocolate down here? Maybe the volunteers were trying to hide it from me? It's obviously leftover from Halloween and that was over a month ago. There's not usually chocolate hanging around that long if I know it's there. A day would be pushing it. Maybe it wasn't such a bad hiding place after all.

The ring is insistent and I have a conscience about ignoring a ringing phone. It could be an emergency. It could be my dad saying he's fallen and can't get up or paramedics who have been called out because he's had another heart scare.

I look at the mannequin's blank face. 'Sorry,' I mutter to it as

I try to prop it against the wall, shove the last half of the Crunchie into my mouth and rush through the back room and out onto the shop floor, leaving behind a series of thuds as the mannequin slides back down the steps I've just dragged it up.

I've forgotten to hit the light switch so the shop floor is in darkness and I trip over a clothing rail and nearly go flying.

'Hello?' I say with my mouth full as I grab the handset from behind the counter. It's far from the polite 'One Light charity shop, how can I help you?' that we're supposed to answer the phone with, but I fully expect the caller to have rung off by now anyway.

'Do you think it will hurt?'

'What?' I say with all eloquence of an inebriated badger, hopping about with the phone in one hand, the other clutching the toe that collided with the clothing rail.

'If I jump off this bridge?'

I choke on the Crunchie.

'Are you okay?' The man's voice on the other end of the line asks.

'Yes, thanks.' I clear my throat a few times, trying to dislodge rouge bits of honeycomb. Only I could greet a suicidal man by choking at him. 'Shouldn't it be me asking you that?'

He lets out a laugh that sounds wet and thick, like he's been crying. 'I'm not the one choking to death. Do you need a glass of water or something?'

'No, no, I'm fine,' I say, wondering if swallowing actual sandpaper might've been more comfortable. 'I'm so sorry, I'd just shoved an entire fun-size Crunchie into my mouth and then tried to speak. If that isn't a recipe for disaster, I don't know what is.'

I don't know why I said that. A recipe for disaster is not me choking on a chocolate bar – it's a guy about to throw himself off a bridge who doesn't realise he's phoned the charity shop for a suicide prevention helpline rather than the suicide prevention helpline itself.

My heart is suddenly pounding and a cold sweat has prickled my forehead. I don't know what to do. I've always been petrified this would happen but never really thought it would. I've always thought that the two numbers are printed worryingly close together on our leaflets. Head Office told me I was worrying too much, but I've often wondered how easy it would be for someone to get our number muddled up with the helpline number and phone here by mistake. And it seems like the answer has just rung.

What am I going to do? I can't take this call. I don't know how to talk someone down off a bridge.

'Oh, I love Crunchies. Don't tell me you still have fun-size ones leftover from Halloween?'

'I think they were hidden from me. I've only just found them.' I'm rambling about nonsense but I don't know what else to say. I know people think chocolate is the answer to most things, but I doubt it's likely to help in this situation, and as much as I'd like to keep talking about Cadbury's honeycomb treat, I can't keep avoiding his first question.

I go to speak but he gets there first. 'Can we just keep talking about chocolate? This is the most normal conversation I've had for days.'

I let out a nervous laugh. 'We can talk about anything you want. Chocolate's always a good topic.'

'Where's your hiding place? I never manage to hide mine successfully, I always remember where it is and scoff the lot. I bought boxes of Milk Tray for the family when they were on offer a couple of weeks ago, and let's just say I've now got to go and buy more before Christmas. You can guess what happened to them, right?'

Another nervous laugh. 'Well, this time, my staff bought them in case any trick or treaters came round before closing time, but none did, so they must've hidden them in the cupboard under the stairs of all places. I was just wrestling a naked mannequin out when I found them. Safe to say there aren't many left now. And I feel a bit sick. Those two points are probably related.'

'Well, if they've been there for a month, you're only testing them for quality, right?'

I giggle again. How can someone about to throw himself off a bridge make me laugh? 'Yes. Testing them *vigorously*.'

He laughs too and the laugh seems to go on for much longer than anything that was actually funny. 'God, I haven't laughed in so long,' he says eventually, sounding out of breath. 'So what are you doing naked wrestling mannequins under the stairs at this time of night? Aren't you in a call centre?'

'Um …'

'Oh god, please don't tell me I phoned the wrong number.' He must be able to hear my hesitation because he suddenly sounds distraught and I hear paper rustling down the line. 'I have, haven't I? There are two numbers on here and the leaflet's all wet and the ink's blurred. God, I'm such an idiot.'

'No, you're not. You're *not*. Trust me, it's our fault, I've been trying to get those leaflets redesigned for years,' I say, feeling panic claw at my chest. What if he's going to hang up and go through with the jump because of a silly mistake?

'I'm so sorry.' He makes a noise of frustration. 'I'm so, so sorry to have disturbed you. Please forget this ever happened. I'll leave you to your naked mannequin wrestling.'

He says the words in such a rush that I can't interrupt him quickly enough. 'Please don't go,' I say, my voice going high at the fear of what he might do. I need to give him the number of the real helpline. There are business cards on the counter right in front of me, it would be easy enough to read out the number and tell him to phone there instead, where there are people who do this all the time and have a lot of training in dealing with these situations. But what if he doesn't phone them? What if he feels stupid for phoning the wrong place? What if he decides to jump rather than make another phone call?

314

I can't tell a suicidal man to hang up and try again, can I?

'Please stay and talk a minute,' I say cautiously. Surely the best thing I can do is talk to him? There are testimonials on the One Light website that say the most important thing in deciding not to go through with a suicide attempt was having someone to talk to, and the charity have run campaigns about how important making small talk with a stranger can be. 'I don't have enough people to talk about chocolate with. And I feel like I shouldn't let you go without clarifying that it's the mannequins who are naked, not me. It's way too cold for that.'

He lets out a guffaw. 'Ah, so if I'd phoned on a summer night, it would have been a different story, huh?'

I laugh too. 'What did I expect from a conversation that's revolved entirely around chocolate, naked mannequins, and wrestling?'

'I think I'd be letting the male species as a whole down if I didn't derive something dirty from a conversation like that.'

'I think we've both done our duty with weird conversations so far tonight,' I say. I need to end this and get him on the phone to an actual counsellor who can help him talk things through, but I don't know how to broach the subject. I can't just say, 'right, here's the number, off you go'. It's too abrupt, it could make him feel rejected, it could make him more likely to jump.

'Where are you?' I ask instead. Maybe getting back onto the subject is a good start.

'The suspension bridge over the Barrow river. It's on the outskirts of Oakbarrow town.'

He's local. I know exactly where he is. Turn right at the end of the high street and go past the churchyard, it's a ten-minute walk away. The old steel bridge on the road that leads out of Oakbarrow. I was up there two days ago putting One Light leaflets out. I leave a few of them weighed down with a stone in the corner of the pavement, next to the safety barrier that was replaced after an accident a few years ago. The replacement part is just a bit lower than the rest of the barrier, the part where anyone thinking of jumping would be most likely to climb over.

'What are you doing up there at this time of night?'

'I don't know. God, I don't know. It seemed so clear when I walked up here, but I got to the edge and looked down, and I couldn't see the water, just blackness in the dark, and I went dizzy so I sat down on the pavement, and I just … I don't know. Sorry, I'm rambling.'

'Not at all,' I say, thinking his voice sounds familiar. He's got an English accent but he puts a little emphasis on his 'r's. It's typical for this part of Gloucestershire. That must be why I think I recognise it.

'I walked across the bridge yesterday and saw a stack of your leaflets. The thought of … you know … jumping has been in my head for a while and I grabbed one and stuffed it in my pocket. As I stood there and looked over the edge tonight, I put my hands in my pockets and my fingers brushed it, and it was like I didn't even remember putting it there.'

That must've been one of the leaflets I put out the day before. It makes me feel weirdly connected to him. This man has reached out in his darkest moment because of something I did. I have a responsibility to help him.

'I sat on the pavement and unfolded it and thought about my dad – he died on this river – and I just felt … compelled to ring you. He'd be so disappointed if he could see me now. He thought life was the most precious thing any of us have.'

'You didn't jump. That's the most important part. Life *is* precious and you chose to sit down and call instead of throwing it away. That's the first step to making things better.'

'I didn't choose to sit down, I thought I was going to pass out.'

'That's okay too. The only thing that matters is that you're here and talking. It's got to be better than the alternative,' I say carefully, trying to sound as neutral as possible.

'I shouldn't be talking about this to you though, should I? I phoned the wrong number. I wouldn't mind betting this is definitely not part of your job description …'

'It's okay, it's absolutely fine.' I'm glad he can't see the expression on my face because it definitely doesn't match the light-hearted tone in my voice. 'It's just the people on the helpline are proper trained counsellors, and I'm not. I don't want to say the wrong thing and make this worse,' I say, deciding honesty is the best policy.

'Please don't hang up,' he says after a long moment of silence. He sounds so cautious, almost afraid and kind of hopeful, that there's no way I could refuse. 'I know I shouldn't be asking you to talk to me but I don't know what to do, and you're reminding me of normal people and normal conversations and feeling normal and you've already made me laugh and it's been so long since I …' His voice goes choked up again and I can hear him sniffle.

'I'm not going anywhere,' I say quickly, trying to reassure him. My hand tightens around the plastic of the handset. In my head, I'm wondering if I could somehow get in touch with the helpline while he's still on the line and try to transfer the call without hanging up on him, but I can't think of a way to do it. The phone in the shop is an old corded one that's attached to the wall behind the counter so no one can accidentally sell it – been there, done that – and my mobile is in my locker upstairs. I'd have to leave him for a few precious minutes to dash up there and get it. It would be too obvious what I was doing. What if he felt like I was just shafting him off onto the next person because I didn't care? If he feels like I can't get rid of him quick enough, it might make this situation worse. Even if I could get my phone and text the helpline and ask them what to say, I'd still have to leave him hanging here in silence while I got right the way across the shop floor, through the back room, up the stairs and into my locker and all the way back again, and who knows what he might do in that time? He phoned because he needs someone to talk to *now*. I can't just leave him.

I wind the cord of the phone around my fingers and sink down into a sitting position. I thunk my head back against the wall behind the counter and listen to the rain pounding on the shop roof. Even Bernard, the homeless man who lives in the churchyard, will have found shelter tonight. 'Aren't you soaked?'

I hear movement and can imagine him lifting an arm and looking at it. 'I am, actually. I hadn't even noticed.'

I don't know what it's like to be in that situation, to feel so bad, so desperate, that there's no way out, but I imagine a little fall of rain is the last thing he's worrying about. I hate the idea of someone sitting on the pavement outside in this weather though. He must be drenched and freezing. I could go up there, take him a warm blanket and a hot cup of tea, but that too would mean leaving the phone, and it would eradicate our anonymity.

Privacy and anonymity are the foundations of the charity. The helpline exists so people in a crisis can open up to an unbiased stranger. Callers are routed through a server that hides the number from the person on the other end. Helpline staff are not allowed to ask the caller's name if they don't share it, and not allowed to give their own name unless asked. He knows I'm not proper helpline staff, but I still work for One Light. Those rules must still apply to me, even if this is a situation that's never happened before.

'Talk to me,' I say gently, terrified that I'm saying the wrong thing. 'Why were you thinking of jumping?'

'We'll be here all night if I start listing the reasons.'

'That's okay. We can be here all night. There's no time limit. What's going on?'

'Everything. I'm a failure at life. My business is going under and I've done everything I can to try to save it, and I don't know what else to do. It was supposed to be a way of honouring my father, but it's taken every bit of money I had, and it's dead. I have no customers. My mum is seventy-seven years old and on her feet at seven o'clock every day to help me out because I can't

318

afford to pay any staff. I'm in debt up to my eyeballs and I got my business rates bill this morning, and I can't afford to pay even a fraction of it. And just to ice the cake, the rates are going up in January and there's *no way* I can pay them.'

Because of the anonymity rules, I can't ask him outright where he works, but if he's in Oakbarrow then chances are it's somewhere nearby. It might even be on this high street.

I sit up on my knees and look over the counter at the darkened road outside. Even the streetlamps have flickered their final death and no one's bothered to mend them. Oakbarrow High Street used to be a hive of activity, especially at this time of year, but now it's deader than the burnt-out bulbs in the streetlights. The truth is that I know how quiet things are. I know how difficult it is to get people through the door. Every day, I expect a phone call from Head Office saying they've decided to shut our branch down.

'Well, it's nearly Christmas,' I say. 'People are out shopping in the big towns at this time of year. Maybe things will pick up in January?'

'There's a new retail park on the roundabout outside of town. It's easy to get to, there's plenty of free parking, and it's got every kind of shop you could imagine. No one needs to come to high streets anymore, no matter the time of year.'

'Yeah, but the retail park is a bit … soulless, isn't it? These business parks are all the same – if you've seen one, you've seen them all. I'd rather go to a little high street full of independent shops that actually mean something to the people who own them. That comes across to shoppers, you know?'

'Well, you must be one of about ten people left in the country who think that way.'

I suddenly feel incredibly sad because he's so right about the high street. I've lived in Oakbarrow all my life. This high street used to be the centre of the universe, especially at this time of year. I remember coming Christmas shopping with my mum when I was little and being amazed by it, the sights, the sounds, the smells. The giant tree they put up in front of the churchyard, always at least ten-foot high, lush green branches weighed down with twinkling lights and ornaments that local schoolchildren had made. It was magical back then. Shopkeepers would stay open late, decorations of reindeer pulling Santa's sleigh ran across the road above our heads, snowflakes twinkled on hangers outside every shop, lampposts were wrapped with tinsel and bows and had bright bulbs that still worked.

I look out the window again. The shop across the road is empty, its windows painted white from inside, the shop next to that has a 'for sale' sign nailed to its front though the 's' has worn off, and the one on the opposite side has had 'closing down sale' notices in its bare windows for the past three years.

Just about the only shops still in business are the charity shop and the bank next door, a coffee shop, a tanning shop, a lingerie shop, and a television repair shop at the upper end of the high street. Even the only pub, that used to be the heart of all village gatherings, has closed in recent years. It used to be called The Blue Drum but some clever vandal has removed the middle five letters, so now it's just The B um. I hear a lot of regular customers talking about wishing The Bum was still open so they could go up it.

It feels like every one of us is only here to await the death knell. Even the mini supermarket that put the independent green-grocer out of business and contributed to the market closure has shut up shop and run for the hills. Or, more specifically, run for the retail park to be with all the other convenient and cheap shops that make high streets everywhere irrelevant.

'I wish there was something I could say to make you feel better, but there's no denying what a state high streets everywhere are in.'

'At least you're honest. Somehow, even hearing that makes me feel better.'

Well, I want to make him feel better but I'm not sure commiserating over the state of things was quite what I had in mind. 'How are you feeling now?'

'Cold. Wet.' I can hear his teeth chattering. 'Stupid for being up here. Stupid for thinking this was the answer. Pathetic for crying down the phone to a stranger.'

'Hey, that's not pathetic.' I wonder if we are strangers. If he works around here, I might know him in passing. I've had this job for four years now, you get to know people who work nearby, and his voice *does* sound familiar. 'When you need help, the bravest thing you can do is reach out and ask for it.'

'Or phone a stranger and talk about naked mannequin wrestling.'

The laugh takes me by surprise. 'Or make them choke on a Crunchie.'

'Or that.' His laugh turns into a sob. 'I shouldn't be up here. I feel like I've let everyone down. My family would be devastated if they knew it had come to this.'

'You haven't let anyone down because you're still here. The only thing your family would care about is you being all right. I know what it's like to lose someone you love. I promise you, there's nothing in the world worse than that. Any business that's failing is just a business, a building, a job. Losing that can be recovered from. *You* are irreplaceable.'

'Thank you.' His voice breaks and I can hear the thickness of tears welling up again. My heart constricts in my chest and I want nothing more than to hug this man I don't even know.

'None of us know how much we matter until it's too late. No matter how bad you feel, you're so important to so many people. One person's life touches so many others.'

'*Do you know It's a Wonderful Life?*'

I feel myself sitting up a bit straighter because he obviously recognised the quote. *It's a Wonderful Life* is not just a film to me. It was my mum's favourite, so much so that she named me

321

Georgia Bailey after it. 'I would be seriously concerned for anyone who *didn't* know *It's a Wonderful Life*. It's an amazing film.'

He makes a noise of agreement.

'It's kind of life-affirming,' I say pointedly. 'It really shows the importance of every life, no matter how insignificant we think we are, our little lives still make a big difference.'

He considers it for a moment. 'You have no idea how much I needed to hear that tonight.'

We sit there in silence for a while, neither of us speaking, and I realise I'm holding the phone handset so tightly that the plastic must be in danger of cracking by now. It feels like a lifeline to him and I could sit here all night just listening to him breathe. His breath has got that shuddery hitch you get after a long cry, and I have never wanted to hug someone so badly in all my life.

At the end of the high street, the church bell dongs for midnight.

'Every time a bell rings,' he murmurs. 'Did you hear that?'

It makes my heart pound harder. It's what I say every time I hear a bell ring too because they make me think of my mum. I love that he knows the film so well because it means so much to me and not many people get that.

'I heard something,' I say, because I don't know whether he's asking if I heard it through the phone or if he realises I'm just down the road.

'That was the Oakbarrow church telling us all it's officially December.'

'Christmas month,' I say.

'Don't remind me. I can't deal with Christmas this year.'

'Why not?'

'It makes me realise that another year has gone by and I've done nothing with my life. You're supposed to be all happy happy, joy joy at Christmas and I've got nothing left in me to give.'

'I wouldn't mind betting that the only reason you've got nothing left is because you're so busy looking after everyone else

322

that you forget to take care of yourself,' I say, because so many men are the same. He's probably a guy who's grown up thinking men must always be strong and never let their feelings show. It's a toxic masculinity that's dangerous to men's mental health. It's why suicide is the biggest killer of men under fifty. Men bottle things up inside and don't let it out until it's too late. I don't know the exact figures off the top of my head, but I do know that a majority of One Light's callers are male because of this exact reason.

'My mum always says that.'

'Mums are always right,' I murmur, wishing mine was still here.

'Sometimes I feel like I'm frightened of being alive.'

My breath catches in my throat. 'Me too.'

'Really?'

'Yeah,' I say slowly, nodding even though he can't see me. 'No one's ever hit the nail on the head like that before. That's exactly how I feel too.'

'I've always wanted to travel but I never have.'

'Me neither. I've never told anyone this but my ultimate dream is to go backpacking around Europe,' I say wondering what it is about him that makes him so easy to talk to.

'Really?' he says again. 'I'd love to do that.'

'I think I'm a bit old for it now, it's kind of a "gap year" thing, isn't it?' I shake my head at myself. I'm too old for daydreams like this, I should've forgotten it years ago. 'It's just a dream anyway. I have responsibilities that I can't just leave.'

'Me too. I was going to travel after college, but family stuff happened and I couldn't leave, then I was going off to uni but more family stuff came up, and it made more sense for me to get a job and stay here, so I'd been saving up for years to do one big trip somewhere, and then my dad died, and I bought the business, and now ... well, I'm still here. I keep feeling like there has to be more to life than this.'

'Me too,' I say.

'Wow, really? Sorry, I keep saying that, don't I? I've never spoken to someone who knew that feeling before.'

'Me neither. And there you go, I just keep repeating some variation of "me too" and "me neither". It doesn't make for the most exciting conversation in the world but I've never said this to anyone before.'

'Me neither,' he says, making us both laugh and my grip on the phone tightens, like if I hold it tight enough he'll be able to feel me squeezing his hand through the handset.

'This isn't what I thought my life would be like,' I admit. 'And I know I can't really complain because I'm so lucky compared to others, but I feel like I'm still waiting for my life to start.'

'I think we might literally be the same person. I'm thirty-seven and I feel exactly the same. I'm too old to still be waiting for my life to begin and too young to be this jaded, but I don't know what to do about it.'

So he's only three years older than me. I couldn't possibly know him, no matter how familiar his voice sounds. I can't think of anyone around that age who could be in such a dark place and hiding it so well.

'Me too,' I whisper.

'We grow up thinking life will be wonderful and amazing and exciting, and it's just quite dull really, isn't it? I keep thinking what if I die before anything wonderful or amazing or exciting happens to me?' He gives a self-deprecating snort. 'And yes, I know throwing yourself off a bridge isn't exactly conducive to that.'

At least he hasn't lost his sense of humour. He lets out a wobbly little giggle and I feel something like butterflies in my tummy. How can I possibly have butterflies over someone I don't even know? Someone who phoned because he was about to jump off a bridge?

'Okay, so … I should go, shouldn't I?' he says after a few moments silence.

'You don't have to. We can carry on talking.' I kind of want him to stay on the line for my sake now. I *love* talking to him. There's something about him that's so easy to chat to and a familiarity that you'd only expect to feel with a friend.

I can hear the smile in his voice. 'As tempting as that sounds, I think I should go home. I'm so cold that I might actually die from hypothermia and, thanks to you, I've realised I don't want to die tonight.'

'Or any other night, right?'

'Nah. I'll stick to killing myself only in daylight hours.'

'I'm glad you can joke about it, but it's not funny. You were really going to—'

'I know,' he whispers. 'But I feel better already just from talking to you, getting it off my chest, feeling like I'm not alone.'

He pauses and I can almost sense how ashamed he feels. I want to tell him that there's no reason to be, but I'm out of my depth and don't know how to word it.

'I can't thank you enough for staying on the line with me. I shouldn't have asked. I'm sure I've totally ruined your night.'

'Oh god, not at all. I've loved every second of talking to you. It's been a wonderful night.'

I can hear a smile in his voice. 'You just sounded so normal, it made me forget everything that's been in my head and just feel normal for a change. I can't remember the last time I felt connected to anyone. As daft as that sounds in our modern world of technology and the internet and being connected *all* the time.'

'It doesn't sound daft at all. It sounds exactly like what I was feeling too.' I wonder how many more times he's going to surprise me tonight. He seems to understand thoughts I've had but never put into words before. 'I think it's something that's easy to forget sometimes. We get so caught up in social media and being as good as everyone else that we forget we don't really "talk" anymore. And if you want to know about modern world, I'm on an old corded phone that's screwed to the wall, rarely seen in Britain since the Seventies. David Attenborough should be doing a documentary about something so ancient.'

He laughs and I'm glad he got a kick out of that because there's something about his laugh that I just want to keep listening to.

'Thank you for reminding me what it feels like to be alive,' he says.

'I think you might have reminded me a little bit too.'

'I keep thinking I know you. Your voice sounds so familiar,' he says softly. 'I don't even know your name.'

My breath catches in my throat, but I think it's probably best not to tell him that he sounds familiar too. If he *is* someone I could one day come across in real life, he's not going to want to be reminded of this night, is he? People can be more open with a stranger. They can tell them things they wouldn't tell a friend. If he thought we might run into each other somewhere, he probably wouldn't have said half the things he said tonight. No matter what connection we have here, it has to end when we put down the phone. 'I don't know yours. And that's the way it's supposed to be. It's often easier to talk to an anonymous stranger. Someone completely non-judgemental and impartial, who's not involved in your life in any way at all. Like ships passing in the night, honking their horn at each other and continuing their journey.'

'Consider your horn duly honked.'

It makes me laugh. 'And yours too.'

'I like that, you know?'

'Horn honking?'

'No, being anonymous. It makes it seem all mysterious and romantic, like the start of a great story. Well, and horn honking. Honking is a good word. People don't honk enough these days.'

'They leave the honking to geese and old-fashioned car horns.'

It makes us both laugh again and I realise I've gone from panicking when I picked up the phone to relaxing with his company. He really is easy to talk to, and now I don't think he's about to do anything stupid, I'm just enjoying the chat.

'You can hang up, you know,' he says. 'I feel like I've wasted your time tonight.'

'Are you kidding? I've really enjoyed it. I didn't think anyone understood half the things I've said to you tonight. *You* made *me* feel more normal too, you know.'

I hear him swallow.

'And I'm not going anywhere until I know you're okay.'

'Okay, okay.' His chuckle gives way to a grunt and a series of groans as I hear him moving. 'God, I've sat there for too long. I think I need oiling. Got any WD40 handy?'

I smile but his attempt at humour is not going to deter me from what's really important here. 'How're you feeling?'

'I don't know. I'm so cold that I can't feel anything from the neck down.'

I wish I'd taken him a coat or something. I should've just gone as soon as I knew where he was. Anonymity be damned.

'I'm okay,' he says before I have a chance to push him any further. 'Really. I'm not going to do anything stupid. I feel better just for having let it all out. I don't think I've ever cried that much in my life, and I watched *Titanic* fourteen times when it came out on video. How can one set of sinuses hold so much snot?' He does an exaggerated sniff as a demonstration.

It makes me smile. 'When you get home, do me a favour and take care of yourself, okay? Apart from cold and wet, you must be drained. You've been through something traumatic tonight.'

'Ah, I wouldn't call talking to you traumatic.'

'Make light of it all you want. Do whatever you need to cope. But you and I both know that trying to brush things under the carpet is how you ended up on that bridge in the first place.'

I think he's going to say something else sarcastic, but he swallows. 'I know.'

'So take care of yourself. When you get in, have a long hot shower or bath. A long cry is draining, so drink a really big glass of water and get something to eat. I don't care if it's healthy or something made of chocolate, but make yourself a cup of tea and eat some biscuits, and snuggle up into bed with a book or a movie or something. Please? You deserve some TLC too.'

'"Waterfalls" or "No Scrubs"?'

'Oh, ha ha,' I say, even though it does make me want to laugh. There's never a bad time for a Nineties music reference.

'Hot shower, warm pyjamas, drink of water, bed, book, tea and biscuits. The Great British cure for everything.' I can hear that he's smiling as he repeats my instructions. 'I wish I knew your name so I could thank you properly, but at the same time, I kind of like not knowing it. So thank you, mysterious stranger, for saving my life. And for the interesting mental images of mannequins wrestling naked in chocolate. Or something. That *is* what you were doing when I called, right?'

I giggle. 'Thank you for a night I'll never forget.'

'Even the rain's stopping,' he says. I can hear him walking now, the wet flop of something against his phone. Maybe his hair? 'What a wonderful night.'

I smile because in a weird way, it was.

I've never spoken to someone who understands me the way he seems to. It feels kind of magical to speak to someone who you can never speak to again, a connection with a stranger I'll never meet, on a night I'll always remember.

'Thank you for everything,' he whispers, his voice catching again. It makes me want to hug him even more than I wanted to hug him anyway which was already immeasurable on the wanting-to-hug-someone scale. 'Goodnight, lovely.'

The phone clicks off and I sit back on my knees, staring at the handset in shock.

Lovely. That's what Leo from It's A Wonderful Latte up the road calls me. I mean, I'm sure it's what he calls every customer but it still makes my heart beat faster every time he says it.

The thought that it could've been him flits across my mind

but I dismiss it instantly. There must be millions of guys who use endearments like that …

It couldn't be, could it?

No way.

No way could someone be suffering so much on the inside and hide it so well on the outside. Leo is the happiest person I know. He's the one bright spot on a dull winter day. He's the reason I buy a coffee every morning on the way to work. His smile makes every overpriced cup worthwhile. He's the brightest, happiest, smiliest, most cheerful guy in town.

No way in a *million* years would he be considering taking his own life.

No way was the guy on the other end of that phone Leo.

# A Letter from the Author

Dear Reader,

Thank you so much for reading *The Little Vintage Carousel by the Sea*. I hope you loved reading about Ness, Nathan, and the carousel, and enjoyed a summer escape to Pearlholme as much as I did, and hopefully fell in love with Nathan like I did while I was writing – of all my book characters, he's definitely the one I most wish was real!

I'd been thinking about this story for a long while, but something just wasn't working with it – I could never figure out what Nathan would be doing in Pearlholme. My friend has been telling me to watch the musical *Carousel* for years, and I've always been convinced it would be old and boring, and appeased him by saying I'd watch it if it was ever on TV, hoping it never would be. Over Christmas last year, it was on TV, and I had no choice but to watch it! Turns out, it's a lovely old film, and the opening scenes on the carousel, with the nostalgic music and decadent romance was the final puzzle piece for this story – by the time the film ended, I knew what Nathan's job would be, and the idea I'd been turning over in my head for months became *The Little Vintage Carousel by the Sea*!

If you enjoyed this story, please consider leaving a review on Amazon. It only has to be a line or two, and it makes such a difference to helping other readers decide whether to pick up the book or not, and it would mean so much to me to know what you think! Did it make you smile, laugh, or cry? I couldn't help giggling a few times while I was writing it!

Thank you again for reading. If you want to get in touch, you can find me on Twitter – usually when I should be writing – @be_the_spark. I would love to hear from you!

Hope to see you again soon in a future book!

Lots of love,

Jaimie

www.ingramcontent.com/pod-product-compliance
Ingram Content Group UK Ltd.
Pitfield, Milton Keynes, MK11 3LW, UK
UKHW022324250325
456726UK00004B/131